A Broken

Winter

Kale Night

A NineStar Press Publication

Published by NineStar Press
P.O. Box 91792,
Albuquerque, New Mexico, 87199 USA.
www.ninestarpress.com

A Broken Winter

Printed in the USA
First Edition
November, 2019

Print ISBN: 978-1-951057-10-7

Also available in eBook, ISBN: 978-1-951057-09-1

Warning: This book contains sexually explicit content, which may only be suitable for mature readers, suicide, violence, abuse/torture (including that of children), mutilation, murder, gore, religious shaming, medical procedures, illness/death of child and parent, kidnapping/abduction, past trauma.

General Auryn Tyrus is tired of serving an emperor who turns political dissidents into expensive steak and claims to have swallowed Ankari's sun. He is fed up with pretending not to know Emperor Haken is buying biological weapons and collecting taxes for a war that doesn't exist. Auryn's role in the entire mirage leads him to drastic choices, but unexpected news halts his plans. Seven-year-old Keita Kaneko, the son of a former lover, is captured by the emperor's special forces. Auryn secretly intervenes and spares Keita from execution.

Keita changes everything. Instead of feeling helpless and oppressed by a self-proclaimed living god, Auryn works to expose the emperor as a fraud. But he knows exactly what will happen if he's discovered, and the extent of Emperor Haken's lies is worse than anticipated. If Auryn expects anyone to believe the truth, he's going to need proof. And a lot of help.

Chapter One

FREEZING TO DEATH took longer than expected. Auryn hadn't moved in over an hour, lying in the snow, staring up at the stars. His toes burned and his bare fingers prickled painfully, flushed red from the cold. He'd considered a variety of other options, including shooting himself in the head, but feared screwing up and adding a traumatic brain injury to his list of grievances. He thought about hanging himself from a peach tree in Building A, but the fruit was being harvested and there were too many people around, even at night.

Forced to decide quickly, he hopped in a snowcrawler and sped off. He could've kept going, travelling beyond the oxygenated zone, opting for death by hypoxia, but he pulled over and picked a final resting place.

The radio in his earpiece crackled. The Special Activities Division were getting closer. It wouldn't be long before they reached their target, terrorist Reisen Kaneko. Auryn hadn't seen Reisen in over a decade, but his fondness for the man remained intact, uneroded by the passage of time. He'd hoped they'd be reunited one day, despite how impossible it was. No chance of that now. Abandoning his delusions meant being left with nothing, crippled under the weight of reality and longing for oblivion.

Countless stars illuminated the sky, radiant mothers to other worlds, a painful reminder of their own orphaned condition. His Holiness Emperor Haken swallowed planet Ankari's sun centuries ago—punishment for widespread civil disobedience, or so the story went. While Emperor Haken's fire-swallowing abilities were never questioned, it was whispered he *may* have simply taken credit for a dying sun's disappearance. This explanation made sense to Auryn, but Reisen loved tearing it apart.

"A sun like ours doesn't die the way most people expect it to. It burns bigger and brighter, swelling like an infected gash, incinerating planets nurtured from their inception. The final act of a deranged mother. Ankari is close enough to the sun that we'd all be burned alive instead of freezing our asses off.

"If the sun did disappear, it wasn't due to natural causes."

The radio blared with activity. *Target location reached.*

This was it. If he had any sense, he'd turn the radio off, but he needed to be sure someone hadn't made a mistake.

Entrance is clear. Living room clear. Kitchen clear.

His heart pounded, chest constricting painfully.

Door's locked. We're going to break it down.

It wasn't supposed to end like this.

There's someone in the bed.

Auryn closed his eyes, inhaling deeply. The cold air choked him, scratching his throat and lungs like tiny, frozen thorns.

It's a fucking kid. We do not have Kaneko. Repeat. We do not have Kaneko.

He struggled into a seated position, limbs stiff and heavy.

Kid says he's Kaneko's son. We're bringing him in for questioning.

He pulled his hat and gloves back on, skin on fire. Reisen's son would be sent to the capital and interrogated, treated not like a human being, but as an opportunity for promotion.

Auryn extracted himself from the snowbank he'd intended to be his tomb. He knew where they'd send the boy when they were done with him. Exhibiting the motor skills of a two-year-old, he climbed into his snowcrawler and turned the machine around, heading back to the Farm.

THIS WASN'T THE way Keita Kaneko envisioned his first trip to the capital—in the back of a police cruiser, with a ring of light around his neck. An electric halo. One of the officers in front operated the controls. She glared at him frequently, furious for no reason. He sat quietly, eager to avoid another shock.

Tinted windows cast a shadow over streets lined with glass towers, drowning them in darkness. Keita pressed his nose against the cold glass, trying to catch a glimpse of the rising sun. He knew it was an illusion, but wanted to see what all the fuss was about. Grids of electrified mesh and high leather seats blocked his view. He craned his neck, trying to gaze out the front window. Metal cuffs gnawed his wrists, eroding layers of skin.

The officers exchanged worried glances, united in their terror of a seven-year-old boy. Keita knew he was in deep trouble. What he didn't know was why—why policemen armed with gas masks and guns stormed into his room in the middle of the night and stole him from his bed. At first, he thought they'd broken into the wrong house and grabbed the wrong boy, but he saw how everyone shuddered when he told them his name. Someone made a mistake. He hadn't done anything wrong. He wasn't even allowed outside. There were monsters outside.

The car stopped. Keita's stomach churned, pressure rising in his chest. The officers marched him towards the police station. He scanned the horizon, hoping for some indication of the coming light, but saw only blackness.

Inside the station they escorted him to a stall with concrete walls and a drain. A guard with thick leather gloves removed Keita's clothing, maintaining as much distance between them as possible. The cold floor stung his feet. He stood with one foot on top of the other, shivering in a corner of the stall. A masked priestess in white robes rubbed his bare skin with coarse sea salt and turned a strong hose on him, blasting him with water. The force of it rubbed his skin raw, like liquid sandpaper. Guards stuffed him into scratchy clothes without drying him, took him to another room, and then shoved him onto a metal chair.

Florescent overhead lights shone uncomfortably bright and filled his vision with colourful dots. Two men in black suits stood in front of him, wearing glasses with dark lenses.

"There's been a mistake," said Keita, rubbing his burning eyes.

"You are Keita Kaneko, son of Dr. Reisen Kaneko, yes?"

"Yes, but—"

"Shut up and listen. When's the last time you saw your father?"

A few days ago, he'd been playing in the basement of his house and entered his dad's laboratory without permission. He accidentally knocked over a beaker of inkworm, the black slime responsible for killing his mother. Tendrils of sludge shot across the tile. It tried to creep away, but he didn't let it escape. He stomped on the slime over and over, cutting his bare feet on the glass, until the inky goo stopped moving. He expected his dad to be furious, but the man hugged him and gently extracted the glass, healing his wounds with a swirl of luminous energy; a spiral galaxy of slowly spinning stars. His dad left shortly afterward, and Keita hadn't seen him since, which wasn't unusual. Dr. Kaneko worked with sick people—rarely sleeping, rarely eating, pausing only to stand by the window and light a cigarette. Keita's dad often went away for days at a time, helping those who needed it. Those who'd been neglected or abused by the emperor.

"Did something happen to him?" asked Keita, voice raised in panic. He couldn't survive without his dad. There'd be no one to protect him from monsters. No one to bring him food or play games with him.

"Take a look." One of the men pushed a button on the table, displaying a photograph on its surface—a lady with part of her head missing, insides leaking outside. Keita's eyes hurt so badly he couldn't see straight. He felt dizzy and disoriented. Deep rusty reds and violent purples blurred together in a sea of human debris.

Keita bit his lip, swallowing the warm, sour fluid rising in his throat. "It looks like a monster got her."

"Your father is the monster."

"He's not." Keita closed his eyes, head reeling. "You don't know what you're talking about."

"Your father has blown up more buildings than most demolition crews, kid. We have witnesses and security footage."

"My dad doesn't kill people. He heals them."

"Does this look like the work of a healer to you?" Another photograph. An elderly woman torn in half. "We're afraid he's very sick. Healthy people don't blow up old ladies." Keita saw himself reflected in the man's glasses, wet and annoyed. Shaggy blond hair stuck to his head in matted clumps. Blue eyes full of invisible stinging sand. "We're not going to hurt him. We're going to help him. You want your father to get better, don't you?"

"My dad isn't sick!" Keita didn't like losing his temper, but he was tired, angry, and in a lot of pain. These idiots weren't listening to him, resistant to the truth. "He's a doctor, I told you! He wouldn't hurt anybody!"

"We can't do our job if you deny the truth, Keita."

The use of his name threw him off, a human gesture from someone who otherwise failed to act the part. They were a bunch of fakers. It was a trick to make him feel like they were on the same side, and he wasn't falling for it. "You're a liar."

"Listen to me." The officer grabbed him by the shoulders, shaking him. "You can either cooperate or face the consequences of being a stubborn little shit." He gripped Keita's arm, twisting it. "Choose wisely."

Keita had nothing more to say.

A WINDOWLESS RAILCAR shuddered along unseen tracks. Bound and gagged, Keita focused on the monotonous vibration of the train, trying to disappear among the hypnotic clacking. He shared the car with an unknown number of passengers. They were silent for a long time, then all at once burst into muffled wails and muted prayers, forming a ghoulish chorus. Their destination was unclear, but he had the terrifying suspicion it was final. After weeks of trying to extract information he didn't have, the government goons finally gave up on him. The experience left him convinced the monsters his dad spoke of wore human skins.

The train stopped. Swift hands unfastened Keita's bindings, removing his blindfold and a chunk of rubber from his mouth. They'd travelled deep underground and entered an immense cavern. An artificial sun beamed overhead, small but bright, filling the cave with light. He recognised it right away—a hologram. Under different circumstances, he would've been thrilled to see it. Holograms tricked people into seeing something that wasn't there. Like the sun that rose in the capital. Everyone knew it wasn't real, but his dad said it gave people hope.

It was much warmer underground than on the surface. High walls wrapped around a massive collection of buildings. The wall surrounding an entrance marked *Building C* was painted with colourful animals. Smiling pigs. Dancing cows. Suddenly, Keita knew where he was. The Farm. The source of all the food in Terasyn.

"Move!" Soldiers with electric cattle prods kept the small group of people in line, herding them towards the building.

They stopped at a station manned by medical personnel, where a woman silently drew his blood, her face concealed behind a gas mask. She failed to warn him of the impending sting and didn't appear to care when he flinched. She shoved him forwards, moving on to the next in line.

He stumbled and collided with the back of a fellow prisoner. She steadied him with a hand. "It's okay, sweetie. I know it hurts."

"I don't recall giving you permission to speak," interrupted a solider, raising the tip of his weapon.

"Sounds like someone needs a nap. Stay close," whispered the lady.

The soldier grabbed her, shoving her against the wall. "Hold on. You're coming with me. Research purposes. I'm developing a vaccine for problematic bitches." He gripped the tattered fabric of her shirt in a fist and squeezed her. "All it takes is a quick stab."

"I'll bet." The woman glared at the solider and spat in his face. He slapped her, forcing her to the ground, plunging a boot into her stomach.

"Leave her alone!" Keita's throat was dry and swollen, his voice barely audible. He pounced and sank his teeth into the soldier's thigh—a long-toothed cat, taking down its prey. He tasted blood and bit down harder. The soldier clubbed him on the head with the hilt of his prod and he hit the ground, moaning.

Keita closed his eyes. He curled up, waiting for the electric sting to come, but a deep, firm voice pre-empted the shock.

"Hyder. Stand down."

"The little bastard took a chunk out of me!"

"You'll live."

He opened his eyes. A tall, blond soldier crouched nearby, healing Hyder's leg, closing the gouges left by Keita's tiger teeth. The soldier wore more medals than the others, more decorations. He must have been more important. Some kind of soldier boss. His eyes studied Keita critically; bright blue and very serious.

"Who's the boy?" asked the soldier boss.

Hyder scanned his collar with an electronic reader. "Kaneko, Keita, sir. Age seven. Terrorist contact; awaiting sacrifice on orders of His Holiness. Only child of known terrorists Kaneko, Reisen and Glass, Naida—deceased."

The soldier boss's gaze softened, but it did nothing to water down Keita's fear. He stood there, shaking, heat slowly draining from his body.

"I'll deal with the kid. Put the young lady back in line where she belongs."

"Yes, sir." The soldier saluted and turned to collect the woman from the floor, forcing her to her feet.

Keita clutched his stormy stomach.

"My name is General Auryn Tyrus. Follow me."

Keita knew he was going to die.

Auryn led him away from the others. Machines worked noisily in the distance, humming and grinding behind bright white walls. Their clatter gave way to the gentle lowing of animals. Keita approached a pigpen and peered inside. He felt Auryn's gaze on him as he leaned over, reaching out to run his fingers over the prickly, leathery skin of the nearest pig.

"Reisen Kaneko is your father, correct?" asked Auryn.

Keita flinched, expecting to be struck. That question meant bad, bad things were going to happen. He pressed his palms to his forehead and shut his eyes tight, breath catching in his throat. When nothing came, he lowered his arms, peeking at Auryn, terrified and confused.

Auryn didn't look angry. He frowned instead. "I'm sorry, son. I'm not interrogating you."

"Why are you being so nice to me?" asked Keita. They were on opposite sides. Auryn worked for Emperor Haken, and the emperor wanted Keita dead. Erased from memory.

"Good question." Auryn crouched beside him, patting a sow on the hindquarters. "I was friends with your father. I know he's not a bad man, despite what people say."

"Why does everyone think my dad is dangerous?"

"It's a lie Emperor Haken told. He wants your father captured because he's afraid of him."

"Why?" Keita swallowed a lump in his throat, blinking rapidly and trying not to cry. He didn't want Auryn to think he was a baby, but his resolve was melting, and he hurt all over. Nothing made sense.

"Your father knows things that could get Emperor Haken into a lot of trouble. As a result, Haken goes to great lengths to discredit your father, minimising the threat of anyone taking him seriously."

"My dad told me Haken is horrible," stammered Keita, shivering, tucking his clammy hands beneath his armpits, trying to warm them.

Auryn stood up. "He's not wrong." Keita's heart pounded rapidly, his breath coming in strangled hitches, gasping for oxygen, swallowing so much air he belched uncontrollably. He worried he'd throw up or piss himself or pass out or do all three at once. "Keita." Auryn picked him up with ease, carrying him away from the animals. "Let's get you fixed up." Keita clung to him, terrified.

HAD ANYONE ASKED Auryn why he was carrying a distraught detainee, he would have told them he was taking Keita for questioning. One final attempt at extracting information. He was grateful that hadn't occurred. He didn't want to give Keita the wrong idea and risk frightening him further. The boy was already trembling in his arms. He unlocked the door to the Director's Quarters and stepped inside. The previous Director of Operations set up housing in the basement of Building D—research and development—away from the barracks, granting him the privacy to do whatever he wanted. Auryn preferred not to think about what went on down here; when he'd first moved in, the floors and walls had been covered in stains of dubious origins.

He carried Keita into the bathroom, standing him next to the sink. "I need to see where you're hurt. Please remove your uniform."

Keita shook his head, protectively clutching the bloody fabric covering him, eyes wide and fearful.

Auryn held his hand out, demonstrating his intentions, light pooling around his fingers, spinning into loose spirals. "Keita. Let me help. Your father would never forgive me for standing around watching you bleed." He focused on healing the wound on Keita's head while the boy shakily manipulated the buttons on his uniform, working his way out of it.

Seven years old. A year younger than his son, Sasha, had been at the time of his death. Buried two months before his eighth birthday.

Sasha's memory haunted him like a relentless ghost, never drifting far from his thoughts. Auryn no longer experienced an erratic fluctuation between anger and grief, as he did in the aftermath of the incident, only a sense of pervasive agony. Without rage, there was nothing to mask the suffering.

Keita's distrust appeared well-founded, his torso a macabre rainbow of colour—purples so dark they were nearly black, green, yellow, hints of blue from within the last few hours. Burn marks circled his wrists and ankles. Dried blood coated his inner thighs, the result of a recent circumcision. Sacrificing someone unclean was unthinkable.

"They cut me." Keita stared at him with swollen blue eyes, searching for an explanation.

"Emperor Haken believes the skin they cut off makes men behave badly. He helps us avoid temptation by removing it." Auryn related to being born outside the system, remembering nothing before arriving at a government orphanage, no idea where he came from or what his parents looked like. His first memory was of being stripped and gawked at, the cold metal of crushing forceps.

Auryn healed Keita with the same meticulousness employed in counting body bags, energy slow draining from his body. He drew a bath and helped Keita into the warm water. Whether it was exhaustion, relief, or absence of pain, the boy's body listed. Keita remained barely awake for the duration of his bath, numbly enduring Auryn's presence.

He dried Keita with a towel and wrapped it around him. Auryn glanced in the mirror, verifying he appeared as worn out as he felt. Despite approaching 75 years of age, he still looked in his mid-20s. After age 26, cellular degeneration slowed to a thin trickle of sand in a human hourglass, barely flowing for at least another 500 years. Emperor Haken's gift of extended life.

Auryn carried Keita to the second bedroom. Had he not seen it for himself, he never would have known the room was used by its previous occupant as a torture chamber/necrophiliac retreat. A fresh coat of paint went a long way.

He sat Keita on the edge of the bed and reached for the pyjamas he'd laid out earlier, blue with white snowflakes, helping him dress.

"Whose clothes are these?" asked Keita, voice thick with sleep, blinking tiredly.

"They belonged to my son."

"Where is he?"

"He died."

"How?" Keita rubbed his eyes with closed fists, crawling beneath the covers.

"That's not a pleasant bedtime story. Get some sleep, Keita. You're safe here. Don't worry."

Keita put his head down and yawned widely. "You must really like my dad."

"He was a good friend." There were plenty of stories Auryn could tell about Reisen, but he'd be forced to omit the best parts. The parts that kept him awake at night.

Chapter Two

YEAR 2056
Six Years Ago

Idyn, Capital of Terasyn

Auryn's son, Sasha, liked to pretend. In Idyn, pretending was easy. An artificial environment encased the city in luxuries like light and warmth, sparing its residents from the relentless cold. The city was a carefully constructed escape from reality. It even rained on occasion, but rain always made Auryn think of Reisen.

Reisen loved the rain.

Auryn watched Sasha fish for aquatic monsters, painfully aware this was as close to contentment as he got.

"Target is responding to the bait!" Sasha set the hook, laughing as he reeled in a thrashing beast. "Objective obtained, sir!" Sasha held the fish in the air, grinning. "Sharkface will finally pay for his crimes."

Auryn snapped a photo, beaming with pride.

Their apartment was on the top floor of a downtown high-rise. During the day, large windows filled the rooms with artificial sunlight, but it never felt quite right. He had no basis for comparison, but was plagued by an innate nagging that real sunshine was stronger, warmer. It didn't feel like basking in the glow of a refrigerator.

Sasha showed his catch to his mother. "Mom, look what I caught! It's Sharkface, Terror of the Sea!"

She ignored him, lost in the preparation of small, intricate pastries. Lately she'd been disinterested and disconnected, occupying her own little world. It would have concerned him if he didn't like when she pretended he didn't exist.

"Can I gut him?" Sasha asked Auryn, beaming up at him, eyes shining with shameless enthusiasm over getting his hands sticky with gore. He liked digging around the flesh-lined cavity in search of roe, or evidence of what the fish had for its final meal.

"Go ahead, son. Be careful with the knife." He ruffled the boy's hair, leaving him to the task. It wasn't the first time Sasha had used a knife; he was well-instructed in proper safety and handling. The precision of his cuts rivalled most butchers.

"You never had a chance against me, Sharkface. You shouldn't have eaten all those people."

"Sasha!" His wife. "What're you doing?"

"Dad said I could cut Sharkface's guts out." Sasha sounded offended. "Didn't you hear him?"

"He did, did he?"

He never heard his wife enter the living room. She tended to creep like a stalking cat. He wasn't sure if it was all the years of military training or something intrinsic to her nature.

"Auryn." The sound of her voice made him cringe. He swallowed his resentment, sentencing it to the pit of his stomach where it would dwell for a while before rising again.

"There's something wrong with our son."

"What's the matter with him?" He saw no reason for concern. His wife enjoyed blowing things out of proportion, making extravagant productions out of nothing. Her goal was usually to make him feel guilty, and when that failed, she went to other options. Like a good soldier, she always had a backup plan.

After years of feigning an interest in her body, their relationship was more like a bad dream than a marriage— a constant barrage of saying and doing things he wanted no part of. The thought of touching her disgusted him. When he had to it was ideally brief and in the dark. Sasha was his only consolation, a bright star in an otherwise aphotic expanse of space.

His wife folded her arms across her chest, glaring. "He plays such violent games. He might as well join the army."

"He may have a hard time enlisting at his age." He didn't hide his amusement, smiling at the idea of something so obscene. The gulf between slitting the throat of a man and a fish was vast. Sasha had a penchant for the macabre, but within normal parameters. It wasn't as if he was slinking around the neighbourhood strangling cats.

"This isn't a joke!" His wife's long, light brown hair hung in wild tangles, hiding her eyes. "Do you want him to end up like us? Have him rounding up people who are branded as sinners because they don't want the government recording everything they do?"

"When did you become so self-loathing?" asked Auryn. "His Holiness Emperor Haken is a God, exempted from the rules of men. Enforcing His will is our primary objective. The undermining of social stability must not be permitted."

"Fuck you." His wife's fingers curved around a vase, snatching it from its resting place. She hurled it hard and struck the wall just above his head, pelting him with shards of porcelain. Auryn suspected he knew why she was angry.

Several months ago, she'd received a promotion and been assigned the task of supervising at the Farm. The farm secretly swallowed anyone unfortunate enough to make the emperor's list. Those whose sins could no longer be forgiven. He'd heard about the list from Reisen and initially refused to believe him. People on the list vanished. Their disappearances were accounted for in different ways, depending on what kind of mood the emperor was in. Sometimes the culprits were radical Ibaran nationalists, intent on eradicating the Terasian population, because being at war with Ibara wasn't enough. They were demons summoned by Ibaran clerics, because believing the people of Ibara were devil-worshipping degenerates was engraved in the collective consciousness, easy to exploit. They were Reisen Kaneko, which was the worst of all possibilities, because Reisen was not an outsider or an opposing force, he was one of them. Reisen didn't hate them for being different. His reasons were more obscure, more terrifying.

Reisen was many things, but a terrorist wasn't one of them. Emperor Haken had to discredit him, to ensure no one would believe Reisen if he came forwards to discuss things like how the inkworm infection spread or what really happened to the sun. Auryn had been telling his wife this for years, but she'd never believed him. Now, on her daily patrols, she was confronted by the faces of Reisen's alleged victims as they were herded to their deaths, and she knew he'd been right all along.

"What broke?" Sasha, his shirt covered in shiny fish scales.

His wife walked past their son without stopping. "It was an accident," she muttered, retreating into the kitchen.

"Dad?"

Auryn smiled. "It's okay, Sasha. Don't worry. Mom's just tired." He hugged his son reassuringly. "Everything's okay." The boy sought out the company of his toy giraffe, Mr. Bumpy, for additional comfort. Last year Emperor Haken released a line of toys featuring long extinct animals, the likes of which they may have the chance to see someday, if humanity behaved itself enough to justify the restoration of the sun. The three of them built a pillow fortress on the couch until dinner was ready.

He couldn't sleep. The city lights dimmed to a barely visible glow, just enough to reassure everyone they would return in the morning. His wife shifted in bed next to him and pressed against his bare back, kissing his neck. He could pretend to be asleep, but she knew better.

"You're so mean to me," she murmured, slipping a hand inside his pyjama bottoms. Her bony, silky fingers felt all wrong. Nothing about her body appealed to him, soft in places that should have been hard. There was no enticing musk, no allure of the familiar.

"Am not," he protested, his cock slowly hardening from the heat and friction of her hand. The reaction was both unwanted and unavoidable, diluting any pleasure he got out of it. An orgasm at the hands of his wife was less fulfilling than alleviating a full bladder and took considerably longer.

"All you do is follow orders."

"This coming from someone who turned in her own sister."

"Reisen corrupted her. I had no choice."

"Do we have to talk about this right now?"

"You never have time, Auryn. Trying to talk to you is like trying to hammer nails into a board with my forehead. It hurts and it's utterly fucking pointless."

"I'll make time, okay?" He wanted her to stop talking. Blocking her out was harder when he had to listen to the sound of her voice.

"Fine." He wondered if he should be more worried than he was, if something more than job frustration was eating away at her. It wouldn't be a bad idea to sit her down and have a serious talk, but it would have to wait until she didn't have his dick in her hand. He didn't want to be within striking range when he got to the root of the problem.

She clawed at his shoulder, rolling him onto his back, and tugged his bottoms off. The warmth of her mouth almost consoled him, but even that made him wish he was somewhere else. As her tongue swept over the crown of his cock, he thought of Reisen.

Auryn awoke with pale morning light shining on him. He couldn't feel it on his bare skin, but knew it was there. He shifted away from his wife, making a break for the edge of the bed, only to be apprehended mid escape, her arms wrapping tightly around him.

"Morning," she murmured, nuzzling his neck. "You're not going into work today, are you?"

"For a little while." It was a day of rest, but he needed to get away from her. Needed time to himself, even if it was sitting in a temple for eight hours, contemplating all the ways in which his soul was damned.

She leaned back, rubbing below the ridge of her brow bone, trying to relieve the pressure in her skull. Another headache. She'd been getting them for years, but lately they'd become more frequent. "Maybe you should see a doctor."

"No." She shook her head. "They'll say they want to keep me overnight for observation, then kill me in my sleep and use my guts to fertilise Emperor Haken's plants."

"You're being paranoid." He placed his hands on her shoulders, trying to be a decent husband. "All the more reason to see a doctor. Want me to make you an appointment?"

"Hold on." She folded her arms across her chest, glowering. "I see what you're trying to do. Make me feel like I'm going crazy. Bet you'd love to lock me in the attic and have Sasha all to yourself."

"You're right where I want you." He caressed her cheek, hoping he sounded sufficiently convincing.

"Promise?" Stretched out on the bed, casting aside the sheets, her hands roved over her body.

"Promise." He did what any dutiful husband would do, preoccupied with thoughts of hanging himself from the showerhead. Afterward, he stood in the bathroom, unsurprised to find himself seriously considering the idea.

The thought of leaving Sasha alone with her was enough to dissuade him, indicating he probably wasn't as miserable as he thought. He tried to think of something more cheerful, but positive thinking required more energy than he was willing to expend.

He brushed his teeth, getting the taste of his wife out of his mouth. He turned the shower on and stepped into the spray. Her scent was all over him. Even with soap and water, he didn't feel clean. Self-disgust was deeply ingrained, part of his skin, impossible to wash away. That didn't prevent him from trying. Auryn scrubbed harder. Water burned as it hit reddened flesh, but it never helped. The heat brought no catharsis.

He tried to clear his mind, to find a moment of clarity, and ended up with his cock in his hand. Reisen's body was etched in his mind, like hieroglyphs carved in rock. Weathered, but still prominent.

Auryn's feelings for Reisen hadn't crept up on him. Reisen intoxicated him from the start. Two long strands of hair grew well past Reisen's ears, dyed a vibrant, unnatural hue of red, trailing down the front of his chest in slender tails. The tails were accented with alternating white and black stripes, like the bands of a snake. His hair was shorter at the top of his head, grouped into slanting black-tipped tapers, long in the back.

Irrationally long.

Reisen's dark eyes told of limitless possibilities and in them Auryn was not lost, but found.

His wife's hair conditioner helped bring him to orgasm.

Auryn dressed and joined his family for breakfast. He hugged Sasha and kissed his wife goodbye, hating her, hating himself, hating everything.

It was late when he returned home, finding the apartment unusually dark. "Sasha? Where is everyone?"

He noticed the smell before reaching the kitchen. Wet, rusty iron that had somehow gone bad. His wife stood with her back to him, chopping mechanically. Dried blood stained the floor, so dark it was almost black, following the grooves between tiles, forming perpendicular lines. Auryn stood there, numb. She turned to him, eyes glazed, lost in a distant inferno.

"Sasha is gone, Auryn. One of the shadow people took over his body. I made sure it wouldn't bother us anymore. I chopped it into little pieces."

He didn't remember much after that. He did recall finding his wife dead in the bathtub and realising he had no idea how she got there. By the time the investigators arrived he'd gathered his senses enough to create a convincingly garbled recollection of how he'd found her that way.

Elia, the prince of Terasyn, wasn't far behind them. He'd known Elia for as long as he could remember, long enough to know the prince knew he was guilty, but there was no discussion of his involvement. No mention of the scratch marks on his neck or the crack in his wife's skull. Instead, Elia went to work, burying the incident, ensuring no word of it was spoken to the media and keeping the news confined to the royal family and those directly involved in the investigation. An autopsy revealed a malignant brain tumour, leading to the official conclusion his wife had taken a bath after killing Sasha during an unfortunate psychotic episode. She'd experienced a seizure, hit her head, and drowned. A plausible scenario. As far as Auryn was aware, no one ever questioned it.

The ensuing grief covered Auryn in a heavy shroud. There wasn't much to say about grief, apart from the fact that it hurt. Everything else was secondary.

Chapter Three

AURYN AWOKE WITH Keita thrashing beside him. He'd fallen asleep next to the boy, afraid of letting him out of sight. Keita cried out in his sleep, turning over again, nearly rolling off the edge of the bed. Auryn grabbed him and woke him, adding to Keita's apparent terror and confusion. Keita fought him, forcing him to pin the boy's arms to his sides, gently squeezing him. The struggle gradually subsided, replaced with hysterical tears. Auryn held him until the crying stopped.

He managed to entice Keita to the kitchen table and began an inspection of the refrigerator's contents. "You must be starving. What do you want to eat?"

Keita shrugged and stared vacantly at the table. Auryn wondered if discussing what had happened to Keita would be of therapeutic value, but didn't want to pry— didn't want to ask questions the boy may be uncomfortable with answering, placing him in the same category as Keita's tormenters.

"Let's see... There's eggs, cheese, bacon, sausage... If you want, I can make pancakes."

Keita shrugged again. Auryn wondered if he knew what any of those things were. Reisen would have had limited access to food supplies, being a wanted criminal and all.

"I know what you might like. Apple pie." Auryn cut Keita a slice—he'd picked the apples himself from a greenhouse in Building A—and topped it with a scoop of vanilla ice cream. "Don't tell your father I let you eat this for breakfast."

Keita wearily studied the confection. It was disconcerting to see someone so sceptical of pie. "When will I see him again?"

"When it's safe."

"How long'll that be?"

"Might be a while." Auryn sat across from Keita, digging into his own slice of pie. Nothing made one feel like a responsible adult quite like having dessert for breakfast. "In the meantime, you can stay here with me, okay?"

"Okay." Keita impaled a chunk of apple and nibbled it tentatively. Small bites turned into big bites, and next thing he knew, Keita was devouring mouthful after mouthful, filling Auryn with a sense of purpose he'd nearly forgotten existed.

Auryn cut Keita off after four slices of pie, concerned the boy's stomach had reached maximum capacity and anything additional would do more harm than good.

"I have to get to work. Stay here and make yourself at home. There's toys in your room." They'd belonged to Sasha. He'd tried to throw them away when he moved and thrown up his lunch instead and, oh god, he couldn't do it. He set the spare bedroom up to look like Sasha's room, for days when he *really* wanted to torture himself, and it worked wonderfully. "Watch TV if you like, but remember Emperor Haken controls everything you see. It's not an accurate picture of the world. There's a lot of lies, particularly about your father. Might be something you want to avoid, but I'll leave that up to you. Any questions?"

Keita peered up at him. "If I get hungry later, can I have more pie?"

"Help yourself."

IN ANTICIPATION OF Keita's arrival, Auryn deleted the record of an earlier visitor. A nine-year-old boy classified as noncompliant—asking too many questions in class, arguing with his teachers. Like most additions to the Farm, the boy and his parents had been taken at night.

The boy's remains were vacuum packed and labelled with Keita's ID number. Almost nothing was wasted. Emperor Haken had a taste for his subjects. Only the head and genitals were exempted from consumption, soaked in consecrated oil and set alight.

Auryn began his daily patrol in Building A—over 200,000 square feet of greenhouses rigged with artificial lights, producing food for roughly 100,000 people on the surface and the animals in Building C. Fast-growing, genetically modified crops maximised output, largely the product of Reisen's research.

Hot, humid air swirled around him, making Auryn's uniform uncomfortably warm so the fabric stuck to his back. Finding staff willing to work under such conditions was easy. It beat working in the capital, where the emperor's growing contempt for a population fumbling towards enlightenment at the speed of limbless babies resulted in fewer luxuries and colder temperatures.

The sun shone overhead, clearly visible through sheets of polycarbonate. An illusion, but an important one. When Emperor Haken swallowed the sun, millennia ago, there was 300 years of absolute darkness. A time of penitence and self-reflection, during which the suicide rate climbed until roughly half the population were dead and Haken reluctantly agreed to give people a glimpse of what they were supposed to be working for. His Holiness was nothing if not merciful.

Climate controls checked out. Crop yields looked good. They kept up with demand and stored what little surplus they had, praying they never needed it. Auryn paused at a peach tree, indulging in a moment of quality control. He liked peaches, though they inspired an inexplicably mixed reaction. The texture seemed off. Too smooth. He wasn't sure what he wanted instead. The fruit tasted fine, but lacked sweetness. It fell short of unreasonable expectations and never failed to confound him. The taste reminded him of something he couldn't identify. Something buried in the back of his mind, resisting recovery.

Once assured everything in Building A was running smoothly, Auryn moved on to Building B—packaging and shipping. As Director of Operations for the Farm, his main interest was efficiency, reaching and maintaining production goals. Any disputes or practices interfering with achieving these goals were not tolerated.

Building C housed a variety of animals—cows, pigs, fish, and chickens. Maintaining them was ridiculously expensive and consumed more far resources than Auryn deemed practical—the largest cows consumed over 60 pounds of feed per day—but Emperor Haken insisted, refusing suggestions for optimisation. The animals of Building C aged quickly, reaching full maturity after several months, after which they were either utilised for breeding purposes or slaughtered.

Chickens were housed in an area jokingly referred to as the "chicken wing," crushed into thousands of tiny cages, beaks trimmed to prevent stress-induced self-mutilation and cannibalism. Cows and pigs lived out the duration of their short lives under the same roof. A small number were spared terrifying confinement and raised in the "Massage Parlour," a special section where the pens weren't overcrowded and the animals occupying them were well cared for. Unlike the others, they were content. Oblivious to their fates. Their muscles and hides were massaged with alcohol on a regular basis, producing meat of exceptional quality with a price tag to match.

Auryn stepped onto the kill floor, at which point he usually caught himself thinking of inventive ways to die, involving things like meathooks and air saws. It felt strange to walk past a hide fleshing machine without experiencing the urge to stop and stick his head inside. Keita needed him, at least for now.

Those like Keita—political dissidents, sexual deviants, heretics, and other "undesirables" inevitably ended up here. Human sacrifices appeased the emperor and his family, buying much-needed patience and tolerance for their subjects. Sacrifices were ritualistically slaughtered in a secure section of the building, hidden from civilian eyes. Civilians never questioned the disappearances of their neighbours, knowing what happened when you doubt the integrity of a living god. An omnipotent being who saw everything. Heard everything. Owned warehouses full of surveillance equipment.

To do his job, Auryn needed to be detached. Being under orders helped dilute any sense of responsibility, but the greatest sense of distance came from progressive desensitisation. He'd seen his first dead body at age twelve—a suicide, jumped out a window, skull split open, brains everywhere. It haunted him for years, but as the disturbing visual was joined by others, it became less visceral, less traumatic. Just a splash of colour on the sidewalk.

Auryn drove a utility vehicle back to Building D and settled into his office, reviewing financial statements for the upcoming budget, losing himself in a sea of numbers. He usually worked late, preferring distraction to being left alone with his thoughts, putting in more hours than required, but for the first time in recent memory, he left his desk early. He descended into the basement and unlocked the door to his quarters, eager to check on Keita.

He found the boy in front of the TV, eyes glued to the screen, listening intently to the news.

"Twenty-seven-year-old Keera Denkawa's body was found this evening in a dumpster on 19th street. Her eyes, ears, and tongue were removed, an all too familiar calling card of terrorist Reisen Kaneko. Occult symbols used in dark magick and demon worship were found burned into her skin and leading experts to conclude she was victim of a perverse sacrifice. Our thoughts and prayers go out to her family."

Auryn switched off the TV. "That's enough of that."

Keita stared at the blank screen. "If my dad didn't hurt her, who did?"

"Do you remember what I told you before I left?"

"Don't believe everything you see on TV," muttered Keita.

"That's right. Saying someone found a dead body doesn't make it so. The only thing we know for sure is that the lady on TV is being paid to say whatever the emperor wants her to."

"Then how do you know what's real?"

Auryn sat beside Keita on the couch, considering a variety of responses before settling on the most honest, but least reassuring. "You don't. That's why you question everything."

Chapter Four

KEITA LAY ON the floor of the interrogation room, cold cement biting him in places where his clothing was burned or torn. It hurt to breathe, his ribs bruised where the men kicked him. His nose stung from the acrid fumes exuded by bright flares, drowning out the stench of blood and urine. He wiggled a loose tooth with his tongue, tasting damp coins. His wrist throbbed, dangling at an unnatural angle.

Keita wiped his eyes on his sleeve. The stupid tears wouldn't stop flowing out of him in a stubborn trickle. He heard the door unlock. Footsteps. Voices.

An explosion of light.

Fire.

Keita kicked and screamed, held tight by strong arms. As the nightmare faded, his terror remained. How long before Auryn decided he was more trouble than he was worth? A rotten kid who cried too much, ate too much. A baby who couldn't sleep through the night without throwing a fit.

Auryn lay next to him, rubbing his back. The repetitive motion soothed him somewhat, but he dared not go back to sleep, lying there breathing harshly in the dark. Auryn squeezed his hand, holding it until the shaking stopped. Keita managed to stop crying, only occasionally gasping for air.

Auryn got up and turned the light on. Keita curled into a ball. This was it. Auryn was finished with him. Should he beg for his life? For one more chance? Auryn opened the closet, digging through it. "Aha. Here it is." A gun, perhaps. Or a big sword. He was afraid to look, but curiosity got the best of him. The last thing he expected to see in Auryn's hands was a toy frog with a propeller sticking out of its back. "Frogcopter. The Froggiest Copter of them all."

Still dressed in his pyjamas, Keita followed Auryn to a section of the basement with high ceilings and lots of open space. After a quick lesson, Keita gripped the controls, carefully navigating the flying frog. The whirring blades inspired a sense of freedom he'd never felt before. Frogcopter could go anywhere. Do anything. He imagined himself in the cockpit, surveying distant worlds, soaring over lakes and mountains, seeing the sun rise from way up high. He flew from one end of the room to the other, excitement swelling in his chest.

"You're very good at that, son." Auryn smiled at him. "Before I met your father, I flew planes for the emperor."

Keita slowed the frog down, hovering in place. "You were in the air force?"

"I joined the military when I was sixteen. They needed volunteers to design and test a series of stealth aircraft intended to fly undetected over Ibaran airspace. I was half engineer, half test pilot." Keita listened intently to every word, captivated by Auryn's obvious love of flying. "I could spend all day up there. I told Haken I wanted to fly higher than anyone. All the way up to the moon."

"My dad has pilot wings. They're silver with a sun in the middle." Keita flew up and up. The moon would be a neat place to visit. Maybe he'd go there one day. "He said someone special gave them to him."

At first, he thought he'd hurt Auryn's feelings. A look of sadness briefly overtook his face, replaced by a slight smile. "I'm glad he kept them."

YEAR 2043
Eighteen Years Ago

Hallowed Mountain Complex, Military Base

"Before you go in, there's something you should know. Your roommate is a bit eccentric. Last guy he shared a room with had to be taken away in a straitjacket."

"Thanks for the warning, but I'm sure I can handle it." Auryn's curiosity overrode any concern. He'd heard Reisen Kaneko could be difficult—stubborn and highly irrational—but this was what he'd trained for. He was ready.

Auryn opened the door. An overhead sprinkler was triggered, soaking everything. Reisen sat in the middle of it all, wearing a white lab coat. Dark, circular sunglasses shielded his eyes from view. Red hair stuck to him in wet tendrils. A large pair of white headphones crowned his head.

Auryn stepped into the room, closing the door behind him. Reisen didn't appear to notice he had company. He approached cautiously, making no sudden movements.

"What are you listening to?" He wasn't sure if Reisen could hear him.

Reisen glanced up at him. "Ludwig Van Beethoven's 'Ode to Joy.' It sounds like something the God of Rain would listen to at high volume to ward off a panic attack, attempting to anchor in a sea of anxiety, exhaling thunder and inhaling lighting."

"I'm not familiar with it."

"I didn't expect you to be. I have the only copy."

Auryn was already soaked, water pooling at his feet. "My name is Colonel Auryn Tyrus. I'm the new chaplain."

"Dr. Reisen Kaneko. Pleasure to meet you, Colonel Tyrus. Does our darling emperor think you'll be a good influence? Help keep me on my best behaviour?"

"His Holiness knows you'd never stray far from the Light. This was the only bunk available."

"How convenient." Reisen removed his headphones, offering them. "Want to listen?"

Auryn put the headphones on, sceptical. "I never thought of gods as having a use for music."

"How else would you expect them to maintain their sanity?" Reisen let the song play for several minutes, then paused it to inform Auryn, "This is my favourite part."

The song was appropriately named. He'd never heard anything so joyful. It wasn't anything like the music Emperor Haken allowed to play on the radio—all boring, one-dimensional noise devoid of personality. Mostly bland piano arrangements with an occasional harp accompaniment. This was triumphant yet vulnerable, encapsulating a range of human emotion over the span of numerous carefully crafted notes. He wanted to listen over and over again. Fortunately, Reisen was happy to share.

Reisen's generous, considerate nature vexed him. Reisen was eccentric, not crazy. Honest, not a pathological manipulator. Humble, not arrogant. Worst of all, he was easy to get along with. Too easy.

It made his mission much harder than anticipated.

"YOU'RE LUCKY THEY let you grow your hair so long. Doesn't it get in the way?" asked Auryn.

Auryn and Reisen sat in their room, drinking tea in the dark. It was late at night, long after everyone was supposed to be asleep.

"Sometimes," replied Reisen, lighting a cigarette. "But I've had long hair as long as I can remember. I hate cutting it. Feels too much like self-mutilation."

"For your sake, I hope no one takes issue with it."

"My mother punched someone who told her it was inappropriate for a young man to look like a little girl. Anger management wasn't her strong suit."

Auryn took a swig of tea, peering over the rim of the cup to watch Reisen's cigarette cling to the corner of his mouth, trying not to stare. His gaze lingered too long on the man's features, compulsively tracing them, memorising them like flight formulas. "I don't remember my parents." Sometimes he ransacked his memory for any trace of life before arriving at the orphanage. He never found anything but isolated crumbs—someone with rough hands, skin dry and cracked, the nauseating smell of rotten meat. The urge to shed his skin. A woman in a green sweater, her face blurred by time, sleeves too long.

"Orphanage kid, eh? What was it like being raised by the government?"

"Everything revolved around discipline and duty. Doing what's best for Terasyn, not for ourselves."

Reisen shook his head. "A fine sentiment for programming robots. Raising children, not so much."

"It was okay. Every now and then the emperor stopped by. I used to play games with Prince Elia."

"Did they involve pulling intestines out of someone's rectum?" Auryn stared at Reisen in horror. To speak of a member of the royal family in such a way was heresy. Reisen grinned crookedly. "Sorry. Elia is a creep."

"Mortals are in no position to criticise the divine."

"I can see why they let you run the chapel, Colonel." Reisen confused him in every way imaginable. "But I'm afraid I disagree. Mortals are obligated to criticise the divine. To question everything. Otherwise we're no better than sheep."

"We're not qualified to think for ourselves," countered Auryn. "We don't know what's best for us. We *are* no better than sheep, and we can't afford to reject the guidance of a competent shepherd."

"Abused sheep have warped ideas of what constitutes a competent shepherd."

Auryn watched Reisen's blasphemous lips move, excited and cursed. He wanted to kiss him, even if it meant damnation, losing everything. "Come with me to the chapel. Pray with me. The gods will give you strength."

"No, thanks, Chaplain. I'm good."

I'm not.

Auryn sighed in frustration, standing. "It's late, anyway. We should sleep." Idle minds produced dangerous thoughts. They crawled back into their bunks. Auryn closed his eyes, trying to get comfortable, tense all over. "Reisen... Did you really drive your last roommate crazy?"

"Nah. You're giving me way more credit than I deserve. He wigged out on his own. I'm just a convenient scapegoat. General Mordha doesn't like me much, I'm afraid. Maybe it's the hair."

The sound of Reisen breathing steadily in the bunk above him usually provided some strange solace, a fragile peace dependent on Auryn's ability to remain focused on its cadence, but at some point during the night, his mind derailed. The list of long and increasingly disturbing things he wanted to do to Reisen became too painful to ignore.

He defiled himself, as quietly as possible, stroking and stroking until bursting, falling asleep with his cock in hand, already beyond redemption.

"YOU WON'T GET away with this." They sat in the mess hall, Reisen smoking and conversing with a portable video game device he often carried. Auryn didn't understand the appeal of pixelated characters and blinking lights, but Reisen could stay immersed in it for hours, pushing buttons long after complaining of sore thumbs.

"Talking to that game again?" asked Auryn as he peered over at the screen. A pulse of jealousy reminded Auryn of his growing fascination with Reisen. He wished he could monopolise as much of Reisen's time as that primitive machine. He wanted to eradicate the space between them, to feel Reisen's hands on him instead of rescuing imaginary princesses.

"Don't judge me," murmured Reisen. He was quiet for a moment, then erupted into righteous indignation. "Seriously, dude! Sixty rupias for a loaf of bread and no discount? Are you out of your fucking mind? Go ahead, make that face! Throw me out! I'm coming right back in there with my flying monkey and he's going to shit all over you."

Auryn jabbed his meatloaf and shifted it around his plate, appetite lacking. At times he caught Reisen looking at him a certain way, with something approaching fondness, but attraction to a member of the same sex was punishable by death, and he wasn't willing to risk being wrong about the nature of those furtive glances.

"Kaneko!" An officer charged into the hall.

"Hang on. I'm being eaten by a flower."

"Now! You're needed in medical. Tyrus... You'd better come, too." That could only mean one thing. Someone was either dying or dead.

They rushed to the hospital, past more security than Auryn had ever seen, all the way down to the isolation ward.

"They're not contagious," the resident doctor was quick to explain. "We, ah...wanted to keep them away from the others." She drew back the curtain to reveal the patient. The soldier's eyes were sunken black pools of tar-like sludge, charring his cheeks as it trickled down his face, lips and tongue grotesquely swollen, each breath a strangled wheeze. "There's six of them. They were patrolling the Ibaran border and got out to inspect an abandoned vehicle. There was an explosion—a bomb containing some kind of parasite."

"Fucking hell." Reisen had a strange vocabulary, often using words Auryn never heard before. *Hell. Christ. Earth.*

The soldier coughed, spraying black bile, gargling, choking. Auryn stepped back. "You *sure* they're not contagious?"

"The parasite is blood-borne."

"How can I help?" asked Reisen.

"We can't figure out an effective treatment. Vermicide isn't working. You work with lots of medicinal plants. Maybe something will ease the infection."

"Send a sample up to my lab. I'll see what I can do."

Auryn knew what his role was. He clasped his hands together and prayed.

Chapter Five

AURYN MADE UP his mind. Instead of allowing Keita to sit alone all day, languishing in front of the TV, he needed something to keep the boy occupied. Something to keep his mind off being tortured. A little distraction went a long way.

A single chemist operated a laboratory in Building D, researching ideal concoctions for treating the food produced and distributed by the Farm. The chemist, Arandano, was mild-mannered, but anti-social, failing to expand his known associates beyond a puffball monkey named Winkie.

Auryn knocked on the metal door several times before Arandano stuck his bald head out.

"Yes?"

"Arandano, my son will be assisting you from now on. He wants to be a chemist when he grows up, and I'd like him to see what he's getting into."

Arandano blinked at him from behind thick, round glasses. "Is he allergic to sergite, derastrium, or ancastrum?"

"Not that I'm aware of."

Arandano wrinkled his nose. "He'll do."

"I realise this is an unusual request. I'll throw in some new equipment for the inconvenience."

A smile spread across Arandano's face, revealing teeth filed into sharp points. "Didja hear that, Winkie?

We're gettin' a new electron microscope." Winkie hopped on Arandano's shoulder, chirping excitedly.

"Until tomorrow, then." Auryn walked off, cautiously optimistic.

THE LABORATORY'S PRIMARY function was engineering chemical compounds produced to treat products manufactured at the Farm. Their purpose was mainly one of sedation, designed to keep the population of Terasyn content and unquestioning. Arandano was also responsible for creating the combination of chemicals circulating in Terasyn's water supply.

Keita clenched his small, sweaty hands at his sides. Auryn gave him an encouraging nudge towards a large steel-plated door. He'd told him to lie, to say he was his son, should the topic come up, but not to worry, because Arandano wasn't in the habit of showing interest in other humans.

"Go on in, Keita. I'll be back in a few hours to check on you."

"H-Hello?" Keita cracked open the door and peered inside.

Auryn anxiously watched him disappear, reminded of Sasha's first day of school.

When time came to collect the boy, he found him napping in a corner of Arandano's lab. Winkie was curled up in Keita's lap, asleep. Keita was eager to return—Arandano asked little of him, more interested in making colourful foam explode out of bottles and microwaving soap than putting the boy to work. Auryn was relieved.

Keita continued struggling with nightmares. Even when awake, he frightened with increasing ease, painfully aware of his surroundings. Loud noises made him shrink inside his skin. Arandano created a chemical concoction designed to reduce the severity of his symptoms, but Keita didn't respond well. He developed headaches so severe he couldn't see straight and frequently experienced a sensation Keita compared to being smashed in the face with a brick, his head snapping back as if he'd physically been struck.

Strange, acrid-smelling cigarettes Arandano smoked provided a mildly comforting alternative. The combination of medicinal herbs created a sense of solace otherwise lost. It didn't take long for Keita to acquire a habit.

By the age of fourteen, Keita had self-medication down to an art.

KEITA'S EYELIDS SAGGED under the load of heavy weights, resistant to opening for more than a few seconds at a time, but he continued fighting a battle he was bound to lose, too stubborn to surrender.

He didn't need sleep. Sleep was bad dreams and rude awakenings. It was also elusive. Trying to sleep indicated to his brain that it was time to review every stupid thing he'd said or done, and search for reasons to panic. Did he remember to change all the garbage cans in the lab? Had he locked Winkie's treat drawer? Had he put any chemicals he'd used back in the right spot? Waking up was equally fun. Waking up triggered an automatic spike in his anxiety levels, as if consciousness itself was somehow distressing. Then he'd think about everything that could go wrong. Today would be the day Keita was discovered, the day Auryn didn't come home, the day they were attacked by terrorists or Ibaran soldiers or blood-drinking mutants. Then he'd really panic. He'd rather stay awake, stay close to Auryn.

The news droned in the background, but he wasn't listening. He rarely did. He didn't want to hear about Reisen's latest crime against humanity. He just wanted to see old photos of his dad fill the screen. *If you see Reisen Kaneko, notify authorities immediately. Do not attempt to approach him. Kaneko is armed and extremely dangerous.* Haken's persistence reassured him Reisen was still out there somewhere. All he could do was hope his dad was okay, eating at least once a day, and going to bed when he got tired, not staying awake for days. Reisen hated sleeping. Said it was a waste of time. There was too much to do.

He lay on the couch, his head almost in Auryn's lap, cheek pressed to his leg. Keita turned his head, brushing his nose against the fabric of Auryn's trousers, breathing deep. He caught the scent of laundry soap, but mostly he smelled Auryn—a faint, pleasant muskiness which both excited and alarmed him.

Certain changes were hard to ignore. His body always felt too warm, too tight, as if he'd been wrapped in hot, wet leather and left under a heat lamp to dry. His pants were always too short, his shoes too small. He coloured his hair stark white and gleefully observed its expansion into new territory.

His dick behaved strangely, sticking up sometimes, desperate for attention. He'd figured out how to appease it, but there was no telling when it might strike. Done pushing his luck, he inhaled another lungful of Auryn and forced himself to sit up, rubbing his eyes with an arm.

"We should try to sleep." Auryn switched off the TV and stood up, stretching.

"Want some company?" asked Keita. Months had passed since they'd slept in the same bed. Now that he was older, Auryn gave him more space, unaware space was the last thing he wanted. He wanted Auryn beside him, to focus on the sound of his breathing instead of all the bad things.

"Sure." Auryn sounded surprised. "Are you feeling all right? You look warm."

"I'm okay." He hated lying to Auryn, but if he told Auryn he wasn't well, Auryn would want to know what was wrong. "Someone has to make sure you don't stay up all night reading crop reports."

"That doesn't sound like something I'd do." Auryn smiled at him, briefly replacing the weight in his chest with lightness.

"Of course not." Keita changed into his pyjamas and brushed his teeth, joining Auryn in bed. He used to be haunted while he slept, terrorised by spectres summoning fire and lightning, but Auryn was always there to fight them off, and after seven years, they'd been weakened, tormenting him less frequently.

He lay with his back to Auryn, breathing softly. Now the future terrified him more than the past. Would Auryn get tired of him? Decide he wasn't worth the risk? How angry and disgusted would Auryn be if he knew how much time Keita spent imagining him naked? What if Haken arrived unexpectedly and walked in on the two of them like this? No excuse would save them. Haken would never believe they were innocent. He'd see the truth in Keita's eyes.

Panic gnawed at his chest, stealing his breath.

Auryn's hand brushed his back, rubbing it reassuringly. "You're safe."

A convincing lie, but Keita's stomach sank. He tried hard to be a man, to be as strong as Auryn, but men didn't need to be comforted like frightened children. Auryn had nothing to show for his efforts, only a roommate with a poisoned soul.

"If Haken found me, what would he do to you?" He had a recurring dream where Auryn was arrested and interrogated, beaten unrecognisable, defiled and reviled. Being unable to do anything about it upset him more than when he'd been the target, as horrified as he was helpless.

Auryn shifted closer, hugging him. "That's the last thing you should be thinking about when you're trying to sleep."

"I can't help it. My brain's a jerk."

"Think of something that makes you happy."

"I try, but bad thoughts always come back."

"Be persistent. Don't let the bad thoughts win. The more you acknowledge them, the more powerful they become."

If Keita wanted to become a man, he'd have to fight for it. "What d'you think about when you're trying to sleep?"

"Being somewhere warm. Sunshine."

"Maybe I'll try that."

Auryn released him from the hug, giving his shoulder a light squeeze.

"Can't hurt."

Keita tried to picture somewhere not covered in snow. He thought of a bright blue sky, the sun beaming overhead, too bright to look at for long. He added trees and flowers and a wide river. It was peaceful, but something was missing. None of those things made him feel safe.

Only with Auryn's addition did he begin to relax.

Chapter Six

YEAR 2072

Auryn made eggs and toast for breakfast. Fresh out of the shower, Keita sat at the table with a towel wrapped around his hips. Hunger apparently trumped getting properly dressed. Keita barely chewed his food, swallowing each bite with mouthfuls of tepid tea. Auryn had seen pigs eat with less urgency. He cracked a smile, offering Keita a slice of pineapple, left over from the young man's eighteenth birthday a few days prior. The sweet, juicy flesh disappeared, whole, into Keita's mouth. Sticky fluid dripped down his chest, leaving a wet streak on his pale skin.

"Go get dressed," instructed Auryn. "There's something I want to teach you."

"I'm going, I'm going." Keita lit a cigarette and wandered off, running a hand through his wet, white hair. His body had evolved beyond the lanky, awkward stage where nothing fit for long, growing into a newly minted adult skin.

There was nothing self-conscious about Keita, a recent change painfully reminiscent of the young man's father. Reisen was similarly indifferent to clothing, wandering their room in his underwear long before Auryn expressed any interest in seeing the bulge of his cock.

Muscular lines in Keita's torso stood out more, no longer buried beneath layers of baby fat. Auryn found himself looking for excuses to touch him, craving physical contact as rudimentary as the brush of a hand or the warmth of Keita's head on his shoulder. The other night Keita had fallen sleep with an arm around him, and the way it made his body ache came as a deplorable shock.

It wasn't Keita's maleness that bothered him. He'd come to an uneasy peace with that aspect of his nature years ago. It wasn't even his age, despite the years between them. What disturbed him was the considerable mental energy he'd used over the years, convincing himself he was an acceptable substitute for Keita's father, *capable* of being a decent father, only to find himself wanting to do unfatherly things. His affection felt warped and inexcusable. The perversion was not in his preference—despite what Emperor Haken had to say on the subject—but his taste in recipient.

"What's this thing you insist on educating me about?" Keita returned, fully dressed. Auryn had less difficulty looking at him. Keita sat next to him on the couch. "It's not another lecture on milk production and lactation curves in cows, is it?"

"No. Nothing like that." Auryn reached out, grazing Keita's jaw with his thumb to remove a smear of shaving cream.

"That's a relief. I don't think I can handle that much mental stimulation without permanent scarring." Keita switched the television on, not out of disrespect, but habit.

"A new study shows the average life expectancy in Terasyn has risen from 582 to 589," droned the newscaster, a monotone young woman. "Accelerated cellular degeneration is not expected to occur until after age 550. Between ages 26 and 372, very little is observable in terms of physical ageing. Life expectancy in Ibara is said to be much lower, falling from 540 to 523."

The report reeked of Prince Elia's relentless media-fuelled propaganda. Auryn could only marvel at the extent the administration went to mislead people.

"A statement released by the Holy Order describes this decrease as resulting from prolonged deviant behaviour and worship of demonic forces. In other words, divine punishment."

"Is that true?" asked Keita. "Are they really being punished?"

"No. Life expectancy is the same in both countries."

"Why make someone from Terasyn think they're going to live longer than someone from Ibara?"

"It helps the war effort. Most people would rather see their taxes go towards the destruction of an inferior than an equal."

"Do reporters in Ibara broadcast stories about what degenerate barbarians we are in comparison?"

"I've never been to Ibara."

"Someone should tell them what we put in our meat."

Auryn pressed a palm to his own forehead, sighing softly as he rose to his feet. "We should get going. I only have the temple reserved for an hour."

"The temple?" Keita looked horrified at the idea of being dragged to church. "Wait, you're not going to teach me a new prayer or something, are you? Because I told Winkie I'd help him change the tires on his forklift. They're balder than Arandano."

"It's a type of prayer, spoken only with blood—a divine contract."

"You're going to teach me magick?" Keita traded his troubled expression for mild curiosity, betraying just enough interest to avoid being seen as enthusiastic. A lingering adolescent quirk.

"Come, I'll show you."

FACES IN THE hallways were often new. Keita rarely saw the same person more than a dozen times; no one remained stationed at the Farm for long, except Auryn. As far as Keita knew, no one questioned his role here, assuming he was a military brat who simply spent a lot of time with his father.

He walked alongside Auryn, finding it easier to match his steps now that his legs were longer. He no longer had to work three times as hard to keep up, nearly as tall as Auryn and still growing.

Winkie whizzed by on his forklift, ferrying a container of chemical waste. The monkey poked his head out to flash them a thumbs up, but Auryn didn't look relieved.

"Those containers are leak-proof and puncture resistant, aren't they?"

"I hope so," replied Keita.

The walk to the temple was begrudgingly taken on days of prayer, but today Keita didn't dread reaching their destination. He'd seen the things Auryn could do with energy and had distant memories of Reisen using mystical powers to treat the wounded, determined to fix everyone.

The holograph towers were malfunctioning, replacing their fake sun with rock walls, a jarring reminder of reality. Several men in white coats stood around scratching their heads, trying to figure out what made the projectors stop working. The air tasted stale, but it was pleasantly warm. At least their climate controls were fully functional.

They paused at the entrance to the temple to remove their shoes, following the sound of running water to the worship hall. Holy water flowed from rows of gold bowls, emptying into a sacred pool where it was used for purification rituals and blessings. They walked past rows of pews, each equipped with its own coil of barbed wire to be wrapped around the fingers of a parishioner with the intention of driving away impious thoughts. Once the mind was purified, or the sermon was over—whichever came first—bloodied hands were washed in the healing waters of the fountain and rinsed clean of injury.

There was no smoking inside the temple and Keita chewed his bottom lip in the absence of a cigarette, anxiety twisting sharp knots in his chest. He drew in a deep breath and exhaled slowly, over and over again. Auryn regarded him with concern, but knew better than to ask him if he was all right. Keita would only deny the obvious. He was okay. He was *fine*. It was only his body turning against him, fighting him from the inside, filling him with unnecessary fire.

Unfamiliar situations and settings amplified the feeling of constant, irrational panic. All he could do was trust Auryn wouldn't subject him to this without good reason, and did so implicitly. The sense of security Auryn offered was the only thing standing between him and a full-blown panic attack.

A private chapel stood to the left of the vestry, accessible only through an armed door. Auryn keyed in the code and ushered him inside. "You can smoke in here, if you want."

"The gods won't strike me dead?" asked Keita, fumbling for a cigarette with shaky hands.

"They'll have to get through me first."

Keita's fingers closed around a silver lighter, flicking back the cover with a metallic *tink*, swiftly bringing his thumb down to strike up the flame. He revelled in the soothing smoke, blue eyes falling to a momentary close.

Carbon monoxide, tar, benzene, hydrogen cyanide, formaldehyde, and Arandano's personal stash—mainly nicotine in composition, but mixed with chemicals difficult to pronounce and a few herbs of unknown origin. A divinely toxic combination.

They sat in front of a large statue of a shrouded woman, her head bowed and palms upturned. The rock was white and immaculately clean, devoid of imperfection. Its surface was intricately carved, right down to the texture of the woman's clothing.

"This is one of three remaining sacred statues of Ibyx, Goddess of Healing," explained Auryn. "It was donated to the temple by Prince Elia, from his personal collection, to commemorate 500 years of operation at the Farm. Like all sacred statues, it has been blessed by the Creator with a spiritual link to Ibyx. To form a contract all that's required is a blood sacrifice—your blood. You'll act as a channel, directing Ibyx's energy for personal use. In this case, her energy is strictly viable for healing purposes, so you won't be storming any castles with it, but it may come in handy the next time Arandano blows something up."

"How does it work?"

"I'll teach you. But first, the easy part. The contract." Auryn approached a small white bowl at the statue's feet. Upon closer inspection Keita realised the bowl was an upturned skullcap, the bone bleached and worn. He finished his cigarette, carefully extinguishing the flame and confining it to his pocket. He looked to Auryn for reassurance. "Don't worry. All you need is a few drops."

The ceremonial dagger was large for such a limited quantity, but true to his word, Auryn pierced only the tip of his index finger and smeared the inside of the receptacle with several crimson drops.

An audible hiss was instantaneous, filling Keita's head with radiant noise, like the sound of an off-air television station, riddled with static. There was something distantly familiar about the sound. He wrote it off as too many nights spent flipping through a limited number of channels. He closed his eyes and covered his ears, wincing as the noise grew louder, only to halt all at once.

It stopped.

Keita opened his eyes. He knew instantly where he was, despite never having seen one—aboard a starship. Sweat dripped from his temples. A pair of armed men held a captive by the arms, one on each side. Their prisoner was, by far, the largest man Keita had ever seen. At least 7'5" tall with large white wings, he was some bizarre combination of human and bird. Glowing chains bound the birdman's hands behind his back. Naked from the waist up, his well-defined muscles and broad shoulders briefly captured Keita's attention.

The birdman's black hair had a bluish tint, descending to his collarbone in thick, straight tendrils, tucked behind pointed ears. His ears had numerous piercings—a set of silver rings along the shell of his ears, linked together with tiny chains. The birdman had a handsome, striking face, bluish-purple eyes, and a perfectly straight nose.

A man paced the length of the control room, gripping a bone saw in his right hand. Keita recognised him as Prince Elia. "You've taken something valuable from me. It's only fair that I take something valuable from you."

"My advice generally comes at a premium," replied the birdman, "but here's a tip for free—go stick your dick in a syphilitic sheep."

Elia withdrew a needle from his cloak. "Hold him tight. He's not going to like this."

He injected the birdman with a clear substance, draining his energy and forcing him to rely on his captors for support. Elia grabbed a wing, placing the blade of the saw as close to the birdman's shoulder as he could get, teeth gnawing through bone with each swipe. The birdman screamed—a shockingly human sound. Elia removed one wing, then the other. He folded them neatly, placing them in a large cooler.

Elia stalked towards the birdman, shoving him hard against the wall. "Fuck things up again, Dezmodeus, and I'll cut your cock off."

"Your mother...would never forgive you."

Elia punched Dezmodeus in the stomach, sending him sprawling on the floor. Keita's body moved on its own, piloted by an invisible captain. Within seconds of Dezmodeus hitting the ground, Keita was at his side, hands pressed to the tattered wounds in his back to try to stop the bleeding. He had no idea what he was doing, energy flowing through his palms and hands tingling like a live wire. Blood welled up between his fingers, undeterred. *Fuck.*

"Let's get out of here," said Elia, turning and walking away. One of the men picked up the cooler with ease and carried it away. The other remained standing, staring, hidden behind a black helmet.

Keita pushed down harder, directing more energy where needed but it made little difference. How did Elia expect Dezmodeus to survive? There was already enough blood on the floor to fill a small adult. He wished Auryn was there. Auryn would know what to do. Maybe this was a test—the Goddess ascertaining his worth, only to be disappointed by the result. It was too much.

The remaining man stepped forwards, joining Keita at Dezmodeus's side. "You're not focused. Concentrate on what you're doing." The voice sounded familiar, but the helmet obscured it, making it hard to identify.

Keita closed his eyes. Focused. Dezmodeus groaned, and he wasn't sure if it was out of pain or relief. The bleeding slowed, wounds closing. Nausea washed over him in waves. When the bleeding finally stopped, he collapsed, barely breathing. Instead of darkness there was light.

When it faded, Keita saw himself, no older than two years old. His clothing was covered in black stains. Inkworm. His mother lay nearby, not moving, her blonde hair covered in slime. He shook her, trying to wake her.

"Momma! Momma!"

The man who'd attacked her was stretched out nearby, facedown. Blood no longer flowed from the gash in his head, coagulating in dark puddles. Stiffening fingers gripped an empty needle.

Reisen burst through the door, sweeping Keita in his arms. Keita clung to him and sobbed. Reisen hugged him tightly, filling his ears with static.

Everything went black.

"Keita!" Auryn's voice. "Are you all right? What happened?"

"Don't know." The temple slowly came into focus. Keita wasn't sure how to respond. The memory faded quickly, leaving him tired and confused. "My ears started hurting."

"Strange. That's not supposed to happen."

"Lucky me. Must be her day off."

He tried to stand, but his legs gave out. Auryn caught him. He wanted to apologise for being too weak, but his mouth wouldn't work. His eyes refused to remain open. He had no idea what was going on, yet having Auryn nearby made it okay. He caved to the allure of sleep, knowing he was safe.

Chapter Seven

LATER THAT EVENING

Kuroi, Capital of Ibara

Black feathers littered the floor of the Ibaran palace. Aggnaroth gripped his sword tighter, palms slick with sweat. Striking Princess Jada was like assaulting a wall of granite—her defences were solid, unyielding. At 7'4" he was two feet taller than her, but it made little difference. When their swords clashed, he stood his ground, undeterred by her skilful handling.

Jada lowered her sword. "You're moulting again."

Nineteen years old and one of the most skilful fighters in Ibara, the princess insisted on working security for her father, Emperor Jaden. Her long black hair was pulled back from her face in a high ponytail, leaving her green eyes unobstructed. A few dark freckles graced her cheeks—errant stars on flawless skin.

She was beautiful beyond measure. A natural wonder.

"I had not noticed," Aggnaroth responded dryly. His people, the Nephilim, were bred for combat, serving the oldest known race, the Lightwalkers. Dark robes hid most of his body, partially concealing his face. He was sensitive about obvious differences in his anatomy, particularly his pointed ears. Humans always looked at him strangely, especially when they were unaccustomed to other races. Heck, humans barely tolerated other humans. Hiding his features only made people curious, but curiosity beat revulsion.

Jada coughed harshly, making him cringe inwardly. She had been sick for a week, growing sicker every day. Living in an isolated environment did little for promoting immunity to infection. Even the common cold was potentially lethal. Masking his concern became increasingly problematic.

"That cough sounds bad, Jada." Emperor Jaden swished the contents of his glass and sipped an amber coloured fluid. Aggnaroth was bound by contract to serve the emperor until his brother, Dezmodeus, repaid a debt of 500 billion dollars. Fortunately, the emperor's family was more interested in having their own Nephilim to play with than castrating Dezmodeus. His brother managed to soldier on without wings, but Aggnaroth feared the loss of his genitalia would prove too much.

"Perhaps I should take Her Majesty to the infirmary," suggested Aggnaroth.

"Let's give her until the morning to get her shit together. If she's not better by then, we'll put her out of her misery."

"You two are hysterical," groaned Jada. She covered his mouth, green eyes closing tight. She made a sickly retching sound, thin tendrils of black ooze leaking between clenched fingers.

Emperor Jaden stared in horrified disbelief. "Inkworm... She's infected! Summon a doctor!"

Aggnaroth tried to appear indifferent, reminding himself to breathe. "There is nothing a doctor can do. You know that."

"I don't give a fuck! You have connections." Jaden's eyes were wild, unhinged. "Find someone who knows what they're dealing with."

"I may know someone who can help."

"Don't stand there, go!"

"Right away, my lord."

Sometimes having a pet Nephilim came in handy.

"EMPEROR JADEN! AGGNAROTH'S returned! He's got someone with him."

Reisen Kaneko took less than a dozen steps into Princess Jada's bedroom before the emperor of Ibara grabbed him by the throat. He slammed him against the wall, pinning him in place.

"You're that brat from Terasyn who blows up old ladies."

"Actually, I kinda like old ladies." Reisen stared back at the emperor calmly, making no attempt to resist. "Not in a sexual way, mind you. Though there's something to be said for the unquestionable value of a hot mouth with no teeth."

Jaden shoved him hard. "You're a criminal. What the fuck makes you think I'll let you near my daughter?"

"I'm not much of a criminal, but attempts to convince people otherwise inevitably end with someone calling me a liar. Which is funny, considering if I was a liar I'd still be working for the government."

"Why do you have such disdain for your emperor?"

"Too many reasons to list."

"Answer the question!"

"Let's start with the most obvious, then. The man has terrible taste in fashion. All those gold sweaters are tacky as hell."

"Enough bullshit!"

"All right, all right. Emperor Haken is an intolerant, malignant narcissist. He's created a culture biased against anyone like me, anyone who doesn't fit into his fucked-up idea of a perfect world. The man should be in extensive therapy, not running a country." Emperor Jaden took a step back, allowing him to move away from the wall. "Now, if you don't mind, I'd like to examine your daughter before it's too late. Interrogating me will bring you less pleasure than tucking her into bed tonight."

Emperor Jaden moved aside, allowing him to pass.

"Thank you."

PRIESTS CLUSTERED AROUND the stricken princess' bed like barnacles glued to the hull of a sinking ship.

Reisen washed his hands in Jada's drinking fountain, grounding them. Twin stone dragons regurgitated a steady stream of water, their marble necks entwined. The water neutralised any disruptive forces, balancing energies. His senses swelled, placing him on high alert. It was possible Emperor Jaden had no intention of allowing him to leave alive, regardless of how things went with the princess. He trusted Aggnaroth, but the others...he suspected he'd be safer utilising a glory hole in a shark tank and hoped to be proven wrong.

Reisen took note of the nearest exits, just in case, and went to work. There was a limited window where an inkworm infection was treatable, before the parasite anchored to its host. After that, there was nothing he could do. He placed a hand on Jada's chest, infusing her body with concentrated pranic energy.

The reaction was immediate.

A gush of blood erupted from Jada's nose. Empress Seki shrieked and charged towards her, arms flailing. Emperor Jaden caught her from behind and held tight. Jada's blood was viscous and dark, the result of toxins excreted by the parasites. Inkworm wouldn't last long in the open, without an energy field to sustain it, but as a precautionary measure, Reisen cupped it in his hands and incinerated it.

There was a feeling of accomplishment that came with treating an infection in a quick, precise manner, negating any further damage. The princess would make a full recovery. Not everyone was so lucky, and the opportunity to destroy the organism instilled in him a much-needed sense of victory. Reisen knew the feeling wouldn't last long but intended to enjoy it while he could.

A thin layer of ash covered his palms. Hatred of anything was a waste of mental resources, but inkworm invoked endless frustration and contempt. Much like Emperor Jaden and his family, with their human masks and empty souls.

Jada stirred. Empress Seki broke free from her husband, throwing her arms around her daughter. Jada opened her eyes, hazy and unfocused. Reisen moved away from the bed, giving them space. He felt a painful stab, a longing for something he couldn't have.

Keita...

He frowned and rubbed the upper bridge of his nose. Emperor Jaden moved from Jada's side, arms crossed.

"Kaneko. We need to discuss your future."

EMPEROR JADEN HAD finally given up searching for the night, but Aggnaroth knew the investigation was far from over. Jaden would turn the palace inside out in pursuit of the person who infected his daughter. He would not stop until evidence was found, the guilty party apprehended and punished accordingly. To avoid this pointless, maniacal quest, Aggnaroth had hoped to frame someone for the deed. Maybe the royal chef, who called him a freak and spat in his food, or the groundskeeper, who was fond of collecting frozen dog excrement and placing it in Aggnaroth's bed to thaw, but decided such deception would weigh too heavily on his conscience. He did not have Dezmodeus's taste for murder.

Jaden would never discover the truth. He had examined the tiny puncture mark on Jada's arm and believed her when she said she had no memory of being injected. For her to have done such a thing to herself was not considered a possibility.

Aggnaroth knocked lightly on Jada's door. He did not want to disturb her if she was asleep.

"You may enter."

He opened the heavy wooden door and stepped inside. He sat on the edge of Jada's bed, carefully caressing her cheek with the underside of his thumb. His long, corkscrew shaped fingernails could easily scratch her. Empress Seki derived so much pleasure from constantly shaping and painting them that he was forbidden to cut them. They were currently metallic blue and purple, decorated with tiny silver stars.

"How do you feel?" he asked.

"A little tired, but okay." She smiled at him, taking his hand and squeezing it. His heart swelled with affection. She was the only one who treated him as an equal. The only one who saw something wrong with regarding an individual as a commodity and personal plaything. It took him a long time to trust her, to believe her compassion was genuine. If infecting oneself with a parasite capable of corrupting one's soul was not a sign of loyalty, Aggnaroth did not know what was.

He stretched out beside her, listening for the sound of approaching footsteps in the hall. He was not sure how Jaden would react to news of his involvement with his daughter. Did not want to find out. It would probably involve sensitive body parts and sharp objects.

"I cannot thank you enough for doing this."

"Aggy." She reached out, pushing his hood back, sliding her fingers through his silver hair. "You know I'd do anything for you." She kissed his mouth, making his wings tingle and heightening his awareness of the chastity cage between his legs, squeezing him uncomfortably tight.

"I know." He closed his eyes. She was the daughter of a warlord, the niece of a psychopath, part of a warmongering, genocidal race. She was also precious, kind, and one of the bravest women he had ever met. Her willingness to expose her family as war criminals was a bonus.

Chapter Eight

YEAR 2044
Twenty-Nine Years Ago

Hallowed Mountain Complex, Military Base

Reisen had been researching the parasite infecting the soldiers in the isolation ward for weeks. Inkworm, he called it. Auryn rarely saw him, to the point of growing concerned for Reisen's well-being. Reisen had a habit of throwing himself into his work and ignoring everything else, even at the expense of sleeping and eating. After several days passed with no sign of him, Auryn decided to investigate.

He found Reisen on the floor of his lab. He was covered in sweat, but showed no sign of infection. No black slime leaking from the corners of his eyes. No muscle spasms. No incoherent rambling.

"The sun," muttered Reisen. "It burns."

Well, two out of three wasn't bad. He helped the man to his feet, wondering if he was experimenting with psychotropic plants again. "Reisen. What happened?"

"Tigers don't like pizza."

"You stupid shit. If General Mordha sees you like this, he'll—" He noticed the syringe first. The dark smear of inkworm second.

"You injected yourself with that crap? Are you insane?!"

"I hope so, because the alternative sucks."

"What's that supposed to mean?" Auryn glowered at Reisen, annoyed with his carelessness.

Reisen pressed against him and murmured in his ear, "Aliens."

"You're not making any sense." He checked Reisen's pulse, cheeks burning, and tuned into his vital signs. His energy felt frantic and dense. "Why would you do this?"

"To prove I'm immune to the infection."

"There isn't some kind of fucking experiment you could do to establish that?"

"I just did it." Reisen hugged him almost painfully tight, dissolving into tears. "God, I'm sorry... So sorry..."

Auryn tensed, unaccustomed to physical affection, but gradually relaxed as Reisen's warmth enveloped his body, bleeding between them. "For what?"

"Everything, everything, everything, everything..."

Auryn sighed heavily, resolving to refrain from asking any further questions until Reisen regained his senses. "You need to eat something and sleep for twelve hours. You'll feel better." There was no telling if Reisen's condition was the result of exposure to inkworm or something else he'd taken. Hopefully sleep would help.

"Ryn..." Reisen gazed at him with such intensity that he felt exposed, the man's dark eyes swollen and depthless. "Don't leave me again. I can't stay here without you. It hurts too much."

"I'm not going anywhere except back to bed and I'm taking you with me." He hauled Reisen to his feet and steadied him. This was exactly the kind of thing he was supposed to report to General Mordha, but that wasn't happening.

Reisen gripped his arms. "All right, but we gotta watch out for gremlins. The one with the stripe is a real dick."

REISEN NEVER TALKED about what the inkworm did to him. He swore he wasn't infected, and as far as Auryn could tell, he was telling the truth, but there was a noticeable change in his attitude. Reisen became withdrawn and antagonistic towards almost everyone, but never Auryn. Auryn wasn't sure what made him an exception, until he saw the way Reisen looked at him— eyes glued to his body like a second skin, eradicating any doubt he had that he was alone in his perversion.

They were in a meeting. General Sycorax was talking the usual crap. They could all sense it, but Reisen was visibly agitated, every carefully manufactured lie another thorn in his flesh.

Sycorax showed off charts. Graphs. "In conclusion, the planet is cooling at a rate of five degrees centigrade per annum and will continue to do so indefinitely, unless collective enlightenment is achieved and His Holiness Emperor Haken deems us worthy of regaining the sun."

"Do you have any idea how stupid you sound?" Reisen said, barely louder than a whisper. Auryn heard him. Kicked him under the table.

"Problem, Kaneko?" asked Sycorax.

"No problem. You're asking me to sit here and forget everything I know about astronomy, astrophysics, and stellar nucleosynthesis. I see nothing wrong with that. However, for future reference, a star doesn't disappear overnight. We can't even consider the possibility that the sun died on its own, because the solar mass of a star likes ours dictates that as it dies, it evolves into a red giant, incinerating everything in range. Seems to me global cooling is the opposite of death by burning, so, seriously... What the fuck?"

Sycorax gritted her teeth. "You're mistaken if you think pseudo-science and blatant heresy have any place in this organisation."

"When I was a kid, I was obsessed with shit." *Reisen. Shut. Up.* "My first act of literary criticism was taking a big steaming dump all over a book I hated, knowing my poor mum would be forced to throw it away and I'd never have to listen to her read it again. I dug holes in my backyard and filled them with shit, a five-year-old warlock brewing concoctions in noxious pits. My nickname for the street leading up to our house was 'poo road.' I'd shit in the bath with my cousins, as one does. When my mother discovered I was using her camera to catalogue my specimens I was forbidden from playing video games for a week. An entire week. If you were looking to torture a six-year-old boy in the eighties, that's the way you went about it. Take away a pair of Italian plumbers and there was nothing left to live for."

At that point, he decided Reisen had officially lost his mind. Maybe it was substance-related—something he was smoking. Maybe he'd folded under pressure, followed his former roommates' example and taken a vacation from reality. Gods, maybe whatever the inkworm did to him finally fried his brain.

"What the fuck is your point?" Sycorax percolated with rage.

"My point is, I'm not a little kid anymore, and I'm tired of shit. Your shit, specifically." Reisen stood up and left, leaving stunned silence in his wake.

Auryn finally said something. "Ah... Kaneko hasn't been feeling well lately. Think he might be sick."

"I don't give a fuck if he's dying. See to it that he gets his priorities straightened out. Beat some sense into him if you have to."

"Yes, ma'am."

He found Reisen stretched out in his bunk. "Have you lost your mind?" he inquired, more afraid than angry. Afraid of what might happen if Reisen's attitude didn't dramatically improve, if he couldn't convince their superiors he was harmless.

"Take your shirt off."

"What?" He hadn't heard correctly.

"I'm running low on algae paper and I'd rather draw on you."

"I'm not rewarding you for acting like a psycho!"

"Don't be like that. They'll get over it."

"Not likely."

"Please?" Reisen reached for him.

Auryn's resistance dissolved. He unbuttoned his shirt, stripping down to a white T-shirt. "I can't believe I'm doing this." His skin radiated a nervous tingle. Reisen studied him with excruciating fondness. "You're exasperating."

"You say that like it's a bad thing." Reisen produced a well of ink, coating the bristles of a rabbit-hair brush. The ink was strangely warm on his skin. Auryn's cheeks burned, heat trickling down his spine and pooling in his groin. He sat as still as possible, grateful Reisen was too engrossed to notice his hardness. Or so he thought, up until the moment Reisen's lips parted against his neck, electrifying him. His cock throbbed painfully, dampening the front of his uniform.

He knew what he would do if he had any sense of self-preservation. He'd get up. Put his shirt back on. Pretend it never happened. Pray for their souls. He turned and kissed Reisen instead.

He'd never kissed a woman, let alone a man. There were plenty of opportunities to share himself with the opposite sex, but looking at a woman was like glancing over a passage in a book he'd lost interest in—he knew she was there, but none of the details registered. Reisen was different. Reisen was always there, painfully apparent.

It didn't take long for guilt to set in, accompanied by the shame of allowing his cock to override his brain. What they were doing was dangerous. Defying the natural order was punishable by death. It was unholy. Emperor Haken said so, and His Holiness had no reason to lie. Gods had an obligation to be honest, lest their flock lose faith in them.

He was risking Reisen's life along with his own and flirting with divine retribution; punishment in the next world as well as this. He broke the kiss and then stared down at the bed, flooded with uncertainty. "I don't know if I can do this."

"Ryn... it's okay." Reisen reached for his hand, holding it. "If you need more time—"

"I don't want more time." It would be squandered. Used to second-guess everything. To convince himself Emperor Haken was right and Reisen was wrong and no unnatural predilection was going to stand between him and following the path of righteousness. To die bitter, frustrated, confused, and alone. "I want you."

Reisen's hand on his cock made him question everything he knew, dissolving years of indoctrination with each stroke, emptying him, damning and saving him.

FOR A WHILE Auryn convinced himself everything was going to be okay, but the illusion of security was easily shattered.

He hadn't seen Reisen in three days. Nothing out of the ordinary, but he worried. Logic dictated if anything happened to Reisen, he'd be the first to know, but a lingering *what if* got beneath his skin and festered. He found Reisen at work in his lab, filling him with equal parts relief and annoyance.

"It's the middle of the night. Take a break, will you?"

"But we're finally getting somewhere."

"We" referred to Reisen's assistant, Naida. Auryn hadn't spoken with her much, but he preferred her company over her sister's; that woman had a talent for making him uncomfortable. Always touching him. Her long, bony fingers like icy talons, conjuring a sense of revulsion so profound he felt nauseous.

"I'm worried about you," he muttered. In the presence of a third party he didn't want his concern to appear unwarranted, but he was uncomfortable with the idea of Reisen working himself to death. Between stress, a lack of sleep, and experimenting with controlled substances, the outlook wasn't exactly favourable.

"You worry too much." Reisen reached up, running his fingers through Auryn's hair.

He recoiled, glaring. "This is exactly what I'm talking about. You're all messed up, acting like some kind of—"

"It's okay. She knows."

It took a moment to process what he was hearing. "You told her?"

"She's surprisingly open-minded."

"And you're surprisingly okay with the prospect of being torn apart by an angry mob."

"You're being paranoid."

"You're not paranoid enough."

"I'm paranoid enough for the both of us," protested Reisen. "That doesn't mean I'm going to hide the way I feel about you from someone who understands."

"Understands? Reisen, you're risking everything for a chick who washes your beakers!"

Naida spoke up, "Lay off him, Auryn. I was upset. I told him I'm attracted to one of the female officers. I figured he might know what's wrong with me, being a doctor and all. He said I'm normal, despite what Haken says, and that he feels the same way about you. He was trying to make me feel better."

"You like women?"

"That's the official diagnosis," replied Naida.

"See? No harm done," insisted Reisen. He kissed his hand, gazing at him intently. "I'm not going to let anyone hurt you."

The contents of a beaker boiled over a flame. A timer went off.

Naida threw her arms in the air. "It's finished!"

Reisen lowered the flame. He reached below the counter and then pulled out plates of cookies, cake, and fresh fruit. The latter was strictly rationed; possessing so much of it felt like a crime. Reisen wouldn't say where he'd gotten it from, only that he'd traded something of equal value.

"What are you working on, anyway?" Auryn asked between bites.

"We're taking a break from playing with worms, analysing samples of *Chlamydomonas reinhardtii*," replied Reisen. "Unicellular green algae."

"That's where we get our oxygen from."

"Right. *C. reinhardtii* can grow without light and has been genetically modified to maximise oxygen output under those conditions, producing oxygen in the absence of photosynthetic plants." Reisen peered into a microscope, examining the slide. "This sample was obtained from the Castlegar facility, which provides oxygen for the capital, yet it's not producing oxygen. It's producing hydrogen. Switching from the production of oxygen to hydrogen isn't necessarily abnormal behaviour for *C. reinhardtii*, but it's supposed to be provided with sufficient levels of sulphur to prevent that from happening."

"What are you saying?"

"Emperor Haken isn't making oxygen. He's making fuel."

"Fuel? There's other farms producing biofuel."

"Those farms are taxed to their limits. If Emperor Haken wanted additional resources, he'd need another source."

"And why would the emperor want additional resources?"

"Hydrogen fuel is ideal for space exploration."

"Space exploration? Reisen, that's insane. Our government hasn't operated a space program in centuries. There's nothing out there of any value to us. Every planet within a circumstellar habitable zone is incapable of sustaining life or too far to make travelling there a realistic option. One oxygen farm manufacturing a bit of hydrogen doesn't mean anything."

"It's not one. It's all of them."

Chapter Nine

AURYN AWOKE AT his desk, having nodded off while analysing the quarterly crop report. He rubbed his eyes, annoyed with himself. Numbers he'd once cherished had become tedious to look at. His focus wandered. He had a hard time staying awake. Auryn wished he could drink coffee, but in the last year his nerves had decided they could no longer tolerate caffeine. It made him shake terribly, his heart pound.

A new message appeared on his computer screen.

Ibara has granted Reisen Kaneko political asylum.

Auryn stared. The shock of the statement numbed him, dimly aware of the heat draining from his extremities, fingers turning cold. He caught a glimpse of movement out of the corner of his eye, a fleeting shadow, but when he turned to look there was nothing there.

Political asylum. This was good news. Reisen would be free to live without fear of persecution.

During his time undercover, Auryn reported to General Mordha once a week. The conversation that followed was all too often the same.

"Have you gathered enough intelligence on Kaneko to properly access the situation?"

"Kaneko is harmless, sir. Any suspicions you may have are ungrounded. I'm aware some of the things he says may be construed as subversive, but he has an inquisitive nature. That's all."

"Yet I continue to receive reports to the contrary."

"With all due respect, sir, your sources don't know him as well as I do. You assigned me to observe him for a reason, and I urge you to value my judgement on the subject."

"Regardless of your experience with covert operations, Colonel Tyrus, I'm concerned. We have good reason to believe Kaneko may present a threat to national security if he decides to go public with any of his wild speculations. This is no place for conspiracy theorists and heretics and Kaneko is marching on increasingly thin ice. If his research wasn't so valuable, His Holiness would have disposed of him long ago."

Auryn closed his eyes, taking a deep breath. He needed to tell Keita. A father and son reunion would be easy enough to arrange. Keita belonged with Reisen.

His heart thudded frantically. He assumed Aggnaroth reached out to Reisen when Princess Jada was infected, but how had he found him so easily? Reisen knew how to disappear. It was the only reason he was still alive. He would have heard otherwise, most likely in the form of a drunken phone call from Prince Elia, complaining about his father throwing a fit over finding Reisen dead in an abandoned subway tunnel, needle in his arm, being denied the pleasure of burning Reisen's ass at the stake. It was hard to believe it was over. Reisen was okay. Somewhere safe. Soon Keita would be safe, too.

What little heat remained in Auryn's body drained out of him. A surge of nausea sent his head spinning. He swallowed a mouthful of bile, gripping his desk for support. He wanted to rejoice in the knowledge Keita would be free, but experienced only grief, as if he'd already gone.

He felt a tap on the toe of his boot and nearly pissed himself, pushing his chair away from his desk. A toy giraffe sat at his feet. *Mr. Bumpy...* Sasha's favourite. Auryn picked up the stuffed animal and held it for a long time, pushing his emotions as far beneath the surface as they would go.

Just breathe.

Auryn shut his computer down for the night. He wasn't going to get anything else done, no matter how badly the lack of productivity irked him. He left Mr. Bumpy in his chair. Mr. Bumpy could run things while he was gone. Maybe even fill out a few reports. Hopefully he'd be all right. If anything happened to him, Sasha would never forgive him.

Auryn headed back to his quarters, finding Keita curled up in his usual spot on the couch, eyes half-lidded. He sat next to him, wanting to share the news about Reisen, but couldn't force the words out without fear of choking on them.

"How do you feel, Kei? Do you remember anything from yesterday, at the temple?"

"We were at the temple yesterday?" Keita looked at him with tired confusion. "Must have blocked it out. It's so boring."

He examined Keita's hand. There was no trace of the cut left by the blood offering, no indication of injury at all. Keita had hurt himself several times over the years and never healed this quickly on his own. It concerned him, but there was nothing he could do about it right now.

"It's not important," he murmured, trying not to fixate on the pale curve of Keita's neck, envisioning his mouth on that impossibly soft skin, whimpers of pleasure rising from Keita's throat. He looked away and clenched his jaw, fighting the urge to punch himself in the face, as if the pain might somehow distract him, granting him a momentary reprieve from reality.

"Ryn..." Keita sat up, wrapping an arm around him. "You okay?"

"Mnh. Just tired."

"Me too." Keita switched off the TV, taking him by the hand. "Lie down with me?"

"I don't know if that's a good idea." Auryn stared at the floor. "Think I might be getting sick." A whisper filled his ears. *You're already sick. Sick, sick, sick.*

"I don't care." Keita tugged at his arm lightly. "Please?"

"Okay..."

Auryn climbed into bed with Keita, rubbing his back until he fell asleep. He got up to get a glass of water and found himself seated at the kitchen table, staring into space. A rotten taste filled his mouth, lingering despite his effort to drown it, guzzling water with no relief.

IT WAS HARD to tell what was pig and what was human, the two species merged into one. Auryn couldn't tell if the pigs were stitched together from human components or if they were people with porcine faces and cloven hooves. They made inhuman sounds, scrounging in the dark for food. Their stomachs, human and creature alike, were sunken and bony—frail skeletons, stretching their sickly skin unnaturally thin.

The creatures reeked of decay; the kind of stench that lingered for weeks after the offending party was removed. A sliver of light spilled from a hole in the roof of the enclosure, forming a bright circle on the straw.

It was the light that attracted them, sparking a stampede, each creature determined to gorge itself on the glow. Gathered in a great heap, each member of the pile fought to be the first to reach the narrow opening.

One creature used human hands to reach the top of the pile. Triumphant, it drove its snout through the ceiling, widening the hole with serrated teeth, tasting freedom.

The creature worked its swollen pink head into the open, basking in the warmth. Its lips twitched and Auryn could have sworn the monstrosity was smiling, shamelessly worshiping the sun.

A metal blade swept across the opening, decapitating the creature. Maggots spilled from the wound, showering the monsters below.

They grew bored of the light, turning their attention to Auryn. Their teeth ripped into his flesh. He fought back, trying to drive them away, but the creatures were much stronger.

He swung wildly, awakening to find Keita blocking his blows.

"Easy, easy. I've got you."

It took him a minute to fully process he wasn't under attack. He'd fallen asleep at the kitchen table.

"Sorry, I..." Auryn exhaled shakily. His skin felt like it had been boiled in hot tar, itching and burning.

"Don't be sorry. I'm the one who should apologise. Should have known waking you like that would be an invitation to remodel my face. Hang on. I'll get you some water."

"I could have hurt you. I could have..."

"If you wanted to hurt me, you wouldn't have bothered to teach me self-defence. Here."

Keita offered him a cold glass of water. He noticed Keita's teeth sinking into the flesh of his bottom lip, absently sucking at the skin, indicating he was thirsty. A habit. Reisen did the same thing.

"You have it," murmured Auryn.

"But..."

"I insist."

Keita drained the glass with big, satisfied gulps. A trickle of water leaked from the corner of his mouth, trailing down his chin. He wiped it away with the back of his hand. Keita was dressed for bed, shirtless, in a pair of white underwear. The bones of his hips were clearly visible, natural muscle tone carving subtle grooves in his body. The work of a divine sculptor. A trail of blond hair drew Auryn's gaze from Keita's navel to his groin, the swell of the younger male's sex. God, Keita had a big cock. Auryn imagined how it might feel in his hand, throbbing to the point of bursting, Keita crying out in bliss.

The thick, loose fabric of Auryn's uniform helped conceal his partial erection. "I should check on the holograph towers," he announced shakily, blood rushing to his head as he stood. A moment of light-headedness struck. He pocketed his hands, pinning his engorged dick to his lower stomach, praying it would go unnoticed. "They're still broken. People can't handle the dark for long. Someone needs to make sure they get fixed. They're no good if they're broken. Excuse me. I'm sorry."

His chest burned. Pressure. Tension building. Couldn't breathe.

Quit panicking, asshole. All your military training and you're more worked up than an asthmatic on their wedding night, in more ways than one.

Pathetic.

Hoping a calm setting would help soothe his nerves, he retreated to the sanctity of temple. At this hour the pews had long grown cold. He anticipated no invasion of privacy. No one was crazy enough to be hanging out with a bunch of defective idols at this hour.

No one except me.

He sank into his usual seat, wrapped a long strand of barbed wire around his right hand, and clenched his fist. If temple was in session the priest would say his blood symbolised apologies for all the things he'd done wrong. The more blood he could wring from his hands, the sorrier he was.

There was never enough blood.

Nor was there a god from whom he wished to beg forgiveness. Only a dead little boy.

Warmth flowed over his hand, sticky pockets of heat. He pulled on the slender tail of blond hair trailing down his neck. A nervous habit. He'd never seen the appeal of long hair, until he met Reisen.

Auryn undid his pants with his free hand and tightened his grip on the barbed wire, going numb. He pumped his erection, desperate to relieve the tension. He tried to focus on Reisen—the heat of his mouth, the friction of their bodies grinding and colliding—but his thoughts continuously derailed, diverting to Keita. Keita was there. Reisen wasn't. Keita was real. Reisen was more like a glorious figment of his imagination.

It wasn't long before his hands were covered in blood and semen. Relief was short-lived. He sat with his head bowed in deference to no one, taking slow, deep breaths. Before exiting the temple, he placed his hands in the sacred fountain and healed the gouges in his flesh. The sound of laughter echoed off the walls, originating from nearby. He found Sasha crouched behind the fountain, scowling and gripping his toy giraffe by the neck.

"You left Mr. Bumpy alone," growled Sasha.

"I left him in charge."

"Mr. Bumpy doesn't want to be in charge! He wants leaves to munch on."

"Lots of leaves in the greenhouses. Take him there."

Sasha glared. "You're trying to get rid of me, aren't you?" He plunged the giraffe's head into the fountain, holding it underwater.

"You're going to drown him, Sasha."

"He needs to be blessed. He's dirty, like you."

"Sasha..."

"You're disgusting."

Auryn turned and walked away, heading for the exit.

"Coward! I hate you!"

Auryn covered his ears with his hands, but it did nothing to dilute the noise.

THE CAVERN WAS black. With the holographic projectors still down, there was nothing to disguise the darkness. The breakdown affected morale and conduct, as if a lack of light was permission to behave badly, to revert to the kind of primitive, uncivilised behaviour characterising the human species in its early stages.

Auryn returned to his quarters and stepped inside. It was early in the morning and he expected Keita to be asleep, but the scent of freshly baked lemon meringue pie greeted him. His favourite. Keita stood at the kitchen counter slicing oranges, placing them in a pitcher of juice, the pie cooling on the counter. For a moment he forgot about how pathetic he was, moved by the younger male's thoughtfulness.

"What's the occasion?"

"You seem a little stressed out." Keita poured him a glass of juice and placed a large slice of pie in front of him. "Thought it might help."

Stressed out. He experienced a sense of bitter relief—he was forgiven for behaving strangely, and unworthy of forgiveness.

Auryn fought the urge to deny anything was wrong. Keita clearly knew otherwise and insulting his intelligence would do neither of them any good.

"You didn't have to do that... Thank you." The pie crust crumbled in his mouth, golden and flaky. It reminded him of cookies Reisen used to make. The filling was refreshing and cool, impregnated with the taste of lemons. "This is really good, Kei." He inhaled slowly, trying to convince himself everything was going to be all right. If he lied to himself often enough, he might begin to believe it. The trick was committing to it.

"Feeling any better?" asked Keita.

"Ah, well..." Auryn wanted to spill everything. To emotionally eviscerate himself, presenting his guts for inspection, leaking tales of government corruption, confessing to conversing with the dead, and admitting to a complete lack of confidence when it came to preventing his remaining grains of sanity from blowing away in a worsening gale. "I'll be all right." Auryn felt tired and filthy. He studied Keita in desperate hope of finding distraction, but found only more shame.

"Why don't you have a girlfriend?" asked Keita.

His cheeks warmed, caught off-guard by the question. "Can't find anyone who'll put up with me."

"You must not be looking very hard. There's nothing wrong with you."

He laughed nervously, stomach flipping, chest constricting, "I have more important things to worry about than finding a girlfriend."

"Don't you get lonely?" Keita scraped his plate for the last of the filling, licking it off his spoon.

"Work keeps me busy. Plus... I have you."

Keita stood and gathered the empty plates, depositing them in the dishwasher. "Things would be easier for you if I wasn't around."

Tell him. Tell him he's free to leave you fucking sheepshit.

"Keita... Easier doesn't always equal better. Having you here with me has been a joy and a privilege."

Without you, I have nothing.

"You're just saying that."

"I mean it." Auryn forced a smile. It must have appeared strained, because Keita looked concerned. He knew Keita cared, but seeing it so clearly in the young man's eyes put a clog his throat.

"What's wrong?" Keita touched his cheek. "Tell me what's bothering you."

"It's nothing." He looked away, swallowing thickly. Keita sounded like Reisen. Reisen often questioned his inability to open up, pressuring him to reveal things better off hidden away. The corners of his eyes burned with tears he refused to shed.

"Why won't you talk to me?"

"It's not like that. I just have nothing to say."

"That's not true. You always make me feel better. I can—"

"That's enough, Keita. Drop it." The harshness of his tone surprised and unsettled him, regretting it instantly.

Keita shrank back, wounded. "Sorry."

"No..." Auryn shook his head incessantly, trying not to scream.

"No?" Keita placed a hand on his shoulder, stroking his neck. "Ryn..."

Auryn stood up. "Your father is no longer wanted in Ibara. He's living there now."

"Good for him." Keita sounded unimpressed. "What's that got to do with anything?"

"You don't have to stay here."

"Seriously? What makes you think I want to leave? The fact that Reisen practically abandoned me to focus on his work? Or is it because he allowed me to be taken by men with gas masks and electroshock weapons while he was conveniently nowhere to be found? Fucking 'Father of the Year'!" He'd never seen Keita so furious. "So, he managed to convince someone important he's too much of a coward to kill anyone, why should I care? You're more of a father to me than he was!"

Auryn flinched, a scalding wall of water crashing over him. Fathers didn't fantasise about their sons. Didn't fixate on sucking them and fucking them. Not unless something was very wrong. Broken. *You're a good boy, Auryn. This is our little secret.* He pulled his hair, unravelling. "I... I don't want to lose you, Kei. But I have no right to keep you."

"That's it, then? You're sending me away?" Angry tears collected in Keita's eyes.

"It's for your own good. I'm not trying to punish you. If you stay here, sooner or later someone is going to figure out you don't belong here."

Keita turned away from him, rubbing his eyes with his sleeve. "I want to stay with you."

"We're leaving in the morning."

Keita stomped down the hall, stopping to kick the crap out of a table, bits of plastic cracking and flying.

Auryn stood by and said nothing, allowing Keita to work the rage out of his system. He understood the need to destroy something.

AURYN STARED INTO an empty suitcase, losing track of time and diverting his focus only when Sasha burst into the room. "Don't even think about it."

"What do you mean?"

"You're not leaving." Sasha looked furious.

He hadn't seriously considered going with Keita. Haken would hunt him down for abandoning his post, but he felt obligated to entertain the idea. "Why not?"

"Reisen doesn't love you anymore." Sasha snapped his suitcase shut. "He won't want you there, 'specially when he finds out you wanna stick your filthy winky in his son."

Auryn winced. "Maybe he—"

"You have to stay here. Mr. Bumpy needs help running things. He's not very smart. His brain is mostly stuffing, you know." Sasha jabbed Auryn in the side with a fingertip. "You put him in charge. He'll ruin everything."

Auryn closed his eyes. Sasha had a point. He was responsible for the death of thousands of people who'd done little more than question Haken's authority, usually in the "privacy" of their own homes. He was mentally unstable and a relentless pervert. He was a murderer. Why would Reisen or Keita would want him around? They were better off without him.

"All right. I'll stay and help Mr. Bumpy."

"Good." Sasha hopped up on the bed, feet dangling over the edge. "You don't wanna make Mr. Bumpy angry."

KEITA COULDN'T SLEEP. It was the last night he'd spend in his own bed. He wanted to feel indifferent about it, but apathy was inapplicable. Auryn had done more than save his life, going out of his way to accommodate him, making him feel loved. Maybe that was why it hurt so much. It felt like he'd been tricked.

A knock at the door. "Keita?"

He considered pretending to be asleep, staying silent, and he held his tongue for several seconds before caving. "What?"

"Can I come in?"

"I don't care." He said nothing when Auryn lay down beside him, and nothing still when he slid an arm around him, until the warmth of the older male's body finally broke him. "Don't make me leave." Keita pressed his face to Auryn's bare chest, inhaling him. He rested his head next to Auryn's, fingers grazing the older male's cheek. "I belong with you." He wanted to kiss him, consequences be damned. He was already being discarded. What difference would it make?

"Your father deserves to know you're alive. I envy him, a bit." Nearly nose to nose, all he needed was another swell of courage to put him over the threshold of cowardice.

"Then come with me!" His voice grew louder, frustration seeping in. "You don't have to stay here alone. You'll get along better with Reisen than I will."

"I can't."

"Why not?"

Auryn shook his head. "I want you to be safe. That's all that matters to me."

"Don't I get a say in this?"

"We all want things we can't have, Kei." Auryn's thumb collected the moisture pooling in the corner of his eye, caressing his cheek.

"It's not fair."

"I know." Auryn inclined his head towards him, their foreheads touching. Keita didn't want to go back to Reisen. Didn't want anything to do with Reisen. He changed the channel whenever the subject of his dad came up. Couldn't stand to see his face. It filled him with a rage so profound it frightened him. He tried to identify the source of his animosity, but failed. He didn't feel abandoned. He understood why Reisen had been absent when the police showed up. As he'd told the interrogators, over and over again, his dad was rarely home. Reisen hadn't done anything wrong. Yet the thought of him made Keita want to break things.

"Can you visit sometime?"

"I'd like to, but... no."

He made a frustrated noise, nestling closer to the older male. He didn't plan on sleeping, doubting his ability to do so under such conditions, but Auryn's presence soothed him, easing the transition into dreamless slumber.

When he awoke, Auryn was gone.

Chapter Ten

KEITA FOUND AURYN seated at the kitchen table, poking at his breakfast with obvious disinterest. He sat across from the older male, placing his backpack on the floor beside him.

"Morning." Auryn barely looked up from his plate, banishing a slice of banana to its outskirts. "Are you ready?"

"Yeah. Let's get this over with." Keita shovelled a few pieces of fruit into his mouth and devoured a bowl of cereal. He took one last look around before following Auryn out the door, lighting a cigarette.

They walked through long, empty corridors. Auryn always knew exactly which way to go to avoid running into other soldiers.

"Arandano will want to know what happened to me," he muttered, keeping his head down. "What are you going to tell him?"

"Haven't thought that far ahead," admitted Auryn. The question took Auryn off-guard and Keita caught a flicker of emotion he couldn't identify on the man's face. He stopped himself from asking about it. Didn't want to know. Didn't care. Convinced himself of all kinds of things, but his conviction was short-lived.

He'd never ridden in a snowcrawler. Normally, he would have enjoyed climbing into the passenger seat and listening to the purr of a motor.

A lift carried them to the surface. Outside the capital there were no holographic projectors or climate controls to create sun and rain, only endless fields of snow.

They drove to Ibara in silence.

The border between the two countries was closed and heavily guarded. No one in. No one out. A tunnel allowed them to cross easily, exactly where the map on his dashboard said it would be, and they emerged a safe distance from the search towers.

Keita's first impression of Kuroi, the Ibaran capital, was the cold. Minor climate adjustments kept the temperature slightly below freezing, encouraging a healthy respect for indoor heating. People dressed strangely, favouring dark colours and ornate decorations, piercing parts of their bodies with no business being full of holes.

Women walked through the snow in high heels, their cleavage pushed up and exposed despite the chill in the air.

He wanted to go home.

Auryn stopped the armoured vehicle near a large snow-covered park, close to the royal palace, and stepped out onto the street. He reluctantly followed. Auryn withdrew an envelope from his jacket and handed it to him.

"Here. This is the address where your father is staying. You also have an Ibaran passport in your own name and some currency."

Keita stared at the envelope, wanting to tear it out of Auryn's hand and grind it into the icy pavement.

"Please... don't hate me." Auryn looked distressed. On the verge of tears.

It finally occurred to him that Auryn might resent this as much as he did. He felt like an idiot for not seeing it sooner, overtaken by a sudden swell of affection. "I don't hate you." He hugged Auryn. Part of him didn't want to give in, compelled to punish him for banishing him, but the impulse was too strong.

"Don't be too hard on your father. Tell him I miss him." Keita nodded, refraining from giving a verbal commitment. He was doing a good job of holding it together until Auryn pulled away from him. That's when the burning started. His eyes on fire. "Take care of yourself, Kei."

He shook despite the warmth provided by his heavy coat, more anxious than cold, haemorrhaging heat. He watched Auryn drive off, tears crystallising on his cheeks.

"MR. BUMPY IS bored." Sasha kicked the back of Auryn's seat.

Thump.

Thump.

Thump.

"Tell him to hang in there, son. We'll be home soon." Auryn sped up. He crossed the border back into Terasyn. Passage between the two countries was easy when you knew the right places to cross. Massive searchlights perched on towering guard posts were all spectacle, seeking armies of invading ghosts.

Instead of heading back to the Farm, he drove deeper into an ancient, petrified forest.

"How long is this going to take?"

Thump.

"Hello? Are you listening?"

Thump.

"Sorry. I'm listening. How's Mr. Bumpy doing?"

"He got too bored. I think he's dead." Sasha scowled in the back seat, shaking Mr. Bumpy.

Auryn hit the brakes. The vehicle skidded to a halt. They were in the middle of nowhere. If Emperor Haken was to be believed, one step outside and he'd be dead; there was no oxygen this far from civilisation, but Auryn suspected otherwise.

"You'd better go bury him, or he'll start to stink."

"But I don't want Mr. Bumpy to go away!"

"Do you love him?"

"Yes."

"Then looking after his remains is the least you can do."

"Oh, all right. I'll do it." Sasha climbed out of the vehicle and slammed the door, dragging Mr. Bumpy behind him, leaving a red smear on the fresh snow. The giraffe's neck twisted at a funny angle, his body slashed with hundreds of intersecting gouges, guts dangling from a widening gash in his abdomen, swollen and purple. "It's your fault he's dead. All your fault! All your fault!"

"I know." Auryn withdrew his phone from his pocket, entering the password.

The explosion was like a second of sunlight, searing heat, then nothing.

Chapter Eleven

EMPEROR JADEN'S PHONE rang. Aggnaroth fished it out of the cradle. "Yes? No, I don't recall being trained to speak to you this way, your Holiness. It comes naturally." He held the phone away from his ear. "It's your brother, sir."

Jaden cringed and then took the phone with the tenderness of someone handling live explosives. "What do you want? I understand that, but—hang on a second! Kaneko cured my daughter of a parasite in *your* possession. I disagree completely. Call me back when you're done acting like a baby. Waaaaah. Waaaah. Oh, really? Is that so? Go eat shit and die, you fucking cannibal."

"Was that Uncle Haken?" asked Jada. Black hair tumbled down her neck in beautiful waves; soft, loose curls he longed to touch.

"You can forget about getting a birthday present from him this year." Jaden poured himself another drink.

Empress Seki gazed out the window, watching the falling snow. "He's going to destroy us all."

IT WAS COLD outside; much colder than underground. Keita zipped his jacket up and took shelter from the wind, lighting a cigarette while his hands were still warm enough to successfully manipulate his lighter. He opened the envelope Auryn had given him before examining its contents. A passport, currency, and an electronic compass with Reisen's address in it, pointing in the direction he needed to go. But he wasn't ready to go yet.

Fuck Reisen.

Keita was half-tempted to throw the compass away and wander around aimlessly until he decided what to do with himself. Anything other than returning to Reisen. The thought of it made his cheeks flush with anger. But the unknown was marginally more terrifying. And if Auryn ever changed his mind and decided to visit, he wanted to be there.

He followed a sidewalk down the brightly lit street. He'd never seen so many shops. He considered entering one with a mouth-watering variety of pastries in the window, but he wasn't sure how much money Auryn had given him, having no concept of Ibaran currency. There were a few bills and some kind of gold certificate. *7,000 ounces.* The number meant nothing.

A man twice Keita's size bumped into him, leather jacket crinkling. The stranger's greasy hair was shaved on the sides, leaving a dark slick on the crown of his head. Images of dragons and demonic creatures rampaged across his jacket. This was the people of Ibara, in all their Godlessness, walking around like drunken freaks with no clue as to proper—

"Sorry about that. I'm always getting in the way." The man smiled apologetically and continued onward.

Keita watched him go, feeling stupid.

A mouth-watering scent emanated from another shop, but he wasn't sure how safe the food was, concerned not so much about cleanliness, but content. If Ibara was anything like Terasyn, you never knew for sure what—or who—you were eating.

Reality began to set in, accompanied by a surge of panic. He was in a strange place, surrounded by strange people, too stubborn to follow instructions.

Behind the shop a narrow alleyway resonated with distressed noises, too high-pitched to be human. He followed the sound and discovered a cat torturing a long-tailed, wide-eyed creature. One of the poor creature's giant eyes hung lose from the socket, attached with strands of inflamed tissue. He grabbed the bloodied bundle of fluff and shielded it from the feline's fury. The cat slashed him, raking its claws across his cheek.

He tucked the animal inside his jacket to keep it warm and followed his compass, rushing to Reisen's house, several blocks away. He stood at Reisen's door, hacking up burning winter air, tasting blood in his throat. He rang the doorbell and waited.

Reisen opened the door, eyes framed in red plastic heart-shaped sunglasses. A lollipop stem protruded from the corner of his mouth.

"Please tell me you're selling those little chocolates with the mint inside."

Keita unzipped his jacket and revealed the injured animal. "I was told you might be able to help."

Reisen looked disappointed. "Sure. Come on in."

The house was remarkably clean. A flag he recalled vividly from childhood was mounted on the wall; a red leaf on a white background, with vertical red bars on either side of it. His throat constricted.

"What's your name?" asked Reisen, taking the wounded creature from him.

"Sasha. Sasha Tyrus."

Reisen treated the animal's wounds with healing energy, repairing the damage. "I'm Reisen. You're not related to Auryn Tyrus, are you?"

"He's my dad."

Reisen went quiet, right hand hovering over the injured animal, full of light and love and crap. "We served in the Terasian army together."

"I heard you prefer blowing up old ladies to serving your country."

"Why is everyone so fixated on the old lady thing?"

Keita folded his arms across his chest. "You're a traitor."

"Jesus." Reisen shook his head and slipped on a pair of sterile gloves. "You remind me of your mother. Hasn't she grown out of being a relentless bitch?"

"My mother is dead."

"Sorry to hear that, strangely enough." Little by little, Reisen eased the luxated eyeball back into its socket. "I won't pretend she and I saw eye-to-eye about anything, except when it came to our admiration of your dad. I'll have to let her sister know."

Sister?

"Why are you in Ibara?" asked Reisen. He used a thin band of blue light to temporarily seal the sleeping creature's injured eyelid shut.

"My dad wanted me to come. He thought I'd be better off here."

"His concern is justified. Terasyn is a fucking mess. Haken is psychotic. Jaden is less of a control freak, but he has a short fuse and a low tolerance for opinions that differ from his own."

"I was fine where I was."

"You may be pleasantly surprised. Plenty of things to do here you'd have a hard time getting away with in Terasyn."

"Like what?"

"Drink whatever you want. Fuck whomever you like. Eat things that aren't filled with drugs designed to dehumanise you. Discuss your dislike of the emperor in public without being turned into expensive steak."

"Those things don't interest me." Keita's cheeks burned. Who did this guy think he was, talking to him like that?

"Are you sure you're Auryn's son?" Reisen regarded him with mock scepticism. "Oh, man. The stories I could tell you."

"You're impossible."

"That's more like it." Reisen smiled faintly. He wrapped the animal in a towel and placed it in a crate, along with some water. "She'll be all right. Just needs to rest." He tossed his gloves in the trash. "I won't hold it against you if you want to leave, but there's someone I'd like to introduce you to first."

"Who?"

"Your aunt."

REISEN LED SASHA into the basement. The kid was really something. None of his father's charm and all his mother's hostility. *C'est tragique.* He didn't know Auryn had a son. He only knew Auryn had married that bitch because a wedding announcement was one of several results generated by an internet search. He'd dealt with the news as well as possible, alternating between drug-induced slumber and eating his feelings.

"I worked with your mother's sister, Naida. We became close friends." Reisen longed to tell the whole story; deliberately omitting things felt dishonest, but he doubted Auryn would appreciate being outed in front of his son. Instead, he settled on an abridged version. "We were working on a cure for inkworm, having been told by our superiors the parasite was being used by Ibara as a form of biological warfare. We discovered this wasn't the case. Naida told your mother what we found. Long story short, your mother accused us both of conspiring against Haken, and your dad helped us escape."

"Reisen? Who's that with you?" Two sets of footsteps descending the stairs caught Naida's attention. It was nice to see her awake and alert. Too often the infection left her weak and tired, sleeping for days at a time. She was unable to leave the hospital bed, connected to so many tubes she looked like a human jellyfish. Her eyes were bandaged, concealing dead, black orbs. He hated seeing her like this, but for as long as she remained determined to stay alive, he would do everything he could to save her. Their affection for one another was not romantic in nature, but no less profound.

"Naida. This is Sasha Tyrus. Your nephew."

"Is he as handsome as his father?"

Reisen smiled. "I don't think he'll have any problems finding a date." Sasha was a good-looking young man, but looked nothing like Auryn. It was just as well. He didn't need that kind of distraction.

He headed for the coffee machine, pouring himself another cup. It was murdering his stomach, but he was going on day three of no sleep and cognitive function was in open rebellion. He observed Sasha with tired eyes, still shielded behind the heart-shaped lenses of his sunglasses.

There was something strange about him. Something he couldn't place.

Sasha sat on the edge of the hospital bed. Naida reached out to touch his face, mapping its contours with her fingers. "You'd better keep your hands to your se—" She halted midspeech, going quiet for several seconds. "Reisen, you idiot. This is our son."

"You... It's not possible." He fumbled with the coffee cup, sending it crashing to the floor. It shattered on contact, splintering across the immaculate, white tile.

"How long did it take you to notice I was gone?" asked the young man. His son? *Keita?* How was that possible? The fucking emperor and his goons took Keita away. Sent him to the Farm, according to his file in the government database. *Deceased.* No one escaped the Farm. "A day? A week? You're such an asshole! It's your fault Auryn made me leave!"

My fault... Auryn... What?

"Wait... I..." Reisen sat down slowly, feeling faint. "How... How do you know Auryn?"

"Auryn saved me. I was sent to the Farm and he took me in. What have *you* done, other than forget me?"

The anger in Keita's voice was painful to endure. "I didn't forget you." He tried his best to sound calm, in control. "Ask your mother how well I dealt with losing you. She'll tell you how grateful she was when I started showering again. Depression does fucked up things to people."

"Since when are the two of you only friends?"

Oh god, he doesn't know.

"Reisen isn't exactly my type," replied Naida. She reached for Keita's hand, holding it with brittle fingers. "You were conceived through in vitro fertilisation. It sounds selfish in retrospect, but after years of running, we finally found a place we thought was safe. I wanted something beautiful and pure. Something that would allow me to forget. You were perfect."

"Is that all I was to you? A temporary distraction?" Keita wiped away furious tears with his arm.

"Of course not, baby." Naida sat up shakily, embracing Keita.

"I thought you were dead."

"That's my fault," Reisen admitted quickly. "I was afraid she wasn't going to make it, and I didn't want to upset you. Naida was injected with inkworm, and by the time I got there, the infection had already progressed to the point where I was unable to cure it. Once the parasite anchors to its host, inkworm's defences are impenetrable. I can try to minimise the damage, but that's all." He wrapped his arms around Keita from behind, hugging him tightly.

"You're crushing me." Keita was quick to fend him off, squirming out of his grasp. A dark trickle leaked from Naida's bandaged eyes. Keita wiped it away, staring at the smear on his thumb. "Inkworm... What is it?"

"It's a blood parasite. Most people have no immunity against this strain. We're too isolated. However, in instances where the prospective host is an aether—an old soul, an ascended master, enlightened, whatever the hell you want to call it—the parasite acts as a catalyst."

"Catalyst for what?"

"It ignites a divine spark, granting access to abilities people normally wouldn't be able to tap into, given the relatively low vibration of planets like this. Their capacity to channel energy is greatly enhanced and contact with the spirit world is established. It also weakens the astral veil, a tightly woven web of energy surrounding each person. Veils keep people locked in the moment, suppressing memories of past lives and knowledge of the discarnate realms. They make us forget who we are. When a veil is torn, anything can slip through."

He doubted Keita had any memory of being injected. Keita never mentioned it, more concerned with why Mommy was covered in black goo and where she'd gone. Probably blocked it out.

"Where does it come from?" asked Keita, his gaze drawn to the dense inky substance with a fascination he understood all too well.

"Inkworm is a mutation of Saphiel, a worm used by the Nephilim to increase their capacity to channel energy and improve their performance in battle."

"Nephilim?"

"An ancient warrior race. They're not native to this planet, but there's a few around."

"How do you know all this?"

"Emperor Jaden owns one of them." He bent to collect the shards of his coffee cup, depositing them in the trash. "Aggnaroth."

Chapter Twelve

AGGNAROTH WALKED THROUGH the halls of the hospital, hoping no one looked at him too closely. A surgical mask covered his face and a doctor's cap hid his hair along with the tips of his distinctive ears. They felt naked without their usual ornamentation—tiny chains, hoops, and armour plating. His wings were hidden beneath his clothing, ritualistically bound, confined by strips of sacred cloth, like holy bandages. The loose-fitting cloaks he wore were designed to conceal their presence, but once a year his feathers underwent a complete moult. It was a time normally reserved for fasting, prayer, and meditation—two months of monk-like dedication for the Nephilim, but he was prohibited from practising his religion.

He had left the Ibaran palace in a hurry after receiving a series of text messages from his brother, Dezmodeus. Dezi had tracked Reisen and Auryn for years, relying on microscopic implants in the skin to relay geographical location and vital signs.

Dezmodeus: 2:54. Uh. Auryn's vitals just went to shit. Standby.

Aggnaroth: 2:54. Is the chip malfunctioning?

Dezmodeus: 2:55. BT=14 °C; BP = 40/14; HR = 260 beats/min. RR =59 breaths/min. WHAT THE FUCK, AGGY?

Aggnaroth vividly recalled the day he met Auryn, despite how long ago it was. Around 90 years. Auryn had worn a vacant, hypnotised expression—a three-year-old boy who smelled like the forest, still under the effects of Dezi's spell. They had left him standing on the doorstep of a Terasian orphanage with a note pinned to his jacket. *My name is Auryn.*

Auryn's room was unguarded. Aggnaroth let himself in. Fish skin bandages covered most of Auryn's body, concealing dark burns and deep gashes. An inkworm injection was an extreme measure, but Auryn would not survive without it. There was a chance he would not survive either way; the process of awakening was too much for some souls to endure, enlightened or not. As the veil of forgetfulness weakened, Auryn would become conscious of the transitory, illusory nature of the world. Memories of past lives would creep in, uninvited and often unwanted. He would be confronted with the largest obstacle of all—himself, and forced to decide if he liked what he saw. It was a risk he preferred to avoid, but Auryn's condition left him with little choice.

On a planet like Ankari, catering to the development of juvenile souls, aethers were a curious anomaly. Aethers were old souls, having earned the distinction of living 100,000 lifetimes in humanoid form. They were the enlightened ones, the ascended masters. Yet when stuffed into human bodies, they were subjected to the same fog of spiritual amnesia and propensity for stupidity as souls who were only beginning their journey.

Inkworm changed everything.

Aggnaroth prepared the injection, locating a suitable site for delivering the dose. If Auryn could not get it together, if he lacked the resilience to endure, everything would fall apart.

Aggnaroth pushed the needle in, injected its contents, and waited.

YEAR 1990
Eighty-two Years Ago

North Bembrook Forest, Calder

The trees stirred. The leaves danced, but Auryn felt no wind. The air was heavy, sticking to him like the sky before it rained, but there were no clouds anywhere, just blue. Blue sky and warm sun.

A forest spirit appeared in the clearing, shaking plant fluff from its fur. It sat nearby—fat, with a face like a rabbit. Tiny antlers rested on its head. Someone had carved pretty blue lines in them with a knife.

The spirit wanted to play. Wanted to take him somewhere exciting. Auryn knew he wasn't supposed to wander off on his own. Big brother didn't like it, but big brother was asleep, and if he had a friend with him, he wouldn't be alone.

The fuzzy sprite bounced and peeped. A squeaky little thing. They ran together through the trees, hopping over slippery roots. Auryn fell. Crashed. Cried. The spirit licked him and made the blood go away. He hugged it, sniffing its fur, smelling shortbread.

They didn't make it far. Auryn got stuck in the deep moss and started to sink. He didn't panic at first, trying to pull his boots out of the black water. He pulled his feet out of his boots, but then he lost his balance and his boots, sticking his socks in the swampy mud. He tried not to cry again.

Big brother never cried. Auryn wanted to be just like him, wanted to scare New Daddy like his brother did. Make New Daddy stop touching. Make him go away.

"Dem!" Auryn called for his brother—one tug from Stout, his brother's mount, and he'd be out of the muck—but it wasn't Dem who came. It was a man made of shadows. The man helped him out of the moss and made the sun go away. Now the sun was always gone, and the air was always cold. There was no more brother or mother.

There was only the Emperor of Terasyn.

AURYN OPENED HIS eyes. They adjusted quickly to the dark, bringing into focus a tall figure standing next to the bed. A doctor. Must have given him an injection, judging by the needle in his hand. Maybe something for the pain. Nothing hurt anymore, his body enveloped by blissful numbness.

"How do you feel?" asked the doctor. His voice sounded familiar. Strangely reassuring.

Auryn examined him closer. The doctor's face was hidden behind a mask, but his otherworldly eyes gave him away. *Aggnaroth.* "I don't know," he replied honestly. "The sun..."

Aggnaroth gently peeled a strip of fish skin off his arm, revealing flawless flesh, no trace of trauma. "Would you like to see it?"

NAIDA WAS ASLEEP. With any luck she'd remain that way for a few hours. Reisen desperately wanted a drink, but with Naida's condition he had an obligation to remain sober. If her health took a turn for the worse, he couldn't be halfway through a case of beer or staring at the ceiling, tripping balls and listening to Pink Floyd. At first it had been refreshing to experience the world with a clear head, but the novelty of sobriety had long-since worn off.

Reisen paced in front of the couch, eventually sinking into the leather cushions with his head in his hands. "Sorry... I'm having a difficult time processing this."

"Makes two of us." The sharpness of Keita's tone cut him. Keita's anger was perfectly justifiable, but the intensity of his son's animosity indicated the possibility of something less obvious at work. Keita may not remember the real reason he hated Reisen so much—if he had, he'd be screaming and throwing things by now—but his rage lingered. Auryn must have done something to trigger a partial awakening. It couldn't have been exposure to inkworm. Must have been something else. It terrified Reisen, knowing one day his son would wake up and despise him more than he already did.

He needed to tread carefully and try to satisfy his curiosity without giving Keita any ideas. "Auryn took good care of you, eh? How is he?"

Keita lit a cigarette. The scent of tobacco swirled around him, with faint traces of a sweet-smelling herb alleged to help calm the nerves but overall as effective as a pool noodle in a sword fight.

"I'm not sure. I think he's been working too hard or something. He's stressed out."

Reisen crossed his arms, staring downwards. He couldn't imagine dealing with the pressure of Auryn's occupation *and* secretly harbouring the son of a convicted—*in absentia*—terrorist.

"I wish there was something we could do." He wondered if Keita asked Auryn to come with him. Pleaded with him the same way he did, with equally poor results. *Come with me. Please.*

"You still care about him?" asked Keita, sounding genuinely surprised.

"That's putting it lightly. I was in love with Auryn for a long time before I finally worked up the nerve to kiss him. A kiss that can land you in the emperor's stomach is one hell of an investment."

"You're lucky you didn't get him killed. What were you thinking?" Keita erupted with the expected amount of indignation.

"It was more instinct than reason."

"Obviously."

"It doesn't bother you, does it? I know Ha—"

"I don't care," interrupted Keita. Reisen wasn't sure how much of Keita's annoyance was directed at him and how much of it applied to the situation in general. All in all, Keita appeared to take being forced to leave Auryn about as well as he did.

"Keita... You feel betrayed by my inability to protect you and that's fair, but let me—"

"I'm not interested in your excuses." Keita stood up. Reisen thought he was going to leave, preparing himself to beg and plead, to do or say whatever it took to prevent Keita from walking out the door, but his son walked over to the crate containing the creature he'd rescued earlier. He removed the sleeping animal, along with a blanket and then sat with it bundled in his lap. "What is this thing, anyway?"

"Everyone calls it a snow monkey, but it's actually a snow haplorrhine. It probably belongs to someone.

They're popular pets. I guess some people like being kept awake all night by incessant chirping. We'll check the community billboard later and see if anyone has reported one missing."

"Whatever."

Keita had a streak of dried blood on his cheek, but no wound to accompany it. "How long ago were you injured?"

"Not long. The cat that mutilated the haplorrhine thing scratched me."

"Do you always heal so fast?"

"No. I heal like a normal person. Scratch must not have been too bad."

"Were you in a temple lately?"

"Auryn took me, I think. Don't remember what happened. What does that have to do with anything?"

God damnit.

"You don't remember because the blades of offering daggers are treated with a naturally occurring chemical compound. Cut yourself with one and the most common side effects are feelings of euphoria and a sense of connectivity to a greater power. Less common side effects are visual and auditory hallucinations, tinnitus, flashbacks, and amnesia. It's meant to imitate a spiritual connection, but for some people, the connection is genuine. Your healing abilities have been enhanced."

"I didn't think the contract worked."

"There are no contracts, Keita. No gods or goddesses. There's only people who can channel energy and people who can't."

The power was their own, not a gift or seal of acceptance. It wasn't something to be borrowed and wielded responsibly, at risk of eternal damnation; it was theirs to do with as they pleased. Of course, Haken didn't want anyone to know that. People were much easier to control when they believed their fate was dictated by outside forces.

Keita lit another cigarette, hands trembling. "How bad is Mom?" He was nervous. Out of his element. Struggling to take steady, even breaths.

"Oh... She's in good spirits for someone with a catheter in her abdomen, ongoing struggles with organ failure, total vision loss, and a major parasitic infection."

"So, you're not helping her. You're prolonging the inevitable."

"It's not my decision. It's hers." Reisen borrowed Keita's cigarette before taking a long drag. Its contents left a lot to be desired. "She thinks I can find a cure."

"Can you?"

"How do you kill something that feeds on the energy of everything around it?"

"I don't know."

"Then you're as educated on the subject as I am." Reisen took another drag. Whatever the herbal ingredient was, it was barely strong enough to placate a fly. Unacceptable. He returned the cigarette; he'd provide his son with better alternatives later.

"Can you exorcise it?" asked Keita.

"On whose authority? The statues people worship at temple? The entities anchored to those places are not gods."

Keita frowned, staring at the floor. "How much longer does she have?"

"A year, at most."

"Great..." Keita's blue eyes filled with tears.

Reisen never thought he'd have the opportunity to revisit the pain of being unable to comfort his son; though it stung no less, he was thankful for the experience.

THEY DESCENDED INTO an uncomfortable silence. Years apart, and there was nothing left to be said. Keita lit another cigarette, his failure to derive any comfort from the smoke a sign of impending doom. He was overwhelmed. It was too much. His mother was alive, but wouldn't remain that way much longer. Reisen was a selfish dick who hadn't even recognised him. Auryn was everything he valued and treasured and without him he felt emotionally bankrupt. He snubbed the cigarette out, having a tough time breathing. Damn thing wasn't helping, anyway.

"Everything's fucked." His eyes burned. Chest full of heavy stones.

Reisen touched his back. He pulled away. "You can't hug me and expect me to forgive you! I needed you, and you weren't there. I'd have to be a fucking moron to trust you again."

"Keita." Reisen was persistent. Didn't listen well. Hugged him anyway. "I'm not asking for forgiveness. I just want to hug my son." He resented Reisen's attempts to comfort him, angrier than he thought possible with rage pulsating in his veins. Keita wept bitterly, trying to choke back tears. Failing miserably. "I'm glad you're here."

Reisen couldn't fool him. He knew better. "Yeah, right. You didn't even know who I was."

"Don't take it personally. I haven't slept in days and probably couldn't pick myself out of a line-up. I'm an idiot. I'm sorry. Let me make it up to you."

"Good luck."

"Oh, ye of little faith. There's someone else I'd like you to meet."

"What? Who?"

"Her name is Mary Jane."

Chapter Thirteen

IN LESS THAN five hours they would be somewhere sunny. Warm. Aggnaroth preferred submarines to land-based vehicles—which made him feel sick—and aircraft—which made him feel sicker. The matter of space travel was better left untouched. His stomach turned just thinking about it.

The scene at the hospital bordered on a mob. Everyone wanted to know the details surrounding Auryn's triumph over death and what was being done to punish the Ibaran scum who reportedly tried to blow him up. The General's recovery was advertised as a miracle. An act of God.

Auryn did not look like he had been touched by God. Quite the opposite. He was lethargic, pale, having a hard time keeping his head up, and vacantly staring out the window. Silent and withdrawn. He looked like a man who wanted to die and resented his inability to do so.

Aggnaroth kept his explanation of what he had done short and to the point, explaining the origins of the inkworm and its various applications. The whole time Auryn barely said a word, never questioning his intentions, which was a sign of resignation if he had ever seen one. The look on Auryn's face dictated he would rather have died in the explosion. The submarine continued along on autopilot. It was painted an offensive yellow that would have delighted Reisen, for all his Earthling sentimentality.

A protective shield covered the island on which they resided, stretching a hundred nautical miles in every direction. It extended underground and absorbed frequent shock waves caused by earthquakes in the region—a hotspot for volcanic activity, the source of geothermal energy used to fill the island's massive power requirements, maintaining holographic towers and climate controls.

They passed through the barrier unhindered.

Dense layers of ice disappeared overhead. The water turned from black to blue. Sunlight filtered through the depths, allowing Aggnaroth to distinguish emerging shapes of aquatic life in the distance. Auryn perked up immediately, peering out the window with interest. Nothing grew too close to the barrier, animals and plants alike repelled with electromagnetic pulses. If anything did get through the shock of below-freezing water was enough to deter them. Discouraging human visitors required less effort. A former quarantine zone for those infected by plague, the island's history invoked sufficient dread to keep even the heartiest explorers away.

Aggnaroth drifted off to sleep. When he awoke Auryn remained fixated on the window, staring into the ocean depths, but looking better. Less inclined to swallow a bullet.

The submarine docked at a base on Pao Island, an island off Rian's western coast. Its human inhabitants were long gone. He did not dare go any farther south, lest Auryn spontaneously combust in the sun.

Auryn stepped onto the sand and removed heavy winter clothing, water lapping at his feet. Aggnaroth was torn between granting the man solitude and getting down to business, opting for the latter.

"I need your help. I do not feel you owe me any favours, considering your intention was to die, and I took that away from you, so I am prepared to offer you something in exchange." Aggnaroth baited the hook and let it fly. "I can reunite you with your family."

Chapter Fourteen

TWO DAYS LATER

North Bembrook Forest, Calder
4,500 Kilometres Outside the Quarantine Zone

An old trail wove through the forest, gnarled with roots partially concealed by thick layers of sphagnum moss. Progress would have been difficult for a less sturdy creature than the velver, a robust yak-like ungulate. A velver had the brawn required for transporting heavy loads and the stamina to travel long distances without rest.

Misha's legs worked tirelessly, dredging up peat moss as he ploughed forwards, shaggy head hanging low to the ground. He fought to gain traction in the exposed soil, gritting his teeth as he scrambled up a steep incline.

Tiernan rewarded his mount with an affectionate pat on the withers. A well-groomed coat of black and white hair carpeted Misha with ample insulation from chilly nights and driving rain. Smooth, spiral-shaped horns were an effective deterrent against most predators, human and animal alike.

They'd left Ainsley early in the morning and set out for Calder's western border, taking them through kilometres of coastal temperate rainforest; centuries wrapped in wood. Bembrook Forest. They passed dilapidated red cedar houses, barely visible in the dense trees, moss-covered frames giving them the appearance of something ageless and organic. Not far away was a meadow, covered in purple wildflowers—the place where Uncle Auryn had last been seen before wandering into the forest and disappearing.

Blue feathers attached to wooden arcs on Tiernan's back rustled in the wind, creating a sound more feared than adored, meant to represent the Holy firebird, a symbol of the Goddess, named for its ability to breathe flames.

Remnants of sleep clung to him, refusing to dissipate after less than an hour's rest. That's when the banging started. Old master Tycho was still in his pyjamas and nearly kicked the door in, breathless and smelling strongly of peach cider.

"There's reports of a blasted bog fiend lurkin' north of Garvey. Massive rack. Fifty points, at least. His Eminence, Ranulf Harmouth, High Elder, wants its head above his fireplace." Tiernan had dressed by the glow of a lamp, assembling his thin armour more from memory than visual cues, glinting ghost-like in the light.

The sound of human activity not far ahead attracted Tiernan's attention. They were likely loggers or homesteaders breaking ground on a new settlement. Innocuous civilians. He approached a clearing, remaining unnoticed in the din of falling trees until Misha lumbered onto the grass. Misha hesitated, proceeding only with a reassuring rub and a few comforting words. "Go on, you big baby."

A burly man looked up from the log he was sawing and smiled widely, displaying rows of tobacco-stained teeth. "Well, well. We don't get paladins around these parts real often. Something goin' on we should be aware of?"

"There's no reason to be concerned," replied Tiernan. He urged Misha forwards at a slow, steady pace, feeling the tension in the velver's frame. Over the years, the animal appeared to have absorbed his aversion to human interaction, growing nervous around people.

"In that case, why don't you join us regular folk for a bit of bush tea? You should see the size of the wild blueberries Egan here picked down by the lake." He gestured towards a sweat-soaked man who mopped his brow with an oily rag.

Tiernan bowed his head politely. "I'll only distract you from a decent day's work, but thank you for the offer."

There were a dozen other people in the clearing, all of whom stopped what they were doing to listen. They looked like average forest-dwellers, dressed mainly in worn animal skins. Only a little girl appeared out of place, around six years old, seated on a newly shorn stump in a brown leather jacket, hugging a small toy rabbit.

"Nonsense. Climb off that hairy beast and sit with us for a while. About time we took a break. Bet you have some interesting stories to tell. Name's Tom."

"That's kind of you, Tom, but I must be on my way."

The man who was bathed in sweat fumbled nervously with his rag, speaking in a hesitant tone. "You sure about this, Tom? His velver's the wrong colour. White, the lady said. Not black and white. Just white."

"Expecting someone?" inquired Tiernan, a hint of panic flaring in his chest.

Tom stalked over to the girl, grabbed her by the arm, and hoisted her roughly to her feet. Dark, dishevelled hair covered much of her face, forming a curtain of tangles.

She scratched the toy rabbit's long ears. Matted fur overlapped its faded brown eyes, giving it a pained, morose stare. Its legs were shrunken, a fraction of their normal size. When the girl looked up her black eyes were visible through her unruly hair—large and terrified.

Tom removed a long knife from a leather holster, holding it to the girl's throat, his eyes fixed on Tiernan. "Get off the bloody velver or watch her bleed."

"What makes you think I care?" Paladins were trained to remain focused on their mission at all costs. Failure to do so was unacceptable. Anyone else would ride away, thinking nothing of it.

"I'm only gonna say this once. Do as I say, or the girl dies. Dismount, and don't try nothing funny." There was a sense of radical conviction in Tom's eyes, warning him against further provocation; Tom knew better than to believe he didn't care. Someone had sold him out, right down to the colour of his mount, but their information lacked attention to detail. Tiernan didn't ride a white velver, traditionally considered a bearer of good luck. Stout had belonged to his dad.

Tiernan dismounted, gently touching a gauntlet-clad hand to Misha's forehead. The velver bellowed and tossed his head disapprovingly.

"Told ya he wouldn't fall for it," said a young woman, arching her spine as she stretched while clutching a hatchet she'd been using to strip off layers of bark.

"Shuddup," hissed Tom. The blade of his knife hovered close to the frightened girl's throat, poised to strike. "Remove your helm."

Tiernan hesitated a moment before doing as instructed, shielding his dark blue eyes from the sun as long white-blond hair tumbling free. A profound sense of vulnerability and shame accompanied the act of exposing his face, like peeling back layers of skin to reveal some maligned, inhuman construction. A paladin's helm was part of their anatomy, never to be removed in public. To do so was taboo and carried the punishment of penance. Anonymity assured a lack of consequences for their actions and fill paladins with a bloated sense of self-importance, bolstering their confidence. In their elaborate armour, paladins were more gods than mortal and expected to be treated as such.

At first, Tom appeared surprised, quickly followed by visible annoyance.

"You do have the wrong paladin," said Egan. "This one's naught but a boy."

Tiernan had recently turned forty-one. Hardly a boy. He'd fought in the field for over three decades and trained fighters numerous times his age, a man in every right, but this was neither the time nor the place to argue semantics.

Tom lowered his knife from the girl's throat, but maintained a tight hold on her, looking less convinced. He turned his head and spat. "What's your name, boy?"

Asking a paladin to identify themselves was an act of treason.

"Tiernan Aran."

"*Sir* Tiernan Aran. You're telling me you're *the* Sir Tiernan Aran." Tom was aghast. "Hero of Crown Hill. Saviour of Lir. Human battering ram. They say he single-handedly took back Taregan's Folly when it was occupied by those blasted fools from Fenton."

"It wasn't that impressive. Most of them were drunk on sacred wine. Throwing up everywhere. It didn't sit well with them, the heathens."

"Impossible. You barely look old enough to piss straight." Tom pointed the knife at him accusingly.

"He's got a pretty mouth," the woman added, prompting an explosion of laughter.

"Bet you couldn't even lift that sword," chided Tom, glancing at the longsword in the scabbard fixed to Misha's side.

"Be happy to give you a demonstration."

"Demonstration. Pah. I should kill you for impersonating your ilk. That's got to go against some code of conduct."

"You may find that difficult to do while hiding behind a little girl."

Tom glared murderously, clenching his teeth. "Take your armour off. All of it."

"If I'd known it was going to be that kind of party, I would have brought refreshments."

"Now!" Tom grabbed the girl by the hair, pulling hard enough to elicit a scream of pain.

Tiernan began the meticulous process of removing the rest of his armour, taking off his gleaming pauldrons and engraved breastplate, stripping down to his underwear.

Scars decorated his torso, a human scratching post. From the neck down he looked less boyish, muscles carved clearly into his skin.

"If you don't want him, can I have him?" asked the woman, prompting another gale of collective laughter.

Tom approached cautiously and pressed the tip of his knife against Tiernan's bare chest, drawing a small circle of blood. "Do you know what we do with liars, boy?"

"Recruit them, I'd imagine."

Tom opened his mouth to protest, but the child knocked him off-balance. She kicked Tom in the shin before twisting out of his grasp and tearing off towards the trees in a mad sprint. Tiernan grabbed Tom by the wrist, turning the knife, plunging its blade into his abdomen, spilling springy coils of intestines with a smooth jerk of his hand. Tom stumbled back, and Tiernan caught him by the shoulder before slitting the carotid artery in his neck, only then allowing him to collapse on the ground.

Tiernan retrieved his longsword from Misha's side before the next attacker struck, decapitating him with a well-practised swing of the heavy double-sided blade. As cumbersome as the sword was, it felt natural in his hands. He'd always been unusually strong, wielding his first metal sword at the age of four under his dad's careful tutelage.

The woman charged, waving her hatchet. He struck her on the back of the head with the hilt of his sword. She crumpled at his feet, unconscious.

A scream erupted behind him, and he turned to see Egan herding the little girl back into the clearing, arms pinned painfully behind her back. He held the child in front of him like a shield, panting heavily from chasing her.

"Drop the fucking sword."

Tiernan gauged the distance between them, analysing the amount of time it would take to reach the man, to thrust the point of his sword through his opponent's torso without risking injury to the girl. If he could wear Egan out just a little more, there was a chance the man might collapse on his own accord—his sweat-soaked face was bright red with exertion and a faint whistle was audible when he breathed. The man twisted the girl's arms at an unnatural angle, and Tiernan threw down his sword, equal parts disgusted and defeated.

"Tie him up, and be careful. Might be who he says he is. Damned brat." Egan kept a determined hold on the girl while Tiernan was secured, bound with tightly woven ropes tied into a series of impossible knots. Egan shoved the girl into someone else's care and half-sat, half-collapsed on a nearby log. He mopped his forehead and continued to breathe like an overexerted dog. "Don't try to escape, or we'll feed the girl to the mountain trolls."

"You'd like an excuse to visit the family, wouldn't you?" asked Tiernan.

Egan rose to his feet with a roar, as if determined to prove his point, but he was held back by strong arms. "Easy, Egan. If he's the one they're looking for, we don't get paid nothing if we hurt him."

"You sure?" a voice groaned. The fallen woman sat up slowly, clutching her head. "I wanna cut his balls off and make little purses out of them." She leaned forwards, head between her legs, and vomited.

Chapter Fifteen

TIERNAN WATCHED MISHA charge off into the forest. Branches cracked and the canopy swayed as the velver crashed through the trees. With luck he'd make it back to Ainsley and the Church would be aware things had gone to shit, send help. They'd have a rough idea where he was. He just had to be patient. Have faith.

"Go after it!" someone shouted.

"You go after it! I don't feel like dyin' today."

Egan tied Tiernan up next to the little girl, her arms and legs similarly cocooned. Her toy rabbit was also bound, fur jutting between coils of rope. Something woven into the fibres drained his strength, making him light-headed. A fire burned in front of them, chewing up discarded branches from fallen trees. She fixated on the flames, observing their constant shifting with a mesmerised look.

Eventually she turned her head to stare at him for a moment in silence before speaking. "Will we be okay, Sir Aran?"

He was taken aback by use of his name, given his identity was still a matter of some speculation. "Call me Tiernan, or Mr. Aran if you must. I'm not fond of the 'sir.'" Speaking to the girl filled him with anxiety. Was he supposed to say something reassuring? Wasn't lying to children a commonly accepted practice? "As for being okay, we have the Goddess on our side. Her Light will guide us and give us strength."

"Amen!"

"What's your name?"

"I'm Mae, that's me."

"Listen, Mae. I'll get you back home as soon as I can."

"Haven't got a home." Mae puffed out her cheeks and wiggled around, trying to loosen the rope to no avail. "They caught you because of me, didn't they?"

"It's not your fault. These people are assholes."

"The Goddess lets you talk like that?"

"I've yet to receive a complaint."

"She never zaps you?"

"No. Not for calling someone an asshole, anyway."

"How old are you?" asked Mae.

"Old enough to be your father. Young enough to squeeze in a few more years of making stupid mistakes."

"You don't look very old." Mae cracked a hint of a smile as she peered at him from behind her dark hair. "Will you be my friend?"

"All right, you've talked me into it."

"I'm not happy right now, but I'm glad I have a friend."

"Positive thinking will get you a long way, kid."

By mid afternoon a group of figures emerged from the trees, clad in black cowls, concealing most of their faces. There were five of them in total, hems of their robes brushing the ground as they walked. They moved into the clearing single file, the sound of their footsteps barely audible even to his sensitive ears.

"Who are they?" asked Mae, observing the strange procession with pursed lips.

"More assholes. Fancy ones."

The procession halted, and the first in line stepped forwards and removed her hood. Her dark hair shone blue in the sun, drawn tightly into a bun perched on the top of her head. Several tendrils of hair hung loosely, descending past her chin and concealing portions of nearly translucent skin. When she saw Tiernan, the corners of her mouth extended into a wide, toothy grin.

Studying him intently, the woman moved in close, cupping the side of his face. "Sir Aran, you must forgive our methods. We desire only your cooperation." The woman had no distinguishing marks of any kind, her age likely somewhere in the early thirties, but Tiernan was reluctant to guess based on physical appearance alone.

"We don't know if it's him," declared Egan, nervously wringing his hands. "The velver we lost was the wrong colour, and he's awfully young. Good with a sword, though. He killed Tom and Markus. Nearly knocked poor Janie's brains out."

"That's all right. There's a test I can perform." The woman smiled resplendently, looking him over the way butchers appraised livestock at the market. Her accent was a blend of many—untraceable. "I understand it's quite an honour to see the man behind all that lovely armour. It should be a crime to hide such a pretty face."

"Don't let it go to your head. I was informed clothing was optional," replied Tiernan, regarding her with a bored stare. Traces of the woman's perfume hung in the air, honey and lavender with an undercurrent of something familiar—the origins of which he couldn't place, an artificial sweetness.

"Who are you?" he asked.

"My identity is none of your concern."

He named her Kijo, a serpent demoness slayed by the Goddess.

Kijo withdrew a bone-handled knife from the confines of her robe, the jagged blade set with round, opaque stones.

"Don't hurt him!" yelled Mae.

"Precious, isn't she?" A look of amusement crossed Kijo's face. "And presumptuous to assume she's not the one I'm going to cut."

Mae shrank back, glaring.

Kijo knelt before Tiernan, puncturing the skin between his toes with the point of her blade. Blood seeped from the narrow slit, darkening the ground. Tiernan masked any displeasure and remained still. He stared into Kijo's pale eyes, searching their faded depths for answers but finding only more questions. She twisted the knife clockwise and the stones imbedded in the blade emitted a reddish glow. Kijo withdrew the blade and then tucked it back into the folds of her robe. The bleeding stopped. Tiernan healed quickly, one of many blessings granted by the Goddess.

"You've got the right man," declared Kijo. "Take your money and leave." She tossed a bag of gold coins on the ground.

"We coulda stabbed him for you. Saved you the trouble." Egan looked offended he'd been deprived of the opportunity.

"Gladly," agreed his female counterpart.

"You haven't fought any paladins, have you?" asked Kijo. "He's not the only one who heals fast. He is, however, unique in other ways."

"What do you want?" questioned Tiernan, focus never wavering from Kijo's face.

"You were selected for your healing abilities, your pain tolerance, and most importantly, your empathy. That's all you need to know."

"Right, right. Wouldn't want to give away too much. I'm much cuter when I'm confused."

Kijo rose to her feet and dusted her knees off, giving orders to the cultists. "Take them underground."

"Wait," he protested. "Let Mae go. I'll do whatever you ask. I swear to Goddess Aisha. My word is my bond."

"I have no doubt breaking your word seems anathema to you now, but that may not be the case for long, and I can't risk a change in attitude. Even a boulder can be ground into dust given enough time and enough force."

The bandits quickly rounded up their things, skulking off into the woods. Two of the cultists collected Tiernan's armour, struggling to lift it. They walked a short distance to the mouth of a cave. It was a tight fit passing through, but once they entered the cavern, they followed a natural decline into an expansive open space. Richly pigmented petroglyphs decorated the walls; galloping horses and hunters battling a gigantic cave bear, some triumphant, others slashed and shredded, depicted with vivid gashes of ochre.

They continued through an elaborate underground labyrinth and walked for quite some time, making it impossible to track all the turns they made. Escaping this place was going to be a serious problem. At what Tiernan assumed was the centre of the labyrinth, guards stood watch over a network of individual rooms carved into stone, doors locked with magick seals. Glowing crystals were mounted at regular intervals, driving off the darkness. One of the cultists veered away from the group, heading in the opposite direction and carrying Mae over his shoulder.

"Take care of her!" Tiernan called out, craning his neck to watch them depart. "Unless choking to death on your own blood happens to be on a list of things you'd like to accomplish."

"She'll be fine, darling," assured Kijo. "Can't have you thinking it's a good idea to end your life to get out of this mess. You die, she dies. You refuse to cooperate, she dies. It's simple. Behave yourself and no harm will come to her."

Tiernan quirked an eyebrow, the cool rock beneath his bare feet turning his toes numb. "How do you sleep at night?"

"Naked," replied Kijo.

They followed the sound of running water and reached a grotto. A stream erupted from a hole in the rock, behind it only blackness and endless murmurs. No more than a foot deep, the water snaked through the natural chamber, coiling around intricate rock formations. Its bottom was resplendent with jagged crystals—translucent with a purple tint.

Swirling mineral concoctions brewed in the pools close to the water's edge. An occasional bubble rose to the surface, spraying a milky green substance when it popped.

"We need to purify you first," said Kijo. "A vessel must be free of moral deficiencies."

"You're going to need a lot of soap. And a priestess."

"I have something better." Kijo moved to a nearby table, filled with numerous ritual components. She retrieved a birch switch, three rods intricately braided and soaked in brine. She lit a brazier. The smoke smelled strongly of cedar shavings and dried sage.

The impact of the frayed rods left blushing streaks in their wake—incongruent lines which swelled and wept down the length of Tiernan's back. Hemp ropes bound his arms behind him, circling his upper shoulders and looping several times around his neck. Coarse woven fibres scratched and bit as the ropes were pulled taut, eroding layers of skin.

Two of the cultists stood resolutely at his left and right, each with an end of rope gripped tightly in their sweaty hands; nameless faces with perpetual grins.

A feeling of momentary helplessness reinforced the perilousness of his predicament. Church protocol was useless, emphasising self-preservation. Orders from the High Priestess would read, "Forget the girl. Continue your mission." But he couldn't do anything to compromise Mae's safety. In terms of priorities, her security ranked above his own, orders be damned.

He exhaled slowly, bare legs pitted with dents where stones had nested. Turning his head, he caught a closer look of the instrument Kijo wielded and jerked forwards as it collided with his back. The braided sticks were joined together at the base, wrapped in leather. Tightly wound strips of blood-stained cloth further reinforced the cohesion. The tips of each rod were splintered, blooming outwards in thin wooden petals.

Under other circumstances, this might have been enjoyable.

Tiernan shifted his weight as much as the restrictive pressure of the ropes would allow; agitated. It wasn't the pain that got to him, but the itch—the maddening itch which arose wherever pearls of blood crept downwards and stagnated.

Pain was a different matter. Pain was fluid and multidimensional; a teacher, a priestess, and a poet. It discouraged physically detrimental acts by implementing practical restrictions and establishing boundaries. To broaden these boundaries was divine. Resolve could be strengthened and reinforced with sturdier materials, resurrected anew on a steadier base. Pain sometimes left reminders, scars which told epic tales with a single streak and turbulent dents found only beneath the surface.

To Tiernan Aran it was merely there.

The ropes tightened around his neck, tugging him forwards roughly, momentarily cutting off the flow of oxygen to his lungs. He balanced on the knobs of his knees, cautiously urging his weight back until the precarious nature of his stance reversed. The ropes slackened, and he inhaled deeply, directing an annoyed glance at the men.

A quietness pervaded. He shook a stone free from his knee and watched it skitter across the floor.

The birch rods continued their assault, flared bristles tearing into his back. Each lash healed and closed within seconds of its creation, leaving only a faint, swollen streak to mark its place. Kijo meticulously collected the blood from each wound prior to its closing, gathering the fluid in a round metal bowl.

Tiernan's feet drifted off to sleep, prickling painfully.

He was forced to a kneeling position in the stream. Kijo halted her assault to focus instead of mixing various powders with blood she'd collected. The warm water lapped at his knees. Sharp, concentrated prickles littered the lengths of his legs thanks to the spiky rocks beneath.

Tiernan listened to the babble of rushing water behind the rock wall; enigmatic banter conducted by countless hurried tongues. It seemed to him that water spoke more freely in the dark.

Kijo untied him. He tensed as her nimble fingers set to work on the drawstring of his underwear, her other hand on his lower back, inhumanly cold.

He knelt midstream while Kijo scrubbed him from head to toe, roughly rubbing a coarse mixture of blood and sand onto his skin. Each second made it more challenging to resist grabbing her by the neck and breaking her head open on a nearby rock, especially given the amount of attention she paid to his genitals, pulling back his foreskin, rubbing him with frosty, gritty fingers.

Tiernan felt sandy and sticky; the opposite of clean. Kijo retrieved a new bowl, made of ivory and filled with honey. She used honey and water to further cleanse him, smearing his body with the sticky substance and scraping every inch of him clean with a thin piece of bone, looking him over with smug satisfaction once she was done.

"I'll get you some new clothes."

"You're a gracious host, my lady."

The clothes were little more than a pair of grey cotton pants, but Tiernan took them without complaint. He dressed without haste, denying her the pleasure of seeing him flustered.

"Have a seat." Kijo gestured towards a short wooden stool. Tiernan sat, wishing he could put his helm back on. It helped shake insecurity, allowing him to retreat inwards. Without it he felt human, vulnerable.

Kijo opened a small, ornate glass box to reveal a round plant with thin white, lace-like leaves. It had a strong, acrid smell and narrow, spiny protrusions giving it an appearance more reminiscent of a sea urchin than a plant. Some of the slender spines had fallen off and Kijo carefully collected them.

Kijo pressed one of the spikes into Tiernan's back, easily piercing the skin with its pointed tip as she pushed inwards. She reverently held each spine in position until his skin healed around it, locking it in place. Instead of his body rejecting the spine like it would any other foreign object, he felt an incessant pull, creating a sharp sting—the pain constant, unwavering, and unexpected. For each spine Kijo inserted, the sting multiplied. His surroundings took on a slow, clockwise spin, blurring everything. His stomach churned.

Tiernan focused on the water pouring into the cavern. He wondered where it came from and where it led. He wondered if it surfaced somewhere or lived its entire life underground, if it ever saw the light.

A trickle of blood crept along his spine. The resulting itch made him squirm. He heard Kijo say something, but her voice was far away, undecipherable.

The water spoke to him through the walls. It sounded like wind whipping through poplar trees, spirits speaking in whispers. *We are not what we think we are.* He collapsed, twitching.

TIERNAN AWOKE WITH a monstrous headache, surrounded by rock—an oubliette, dark and silent. The silence was countered only by the sound of his breathing and the rhythmic drumming of his heart, still beating uncomfortably fast. The spines in his back remained firmly rooted in place. They produced a burning sensation, as if his skin had been soaked in kerosene and set alight. Stone walls offered no indication of what dwelt beyond their borders, acting only as a container, coddling the dark. The blackness was an immaculate construction.

There was no adjusting to its density—no brightening of his surroundings.

Tiernan used the last of his prana reserves to conjure the Light of the Goddess, a bright spark which lit up the cave, hurting his eyes. The room was no more than four meters long and four meters wide. A thin straw mat comprised the entirety of his frugal furnishings. No sign of a door; it was likely enchanted to blend in. The rock walls were cool against his fingertips, smelling ancient and damp. At the base of one was a depression in the ground, filled with water. The water flowed in from a small opening and out another, arranged in such a way Tiernan assumed was designed for removing bodily waste. At least his captors weren't going to allow him to drown in his own shit.

Still, to say the situation was bad would be optimistic.

Pain made focusing on anything a challenge, and Tiernan's mind bounced erratically from one thought to another, stressing over things beyond his control.

How's Mae?

Did Misha make it back?

What do these assholes want?

What he needed was a distraction. Something to halt the cycle of rumination and release the tension. He slid a hand in his pants, rubbing the tip of his cock, stroking himself with no effect, numb to pleasure.

Forced to play with a different organ, Tiernan retreated to a place in the far reaches of his mind, fixating on stories his dad told him as a child. He wasn't sure if his dad made them up, or if they were true, but they were stated with absolute conviction, as if they were the word of the Goddess.

"King Karnifer ruled back when all the lands in the great continent of Achius were one. He loved to hunt in the forest. He was out hunting one day when he happened across a baby ghoul suckling the decaying breast of its mother. He was struck with sympathy for the creature and decided to raise it as his own. Great idea, huh? It was rumoured his wife, the queen, was unable to bear children, but if you ask me, there's something incredibly sexist about the assumption her body was the one at fault.

"Anyhow, the king brought the little ghoul home and tried to raise it like a normal kid. You can imagine how well that turned out. The creature didn't play nicely with other children. It ate the court jester and didn't feel bad about it in the morning.

"King Karnifer was distraught. He believed he could tailor the nature of an inhuman species to match his own. The king returned from a hunt one day and found the queen strung up by her own guts with her skin peeled off. The point is, Ti, never assume someone else is going to change just because you want them to. The universe doesn't bow to your wishes, nor should it." It was a strange thing for a paladin to say. They were taught they deserved the universe's affection. Earned it with blood and sacrifice.

The pain intensified, delving deeper. He couldn't see what the plant was doing to him, but feeling around revealed blisters full of serum forming in craters around each spike. Glowing lights filled the cave, an endless field of stars.

A violent shudder wracked Tiernan's body. He tried to focus, to get a sense of the invader's intentions but only felt how badly it wanted him to suffer as their tiny roots twisted around his spinal cord. As if retaliating for his reconnaissance, the plant excreted a toxin, turning his brain into melted cotton. The pain remained, but became easier to ignore.

An orange light flickered in the dark and then vanished unexpectedly, swallowed by the pitch. The taste of ashes filled his mouth.

It reminded him of something.

Embers caught the breeze and skirted the dry grass, setting stalks aflame. Summer seeds crackled and ruptured. A spark caressed Tiernan's armoured cheek, marking the metal with a dot of ash. Grass fires died as suddenly as they started. Cappa, a paladin six years his senior, turned away from the field, retching; the smell was getting to him.

Half an hour earlier, a group of villagers had huddled together in the field and burst into balls of incandescent light; protests personified in flame. They were too late to intervene, just passing through on their way back to Ainsley. When they inquired about the motivation behind it, no one would tell the two paladins anything, apart from an elderly man who proclaimed, "Nutters, the lot of 'em. Saves us the trouble of burnin' 'em."

The stars looked different to him after that. Self-immolation. Mass suicide. Protests personified in flame. A sky full of injustice.

For what reason do you burn?

Chapter Sixteen

YEAR 2050
Twenty-three Years Ago

Ainsley, Calder

Tiernan awoke to the sound of water hissing through pipes. It came as a surprise—weeks had passed since his dad, Demetrius, showed interest in doing anything remotely human, bathing included.

Six years ago, several days after Tiernan's twelfth birthday, his mother was accused of murdering a Church elder. She disappeared, never to be heard from again. The uncertainty surrounding her absence left a gaping wound in Dem and over the years it festered. Tiernan stood by helplessly while Dem lost interest, hope, and himself.

Had his mother died, he suspected Dem would have learned to live with it, moved on. Instead, Dem deteriorated from a confident warrior into someone who considered eating a chore, slept either way too much or way too little, and stopped showing up at Temple. The Church gave up on him without much fuss—Tiernan wasn't sure why. Failing to report for duty was a serious offence, but to his knowledge no one questioned Dem's absence. No one banged on the door, demanding his return.

The water stopped. Tiernan pulled his sheets down and stretched out naked. The sun warmed and aroused him, hardening his cock. He thought about Cappa, an older paladin who worked in the Church's disciplinary department, enforcing punishment for those found in violation of Divine Law. They'd first met two years ago and gradually overcame their initial animosity, discovering they enjoyed fucking as much as fighting. Tiernan subsequently lost count of the number of times he'd been fucked in a prayer position, Cappa's calloused fingers stroking him, making offerings of scattered pearls.

An orgasm first thing in the morning was an ideal way to start the day.

Tiernan took a shower to cool off, dressed, and started breakfast, frying pork sausages and eggs. By the time he finished, Dem appeared, wearing loose-fitting pyjamas and looking clean, but miserable. His blond hair was longer than it had been in years, past his shoulders. Dem didn't get far before Tiernan ambushed him, pulling him into a tight hug. He'd become powerless to do anything except remind Dem how much he was loved.

"Morning. Want something to eat?" He already knew the answer, but he had to try.

"Not hungry."

"There might be some blueberry cake left."

"No."

Tiernan hugged Dem tighter. "You smell nice."

Dem tensed. "I thought I'd feel better if I took a bath. Can't recall how long it's been... But I don't. If anything, I feel worse, because it didn't change how dirty and disgusting I feel, and I'm reminded how fucking pointless everything is." Dem sniffed softly, blue eyes filling with tears. "What's wrong with me?" Only in recent months had Dem begun to acknowledge there was a problem, as if all this was somehow normal.

"I don't know." There had to be something he could do. Some way he could help. He was afraid it would all become too much, and Dem would decide he'd had enough. "But I don't want to lose you."

"I wouldn't do that to you." Dem wiped his eyes with his sleeve, trying to gather his resolve. "Don't worry."

THE BEST APOTHECARY in Ainsley kept weird hours, forcing Tiernan to delay his attendance of morning prayer. If he waited until general dismissal, the shop would be closed.

Large glass windows dominated the building's exterior, showing off rows of curious concoctions in colourful bottles. Ribbons of incense wafted through the air, woody with a pleasant musk.

The apothecary, Dezmodeus Azmodian, sat behind the counter, head in hands and face mostly shrouded behind a black cowl. Dezmodeus was notorious for his involvement with a lot more than finely crafted potions. Kidnapping. Murder. Extortion. Trafficking children. The list of crimes he was rumoured to have committed read like an encyclopaedia of fucked-up things to do to people. For all his alleged talents, Dezmodeus didn't appear to notice Tiernan standing there. Tiernan cleared his throat. Dezmodeus sat upright, tired eyes wide with momentary shock. He shook his head emphatically, smacking himself on the forehead.

"Thought I was hallucinating for a second... Can I help you with something?"

"What would you recommend for someone who's miserable all the time?"

"Your old man's not feeling any better, huh?"

The question threw Tiernan off; Dezmodeus's knowledge of his father's condition was unexpected. "I don't think he wants to be here anymore."

"I see." Dezmodeus stood up, rubbing his back with a wince. Though Dezmodeus was tall, over seven feet, his posture wasn't straight. He stood with a noticeable hunch, making him appear shorter than he was. He shuffled from one ingredient to another, collecting them in a leather pouch. His pointed ears were more elven than human, six silver rings piercing the helix and one in each lobe. "Three drops moonflower extract in the morning, one cup *aqua vitae* morning/noon/night, glimmer root tea for whenever he's feeling particularly useless, and two capsules of free-range leviathan oil, not that farmed shit, with each meal. I'll give him enough for two months. Come back when he runs out and we can make any necessary adjustments." Dezmodeus grabbed a piece of parchment, writing out instructions.

"What if it doesn't work?"

"Let me know." The firmness of Dezmodeus's tone surprised him. "Can't have people thinking my remedies are ineffective. I've got a reputation to uphold." Dezmodeus rotated his shoulder, rubbing it irritably. "That'll be two pieces of silver."

Tiernan was curious as to why the man was in such obvious pain, but knew better than to ask. He placed the coins on the counter. The morning prayer bell chimed. A smile crossed Tiernan's lips and Dezmodeus regarded him strangely.

"Aren't you forced to repent if you're late for prayer?" asked Dezmodeus.

"Yeah." Tiernan took the leather pouch and headed for the door, heart pounding. "Thanks for your help."

"Give my regards to your old man."

"YOU WERE TEN minutes late." Cappa grabbed Tiernan the moment they entered the inner sanctum, pinning him against the heavy gopherwood door, sliding the deadbolt into place. Cappa had that authoritative look in his deep brown eyes, sending a surge of heat to Tiernan's groin, cock hardening in his white prayer clothes. "What do you have to say in your defence?"

"The Goddess isn't my only priority," proclaimed Tiernan, inhaling sharply as Cappa's hand crept inside his shirt, pinching a nipple. "There was something I needed to do."

"You serve the Goddess, remember?" Cappa grinned playfully, speaking with false conviction—neither of them believed the Goddess gave a shit, but they both got off on pretending otherwise. "There's no higher priority than Her Holiness." Cappa took a step back, eying him impiously. "Take your clothes off, Tiernan." This form of "punishment" was unorthodox at best. Sex on Temple grounds was forbidden, except in the bathhouse, where debauchery was considered blowing off steam.

Tiernan slipped his shirt over his head and lowered his trousers. His heart skipped a beat as he exposed himself, dick drooling precum. His skin prickled, electric with excitement.

"Approach the altar," ordered Cappa. Tiernan stepped up to the large rectangular slab of flawless white marble. Cappa stood behind him and bent him over, pressing him against the cold stone. Cappa's hands roamed Tiernan's body, caressing his thighs and hips, tracing him like a dutiful cartographer. He drizzled warm consecrated oil over Tiernan's ass, rubbing it in. The oil had a sappy aroma and ensured his skin wouldn't heal in accordance with the Goddess's blessing, which would normally take all the fun out of what Cappa was about to do to it.

Cappa entered him with a slick finger, giving his prostate a fleeting massage, just enough to leave him groaning and wanting more. Tiernan received it in the form of a curved wand of rose quartz, a sequence of orbs of increasing size, the largest no bigger than an inch and a half in diameter, flared at the base to prevent an awkward trip to the Church clinic. Tiernan drew in a slow, deep breath, the kind generally reserved for when he was about to put an arrow through someone's heart, focusing on relaxing his muscles. Cappa pushed the first bead inside him. The generously anointed crystal produced a faint tingle as it stretched him. Two more and Cappa paused, smoothing his fingers over Tiernan's backside.

"All right?"

"Keep going," groaned Tiernan, eager for all of it. Cappa eased the rest of the wand inside him, filling him.

The first swats were light. The first time Cappa ever spanked him, he'd climaxed after a few slaps, equally embarrassed and aroused. He'd come a long way since then, but whenever Cappa stopped smacking his ass, tenderly rubbing his swollen skin, Tiernan's resolve was sorely tested.

He adjusted to the treatment and Cappa struck him harder, until each blow had him squirming and doing his damnedest not to ejaculate all over the altar. Cappa grabbed a candle, dripping hot black wax on his backside. The sting sent shocks of pleasure through him, his body tensing, balls tightening, legs shaking. Cappa set the candle aside and then removed the wand from Tiernan's ass, leaving him panting and on fire, needing to come so fucking badly it hurt.

"Turn over," said Cappa.

Tiernan flipped onto his back, swollen cock bobbing.

"Stroke yourself. *Slowly*. Don't come." Tiernan did as instructed, lifting his head to get a good look at Cappa, all sweaty and hard, wild brown hair sticking to his tan skin.

Cappa undressed quickly, splashing holy water over his face before oiling up his cock, positioning himself between Tiernan's legs and pushing inside. Tiernan slid his legs over Cappa's broad shoulders, willing his body to relax. Cappa stroked the inside of Tiernan's thighs, sliding in deeper.

"Doing okay?"

"Mmhm... I want all of you," replied Tiernan, stroking himself faster than he should, excitement threatening to explode out of him. Cappa grabbed his thighs, sinking deep inside him.

"Fuck, yes." Tiernan groaned deeply, shamelessly, shuddering with the effort required to hold back.

"Hands off." Cappa reached for Tiernan's cock, taking over, wrapping his thumb and forefinger around the base of his erection. He conjured a bright blue band of light to prevent Tiernan from ejaculating without impairing his ability to achieve orgasm. Determined to test its efficiency, Cappa rubbed the throbbing crown of Tiernan's cock, caressing its sensitive underside with his thumb. Cappa channelled energy to his hand, creating a voltaic tingle that triggered a massive orgasm, and while he came and came, Cappa fucked him, riding out waves of muscle contractions.

Instead of relaxing Tiernan, the release had the opposite effect, making him wilder. He bucked his hips, meeting Cappa's thrusts, urging the man's dick to penetrate him harder and deeper, the sound of their frenzied fucking reverberating off sacred walls.

"Cappa..." He could barely think, let alone speak. The pressure in his groin was becoming too much.

"Had enough?"

"Almost."

"Let me hear it, then."

Tiernan groaned. "Don't want to. Too many words."

"Say it." Cappa squeezed his throbbing balls in just the right way.

Tiernan groaned and threw his head back in surrender, reciting the prayer of penance. "I have wronged you, my Sovereign." He paused, gasping for breath, panting heavily. "I chose darkness over light...aah...Cappa...and lost myself in the shadows."

"Go on," grunted Cappa. A guttural groan betrayed how close he was.

"I ignored your Will for selfish reasons...and failed to withstand the allure of deviance... I am weak and unworthy of your Eternal Love. Oh, fuck... Oh, fuck..."

"Tiernan... You're so close." Cappa's skin gleamed with sweat, his scent contributing to an intoxicating stupor, making it harder to force out the remaining prayer.

"I apologise...not out of fear...but out of devotion. I beseech you...have mercy on my soul."

"I beseech you...to have mercy...on my *filthy* soul," corrected Cappa, releasing the ring of energy as he sank into Tiernan and pumped his cock.

Tiernan erupted with offerings, full of radiant light.

Cappa came hard, crawling up on the altar after pulling out. He collapsed next to him, momentarily dazed. When Cappa regained his senses, he kissed Tiernan, running his fingers through his hair. "The Goddess appreciates your sacrifice and forgives your transgressions." Cappa caressed Tiernan's chest, dragging his short nails over it. "Wanna go for a drink after dismissal?"

"I can't, sorry. Gotta go straight home." Tiernan always refused Cappa on grounds of looking after Dem, but the truth was Dem didn't so much need a babysitter as Tiernan needed an excuse to avoid Cappa. Fooling around at work was fine, but spending time together in a potentially meaningful way didn't appeal to him.

"How's your father doin'?"

"He's gotten a lot worse since his spellcasting abilities went to shit. He can't concentrate enough to properly channel energy. It makes him feel worthless and I don't know how to fix that."

"There's only so much you can do. The rest is up to him."

"That's the problem. He's lost the will to fight. Given up on everything. He can't do it on his own." Cappa reached for his hand, but Tiernan pulled away; he rolled over, getting up, cleaning himself up at the fountain. "I'll figure something out."

"Anything I can do to help?"

"No." He pulled his clothes back on, wobbly on his legs. "Thanks for the reprimand. I should be late more often."

"Looking forward to it."

TIERNAN RETURNED HOME to find Dem seated at the kitchen table, drunk on expensive scotch. Sometimes, when driven to this form of self-medication, alcohol temporarily improved Dem's disposition. Sometimes it made things worse.

Tiernan sat across from Dem, placing the leather pouch on the table. "I got this for you. Hopefully it helps."

Dem traced a fingertip over a wax seal on the pouch—a skeletal fish—means of identifying one merchant from another. "You went to see Dezi?"

"I figured he'd have the best selection, as far as mind-altering substances go. He said to give you his regards. You know the guy?"

"We used to hang out together." Dem drained his glass and filled it again, then poured one for Tiernan.

Tiernan drank deeply. "What's wrong with him? He looks like he's in pain."

"Oh, yes. The Anorian Incident."

"Anorian Incident?"

"The Anorians live up north. Far away. Dezi was transporting a shipment of azurelite on their behalf, and the shipment was hijacked. The Anorians believed Dezi was working with the hijackers and cut off his wings as punishment."

"Wings? Did I hear that right?"

"Dezi's one of the Nephilim—winged warriors. Nephilim are a specific type of soul, created by the Lightwalkers. In human bodies they develop incredibly sharp senses and take on more Nephilim characteristics as they age. They gain the ability to heal quickly. Something to do with the vibration of their soul altering their DNA. If they live to a thousand, they grow wings and no longer qualify as human. Arodontus Pike wrote about them in the Book of Forgotten Legends, remember? Love that book. Anyhow, a group of Nephilim were banished here on Ankari for defying the Lightwalkers."

Dem was deep in drunken storytelling mode, but Tiernan gladly humoured him. "Defying them how?"

"They expressed their displeasure over various Lightwalker policies, like The Right to Divine Love, which stipulates each soul shall be granted a partner whose eternal affection mirrors the love the Lightwalkers have for their creations. That's why souls are always created in pairs, called Eternal Flames."

"What's so bad about that?"

"Turns out, even eternal love isn't always unconditional. People grow apart. Some people never grow together in the first place. Couples of the same sex are never created intentionally and when it happens by supposed error, they're treated with disrespect and revulsion, expected to remain celibate and alone. Did I mention it's only acceptable to sleep with your Eternal Flame? Better hope you have the same kinks, or you're condemned to an eternity of boring sex. Anyhow, a group of Nephilim protested when a Lightwalker judge ordered a Nephilim woman to return to her Flame, despite substantial evidence he was abusing her. The judge informed her even if such heinous accusations were true, it was her duty as his Flame to love him unconditionally and fix him. Her failure in that department justified his wrath."

"I take it back. That's awful."

"The offending Nephilim were banished for opposing the judge, which any idiot could see coming. It was their intention."

"You think they pissed the Lightwalkers off deliberately?"

"Yeah. I do." Dem took a drink, eyes closing in momentary contentment. "The defendant called the judge a fucking cockweed and her friends and family erupted into applause, expressing their own colourful opinions of the judge's verdict. Everyone who spoke out was banished. Twelve in total. They were smart enough to know the consequences of their actions. They weren't lashing out irrationally. They were asking for it."

"Why would they *want* to be banished?"

"They can't remember." Dem opened the medicine pouch, extracting ingredients, examining each of them. "Leviathan oil? Not that farmed shit, I hope... No, it's good." Dem screwed the top off a metal canister, sniffing its contents, a faint smile spreading over his face. "These tea leaves are very shiny."

"Think they'll make your shit sparkle?"

"I'll let you know." Dem stuck his thumb in the tin, coating it with glittery silver powder, smearing it across Tiernan's forehead.

Tiernan retaliated, wiping the powder off with the back of his hand and applying it to Dem's cheek. Dem laughed for the first time in recent memory, filling him with hope.

IN THE MORNING Tiernan was shocked to find Dem up first. Up and making breakfast, no less. Looking a bit hungover, but otherwise thrumming with more life than Tiernan had seen him show in a long time. "I might go do a few errands later, if I can work up the courage to leave the house." How strange to hear Dem say that—a man who'd fought bravely in countless battles, slayed powerful demons and lifted ancient curses. Afraid to go outside.

"I have faith in you. The Goddess will give you strength." He kissed Dem's forehead, hugging him tightly.

TIERNAN KNEW SOMETHING was wrong the moment he entered the house. The smell of blood hung thick in the air, permeating everything. His body went cold, then unbearably hot.

He found Dem sprawled on the floor of his bedroom, wrists slashed with deep gouges stretching the full length of his forearm. Blood pooled on the wooden planks, dripping between them. An empty bottle of anticoagulant sat on Dem's nightstand. Though unable to speak, it said plenty. Dem's commitment to dying was serious. No mistakes. No second chances.

Tiernan stood there for a long time, feeling nothing, and then, all at once, everything.

TIERNAN STOOD IN front of a fountain depicting Goddess Aisha defeating Wert, the water demon. It was supposed to fill him with courage and a sense that anything was possible, but it did neither. Others found it quite peaceful, which Tiernan could see if you ignored the look of twisted agony on Wert's face, his intestines spilling out. Or maybe that was what they liked about it. Sadistic assholes, the lot of them. Well, Cappa was an exception. The only exception.

He closed his eyes, listening to the sound of the water flowing through stone. He heard someone approach and opened his eyes to see Cappa coming his way. They stood in silence for several minutes before Cappa finally spoke, "Sorry about your father."

"Don't waste your sympathy."

Cappa touched his hand. Tiernan recoiled as if he'd been burned. "It wasn't your fault, Tiernan."

"Fuck you." Rage flooded in, an unstoppable torrent, drowning everything. He wanted to verbally tear Cappa apart, to impart hurtful tirade after tirade, to break him down to nothing, but couldn't find the words required to do so. There was nothing so ugly he could say that would have any truth, any validity, and that only frustrated him more.

"You have every right to be angry, Tiernan. Even if it's slightly misdirected."

"You can't absolve me of guilt when you don't know what happened. He was acting strange...seemed sorta content... I should have known better than to leave him alone."

"People who are sorta content don't usually kill themselves, Tiernan. Leaving him alone wasn't a poor decision, it was a sign of trust. I'm sorry your father violated that trust. That's right, I said it again. You have my sympathy whether you like it or not."

It was too much. Tiernan stepped away from the fountain, heading for the exit. "I can't deal with you right now."

"I'm leaving on a mission to Fenton tomorrow. I'll see you when I get back."

Tiernan stopped. Anger trickled out of him slowly, like water from a leaky tap. Fenton was dangerous. Cursed. "Be careful."

"I will."

Tiernan stalked off, hands in his pockets. He hated himself for caring so much, when it was exactly what he'd been trying to avoid. He was too emotionally invested. If anything happened to Cappa...

Chapter Seventeen

TIERNAN AWOKE IN another part of the cave, lying on his stomach on a metal cot. No pain. Kijo stood over him, examining his back. She spoke at length with another woman in a language he could neither place nor understand. It took a while for feeling to return to his extremities and his eyes even longer to adjust.

"Look who's awake." Kijo stood over him, arms crossed. "You've done well, Sir Aran. The nesting pockets look perfect. I've never seen Finnegan's Lace grow so quickly."

"Happy to be of service. Wait...nesting pockets?"

"Hand me the first pupae, Lysa."

The other woman—*Lysa. No need to invent an offensive nickname for this one*—avoided eye contact with him, staring downwards while brushing a strand of waist-length, brown hair away from her face. She retrieved a small tin box from a nearby table and removed the lid, delicately extracting a chrysalis with a pair of tweezers. The hardened outer shell shone metallic bluish green sheen and twinkled in the light.

Tiernan swallowed a mouthful of bile, throat burning. He reminded himself this was all part of the Goddess's plan. Had to be. His job was to endure the unspeakable with dignity and grace.

Kijo sliced open one of the nesting pockets with a long, sharp fingernail and pressed the chrysalis against the wound in Tiernan's back. There was a brief sensation of suction as the pupa anchored itself to him, then a sting as the skin stretched closed, a clear membrane reforming over the gap. She repeated this for twelve pupae, falling silent until finished.

"The butterfly pupae need to be kept at a specific temperature and provided with a nourishing environment specific to their needs."

"Ever heard of an incubator?"

"You are my incubator, Sir Aran."

"Why butterflies?"

"Butterflies are unfit to rule kingdoms."

"Thanks for clarifying." Tiernan closed his eyes, battling back a surge of dizziness. Whatever that psycho, pain-addicted plant did to him, his body wasn't healing the way it should. His pranic reserves were drained, leaving him with barely enough energy to remain conscious and coherent. "I want to see Mae. Gotta make sure you haven't eaten her."

Kijo left to retrieve Mae, leaving him alone with Lysa. She gave him a cup of water which he struggled to swallow, choking on most of it. She glanced around the room as if confirming they were alone, then leaned in close. "Listen to me, Sir Aran—"

"What choice do I have?"

"After the butterflies hatch, you'll be granted a recovery period to regain your strength for the next batch. As soon as your condition permits it, I'll help you and Mae escape."

"Why would you do that?"

"Let's just say I don't agree with Lamashtu or her methods."

"What's she going to do with the butterflies?" asked Tiernan.

"They'll be released in Enra. The butterflies are infected with the dragon's tooth fungus, which they'll spread to human hosts. The fungus causes hallucinations and inspires violent, irrational behaviour. It kills its human hosts in less than ten hours, growing from their body and releasing infectious spores."

"Well, that's cheerful. And I was afraid she was gonna do something terrible."

"Lamashtu intends to create fear and chaos, prompting a nationwide evacuation. She recently discovered an azurelite cluster in southern Enra—that's what she's after. She wants to mine it without anyone knowing it's there, especially the Enrian government."

"Azurelite... That's expensive stuff."

"Yes. Azurelite is highly concentrated energy. Its applications are unlimited. Buyers pay exorbitant amounts of money for it. Its current value on the black market is roughly a hundred thousand dollars, per ounce. We have clients up north who are looking to procure a large quantity."

Lysa moved away from him, sensing something he couldn't, seeming disinterested when Kijo—*Lamashtu*—returned with Mae. Mae looked pale but otherwise fine, clutching her toy rabbit by the ears.

She stared at Tiernan, frowning deeply. "You don't look so good."

Mae whirled around to face Lamashtu. "What did you do to him? You evil witch! I hope someone burns you and spits on your ashes!" The girl swung, striking Lamashtu with a fist, kicking wildly. "I hate you!" Lysa pulled her away to hug her close to her chest.

"There you have it," declared Lamashtu. "Alive and well. See to it that the little monster stays that way."

Chapter Eighteen

HOURS. DAYS. IT didn't matter anymore. One moment became indistinguishable from the next. Tiernan no longer conjured the light of the Goddess. It burned his eyes and required too much energy.

He brushed his fingertips along the cave wall, tracing its surface. If he stared for long enough, shapes materialised in the darkness, taking on a life of their own. Trade winds agitated the leaves of red alder trees, circulating the scent of salt. For a while he sat among the trees, watching them sway hypnotically. The sound of gulls drew him towards the sea. Water stretched on forever, melting into sky.

Fires burned all over the beach. Pots of green-shelled clams simmered over the blazes, brewed with chopped wild onions and black garlic. Heat forced the shells apart, exposing their succulent inhabitants. Children snatched clams from the pots, shells still steaming. They devoured the meat, leaking drizzles of warm juice from the corners of their mouths. When they weren't gorging themselves, the youths convened around fish gutting stations, filling their hands with slick strands of intestine and other organs. The children fed slippery piles of entrails into the flames and studied the smouldering remains intently, divining their futures.

Tiernan followed a path along the shore, eventually working his way inland, passing a large stone temple in trees, a place of worship and confusion. He continued down the path, observing the rise of a city in the distance. *Everhollow Heath.* The ancient capital of Feoras, a small country destroyed in the first Great War. Tiernan recognised it from drawings in the books his father read to him. A grand castle, home of King Karnifer, occupied the centre of the city.

Next to the castle gate stood Sovereign Aisha. The Goddess herself.

Aisha defeated the serpent demoness Kijo. Kijo hated the light. She transformed into a snake and devoured everything in sight, determined to grow large enough to coil around the sun and block it out. She grew larger and larger, until she was able to smother the sun. The Goddess distracted Kijo with a mongoose infested asteroid and cut her heart out, the remnants of which were called Eevire— their small, misshapen moon, which even now resembled a heart.

"Tiernan. Come here." The Goddess called to him, her hair reminiscent of bright flames, a mosaic of reds and oranges with an occasional streak of bluish purple. Her glossy black armour shone in the sun. Before her death and induction into the holy pantheon, she'd served as a general in King Karnifer's army.

Tiernan approached and bowed his head respectfully. "I was beginning to think you'd abandoned me."

"It wasn't abandonment; it was whisky. Way, way too much whisky. I feel like a velver crawled inside my head and trampled my brain." She took him by the hand. "I'll show you around."

Aisha's idea of a tour turned out to be sitting at the race track with a pint of beer, which worked fine for him. Velvers were outfitted with colourful saddles, harnesses looping through rings in their noses. Imprints from their hooves covered the track, where the animals were perfectly suited to gaining traction in the muddy gravel. People often bet on the races, shouting in encouragement or despair as eager velvers fought to secure the lead. Gamblers typically spent their winnings paying for the losers' drinks.

The races were an excuse to drink and socialise and attracted crowds in large numbers. Even King Karnifer attended, ritualistically urinating on the large circular track before the races commenced. Dusk approached in shades of apricot, swaddling the slowly sinking sun. Rows of silver hanging lanterns bloomed with light, flushing shadows from pavilions where people waited anxiously.

A bell chimed. A cacophony of shouting and stampeding hooves rose as velvers took off down the track, their riders not directing the animals so much as holding on to avoid falling and being crushed in a whirlwind of hooves. Aisha finished her pint and put her feet on the table. She observed the races with interest, but never bet on them. After the last race, they headed out and passed a man with unruly brown hair who Tiernan recognised from illustrations as the Dane of Canterly, a notorious lecher who allegedly shared a unique relationship with his horses.

A dog sat patiently outside the track, waiting for its master. As they passed, Tiernan cautiously lowered a hand to the canine's level and it greeted him with a lick. He stroked the dog's coppery brindled fur, wiry to the touch. The animal was alert, with an intelligent look in its blue eyes. He recognised the breed of dog as those utilised by knights for their cleverness and athleticism. They made short work of pursuing fleet-footed criminals, especially those unburdened by heavy armour, and their keen sense of smell made the dregs of society easy to track.

"I have to show you King Karnifer's new pets," said Aisha, lighting a pipeful of something sweeter smelling than tobacco. "Since the death of his wife, his majesty has become unstable. He purchased two crates full of butterflies from a blind Seeress and released them in the castle gardens. These things aren't normal, Tiernan. There's something acidic in their... I wanna say saliva. Do butterflies have saliva? Either way, they dissolve the flesh off living things and lap up the goo."

Tiernan shuddered.

Aisha touched his shoulder. "Oh, don't worry. Yours won't do that."

"No, they'll just turn people into psychotic murderers who get eaten alive by a fungus." They walked towards the castle. The scent of rain hung in the air, sticking to his skin, and for once the absence of his armour didn't bother him. The illusion of freedom was so profound he almost believed it.

Aisha offered her pipe. "Life is always a gamble. Sometimes you own an empire of outhouses and sometimes you're the one who cleans them. Negative experiences are just as valuable as positive ones. Balance is necessary to achieve enlightenment. Not everyone is entitled to a happy ending."

"That doesn't make me feel any better." Aisha took the pipe and inhaled the sweet smoke. "Shitty things happen to people, but that doesn't mean I'm comfortable with being the reason they're suffering."

The neared the castle gardens. A sculpture towered over rows of thorny shrubs, cobbled together with chunks of iron in vague resemblance of a man. It clutched a sign reading, "Do not disturb the butterflies. — KK" The moon loomed in the distance, bright and swollen.

Aisha approached a white metal cage, unlocking it, removing a bucket. Tiernan peered inside. A writhing mass of naked baby mice clambered over one another, pawing at the walls of the bucket.

"The butterflies like mice the best, especially baby ones. Not sure why." Aisha carried the bucket towards majestic fruit trees, one of which was covered with hundreds of brightly coloured butterflies.

Aisha reached into the bucket and drew back her arm, hurling mice at the tree.

All at once butterflies descended from their perches. They landed on the rodents in droves, painlessly piercing flesh with their proboscises. The mice collapsed. Skin and muscle were liquefied and consumed like nectar until all that remained was bones.

The butterflies slept.

HE MUST HAVE fallen asleep outside, because the morning sun warmed Tiernan's face—a strange, unsettling sensation he wasn't sure he liked. Something nagged at him, the distant knowledge he was not lying in the grass, but being held prisoner in a cave by a bunch of stupid shitheads, but he tried to ignore it, pushing it away to focus on the sun.

Aisha sat nearby, her legs crossed, chest puffed outward menacingly, her expression one of intense concentration.

Tiernan sat up, rubbing the back of his neck. Most of the butterflies were still asleep, but a few ventured forth to drink from the crystalline pools of dew scattered among the greenery.

"Why don't the butterflies eat us?" He rubbed his forehead tenderly; apparently even psychosis-induced drinking hurt the next day...or two. He had no idea much time had passed, but sensed it may have been more than a single night. The garden showed an impossible amount of growth, lilacs gone from shy buds to bursting flowers, vines crawling over everything.

"Their creator ensured they have no appetite for human flesh."

"That's reassuring, I guess. How did a general in the Feorian army end up babysitting carnivorous butterflies?"

"King Karnifer belongs in a room with padded walls. Apart from that, I'd say bad luck. Doesn't pay to be in the wrong place at the wrong time."

"What's he want them for?"

"I'm afraid to ask."

As it grew warmer, more butterflies awakened. He noted several travelling in their direction and looked to Aisha for some indication of how to react. She tucked a long blade of grass into the corner of her mouth and stretched her legs outwards, unconcerned.

Tiernan turned his attention to the sky, watching the clouds. It was soothing to track their movement across an endless field of blue, forms constantly changing. Hearing Aisha laugh, he turned his head. She grinned smugly as a butterfly perched on her bottom lip, ruffling its wings.

She laughed softly, trying to speak without disturbing the creature. "It tickles."

The butterfly flew off without incident and Aisha went to work. She locked a catapult into position and said, "Time to test my rodent launcher."

To demonstrate the contraption in action, she loaded it with a terracotta ball containing a dozen mice. She pulled the lever and the arm snapped forwards, sending the ball hurtling through the air. It landed among the trees, shattering and releasing the imprisoned rodents, now dead from the impact. The butterflies showed no interest in them. Aisha sighed and stared sourly at the hungry insects.

"Back to the buckets, I'm afraid. It was worth a try."

The butterflies locked legs and spun through the air, colliding in colourful swarms, stirring up clouds of dusty scales. Aisha held out her hand, allowing the silky powder to collect in her open palm. "I was always told if the dust came off a butterfly's wings, it would never be able to fly." She shifted her focus to Tiernan, forsaking seriousness for tenderness. "It's not true."

THE BUTTERFLIES HUNG upside down in a cage comprised of tiny bones. Their red and black wings were not yet equipped for flight, stiffening slowly as gravity transferred fluid from their abdomens. Six males. Six females. A man stood watch over them. Henri Allan. Born in Fencaster. 34 years old. The butterflies knew everything about him. He was easy to read, his thoughts exposed. They saw the world as Henri saw it. He'd drawn the short twig, taking on guard duty while the others celebrated the new arrivals. He hoped someone would take pity on him and bring him a flagon of blueberry wine and some roasted wild boar, caught earlier in the forest, but so far, he'd been disappointed.

Henri believed the butterflies must be very special to make kidnapping and torturing a paladin worth the risk. He studied the pattern on their wings, dark circles with a ring of white, like large all-seeing eyes, tiny scales woven into an intricate tapestry. He needed to touch, to feel the shiny dust coating his skin. The butterflies called to him. Henri reached into the cage, holding a finger out. His momma always warned him about strange spirits, but what did she know? She'd died broke and alone. Butterfly Amir descended, perching on the tip of his finger.

Amir inserted his proboscis and injected a small dose of venom. He gave the venom a few seconds to numb the skin, then began to feed.

It didn't take long for Henri to hear the hum, like a chorus of finely tuned human voices, lulling him to sleep. He staggered on his feet, searching for the source, turning a corner of the cave, coming face-to-face with a massive gorginox. It nearly filled the cavern, regarding him with glowing red eyes, its scorpion-like body covered with stony mineral-rich spires, jagged and white. The venom produced hallucinations so realistic Henri never questioned them. He turned and ran. The beast charged, still humming, impaling his chest with its stinger. The gorginox thrashed its tail, battering Henri against the cave wall, crushing his bones.

Amir regurgitated the blood he'd swallowed and shared it with the others. The butterflies feasted.

A woman entered the room. Lamashtu. The reason they were trapped in these tiny bodies, craving chaos and destruction. She'd heard Henri screaming and wanted to know what happened. She spotted Henri's body in a mangled heap, slumped against the wall, threw back her head, and laughed.

Chapter Nineteen

TIERNAN WAS DIMLY aware of being moved—half-herded, half-dragged like an unwilling cow to the slaughter. Vivid blue dye stained his skin, excreted by the butterflies after hatching.

Lysa led him through the elaborate network of tunnels, easily finding her way. Deeply disoriented, he relied on her sense of direction. He couldn't tell which tunnels led towards the surface and which led deeper into the underground maze, exacerbating any plans for escape.

"You may get cleaned up, if you wish. We'll prepare for the next batch of butterflies while you heal. You'll be staying with Mae until you regain your strength."

She lowered her voice, whispering to him, "I'll get you out of here as soon as I can."

THE WATER BURNED, though it was barely warm. A small waterfall wept down the cave wall, providing enough water to wash. Tiernan's entire body ached; even the follicles of his hair hurt, right down to the scalp. The filth was so engrained it resisted removal. No amount of scrubbing could wash it away, the dirt internalised. Normally he loved the water, but this bordered on torture.

He scratched off sludge-like rolls of grey skin, tracing familiar scars—old wounds healed into stark lines and hasty strokes. One scar on the back of his neck originated from an Igurak thug trying to decapitate him with a thin wire. Another resulted from a bullet tearing through his leg when a drunken innkeeper accidentally shot him.

Guns were seldom used in Calder. The Church considered them abhorrent, impersonal killing machines, rigorously enforcing their centuries-old ban. High Priestess Camila said it took the honour out of human conflicts, making it possible for untrained and unspecialised men and women to kill strangers in large numbers, without ever looking them in the eye, or at least peering into the gap of their helm.

Tiernan reached for his cock, trying to soothe his nerves. An image of Henri invaded his mind—head crushed and chest torn open, rendering his dick useless.

Tiernan remained in the water for a long time, fingers and toes wrinkled to the texture of walnuts. He dried himself before changing into fresh clothes. He passed the time in a daze and barely noticed when Lysa returned. She led him to Mae's room in silence. The thought of seeing Mae both delighted and horrified him. It would be nice to have someone to talk to, but he didn't want Mae to see him like this, resembling the dead more so than the living.

Mae was a spectre stretched over a human frame, a tired and frustrated child in dire need of the sun, but she beamed at the sight of him. Lysa locked them in. The room was dimly lit, ivory white with smooth walls, much larger than he was used to. A pair of thick mattresses sat side-by-side, covered with warm sheets. A curtained area in the corner served as the bathroom.

Tiernan sat down beside Mae, legs no longer willing to support him. "How are you holding up?"

"Better than you." She squinted at him, gently prodding his back.

Tiernan winced. Mae grabbed his shirt and then lifted it.

"H-Hey!" He tried to fend her off, but she easily overpowered him. Not the least bit embarrassing. There was a moment of silence as she studied the wounds on his back, still fresh from the butterflies.

Mae growled softly. "That lying old bone bag! She said she wouldn't hurt you anymore. I'm gonna smash her face in!"

"I like your spirit, but that's probably a bad idea."

"That mean ol' witch makes me so mad." Mae hugged Nika close to her chest, scowling.

"Where are you from, Mae?"

"Achaius. Daddy got killed in the war. Mommy drank too much and fell down the stairs. She died. Now it's just me and Nika. We were sleeping in the street when Lamashtu grabbed us. She said if I didn't behave, she'd pull my brains out my nose with a hook and feed them to Nika."

Tiernan lay down on the mattress, stretching out on his stomach, pressing his cheek to a pillow. "We're going to get out of here, one way or another."

He needed to think positive thoughts, to find strength in the Goddess. His back felt like it had been slashed a thousand times with hot knives, the sear lingering.

Mae stretched out next to him, resting Nika on her chest. "Lysa's gonna help, right?"

"She wants to, or so she says. Do you know much about her?"

"She spends a lot of time with Cia. I like Cia. When Lamashtu took me, she wanted to sacrifice me, but Cia talked her out of it. She said I'd be perfect for keeping you in line. She's like Lysa—she doesn't want to hurt anybody."

Tiernan sighed, rubbing his temples.

"Nika likes face rubs." Mae held Nika out expectantly, dangling him in front of Tiernan. "Rub his face. You'll feel better. Nika's good at fixing people."

He eyed the toy anxiously, patting it on the head.

Mae wrinkled her nose at him, puffing her cheeks outward, "You don't listen too good." Nika hopped along his arm, moving towards his head. "Get him, Nika!" The rabbit attacked his face, brushing their noses together.

"That tickles, damnit!" Tiernan buried his face in the pillow. The sound of Mae's laughter filled the cave. Strangely enough, he did feel a bit better.

THE BUTTERFLY KNEW exactly where it was going—Heim, a small fishing village on Enra's rugged coastline. Heim was renowned for throwing elaborate feasts. Candied salmon was never in short supply, frequently employed to motivate petulant children. Fish was the main staple, its preparation varying in accordance with the method of preservation, be it pickled, salted, smoked, dried, or fermented in barrels of brine. Year round, freshwater trout were baked in clay ovens with sprigs of dill and lemon root herbal infusions, served with wild strawberry and rhubarb pie.

Long, slender piers extended from the shore outwards, stretching into the sea. Fishermen lined the planks, standing with practised balance in waterproof boots. Chopped shrimp was scooped from buckets of chum and flung into the waves, summoning hungry fish to the shallows. There was no shortage of job opportunities around Heim, from hunting game in the forest to harvesting wild grains, even polishing driftwood for city art dealers to buy at exorbitant prices, but it was always the same people who showed up at the piers, drawn by the sea and the thrill of the catch.

Rich Henning was already out at the end of the sixth pier where he and Thom always fished. Rich and Thom had been best friends since they were old enough to hold a fishing rod. Each day they competed to see who caught the most fish. With Thom being late for work, Rich already had the advantage. "About time you showed up."

"Those words must run in the family, because your ma keeps tellin' me the same thing."

Thom dodged the heel of Rich's boot and went to work, scanning the water for signs of life. He tossed a bulging fistful of shrimp into the sea. Nearby aespis were irresistibly drawn to the scent and flocked to trace its origins in swarms. The fish were several feet across, flat with a slight curve at the edges, bronze in colouration. Tightly woven strands of sinew, coated with pine sap, tethered Thom's spear to the pier. The rope coiled around a metal crank, allowing the catch to be reeled in—a helpful tool, given the average weight of an aespis coming in at just under eighty pounds. When an aespis broke the surface of the water, thrashing wildly in the air, their scales glinted like burnished armour in the sun.

The butterfly sailed past Rich's shoulder on richly pigment wings, flashing symmetrical splotches of red and black. It circled the men unseen and landed on the back of Thom's neck, a benign ornament, too unthreatening to merit attention. Even when the butterfly bit him, Thom failed to notice. Spear in hand, he scanned the water for a potential target, but his focus quickly deteriorated. Instead of scanning smoothly, his eyes darted erratically over the surface of the water. Among the familiar outlines of numerous aespis, Thom noticed a dark shadow moving through the water, roughly the size of a small child. In front of the shadow, a bluish green light swayed hypnotically, making him drowsy. Prickles of warmth erupted all over his body. For several seconds the sensation continued, then stopped abruptly. There was nothing unusual in the water, no soporific light.

Had he fallen asleep? If Thom drifted off on the job, he'd never hear the end of it. He could practically hear Rich berating him, "Fish start biting at dawn, for gods' sake. How many times have I told you not to let Lynda keep you up all night?"

"You see that?" asked Thom dazedly, but Rich wasn't listening.

Shifting his weight from one foot to another, Rich placed his balance entirely on one leg, stretching an arm outwards as if to envelop an invisible lover, and for a moment it looked like Thom's friend was going to start dancing. Instead, Rich collapsed on the planks of the pier, twitching violently, arching and flopping like a suffocating fish. Thom watched intently, mesmerised, until Rich smashed into the pier face-first, blood fountaining from his nose, and went still. Only then did panic begin to set in.

"No, no, no. Rich!" Thom pressed a hand to his friend's neck and searched for a pulse. He found one—strong, regular. Rich lifted his head slowly. His eyes were unnaturally large, dark orbs of volcanic glass. Thom could see himself reflected in those eyes, but his reflection was distorted—elongated and hazy. Fragments of the deformed image broke off, collapsing into nothing, leaving only vast empty space. He could see all the way back to the throne of the soul. Rich was gone, evicted from his own body, and in his place sat a monstrous fish.

Teazio. An aquatic demon who lured people into the water with her light—the ghost lamp. Anyone unfortunate enough to herald the call of the light was eaten alive. Thom couldn't figure out how Teazio had done it. Somehow, Rich's spirit had been violently yanked out of his body. He could see where the strand of pale, shimmery cord used for anchoring the soul had broken, fraying the tightly braided cords. Adrift without the ability to properly navigate, Rich's soul was lost, and Teazio was in control. All that remained of Thom's friend was a shell with an unauthorised occupant. Rage welled up inside him, directing a rush of heat to his head. His heartbeat echoed loudly in his ears, like the pounding of war drums.

The tip of Thom's harpoon slid easily into Rich's neck. He twisted it and rotated the barbs in a clockwise motion. Luminous ooze, filled with radiant light, poured from the wound, splattering the pier. Thom gave the harpoon a final jerk and extracted it, triumphant. The body once occupied by his best friend gurgled sea foam and convulsed. Thom ran his fingers through the glowing puddles, caressing the warm, silky fluid. He painted his cheeks, marking himself as a champion. Thom Fowler, slayer of demons.

"Thom..."

Startled, Thom looked up. Ina, one of the village's most prolific fishermen, stood behind him, arms folded tensely across her chest, a look of profound concern on her ashen face.

"Teazio killed Rich," Thom affirmed, holding up his hands to show the luminescent substance coating his fingers, evidence of the unthinkable act which had taken place.

"Teazio?" Ina looked confused, eyebrows forming creases in her forehead as they furrowed.

"Teazio. She took over Rich's body. I had to do it."

"Why would Teazio... Thom, you're not making any sense."

Thom studied Ina suspiciously, fighting to ascertain the reason for her denial. He'd seen it for himself. The proof was all over his fingers, drying on his cheeks in victorious streaks. When he spotted the fur growing along the shell of Ina's ear, he realised his mistake. She was one of them—dispossessed, a creature with no rightful soul. Thick, dark hair sprouted all over her body and a prominent hump rose between the blades of her shoulders. Claws protruded from the tips of her fishing gloves, gnarled and cracked. Globs of snot gathered in the corners of Ina's eyes. Her wolf jaws snapped, sending flecks of drool airborne, and he caught the odour of something dead—the inevitability of decay, an eternity of filth.

"Away with you, wolf!" cried Thom, brandishing his spear.

Ina's ears twitched, and much to Thom's surprise, she plodded away, pausing briefly to look back at him before moving forwards again, tail wedged securely between her legs.

Other villagers gathered around the piers, watching him. He knew each of them by name, but could barely recognise them now, their heavy paws tearing up the beach as they paced, frantic. Their howls filled his ears with incandescent noise. The sound crushed his insides, creating a sensation of constant, unbearable pressure. Thom's digestive system twisted into impossible knots, erupting through his abdomen. There was no pain, only persistent surges of blood. His blood. Thom could see the elaborate kinks crafted into his guts, contorted in resemblance of paper cranes—sections of intestinal wall pulled taut and elaborately folded. The cranes shook themselves loose from exposed intestines, spilling into the ocean, where they floated increasingly lower in the water, slowly drowning.

Catching the scent of blood in the air, the wolves closed the gap between them, encroaching on the pier, prowling along the narrow strip of wood. Thom plunged off the edge of the pier, following the cranes to the bottom of the sea, where he could no longer hear the howling. His lungs soon screamed for oxygen and his chest convulsed, but he remained beneath the water, where it was safe.

On the beach the crowd of concerned citizens grew. In their midst the butterfly was inconspicuous, invisible to unsuspecting eyes, as if unfit to create disorder.

"What did he say, Ina?"

"Why would Thom kill Rich?"

"Where'd he go?"

"Someone should go check on Lynda."

The butterfly followed the town blacksmith home, watching as she hugged her husband and daughter. The blacksmith never felt the tiny proboscis pierce her shoulder.

It would take several hours before Heim began to burn.

TIERNAN AWOKE FEVERISH and disoriented. Mae sat nearby, humming softly to herself. She'd soaked a sock in cold water and placed it on his forehead. She peered at him with a mixture of curiosity and concern, biting her bottom lip. "Did you have a weird dream?"

"Weird is an understatement." Tiernan rubbed the bridge of his nose, trying to ease a stabbing headache, removing the sock from his forehead.

"Does your head hurt? Maybe Nika can help."

"I'm fine."

"You don't look fine."

Worried lines etched in Mae's pale face triggered a confusing landslide of emotion. His own pain somehow mattered less than hers. He wanted to make her smile, to make her laugh, even at the price of his own dignity, or what little of it remained.

"Don't worry about me. Wanna play a game?"

Tiernan and Mae went on an expedition. They passed through an old, dark forest, full of low-hanging moss. Pale green tendrils wrapped around them, forcing them to wander in the dark. Mae held on tight as Tiernan gradually pried the dangling moss away, progressing deeper into the forest. They hid under a bridge as a small army rode across it, on their way to depose King Karnifer. The king had officially gone insane, wasting vast quantities of gold on parties held in honour of the Great Forest Sloth. You couldn't be crazy and rule forever. Sooner or later someone was going to take notice and decide to do something about it.

The allure of buried treasure drove them out of hiding, continuing onward. He taught Mae a song he'd heard knights sing on many occasions, usually while under the influence of alcohol.

> *A great and mighty turtle*
> *Sailed smoothly with the wind.*
> *His sails were made of silver*
> *And his hold was full of gin.*

He slept all day and drank all night.
When he saw land he yelled,
"Round up your daughters
And lock them up tight!"

They tossed Nika between them, catching him by the ears. Sheets were torn off the beds and pulled off their heads, converted into tents which shook with the wind and muted the howls of wolves in the night. They battled vicious water demons and fought gigantic snakes. In the end, they were always victorious.

They built an imaginary fire in the middle of the room and sat, roasting invisible pheasant, taking turns rotating it on a spit.

Tiernan scanned the sky, one hand raised over his eyes to block out the sun, the other pointing. "Look, Mae. I think that might be a dragon."

"I love dragons!" Mae sprang up with a manic gleam in her eyes. "I wish I could ride one. I have dreams about them all the time. Flying over the red, red desert. It's so much fun!" She bounced excitedly. "Catch it for me! Catch it for me!"

"We'll see if it comes closer. And how fireproof I'm feeling."

Mae twirled around. "Hurray! Nika! Nika! I won't let you get burned."

Tiernan threw another log on the fire, losing himself in the flames, their hypnotic flickering lulling him into a state of almost contentment.

Chapter Twenty

A FLASH OF lighting momentarily blinded the butterfly. It recovered quickly, landing in a woman's hair, burrowing into the greasy auburn strands and locating the nape of her neck.

A storm was approaching, that much was clear. Heather Browning had never seen anything like it. Enra's inner plains were subject to bizarre weather patterns due to their proximity to the Cathcart Mountains, but sudden summer thundershowers were nothing in comparison to the bank of clouds rolling towards her. Heavy, bloated thunderheads were interspersed with clusters of pink and purple light and filled with flocks of screeching seagulls— a rare sight so far from the sea. Electric blue ribbons wove between them, anchoring the birds to crackling currents of energy, spinning them into luminous spheres. The scent of ozone filled the air.

Heather plunged her shovel into the dry ground and stared into the grave she'd spent the better part of an hour revealing. The bodies had already shrivelled and dried. *Mrs. and Mrs. Toliver,* the gravestone read. *Beared to death.* She was unsure if it was a misspelling, or if an actual bear had been involved. It was the largest tombstone she'd ever seen. The gravesite was a great find; there was no sign of bodies being dug up anywhere in the area—uncharted territory, as far as a grave robber was concerned.

It was difficult to tell whether the Tolivers were buried in their best attire, given the state of their clothing—torn, dusty scraps. Even in the grave the dust somehow worked its way in, ever-present. The Tolivers wore matching gold bracelets. It wasn't uncommon for couples to pick identical articles of jewellery when they made the decision to get married. If they could agree on a jewellery type, style, metal, and design elements of a piece they were equally comfortable wearing, it was said they were well-suited to surviving the trials and tribulations of marriage.

Heather pried the bracelets loose along with a few trinkets—rudimentary grave goods, blessedly common in recent years. She found the figurine of a tiny silver goat and a gold-encrusted scorpion, intended to bring good fortune in the next life. Whatever the future may bring for the Tolivers, Heather would put the monetary boon to good use in the present.

An explosion of thunder boomed, closer now. Rain fell, darkening the red sand. Heather hurried back to her motorised bike—one large wheel in front, two in the back. It was rusted with age and exposure to occasional showers. Ironfalds, a remote outpost at the edge of the desert, wasn't far off. Heather kicked the trike into gear and took off, stirring up a cloud of pestilential dust in her wake. The storm followed her, bringing the birds with it.

If birds could speak in doggerel, surely it would have sounded something like this; the cacophonic shrieking of a thousand tongues swollen under the weight of discordant, mismatched words. Ugly words. Heather got the impression even if she could understand what the birds were saying, she wouldn't want to know.

It isn't until they were almost upon her that she realised the birds were screaming.

They swarmed over her, picking the flesh off her bones.

Tevin Hawk watched Heather ride through Main Street. She waved her arms frantically, screaming at nothing. "Get them off! Get them off!" Her trike crashed into a grain silo and exploded in flame, spitting chunks of metal into the street.

The butterfly nipped Tevin's arm. He was nothing more than a human target, another invader slated for extermination. Tevin moved towards the destroyed silo, searching for any sign of life among the wreckage. He found Heather, her skin charred crispy and black. A glint of something caught his eye. Gold. He reached for it, stooping low to the ground. Heather's fingers punched through his rib cage, wrapped around his heart, and squeezed.

TIERNAN FEIGNED SLEEP in response to the sound of footsteps beside the bed.

"He's not well." Lysa pulled a blanket over him.

"Why isn't his condition improving?" Lamashtu sounded irate, less controlled than usual.

"I'm not sure. The nesting pockets have barely healed and can't be reused. If you allow Finnegan's Lace to bloom again, it'll kill him. He needs a nutrient rich diet and more time to heal."

"You assured me this wouldn't be a problem."

"I underestimated how long it would take for the butterflies to hatch. It almost killed him. Perhaps twelve is enough."

"Twelve is not enough. Stick with the plan and do something about his health. We can't afford to lose him."

WHILE TIERNAN SLEPT he watched a group of hunters wander through the swamps of Rian, shooting each other when their companions transformed into their prey. In the village of Shaze, a woman drilled holes in the skulls of her husband and newborn daughter, releasing them into the lake where she believed they would live on forever as freshwater dolphins.

SOMEONE WAS AT the door. Still half-asleep, Tiernan tried to sit up, but lacked the strength to do so. A guard entered the room, fully armoured, a giant of a man. He placed a food tray on the floor, beige slop sloshing in wooden bowls. Tiernan's stomach growled but the food held no appeal. He wanted a fat, juicy steak and an overflowing plate of salty, fried potatoes.

"Some paladin you are," commented the guard. "A blind kitten could kick your ass."

Mae marched towards the guard, glaring up at him. "Don't talk to him like that."

"What are you gonna do about it, shrimp?" He prodded Mae in the chest, the force of it prompting her to take a step back.

"Do not touch me." Mae's tone was surprisingly stern.

"Don't tell me what to do, brat."

Tiernan tried again to get up, but he was too weak, too woozy. It hurt too much to move. "You need to leave."

The guard laughed. "I could fuck this bitch right in front of you. Split her wide open. And you couldn't do a damn thing about it."

"I'm counting to five." Mae clenched her fists at her sides, exhaling slowly. "You better not still be here when I get there."

"Or what?"

"One, two, three..."

"You can count, urchin. I'm impressed."

"Four."

"I'm shaking. Don't hurt me, please."

"Five." Mae dropped low to the ground, sweeping the guard's legs out from underneath him. He hit the ground with a crash. She sprang on him, cat-like in speed and agility, taking his armoured head in her hands and bashing it against the floor. *Smash. Smash. Smash.* The man's brains wept through the slits in his helmet in grey globules. Like a ruptured ink sack, foul-smelling black fluid welled up from the exposed cranial cavity, saturating bloodless brain matter.

The guard groaned and tried to remove his helm, but the warped metal was impacted in such a way that made it impossible to yank free. Unable to see, he grabbed blindly for wayward clumps of brain, attempting to shovel them back into the narrow gap.

Tiernan had seen a lot of things over the years—a woman struggling to retain the contents of her abdomen, slick entrails stubbornly springing free upon each attempt to restore them to their resting place; a man with no legs and no arms worming his way along the ground as he bled out. Feats of seemingly impossible endurance, but this was different. This was no ordinary display of perseverance.

The guard gave up trying to remove his helm and slumped against the wall, whimpering. He rocked slowly, holding his hands over his face, black slime oozing between his fingers. Mae watched with the detachment of a child who had seen much worse. She opened her right hand, fingers flat, palm facing upwards. Streams of light arced from her fingertips, producing a ghostly glow. The light formed a slowly rotating spiral, an army of stars. Approaching from behind, Mae placed a glowing hand on the guard's shoulder. The light was absorbed instantly, spreading through the cultist's body like wildfire. He jerked spasmodically, crashing onto his hands and knees, vomiting luminous sludge.

Large, swollen boils rose from the surface of his skin, filled with black pus. The inky substance erupted, fizzling on the floor of the cave like hot tar. Mae gasped and ran for the bed, grabbing the blankets. Tiernan tugged them over their heads, shielding them from a spray of fluid. A siren-like wail filled the cave, inhuman in pitch and frequency, shrieking until his ears were riddled with static. It didn't trail off or waver, dying out all at once.

"Is it safe now?" whispered Mae.

Raising a corner of the blanket, Tiernan looked at the fallen guard. The cultist's body was withered in the confines of his armour, emitting thin tendrils of smoke.

The high-pitched screeching brought Lamashtu to the room, her eyes wide, tongue swaddled in temporary silence as she gazed at her shrivelled comrade.

"What happened?" she finally asked. Lysa appeared behind her.

"The mean man exploded everywhere." Mae stuck out her bottom lip, clinging to Tiernan. "He said he was gonna hurt me. Tiernan stopped him." Lamashtu studied them critically. Tiernan assumed she accepted Mae's version of events, but she left without saying a word.

"What *really* happened?" asked Lysa.

"He was being a jerk to Tiernan," replied Mae. "I killed him."

Lysa crossed her arms behind her back, full lips pursing in concentration. "Are you okay?"

"Yep."

"It won't take Lamashtu long to figure out what happened. I told you not to use any of the magick Cia taught you."

"I wasn't thinking about that!"

Lysa grunted. "Obviously. It's not ideal, but we should leave now. We may not get another chance. The problem is Tiernan's not nearly as strong as he should be."

"He's pretty heavy. I don't think we can carry him."

Lysa removed a tiny tincture from her pocket, handing it to him. "This will help."

The concoction smelled awful and tasted worst, like rancid cloves, bringing up the meagre contents of his stomach. He closed his eyes, waiting for everything to stop spinning.

Energy surged through him, restoring some of his strength. He was nowhere near functioning at full capacity, lacking sufficient prana reserves for advanced spellcasting, but felt well enough to put up a fight. The room went still.

Lysa stood in front of the door seal. "We need to hurry. There're two guards stationed outside. Let me take care of them."

Tiernan picked up Mae, his heart thudding. Lysa unsealed the door, allowing her to pass through the rock wall. Instead of closing it behind her, she left the door open. She stood between the guards and seized their wrists, pumping enough lightning into their bodies to drop them instantly.

"This way." She turned to the right, taking off down the narrow passageway. Tiernan carried Mae, assuring her little legs didn't slow them down and keeping her close. The stone labyrinth didn't faze Lysa. She confidently charged around each turn until they reached a dead end, or so it appeared. "When Lamashtu finds out we're missing, she'll be on our trail like a rabid wolfhound."

"How long do you think we have until she notices?" asked Tiernan. The cave rumbled like an angry stomach, briefly shaking, raining a fine shower of sand on them. "I guess that answers my question."

Lysa pressed her hands to the wall and flooded it with energy. Cracks appeared, fissures of blue light running through the rock. The wall crumpled at their feet and when they stepped over the rubble, reaching the other side, the wall reformed behind them, stitching itself back together. The shortcut led to a long, narrow rock bridge arching over a bottomless pit. They rushed across and made it almost halfway before Kijo appeared.

"I've inscribed the bridge... with explosive runes." Lysa gasped for breath between words, winded. "As soon as we get across... I'll blow it up."

Mae cheered and tightened her arms around Lysa's neck. "That'll teach her!"

Kijo came at them like a bullet. She covered most of the distance in the time it took them to reach the other side. As soon as they reached the other side, Lysa activated the runes. The bridge exploded, rock flying everywhere, hurtling Lamashtu into the darkness. Debris bounced off a protective shield Lysa cast around them. A distant *thunk, thunk, splash* indicated the pit wasn't as bottomless as he'd thought.

They rested for a moment, speechless and panting, before wriggling through a narrow passageway. Light shone in the distance, illuminating dark, damp granite. Water spilled from the rocks above and formed a small stream that flowed lazily towards the forest. They picked their way around the waterfall, hopping over rocks, and finally reached freedom. Grass felt foreign beneath his bare feet, prickly and strange. The sun burned his eyes.

The mouth of the cave collapsed behind them, triggered by more of Lysa's runes. "Some of them may find their way out eventually, but we'll be long gone by then." She paused to catch her breath, gulping air. "Your velver was recently spotted in the area. He refuses to leave."

Tiernan groaned. "That idiot."

"Try calling him."

He cupped his hands around his mouth, calling as loudly as he could, "Misha!"

Nothing. He called again and listened intently, detecting the sound of a large animal crashing through the bush. *Misha.*

Tiernan didn't know how Misha had gone so long without losing all his tack, but he owed the Goddess thanks for the favour. He ran his hands over Misha's fur, feeling arrowheads lodged in his thick hide, extracting them without hurting him.

Mae stood nearby, hands tucked under her armpits, staring downward. Tiernan crouched in front of her and took her hand. "Mae, do you want to come with me?"

"Yes!" A look of relief swept over her face and she threw her arms around his neck.

Lysa moved away from them, eager to be on her way; he could tell from a scent on the breeze the Altricial had horses nearby. "The butterflies won't torment you for much longer. Their mission is almost complete. I'm sorry you had to get involved in all this."

"Bye, Ly-Ly!" Mae waved enthusiastically.

"Thanks for your help." Tiernan scratched below the bottom of Misha's knee, signalling him to raise his hoof, allowing him to inspect each one. Only when he was satisfied with their condition did he grab Mae and climb aboard Misha's back, riding off.

Chapter Twenty-One

TIERNAN RODE BACK to Ainsley in record time. Ainsley, Calder's capital, was built on an island in the middle of Crimson Lake, surrounded by four massive stone walls. It had never been invaded, never occupied by outsiders. A bridge of Light connected the island to the mainland. Any hint of trouble and the bridge was dispelled; the island contained enough resources to be self-sufficient for years. Access to anywhere in Calder, which was owned and governed by the Church of Light, was restricted to those willing to swear fealty to the Goddess and those wealthy enough to secure an entry pass despite their lack of conviction.

City guards stopped them at the gate, their swords glowing with arcane enchantments. "Identify yourself."

"My name's Tiernan Aran. This is Misha and my friend Mae. I'm a paladin."

A guard stared him down, making a low growl at the back of his throat, like a dog on the defensive. The guard approached Misha slowly and carefully, turning his ear inside out, examining the number tattooed inside. "7894."

Another guard pulled out a leather book, one of many lining shelves on the wall, scanning columns of numbers. "7894... Misha Mish the Mishiest One, registered to Sir Tiernan Aran. Paladin."

"Four-year-olds shouldn't be allowed to name velvers," remarked Tiernan, patting Misha's flank.

"Deepest apologies for the inconvenience, sir." The guards scrambled out of the way, opening the gate. "Have a pleasant evening."

"No need to apologise. I'd be concerned if you guys weren't stopping dirty weirdos from riding into town with little girls. Keep up the good work."

Instead of going to the stable, where Misha's presence would alert everyone to his return, Tiernan rode home, letting Misha through the back gate and into the yard. He helped Mae onto solid ground. She sat for a few minutes and regained her bearings, the usual response of anyone who'd spent more than two hours on a velver.

There was plenty for Misha to eat, but Tiernan feared for the safety of his garden. It was so overgrown with weeds maybe Misha wouldn't notice the zucchini blossoms and tomatoes lurking within. Hopefully the fruit trees would provide sufficient distraction. He showed Misha where a tree that produced small, sweet pears grew and removed the velver's tack. It was nice to care for Misha on his own, without stablehands swarming over him. Stablehands lavished velvers with care and attention, ensuring they were always at their best, ready for battle. He massaged Misha's legs and examined his feet.

"How come you keep lookin' at his feets?" asked Mae, resting against an old maple.

"To make sure they're not hurting him. Velvers are tough, but you must take good care of their feet. I check for swelling, warts, cracks, abscesses, and cuts from things like rocks and thorns."

He took the garden hose and turned it on, hosing down Misha's chest, neck, and legs, cooling him off. He walked Misha around the yard, then sprayed him again.

He sent a fine spray of mist in Mae's direction and she threw her arms up in defence, squealing. She scrambled to her feet and stepped on his toes, trying to wrench the hose away from him, soaking them both.

Misha's fur needed grooming, but he lacked the proper tools. It would have to wait until morning. Wouldn't hurt the brat to go one more night without a haircut.

Before going inside Tiernan left Misha with a stern warning, pressing his hands to the velver's cheeks, their faces touching. "Don't eat all my fucking tomatoes."

The sun sank low in the sky, flushing the horizon with shades of red and yellow. He picked up Mae and carried her inside.

Little had changed while Tiernan was gone, the passage of time marked by layers of dust over everything. He wondered how long he'd been gone. A month, maybe. It seemed like forever, yet he suspected it felt longer than it was.

"How many families live in this house? Where is everybody?" asked Mae.

"It's just me."

Mae wandered around while he looked for something she could wear to bed, selecting a long, white T-shirt made from bamboo, incredibly soft.

He found her standing in his parents' old room, sniffing a vial of his mother's perfume, carefully clutching the clear glass bottle. Mae grinned at him. "It smells like Miss Cia!"

Tiernan froze, heat draining from his body. The elixir was his mother's recipe. She'd distilled the essential oils herself. "From the Altricial? The one who talked Lamashtu out of sacrificing you?"

"Yup." Mae pushed the glass stopper back in and set the bottle down on the oak dresser.

"What does she look like?"

"Her eyes are purple, and she's got white hair. Like the snow. She's waaaay taller than me."

Impossible...

Tiernan sat on the edge of the bed. Mae sat next to him and leaned over. "What's wrong?"

Was that what had become of his mother? Living under an assumed identity with a bunch of deranged occultists?

Mae leaned closer, rubbing Nika's worn nose against his neck. "Hello?"

A confusing array of emotions stormed through him. Hurt. Betrayal. Gratitude. *Mae said Cia was friends with Lysa... Maybe that's why...*

Tiernan shook his head, inhaled deeply, and wrinkled his nose, pushing Nika away. "Nika needs a bath."

Mae looked at him strangely. Obviously not the response she was looking for, but her curiosity kicked in. "Do you have a real bathtub?"

"What else would I bathe in?"

"A bucket." Mae looked him over and giggled softly. "A big bucket."

He showed Mae the bathroom. The sight of the large stone bathtub had her jumping up and down. "Great stars! A whole tub!"

She started throwing off her clothes before he could get the water started. She set Nika on the edge and climbed in, waiting patiently as the water level rose around her. He added a squirt of shampoo to the water and Mae went to work gleefully creating mountains of bubbles. The tub finally filled and he turned the faucet off.

Mae peered at him, eyes just above the water line, striking suddenly, hurling water. "Splash attack!"

Already soaked, he stepped into the tub fully clothed. Tiernan sank into the water, splashing Mae in retaliation.

Mae scooped up bubbles, piling them on his head. He made her a pointy bubble beard. She grabbed Nika, holding him up. "Look at me. I'm an old man."

Tiernan squirted shampoo onto Nika's stiff, dirty fur and Mae massaged it in. She dunked Nika beneath the water, clearing a patch in the bubbles to wash the soap off.

"I don't wanna hold him under too long," she said. "He's afraid he'll go to sleep and get chopped up."

"Why would someone chop him up?"

"His momma thinks he's bad."

"Why does she think that?"

"She gets confused." Mae pulled Nika up, squeezing as much water as she could get out of him, giggling. "It looks like he's peeing."

Tiernan got out of the tub first, squelching over to the other side of a rock wall, removing his wet clothes. He caught sight of his back and winced. The skin was blistered and bruised. The outline of dainty white leaves were visible beneath the surface. He'd hoped his body would take care of the invader on its own, now that he was out of the cave. If the infernal plant showed no sign of weakening in the morning he'd have to break down and consult a Magus.

He slipped on a thin white robe. Mae dried herself off and put on the T-shirt Tiernan found. It extended well past her knees, swallowing her thin body. He sat her down and ran a comb through her hair, trying not to pull too hard as he worked out the knots. He gathered the dark, damp strands, and braided them loosely, all the way down the back of her head.

Mae admired the braid in the mirror, beaming. "I look like a princess!" She kissed his cheek and slunk off to retrieve Nika. "He's soaked."

"Can I hang him outside? He'll dry faster."

"Misha will protect him, right?"

"Sure will. Wait for me in the kitchen."

He hung Nika on the clothesline, a clothespin clasping each ear. Misha snored nearby, sprawled at the base of an apple tree.

Tiernan traded his robe for pyjamas and joined Mae in the kitchen. The fridge was mercifully devoid of alien lifeforms, having been empty apart from a jar of strawberry jam. Everything stored in the cupboards had a reasonably long shelf life and was still in a condition where it could be consumed without being thrown up again.

"Hungry?" he asked Mae.

She sat at the kitchen table, arms folded over its surface, resting her head against them. She looked exhausted, as if the water had sucked all the energy out of her. "Nope."

"Come on. You gotta eat something."

"What are you having?"

"Seeing as our options are limited, I'm leaning towards the traditional feast of kings." He dug through the cupboard, retrieving a package of beef jerky and a can of salted almonds. He ate several handfuls of each, while Mae ate enough to humour him, making a visible effort to do so, her eyes drooping.

Tiernan wrapped Mae in a blanket and sat with her on the couch. "We'll get you some proper clothes in the morning and have a big breakfast, then I have to take Misha to the stables and let the Church know I'm back. They may not be very happy with me."

"Why would they be mad?"

"Because I helped Lamashtu with her bug farming project instead of completing my mission."

"They won't hurt you, will they?"

"No," he lied, hugging Mae, holding her close. She fell asleep in his arms. He closed his eyes, unintentionally drifting off, exhausted, and awoke several hours later with Mae latched onto him, her breathing laboured, her body covered in sweat.

"Hurts," she muttered.

"Where does it hurt?"

Mae placed a hand over her heart. He pressed an ear to her chest, listening to her heartbeat, detecting an audible *whoosh* between beats, as if her heart was full of turbulent air. Her forehead burned.

He got up and carried Mae outside. "Misha's going to take us to a Magus and someone much smarter than I am will help you feel better."

"Okay."

Tiernan retrieved Nika from the clothesline before waking up Misha, and then climbed aboard with Mae, hurrying to the hospital. He tied Misha up outside and approached the front desk, Mae slumped in his arms.

"My friend here isn't feeling well." *There's something wrong with her heart.* He didn't elaborate. Didn't want to scare Mae, or himself. He filled out the necessary paperwork as best he could; Mae had no idea when her birthday was. She'd never celebrated it.

An apprentice led them to a room where they waited for a Magus. He set Mae on the bed and sat beside her.

After several excruciating minutes a Magus entered the room. Ornate bone earrings hung from the man's ears, swirls of ivory. Long, straight black hair descended past his shoulders in thick, loose strands, contrasting white robes.

"Hello." The man lowered his head politely. "I'm Magus Arishkii Sedgewren." A tattoo a few centimetres thick extended from the base of one ear to the other, crossing the bridge of his nose, a dark blue band of intimate lines woven across brown skin. "Call me Ari."

"I'm Tiernan. This is Mae. Her chest hurts."

"Let's take a look. You're in luck, Mae. This hospital has the best ice cream in town." Ari placed a hand on Mae's chest, purple energy radiating off splayed fingers. Tiernan tried to read the Magus's expression, but his face remained frustratingly neutral. "Mae, your ears are going to feel a bit fuzzy. You won't be able to hear anything for a few minutes." Ari brushed the undersides of his thumbs over Mae's earlobes, marking them with a temporary rune. Axil. *Silence.*

Mae lay down, curling into a foetal position. "'kay."

"Are you her father?" asked Ari.

"No. Her guardian. Her parents are deceased."

"Are you aware of her medical history?"

"No."

"Mae was born with a rather large hole in her heart, which has contributed to a bad bacterial infection. The bacteria have formed growths which are interfering with blood flow to the valves in her heart. White blood cells are unable to reach the site of infection, which means there's nothing to fight off the bacteria." Tiernan's vision blurred briefly and the amount of energy required to remain focused on Ari bordered on unattainable. "I'm going to administer a high dose of antibiotics intravenously, but I'm afraid it won't help."

"Try it and see what happens. We'll go from there."

"The extent of the deformity... I'm surprised she's lived this long, to be honest. She's a tough little girl."

Tiernan watched Mae, unnerved by how quiet she was. Ari removed the runes and restored her hearing, but she remained silent. As Ari predicted, the antibiotics had no effect. Mae's condition deteriorated. She slipped further away and the voices in his head grew louder. He cursed his stupidity for cowering from the Church instead of bringing Mae straight to the hospital. He should have known something was wrong. *Fucking idiot.*

Ari reactivated the ruins, ensuring Mae didn't hear what came next. "The blockage is getting worse. It won't be long before she suffers from either a heart attack or a stroke. I'm sorry, Tiernan."

"If the Goddess wills it." Tiernan's words sounded hollow, lacking conviction.

"If you'd like, there's something I can give Mae to ease her transition. She'll experience a temporary surge of energy, no pain... Once she burns through her energy reserves, she'll go to sleep. You'd have about an hour to properly say goodbye."

"The Church permits this?"

"Ah, well, the Church doesn't like people interfering with Divine Will. I don't like watching children die in agony. We managed to come to a compromise."

"Do it."

Ari injected Mae's shoulder with clear fluid, holding a cotton swab over the puncture point.

Mae's eyes fluttered open. She glanced from Ari to Tiernan, then back to Ari, grasping at his necklace, thinly cut segments of poisonous cone shells, white with black spots. "Pretty shells! Where'd you get 'em?"

"On the beach near my family's home. We lived by the ocean."

"I wanna go to the ocean. Tiernan! Will you take me?"

He wanted to say something, but the words stuck in his throat, choking him.

Ari came to his rescue, taking Mae by the hand. "Have you ever seen a helio tree, Mae?"

"A helio tree! No, never!"

"Let's fix that right now."

Mae skipped down the hall, holding Tiernan's left hand and Ari's right, swinging between them, Nika's ears tied securely around her wrist. They reached a large arboretum, light streaming through the glass ceiling. A diverse range of trees and shrubs filled the room, along with a circular fish pond containing an array of brightly coloured fish, orange and red scales accented with silver and black. At the far end sat a helio tree, golden leaves shimmering in the sunlight. Mae ran towards it, running her fingers over the pale, papery bark. Thousands of years ago the Goddess Aisha planted the original helio tree, from which all others were descended, infusing its leaves with gold dust and sacred energy. Only a few existed. Tiernan had only ever seen them in temples.

"It's so shiny!" cried Mae, caressing a leaf.

Tiernan focused on his breathing, light-headed.

Mae hugged the tree before scampering off to investigate the fish pond. She sat at its edge and put her feet in the water. Her splashing attracted the attention of the fish, which nibbled delicately at the dead skin on her feet, provoking laughter.

Another Magus showed up, looking for Ari. "I'll be there in a minute," he told her. "I have to say goodbye to Mae." A knowing look crossed her face and she excused herself, waiting in the hall.

Ari crouched next to Mae. "I need to go help someone else now. I'm glad you're feeling better." He removed the string of shells from around his neck, placing it around hers.

Mae beamed, delighted. "Thank you!" She hugged him, holding up Nika. "Will you rub Nika's face? He loves that." She looked to Tiernan, sticking out her tongue. "Tiernan won't do it."

Tiernan crossed his arms. "Tiernan doesn't take orders from rabbits."

"Nika is an unusual name for a rabbit," replied Ari.

"It means rabbit, silly."

"It does? In what language?"

"Oterai."

"Where did you learn Oterai?"

"I only know a few words. I don't remember where I learned them."

"Do you like dragons, Mae?"

"Oh, yes! But they're fierce! You have to be very brave to catch one, like Tiernan."

Ari rubbed Nika's nose with his own, giving Mae's braid a playful tug. "I'll be back later to check on you." Ari glanced at Tiernan as he spoke and Tiernan knew it wasn't Mae he'd be checking on.

"See you later!" Mae tackled Tiernan, showing off her shells. "Look what he gave me!"

"Beautiful." He tried to smile, with minimal success.

"How come you look so sad?"

"I'm not sad."

"You are, too."

"Am not."

"Liar."

He sighed heavily, concocting an alternative to the truth, "I didn't want the cute Magus to leave."

Mae giggled and grinned at him. "Don't worry. He'll be back." She grabbed him by the arm, shaking it. "Play with me. You can be my dragon."

She could have asked him to stand on his head and recite the morning prayer backwards and he would have done it. He got on all fours and Mae hopped up on his back. For the next hour they explored the arboretum, appeasing water demons with fish food and examining plants Tiernan had never seen before. One had broad blue leaves and smelled like mint. Another was a silvery shrub with brightly coloured red flowers, soft and bristly, like bloodstained paint brushes. Mae investigated a thicket of purple reeds and emerged, stricken with a curse that could only be cured by copious amounts of tickling. He braided her a crown out of whistle reed, one of the few things he recognised.

Eventually she started to get tired. "Can we go back to the helio tree?" They sprawled out among the fallen leaves, metallic gold even in death, glowing faintly. The helio tree routinely shed old leaves to make way for new ones, regardless of the time of year, engaged in a constant cycle of death and rebirth.

"I'm tired." Mae rubbed her eyes and yawned.

"You can sleep if you want to." His voice cracked. He hoped she was too tired to notice.

"Will you wake me up when Ari gets back?"

"Sure."

Mae held Nika up and pushed him close. "Rub his face."

Tiernan touched his forehead to the rabbit's furry face and nuzzled the worn tufts, rubbing their noses together.

"He likes that." Mae grinned on Nika's behalf. She fumbled with the rabbit, having a hard time moving. "You can hold him. He's not heavy." She patted Nika's head. "Be a good boy, Nika. Tiernan will look after you." Her chest rose and fell several more times, then grew still.

Tiernan remained next to her, yet somewhere far removed, no longer occupying his own body. Numb.

Chapter Twenty-Two

MAGUS ARISHKII SEDGEWREN glanced at his watch. Mae would be reunited with the Creator by now. Every loss was hard, but his inability to help weighed heavily on his conscience. Logic dictated there was only so much he could do, especially in a case where the child's mother clearly hadn't allowed pregnancy to curb her taste for alcohol, resulting in a number of birth defects, but rationalising it didn't make it hurt any less.

Their time together had been brief, but Mae was obviously an unusual child. He would've loved to find out how she learned a dead language. The last of the Oterai had been killed several thousand years ago in Rian, rounded up and burned alive by the royal family, who believed the Oterai were responsible for an outbreak of the plague. Rian also had the distinction of being the only country in the world with dragons, up until they were hunted to extinction a decade or so before the Oterai genocide.

He didn't have long to dwell on it. Vica burst into the laboratory, looking uncharacteristically rattled, trembling visibly.

"What's going on?" he asked.

"There's a paladin in room 28. Sir Basil Denholm. Director Thrush wants you to look at him."

"A paladin? Why would they bring a paladin here?"

"Church Clerics at the Temple have their hands full right now. Bunch of priests with alcohol poisoning."

Ari wasn't sure what he'd done to deserve this. Paladins were to be avoided at all costs. Rude, irrational bullies who beat up merchants who didn't offer them discounts. He reviewed Basil's paperwork, shaking his head the whole time.

Ari drew in a deep, fortifying breath before entering the room. The paladin wore a white hospital gown and swung his legs in agitation. "Sir Basil Denholm? I'm Magus Sedgewren. I understand you're not feeling well."

"You assholes got no right to keep me here! I demand to be released immediately!" Basil shook, dripping with sweat. He looked like he was going to burst out of his skin.

"I need to examine you first. The faster we get this done, the sooner you can go. When did you start feeling strange?"

"I told you people already! Ain't nothing strange going on wit' me."

"Publicly peeing on children is normal behaviour for you?" *Fucking paladins.*

"I do what I want!" Basil growled low in his throat. Ari was grateful Basil was sedated. "Ain't nobody got the right to judge me. Fuckin' little brats were askin' for it. Noisy bastards."

"Do you understand why people might be alarmed by your actions?"

"Alarmed! Pah! What kind of a world we livin' in when a man can't let loose in public? I fought for this country. Drank me the Elixir of the Goddess like everybody else and they weren't chosen. It was me! Aisha picked me! I am the light of divine wrath. I am the vanquisher of shadows!"

"When's the last time you slept?"

"I got more important shit to do than keep track o' stuff like that."

"Right. You're obviously a busy man. I'm going to check for anything unusual, then you can be on your way."

"You? No way. Send in someone with a cunt. I'll get a handful of her titties while she pokes and prods me. Then I can poke and prod her."

"It'll only take a second, sir."

Ari held out a hand, fingers splayed, pressing a hand to Basil's chest. The first and most obvious thing he sensed was the paladin's vital signs. Heartbeat slightly elevated. Blood pressure moderate—too much salty food, but nothing life-threatening. Body temperature normal. Tired. Much too tired. Minimum of three days without sleep. Anything more was harder to see. Basil's organ function was suboptimal. Ari looked deeper, concentrating harder. He felt light-headed and disconnected from his body. Everything blurred into the background until the mechanics of Basil's body, every structure and system of operation, became clear to him. Only then could he distinguish the tiny, barely visible lines strewn throughout his arteries and veins. Hiding in the blood.

He pulled out of the trance and grabbed a form for Basil to sign. "I'm going to need a few blood samples. Sign this, please."

"Ain't signin' my soul away to no Magus."

"I have no interest in your soul, just your blood. You can volunteer it willingly or I can have you transferred to the psychiatric ward where you won't have much choice in the matter. Bear in mind being strapped to a bed with a tube in your penis will impair your ability to urinate on people and molest women."

"Gimme the pen."

Ari read Basil's intentions long before the paladin swung, sweaty fingers gripping the pen like a dagger. He aimed for Ari's neck, trying to drive the point of the pen into his carotid. Ari blocked the attempt with his arm, knocking the man out with a blow to the jaw.

"Can't say I didn't give him a choice." He stuck his head out into the hall and called for back-up. "I need a patient transferred to the mental ward."

ARI ENTERED THE arboretum, finding Tiernan being escorted out by two paladins, Mae's lifeless body in his arms.

"What's going on here?"

The paladins glowered at him. "This doesn't concern you, Magus. Move along."

Ari stood his ground, painfully aware of the degree of stupidity involved in doing so. "As long as you're in my hospital it does."

The paladins exchanged glances. "We dropped off Sir Denholm and noticed Sir Aran's velver out front. He went AWOL four months ago. I imagine the Elders would like to have a chat with him."

Sir Aran?

"*Four months?*" Tiernan's eyes widened in horror. "I was gone *four months*? What fucking day is it?"

"The fifth of Samas."

Tiernan groaned. "Guess I'm going with these guys."

There had to be a mistake. Tiernan couldn't be a paladin. His behaviour was far too human.

Tiernan handed Mae to him. "Would you mind saving her ashes for me?"

"I... Of course. It's no trouble."

"Come along now. Everyone'll be surprised to see you alive."

Ari watched them go, still in disbelief.

TINY BLACK WORMS present in Basil's blood sample required use of a magnifying lens to study.

The worms excreted a toxic chemical into the bloodstream, likely the source of Basil's erratic behaviour. Beyond that, Ari couldn't tell how Basil'd been infected or where the parasite originated from.

Frequent thoughts of Mae, lying in the crematorium, and Tiernan, a curious anomaly, made focusing difficult. He took a short break to get some fresh air and fed the streethawks on the roof while trying to think of anything other than questions he had no answers to and failing miserably.

Ari returned to his lab and ordered another round of samples, injecting a rat with infected blood. Within seconds, the rat staggered around drunkenly, secreting a dark, sticky substance from its eyes and nose. Its blood turned black, filled with toxins. The rat's condition worsened rapidly, body further degenerating and mental state declining. It spun in incessant circles and snapped its jaws at nothing, charging invisible spectres. When the rat decided to chew its foot off, Ari put it out of its misery.

It wasn't hard to see why Basil was having a rough day. Recommended treatment: vermicide to kill the worms and plenty of rest.

He injected another rat. Treated it. The infection remained, but the number of worms dramatically decreased. The rat displayed elevated levels of aggression and increased strength. It nearly bit the tip of Ari's finger off, piercing his leather glove.

The paladin's sword carved an effortless swathe through the air, crashing towards him. Ari raised his own sword to block the blow, surprised to see himself clad in identical armour. His attacker was fast and aggressive, leaving him no opening to retaliate, forcing him on the defensive. If he could hold his nerve, keep up, the other paladin was bound to get tired eventually, start making mistakes. He was glad he was taller and heavier than his opponent; had their sizes been reversed, the barrage would have been too much to withstand. Sure, technique counted for a lot, but so did being a big fucker.

A quick glance of his surroundings revealed targets riddled with arrows, wooden dummies slashed to shit, racks of weapons. Training grounds. The other paladin's assault finally faltered, allowing him to strike back, turning things in his favour. Worn out, his opponent struggled to counter his attacks. He hit the paladin hard across the chest, chipping his sword on his opponent's armour, knocking him back, shoving him against a wall. He wanted to exult in his victory, but a much different compulsion struck him. He pinned the other paladin in place, removing their helm. Tiernan stared at him, pale cheeks flushed darkly. Tiernan looked younger than he did now, but not so much that Ari hesitated before kissing him. He was surprised by the force of Tiernan's lips, crushing against his own, flooding him with immediate warmth. The kiss made him feel like he was drowning, and quite content to do so. There were worse ways to die than with a beautiful blond's tongue in his mouth.

Ari opened his eyes, finger throbbing. He removed the glove and disinfected the wound with iodine. After healing it he conducted a thorough scan, checking for any sign of infection, finding nothing to indicate the worms had found a new host.

Thankyouthankyouthankyou.

Yet the parasite had affected him. He recognised Tiernan in his vision, but hadn't seen his own face. He was tempted to let the rat bite him again, see what came up, but experience told him it was better not to mess with something esoteric until you knew exactly what you were messing with.

He needed to find out more. He also needed to eat something. It was hard to concentrate on an empty stomach and he needed all the brain power he could get. He headed for the cafeteria, trying not to think about Tiernan, the fervent heat of his mouth. It was too much distraction. There was far too much work to be done.

Chapter Twenty-Three

THE HIGH COUNCIL sat on elevated benches, eyes collectively narrowing as Tiernan entered the chamber. He held Nika in one hand, squeezing him too hard. The Elders always looked at him like he was guilty of dragging them away from a party offering unlimited alcohol consumption and eager temple maidens, depriving them of full stomachs and empty nutsacks.

"Sir Aran. How gracious of you to join us." Elder Bryn sounded tired of him already.

"You honour me with praise."

"Go ahead. Explain yourself."

Tiernan exhaled slowly. "I've been trapped in a cave for the last four months by a group of deranged occultists known as the Altricial. I helped them produce a biological weapon in return for the safety of a little girl who died an hour ago."

"What kind of weapon?"

"Infectious butterflies that turn their victims into violent psychopaths. They're flying around Enra. The Altricial want to take possession of an azurelite mine there."

Elder Pine stared at his nails and picked out dirt trapped underneath them. "Enra is being evacuated. The Goddess has advised us not to get involved."

"That's bullshit."

"Watch your language." Elder Blackstone rose to his feet. "You cooperated with a terrorist organisation instead of following your mission. You're lucky you're not standing here on trial for treason and apostasy. That kid you saved has cost over 5,000 lives in Enra and counting. You've acted selfishly and disregarded orders. Your soul can only be cleansed with pain."

"Then it should be squeaky fucking clean by now."

"WALK!"

Tiernan winced as the heavy leather whip struck. Thick velver hide gave it a nasty bite. He took his first step. The snake's muscles ripped beneath his bare feet. Its scales gleamed metallic green, sharp enough to shred his feet, already sticky with venomous secretions. Nearly a foot thick and 30 feet long, the snake paid no attention to him, relaxed and inert. He wasn't afraid of much, but the majestic reptile scared the shit out of him. He hated snakes. Always had. Yet he'd never had a bad experience with one, until now.

His clothing, made from the coarse, prickly hair of a quill bear, made his body feel like it was on fire. It itched and burned, reminding him of what a terrible thing he'd done. Compromised his dignity and integrity. Brought shame on the Holy Order. Offended the Goddess with his vulgar disregard for Her will. The usual.

He'd managed to go this long without getting caught doing anything serious enough to merit this form of punishment. He took another step, walking along the snake's back. If he stepped off, he'd be whipped and forced to start over. The only acceptable reason for getting off the viridian viper was the moment of ascendancy, when his body absorbed enough of the snake's venom to render him unconscious.

The venom was already getting to him. Waves of nausea coalesced into a constant sensation of queasiness. The temple wavered in and out of focus. Bright splashes of colour danced before his eyes. More steps. Walking on razor blades.

Pain ripped through him, bringing him crashing to the ground. Then white, radiant light.

THE DESERT LOOKED like it went on forever, an endless red smear. The sun shone at full force, baking everything, forcing Tiernan to take shelter among a group of tall rust-coloured rocks, wilting in the shade. No one bothered to inform him viridian viper venom produced visions. Maybe this wouldn't be so bad. The environment didn't look familiar, yet it invoked a strange sense of intimacy, an affection for a land he couldn't identify.

The howl of a large wolf drew his attention away from the scenery. The animal descended from the ledge above him, at least three meters long, not including the tail, with teeth as thick as his arm. Its body was covered in white, shiny fur. The wolf pounced, knocking him flat on his back, and he knew he was going to die.

He closed his eyes, awaiting fangs sinking into his neck. A warm tongue lashed against his cheek, licking his skin. Tiernan cracked an eye open, staring up at the massive predator. The wolf gave his cheek another thrashing, then jumped off him, slinking through a narrow canyon. It sat, waiting for him, tail sweeping slowly across the sand until he was on his feet, following close behind. The wolf led him to a camp pitched at a small oasis, and Tiernan went to work frying bacon while his companion lounged in the shade, drooling.

The sun set, darkening the land. The temperature dropped. Tiernan threw more wood on the fire, wrapping himself in furs, and lay back, staring at more stars than he'd ever seen. For the first time, he observed a purple glow in the distance, surrounding swarms of stars. It looked as if the sky had been sliced open, allowing countless stars to pour from the Great Beyond, then sewn shut again, leaving a shadowy scar. He stared at the sky, peaceful, his mind blank, too full of wonder to accommodate dark thoughts.

A ball of fire appeared in the distance, streaking towards the ground. A meteor, he was sure of it, until the object came closer, and he realised it wasn't natural. It looked like a massive wingless airplane, though his knowledge of aircraft was limited. He'd only ever seen one plane. Around a decade ago, a plane from Heran violated Calderian airspace, a designated no-fly zone. The High Priestess shot it down with a Missile of Light and the plane plunged out of the sky, burning.

The object crashed into distant dunes. Tiernan's first impulse was to investigate the crash site, but strange lights moved across the desert, travelling low to the ground, in the direction of the crash, and instinct warned him to hold back. He slept, waiting until the morning before climbing aboard a sled, the wolf pulling him in the direction he'd seen the vessel go down.

The dunes near their destination had been flattened, slowing the vessel as it slammed into the desert. He located the wreckage a surprising distance away; whatever it was, it took a long time to slow down. Even upon closer inspection, he couldn't identify what it was, apart from a mangled heap of metal somehow capable of flight. Strange, parallel tracks surrounded the wreckage, smooth lines pressed into the sand. The tracks congregated in one spot, with at least a dozen sets of footprints. Blood stained the sand. He scanned the debris, searching for anything that might help him figure out what happened, finding only a series of strange symbols etched on a piece of metal.

Minokawa.

WAKING UP WAS slow and excruciating, his head in a sharp fog, shredding everything. Tiernan felt like he'd been trampled by a herd of stampeding velvers.

"Apologise for your sins!" Elder Blackstone stood over him, screaming, spit flying.

Tiernan turned towards a life-sized statue of the Goddess and knelt, body bent forwards, head bowed. "I have wronged you, my Sovereign. I chose darkness over light and lost myself in the shadows. I ignored your Will for selfish reasons and failed to withstand the allure of deviance. I am weak and unworthy of your Eternal Love. I apologise not out of fear, but out of devotion. I beseech you to have mercy on my soul."

"I beseech you to have mercy on my *filthy* soul!" corrected Elder Blackstone, striking him with the whip.

"Thanks. I always forget that part."

Chapter Twenty-Four

TIERNAN SHUFFLED THROUGH the streets. People hurried past. Mothers shielded their children's eyes. Their horror barely registered. Nothing to see here. Only a walking corpse, wearing pyjamas and bloody, squishy sandals. His feet burned, cut to shreds. His vision wavered in an out of focus and his head spun. *Stupid snake.* He entered the hospital and leaned against the front desk, trying not to throw up all over it.

"Ari… "

"I'll go find him. Wait here."

He sat in the waiting room, dimly aware of being wet, covered in sweat. His teeth chattered. He stared at the ground and watched blood pool around his feet, holding Nika so tight his hand went numb. He was supposed to use this time to reflect on his transgressions and bolster his resolve to avoid violating Church protocol in the future, but couldn't bring himself to care.

"Hey. Tiernan."

He looked up, recognising Ari's voice, but not the whirling blur in front of him. "Hmn?"

"What the fuck did they do to you?"

"Georgie."

"… Georgie?"

"He's a viridian viper. He bit me, the jerk."

"If you were a normal human being, you'd be dead right now."

"Lucky me." Tiernan swayed. "Do you have Mae's ashes?"

"I'll take you to them." Ari took his arm, helping him stand, leading him down the hall to a brightly lit room identical to the one Mae had been in. They stepped inside, and Ari handed him a plain cedar box, the wood still fragrant.

"Thanks." Tiernan turned to leave.

Ari grabbed him by the wrist, pushing him towards the bed. "Sit. You've been bitten by the deadliest snake in the world and you look undead. If you leave in this condition someone is going to mistake you for a ghoul and dismember you."

Tiernan sat, placing the box on the bed beside him. "I'm fine."

Ari removed Tiernan's bloody sandals, gingerly touching his feet. "Clearly. I thought paladins were supposed to heal quickly. Does it usually take this long?"

"No." A wave of dizziness washed over him and Tiernan closed his eyes. "It's the Finnegan's Lace... I can't heal properly. "

"I thought Finnegan's Lace was extinct. Did you ingest it orally?"

Tiernan removed his shirt, exposing his back. Remains of the nesting pockets were visible in large swollen red blisters, some covered by a translucent membrane, others torn and leaking clear fluid. The plant's roots stood stark beneath his pale skin.

Ari inhaled sharply. "How long have you been walking around like this?"

"Four months, apparently."

"Doesn't it hurt?"

"Not as bad as it used to."

"Did the Church do this to you?"

"No. A different group of assholes."

Ari squeezed his hand, a gesture so comforting and undeserved it made him feel worse.

"It's not a big deal, really."

"I can't tell if you're stubborn or masochistic. Either way, I can't have you torturing yourself on my watch. I can fix this." Ari touched his back, examining him. "Looks like there's twelve distinct root systems, each linked to a spot on your back. I'm going to inject each site with saline solution. It's a natural herbicide. Should do the trick. What concerns me is the sac of toxins attached to each plant. They're going to burst when the plant shrivels. What affect do they have on you?"

"It's actually kinda nice...makes me stop caring that everything hurts."

"That's a relief." Ari stood up. "I'll go get everything I need. Won't take long."

"Fine." Tiernan was too tired to argue. Just remaining seated took everything out of him. It occurred to him to escape, to leave before Ari healed him in ways he didn't deserve, but he doubted he'd make it farther than the door.

Ari returned, injecting each nesting site. As the plant died, the toxin sacs ruptured, making him gloriously apathetic to the sensation of his back being ripped to shreds by angry shards of glass, flayed alive. He zoned out for a while, thinking about nothing, being no one, until he came around, slick with sweat, his breathing laboured as his chest collapsed on itself.

"Easy." Ari placed a hand on his shoulder, steadying him. "It'll get better."

But it wouldn't. He'd killed 5,000 people—and counting. Nothing he did would change that.

Tiernan couldn't breathe. Couldn't talk. He gasped for air, vision blurring. He closed his eyes, trying to stop the burning. "Tiernan. Inhale slowly." He did as he was told. "Hold it for a few seconds, then exhale slowly." Much easier than it sounded. "Try it again." He did. And again, and again. Until his breathing slowed, and the crushing sensation abated.

Ari pressed a hand to Tiernan's forehead. "The venom's wearing off."

"Good. I can go home and drink myself to sleep."

"I don't think so. You're staying where I can keep an eye on you, at least until the morning. I can give you something to help you sleep."

Ari opened a drawer filled with glass containers, each brimming with herbs or roots, various potion reagents. He crushed several ingredients in a stone crucible, placing them in a mesh pouch he covered with boiling water and allowed to steep. Strong, musty vapours permeated the air.

Ari handed him the cup. "Here. Drink this."

"Bossy."

"Drink it."

Tiernan drank every drop, face twisting in displeasure "You've got a lot of nerve ordering a paladin around, forcing them to drink stuff that tastes like dirty socks." He lay down, already tired.

Ari sat in a chair next to him, wiping blood off his face with a warm, wet cloth. "You're not like other paladins. And I suspect you enjoy being ordered around."

"Depends on who's giving the orders." Tiernan held Nika close to his chest, eyes too heavy to remain open.

"Sleep. You'll feel better in the morning."

Tiernan tried to defy the instructions on principle, but the combined effect of the medicine and the soothing motion of Ari's cloth on the back of his neck crippled his resistance, leading him to dreamless slumber.

ARI STAYED WITH Tiernan all night, at one point falling asleep in his chair and waking up with a painful crick in the neck. He worked the tension out of his muscles and scowled at the time, already five minutes into his shift. With Tiernan still asleep, he left to check on Basil. He'd given him a strong dose of vermicide, resulting in significant changes to Basil's disposition.

"How are you feeling?" asked Ari.

"Better." Basil looked and sounded more subdued, less agitated. "Can I go home? I gotta get cleaned up. Don't wanna be late for morning prayer."

Ari conducted a final scan. The vermicide greatly reduced the severity of the infection, but the worms remained, almost impossible to detect. If he hadn't known exactly what he was looking for, he never would have found them.

"Yeah, you can go."

He couldn't hold someone for being full of worms. He'd be forced to detain half of Calder.

Basil cleared out in a hurry. Ari grabbed a blueberry muffin from the cafeteria and inhaled it on his way back to Tiernan. The paladin was mostly awake, rubbing his beautiful blue eyes and gazing at him wearily.

"You're still working?" asked Tiernan, sitting up.

"Just started."

"What time is it?"

"Seven in the morning."

"But you were with me all night."

"By choice, not necessity."

"You didn't have to do that." Tiernan frowned.

"I wanted to." Ari sat beside him. "Tiernan, do you know Basil Denholm?"

"Unfortunately, yes."

"Is he always violent and disrespectful?"

"You're aware that he's a paladin, yes?"

"I know, but you're not like that."

"Guess I'm weird." Tiernan shrugged. "I don't thrive on seeing how miserable my behaviour can make other people. The Light of the Goddess is a blessing and a burden. People don't handle the burden part so well."

"Has Basil been like this as long as you've known him?"

"Yeah. Sometimes it's worse than others, but for the most part he's happiest when he's decapitating people for looking at him funny. I wouldn't worry about it. Everyone gets cranky before Hare'thine."

"Hare'thine?"

"A paladin ritual. Happens four times a year. The priests prepare an elixir called Blood of the Moon and force everyone to drink it, which is by no means the weirdest part. In the weeks leading up to Hare'thine, everyone forgets how to behave. Once they get their dose of moon blood, they're reminded the Goddess loves and forgives them, and for a while they go back to being insatiable assholes instead of crazy shitheads."

"Huh..." *Sounds like the Church is giving them something to ease the infection.* "I should get back to work. You're free to leave, but take it easy, okay? Stop by sometime. You know where to find me."

"Thank you, Ari."

MRS. DENHOLM WAS recently widowed. Her apartment was small and clean and smelled of fresh flowers. Ari got her address from Basil's paperwork—his emergency contact was his mother. The living room was filled with photographs of Basil. Cameras were illegal in Calder and difficult to obtain—the Church said they promoted vanity— but Mrs. Denholm displayed the photos with pride. Most of them were from when Basil was younger. Basil as a gangly teenager, showing nearly every tooth in his mouth when he smiled. Basil as a boy, hugging the fattest, angriest looking cat Ari had ever seen. Basil posing with his arms around his parents' shoulders. In every photo he looked happy. Normal. Not the kind of guy who, up until twelve hours ago, preferred spitting his food at Magi and their assistants over swallowing it.

Mrs. Denholm refilled Ari's tea cup and set out more cookies, relying heavily on the use of a cane to help her around the kitchen. He'd already been gone too long— while he was allowed a lunch break, he was supposed to remain on hospital property, readily available.

"I can't thank you enough for stopping by to give me an update on my Basil, Magus," she exclaimed. "He was a sickly boy. Always had a case of the sniffles."

"You're welcome, Mrs. Denholm. Before I go, I was wondering if you could tell me a bit about what Basil was like before he became a paladin. Was he always so brave?"

"Oh, yes. Very brave. Only..." The elderly woman's expression darkened, ancient eyes turning downwards. "When Basil was young, he didn't have any worries. He was a very happy, polite boy. But becoming a paladin changes a man. It's a heavy load to carry. The Goddess places a tremendous burden on them all. Some days I worry the burden may be too great, but the Goddess gives us faith."

That was all Ari needed to hear.

"We're all grateful for his sacrifice, ma'am."

"I know, dear." Mrs. Denholm reached across the table and patted his hand, smiling sadly. "I know."

TIERNAN LAY IN bed, listless, his mind in a dozen places at once, unable to focus on one thing for long. One minute he was contemplating what to do with Mae's ashes, her absence a giant hole into which everything collapsed. The next he was overflowing with anger, furious at both himself and the Church. Their refusal to do anything to help the people of Enra was a painfully sore point of contention. What he needed was to relax, to release the annoying, unwanted emotions rampaging through his head, or at least a temporary distraction.

He tried to coax a reaction out of his cock, but it resisted every call to arms, blood flow restricted by an unseen force. The friction created by his hand almost felt good, but without anything to show for it he was left frustrated and pissed off.

His first impulse was to hit someone, anyone, and keep hitting them until their bewilderment and rage matched his own.

He listened to the sound of his bedside clock ticking with growing irritation. Each tick extended a teasing instance of noiselessness followed by a jarring mechanical click. He muffled the clock beneath a nearby pillow, and still, maddeningly, it ticked. A ceaseless heartbeat wrapped in metal. Finally, he smashed it against the edge of his nightstand, scattering gears and glass.

He got up and made his way outside, engaging in open warfare with the weeds invading his garden. He plucked them out by the roots, tossing the clumps in a pile. Thistles and thorns bloodied his hands, making their extraction more rewarding, the pain teasing him with the potential for catharsis.

Once he'd cleared out the weeds, their discarded carcasses wilting in a large pile, he was finally able to survey the garden's condition. He could practically hear the rows of peas and beans breathing sighs of relief. Lettuce, carrots, and onions were ready to be harvested, along with a patch of oversized zucchini and vines laden with luscious tomatoes. It was far more food than he could ever consume on his own. He grabbed a basket from the house and stuffed it as full as possible, carrying it to the hospital after cleaning himself up.

Ari looked pleasantly surprised to see him.

"I brought you a few things." Tiernan held out the basket. "Wanted to thank you properly."

"Did you grow these? They're huge."

"I can't take any credit. They've thrived despite my neglect."

"A garden's love tends to be unconditional."

"The zucchini's a bit too big. Might taste a little woody."

"I don't mind." A hint of colour bloomed on Ari's cheeks. "Thanks."

"You're welcome."

"I have tomorrow off. I was planning on going fishing..." Ari rubbed the back of his own neck. "Any chance you'd like to come?"

"Aah... I don't know."

"I have everything we need, and the weather should be nice. You could use some sun."

Tiernan hesitated. "I guess." He studied Ari intently for the first time, admiring his strong jawline and high cheekbones, that perfectly straight nose, tattooed in perfect symmetry. He was easy to look at. Too easy.

"I'll understand if you don't feel up to it, but otherwise I'll meet you at the south gate at noon."

"Want me to bring anything?"

"Just yourself." Ari smiled, squeezing his arm. "See you tomorrow."

Chapter Twenty-Five

THE WIND BLEW north, conveniently carrying butterfly Amir the direction he wanted. ECTOSA. Enra's capital. The evacuation was still in progress, cars streaming out of the city and congested the streets. Horns blared. The last plane took off hours ago with no guarantee it would be allowed to land anywhere outside the country. The air was thick with so much panic the butterfly tasted it, metallic and cold, and no one from Ectosa had been bitten yet.

Not everyone intended to leave the city, wandering through the streets, searching for jewellery stores and banks. Government buildings were barricaded shut. Amir was drawn to a large park in the centre of town. He caught an intoxicating scent, adjusting its course to zero in on the source of the exciting aroma. The other butterflies joined him, wanting the same thing. They landed on silky red petals and scrambled for a taste of the fragrant, spicy pollen, drinking greedily. When they'd had their fill, they stretched out in the sun and a lady—Hestia Aran, who cursed them for what they'd done to her son, as if they weren't cursed already—collected them, placing them in a glass box where they quickly went to sleep.

TIERNAN AWOKE WITH a dull throb resonating between his eyes. Surges of nausea knotted his stomach into a series of intricate twists. Overnight something had nested in his chest, invoking tightness and shortness of breath, an ache his body was unable to heal. Unable or unwilling. Bits of bad dreams stood out, dark and distended in his mind, infected shadows. They slowly retreated, but the impression they left was indelible.

He lay there for a while before realising he had no idea what time it was, his clock in pieces on the floor. He got up to check the kitchen clock. *11:29.* He wavered between going back to bed and spending the day hating everything and fishing with a generous Magus who'd be inconvenienced by his absence, eventually giving in to the latter. He showered and dressed before walking to the stable. Misha was neatly trimmed and primped, with small blue wooden beads woven into his mane. He climbed aboard and rode Misha to the south gate.

Ari was already there, waiting for him astride a black velver. He wore a dark blue sleeved shirt, leaving his chest partially exposed, tiny nacre buttons begging to be further undone, black leather pants hugging perfectly shaped legs. His dark hair was free-flowing and impossibly shiny.

"Hey." He'd never seen anyone look so happy to see him. "I was afraid I was going to have to eat all this food and drink all this beer by myself."

"Sorry to keep you waiting. I lost track of time."

"No harm done."

It was an hour's ride to the western arm of the Denfold River. When they reached their destination, Misha followed Tiernan along the river bank, playfully butting his back. He grabbed Misha by the horns, wrestling with the beast in the smooth gravel, forcing the velver back a few steps. Misha put up a good fight, and Tiernan rewarded him with a handful of wild apples. Ari laughed at the faces Misha made as he chewed, the fruit *barely* sweet enough to enjoy.

Ari stood at the water's edge and placed a bundle of neatly wrapped leaves on a submerged, silvery rock. "An offering to the spirits of the river." He ran his fingers through the water, making a series of graceful clockwise swirls. "Your names may be forgotten, but your voices are still heard."

Tiernan followed his example and removed a folded knife from his pocket, nicking his hand and spilling blood into the water. "Holy Mother, bless your children. Allow us to partake of your bounty with gratitude and humbleness." He met Ari's look of horrified intrigue with a shrug. "Doesn't hurt to have a little extra assistance."

He helped Ari unpack their gear, hoping he wouldn't make a fool out of himself. He hadn't gone fishing since his dad died. Tiernan threaded a fat earthworm onto his hook, feeling slightly sorry for the creature.

"How long have you worked at the hospital?" asked Tiernan.

"The Church offered me a job last year. There aren't enough Magi in Calder to meet the demand, so they grant work permits to outsiders like me."

His gaze lingered on Ari, only to be caught staring, quickly attempting to justify it. "You're the youngest Magus I've ever seen. How old are you?"

"Nineteen. You?"

"I'll be forty-two next month."

"No way. You look the same age as me. Must be negligible senescence... Your healing abilities repair damaged DNA, making you age slower. That's incredible."

"It's frustrating. My midlife crisis will be mistaken for teenage rebellion."

Ari smiled at him, invoking a stab of guilt. There were so many other things he could have been doing, *should* have been doing, like atoning for his actions and properly mourning Mae, not spending time with a Magus who looked far too attractive in leather. Someone who made him forget.

"Do you live alone?" asked Ari.

"I've been on my own for a while." Tiernan paused, unsure if he was willing to elaborate, but it came pouring out of him in a flood. "My dad killed himself. My mother is a wanted criminal. My grandfather died in a fire, trying to rescue his velver from a burning stable, and my grandmother remarried some asshole who I'm 90% sure molested my dad. The asshole was assassinated by a flower girl who knew as much about dissection as she did azaleas, and Grandmother drowned in a bog. I had an uncle, but he disappeared when he was a kid. Went into the forest and never came out." Tiernan reeled his line in, unsatisfied with its position. "It was probably for the best." He cast out again and turned the reel, snapping the bail back into place.

"You make my family sound normal, and my parents gave $2.2 million dollars' worth of gold to a psychopath." Ari removed his leather sandals and sat at the water's edge, curling his toes in the wet sand.

Tiernan sat beside him. "How'd *that* happen?"

"They believed he was a god. Thought he was telling the truth when he said he'd make the afterlife a more comfortable place for them."

"How do you convince someone you're a god?"

"Helps if you're able to predict the future, or at least create the illusion of doing so. Knowing things about people they'd never say out loud is a plus, along with performing so-called miracles. Feeding your followers lots of psychotropic plants also goes a long way." Ari grinned crookedly. "Never underestimate the power of mass hysteria. Hey, you've got a bite."

A sharp tug bent the end of his rod. He set the hook and reeled wildly. The fish resisted, thrashing and stripping line, but the hook held. It wasn't long before the fish was flopping on shore, around 50 cm long, rainbow-tinted scales gleaming. They bled the fish and put it on ice.

"Do you like smoked trout?" asked Ari.

"Love it. Haven't had it in a while."

"If we catch a few more, I can fix that."

Ari caught the next one and after an extended lull they sat in the shade of a gigantic uprooted tree, bleached white from the sun. They ate the sandwiches Ari made—delicious thinly sliced roasted beef with horseradish and cheese, a light dusting of flour on sourdough buns, and drank slightly bitter, deeply refreshing beer. Tiernan was grateful Ari refrained from asking him anything about where he'd been for the last four months or what happened to him, happy to learn more about Ari instead.

"You must deal with a lot of weird stuff at the hospital, huh?"

"Oh, yeah. You think you've seen everything, then you're treating a guy with potatoes stuck up his ass." They both laughed. "People feel compelled to insert all kinds of things into their rectum."

"I try to stick to the basics."

"That's very wise."

"Sadly, a potato isn't the most unusual thing I've pulled out of someone."

"What is?" asked Tiernan.

"Horse teeth."

"That's... Wow, yeah." Laughter filled him again, turning his stomach, making him queasy, as if he'd eaten something unfamiliar.

By the time it got dark, they accumulated a dozen rainbow trout, more than enough for Ari to smoke. They rode back to Ainsley, stopping after the gate before going their separate ways.

"Thanks for coming with me." Ari shifted in his saddle, tucking a strand of hair behind his ear. "I enjoy your company."

Tiernan wasn't sure what to say, an uncomfortable heat rising in his cheeks. "Likewise."

"Stop by the hospital in a few days—I'll give you your share of the trout."

"Sure. See you then." He rode off, relieved to put some distance between them, tension mounting in his chest, heart racing. He didn't look back, returning Misha to the stable and wandering home, the streets quiet and illuminated with white lanterns.

When he got home, he noticed the flag raised on his mailbox, indicating he had orders to pick up at the temple. Given the success of his previous mission, he barely slept, waiting until first light before dragging himself out of bed and making his way to the temple.

Chapter Twenty-Six

TIERNAN ALWAYS FOUND the temple rather decadent for a deity who was supposed to inspire humility and the rejection of materialism, reflecting the taste of those who ran the Church rather than the Goddess. He entered the main hall. White marble walls were streaked with silvery lines, the floor a shiny glass-like material, layered over pale stone rich in mica deposits. Crystal chandeliers descended from the ceiling, made with glowing azurelite.

The altar overflowed with offerings, everything from bottles of wine to fresh produce, silver platters of exotic fruits and cheeses.

A fountain of opaque, pale blue fluid bubbled not far away. The famous Elixir of the Goddess. Prospective paladins had to drink it. What happened next wasn't public information—a closely guarded secret, part of a sacred ritual. Even those rejected by the Goddess were sworn never to discuss it. Those who did were struck down in mysterious ways.

He entered the mission office. Sir Adler sat behind the desk, her usual scowling self.

"Picking up orders for Tiernan Aran."

She handed him a scroll and went back to her paperwork. Tiernan nervously unfurled the document and then scanned it. Instead of the usual breakdown of details, including the name of the client and nature of the mission, a single sentence graced the paper.

To receive mission details, visit Azmodian's Apothecary.

WHAT LITTLE CALM Tiernan managed to instil evaporated, replaced with raw panic. Irrational, surely, but his previous mission had gone *so* well. His hands shook. The sound of his own strained, irregular breathing filled his helm. He entered the apothecary, spotting Dezmodeus behind the counter. Dezmodeus stood, clutching his shoulder, glasses perched on the end of his nose.

"We've never been properly introduced. I am Dezmodeus Azmodian. If you wouldn't mind accompanying me upstairs, I can explain."

Tiernan reluctantly followed. Dezmodeus looked like he could crush his head without breaking a sweat and snap his spine in half before he felt a thing, despite being in obvious pain.

Dezmodeus headed for the stairs, glancing back at him as if reading his mind. "If I wanted to kill you, I wouldn't do it here. Too many witnesses."

Dezmodeus made it halfway up the stairs, then stopped. He sat down with a grunt, rubbing his back, face twisted in pain. After a minute of heavy breathing, he was on his feet again and Tiernan felt somewhat less threatened.

They entered the room at the end of the hall. A man sat at a wooden table, staring out the window. Built like a paladin. Blond. He turned to look at Tiernan, filling his chest with a sharp, unexpected pain.

The man bore a striking resemblance to his father. Tiernan's mind struggled to process what he was seeing, eventually providing him with a name, his voice barely audible over the percussive thundering in his head. "Uncle Auryn?"

"Tiernan." The man nodded and smiled warmly.

"You'd better sit down," said Dezmodeus.

"What happened?" Tiernan stared at Auryn in shock, removing his helm. "Everyone thought you were dead." He'd always assumed his uncle had been eaten by bears. Or trolls.

Dezmodeus raised his hand. "That's my bad. I abducted him. Took him to an isolated island in northern Rian, where he grew up in a government orphanage."

"*Why?*"

"He was better off being raised by a delusional dictator than your stepgrandfather. And we needed someone on the inside." Tiernan's confusion grew. Dezmodeus poured him a glass of strong-smelling liquor and handed it to him. "The island is occupied illegally by the Anorians, an alien race. Universal Law prohibits interaction between humans and aliens until humanity attains a certain level of spiritual advancement."

"I've been gathering evidence to help expose them," said Auryn.

Dezmodeus continued. "The leader of the Anorians, Haruki Kumara, is president of Penumbra Technologies, which markets holographic technology for discerning despots eager to manipulate the masses. They also dabble in biological weaponry and real estate, invading planets and selling them to the highest bidder." Dezmodeus poured himself a drink, knocking it back. "Haruki has two sons, Haken and Jaden, who split the rule of the island Auryn lives on." Dezmodeus set his empty glass down and stretched, rotating his shoulders. "Any questions?"

Tiernan sipped the fiery fluid, nearly choking on it. "What's my mission?"

Auryn spoke up. "I'd like to take you to see your mama, if you're all right with that."

Tiernan took a deep breath and another drink. "She's with the Altricial, isn't she?"

"How'd you know?

"Mae got into her perfume...said it smelled like Cia." A lump formed in his throat. He washed it down quickly, leaving an ache in his chest.

"She attempted to dissuade Lamashtu from using you," said Dezmodeus. "But there was only so much she could do without blowing her cover."

"Why'd she kill Elder Barthus?"

"It's better if she tells you. Excuse me for a moment." Dezmodeus left, leaving him alone with Auryn.

"I'm sorry my dad isn't here." Tiernan stared at his hands, frowning. "Must be disappointing to hear your family's all gone, except me."

Auryn shook his head and gently touched Tiernan's hand. "You're here. That's more than enough."

Dezi wandered back in, scowling at his phone. "My weirdo brother wants me to take a picture of you, Tiernan."

"Me? Why?"

"Says he's curious what you look like. Creepy old man."

"He's two hours older than you," pointed out Auryn.

"Quiet, you."

Tiernan snickered in amusement. "I don't mind." He'd never had his picture taken before. What was Dezi's brother like? If he was anything like Dezi, he felt sorry for their parents.

Dezi snapped a photo with the camera on his phone and five minutes later he received a response, taking the opportunity to read it aloud. "Thank you. He is beautiful. Looks like his uncle. Do not let him escape without feeding him."

It was the first time a man he'd never met made him blush.

TIERNAN AWOKE HUNGOVER and nervous, an obese phantom sitting on his chest. He was supposed to meet Auryn back at Dezmodeus's place, but there was something he needed to do first. He showered and dressed before heading to the hospital to find Ari.

"This is a pleasant surprise." Ari smiled at him, tilting his head slightly. "You're not sick, are you?"

"No." Tiernan pocketed his hands, awkwardly meeting Ari's gaze. "I'm leaving on a mission. Didn't want you to think I was avoiding you."

"Much appreciated. Where're you going?"

"My uncle is taking me to see my mother."

"Your uncle who disappeared?"

"Yeah. Turns out he was abducted. I met him yesterday."

"And he knows where your mom is?"

"Yeah."

"Hey, that's great news. I'm happy for you." Ari's smile contrasted with the rest of him, his uniform streaked with blood, hair sticking up in places, dark shadows beneath his eyes.

"Long day?"

Ari nodded. Tiernan licked his thumb, wiping a smear of blood off his cheek. Ari inclined his head towards him, closing his eyes. "Thanks."

Tiernan forced his hand back into his pocket, fighting the urge to run his fingers through Ari's hair and caress the thick, shiny strands. "Anyway, I'll see you when I get back."

Ari opened his eyes, regarding him with a degree of affection that both terrified and excited him. "Looking forward to it. Have a safe trip."

"Later." Tiernan turned away, forcing himself to walk slowly, fighting the urge to run.

Chapter Twenty-Seven

TIERNAN REALISED HE hated flying during take off. His stomach climbed into his throat and threatened to escape. Everything spun out of focus and a feverish heat gripped him, making him desperate for air. Uncle Auryn gave him a tablet to counteract the effect, and within ten minutes he was fine, staring out the window at the grey, cloudless sky, too high to see the ground.

He mentally repeated what Auryn told him. *This aircraft is designed to remain undetected by enemy surveillance. We'll be fine.* Still, he thought of the Heranian pilot who fell asleep at the controls and drifted into Calderian airspace, only to be shot down like a metal game bird. What an awful way to go.

Tiernan sipped from a glass water bottle, glancing often at Auryn while trying not to stare. Not only did Auryn look like his dad, he felt eerily at ease in his presence, as if they'd known each other for ages. "Are you married?"

"No." Auryn shook his head. "I was, but it didn't end well." Before Tiernan could offer his condolences, Auryn continued, "What about you? Are you seeing anyone?"

"No. I met someone recently, but I don't know... He reminds me of someone."

"Oh?"

With a gentle prod, he disgorged everything. "Cappa Andali. We were... He was..." Or tried to, at least. "He meant a lot to me. He was always looking out for me, telling me what to do. He was considerate and helpful and genuinely cared about others. He was killed in Fenton." He breathed deeply, trying to shake the building panic. "Ari's a lot like him. It scares the shit out of me."

"You're not used to someone taking care of you, are you?"

"No. The attention feels undeserved, like I'm unworthy of it. He makes me forget how miserable I am, and I'm not convinced I deserve that."

"You're too hard on yourself."

"People are dying because of me, Auryn. If I reject suffering, I reject atoning for everything I've done."

"Beating yourself up won't fix anything. It'll just diminish your ability to do something about it."

Tiernan stared at gauges in the cockpit, wondering what they all meant.

"I know what it's like to be responsible for things you're not proud of." Auryn's tone convinced him he spoke truthfully. "I've supervised the execution of women and children for crimes they didn't commit. I've made thousands of people disappear. I can attempt to justify it by saying I was only following orders, but it doesn't change anything. It doesn't bring anyone back. It doesn't give their families any closure, and I have to live with that."

"How do you do it?"

"Some days are better than others." Auryn lapsed into momentary silence. "Give Ari a chance. His support will make all the difference."

Tiernan sighed in defeat. He'd be foolish not to take Auryn's advice. Allowing a brilliant Magus to lick his wounds may be devoid of redemptive qualities, but it would help. If anyone knew how to correct his lack of vigour, it would be Ari. That alone would eliminate considerable anger and frustration, if he could ever broach the subject.

"You're right, it's just...hard. Being in a relationship is like putting all your time and energy into building a big, beautiful home, knowing someday it's either going to fall apart or be taken away from you."

"Doesn't mean it's better to be homeless. You can't allow what may or may not happen in the future to deter you from living in the present. It becomes an excuse to remain stagnant."

"I'm trying."

"Keep at it. It'll get better."

"I hope so." The plane descended, and the ground came into view. Vast dunes of red sand stretched over parched ground. Clumps of small, scrubby trees surrounded sporadic springs. The landscape was unlike anything he'd ever seen, yet looked familiar. "Have you been here before?"

"No," replied Auryn, "but I feel like I have."

"Yeah... Me, too. I had a vision recently...looked a lot like here. Something crashed in the desert. I'm not sure what it was."

Auryn inhaled sharply. "The Minokawa."

"Yeah. How'd you know?"

"I was onboard when it crashed."

AURYN HALTED IN front of a door at the Crocus Inn, but didn't knock. "I'll give you two some time alone. Think I'll go for a walk. See how long it takes to get lost."

Tiernan preferred he stay, but wasn't going to admit it. "Don't get *too* lost. If you disappear on my watch, I'll be perpetuating a rather disturbing family tradition."

Auryn grinned at him and walked off. "I'll try not to."

Tiernan stood in front of the door for a long time before finally rapping his knuckles on the pale wood. Hestia Aran opened the door. She stared at him for a moment before drawing him into a tight hug. He stood there, arms at his sides, neither pulling away nor reciprocating, unsure. She held him for ages before finally taking him by the hand and pulling him inside.

"Can I get you something to drink?" she asked.

Tiernan walked up to the bar and helped himself to a bottle of whisky, then sat down.

"I was afraid you wouldn't come."

"Can't imagine why." One of his childhood ambitions had been to grow as tall as his mother, but he'd fallen a few inches short. Her white-blonde hair was cut short, curving beneath her chin.

"Did you lose your uncle?"

"He wandered off again."

Hestia turned towards the window, gazing down at the street. "I didn't kill Elder Barthus. He died from a drug overdose. Some industrious souls saw his passing as an opportunity to frame me for the crime."

"Frame you? Why?"

"You're better off not knowing, at least for now."

"You're honestly not going to tell me?"

"Considering it got your father killed, I'm afraid I must be firm on that."

"Killed... He killed himself. I thought you knew that."

"Tiernan, your father didn't kill himself. The Church goes after anyone who compromises their position."

"No... I saw him... He..."

"You saw what they wanted you to see. They made it look like Dem took his own life and apparently did a damn fine job."

"How do you know that?"

"Dem wouldn't kill himself, no matter how miserable he was. He knew what would happen if he did."

"What's that?"

"When we die, we don't go where we're supposed to. The Anorians have an energy barrier in place that traps discarnate souls, disorienting them. He'd be handing himself over to the enemy."

Tiernan took another swig of whisky, then another, mind swirling. "Did you ask Lysa to rescue me?"

"I did. She's the only one in the Altricial who knows you're my son."

"Any idea where she is?"

"No, but she's managed to avoid the Altricial so far."

"Why'd they target me?"

"They obtained records of all 52 paladins and yours stood out. You got into trouble often, for things like protecting the children of war criminals and refusing to execute thieves. Unlike the others, you appear impervious to the burden of Light. It's rumoured only those with Nephilim blood can withstand it."

"Nephilim blood? From where?"

"My side of the family. Your grandfather Asheron and grandmother Uma are Nephilim. Nephilim blood is a requirement for the butterfly ritual."

"Where're the butterflies now?"

"Asleep. They won't bother you again."

He drank deeply, relishing the burn.

"Tiernan... I'm sorry about Mae."

A stab of pain shot through his chest. He tried to ignore it, as if the wound belonged to someone else. "You know about that?"

"I felt her energy expire. I know it's hard to accept, but living in a cave with you was a significant improvement to her overall quality of life. It's what she wanted. Mae's spirit is rather fond of you."

"What do you mean?"

"Let's go for a walk."

THE MARKET WAS a hub of activity. Vendors cried out in promotion of their wares. The scent of spices and frying food filled the air. Stands lined the walkways, selling everything—jewellery made from green glass found in the desert, brightly dyed fabrics, live lizards and insects, clay pottery, dried fruit and nuts. Most of the produce was unidentifiable except for a basket of tomatoes and a pumpkin.

"Let me know if you see anything you want." Hestia stayed close, holding Tiernan's hand.

He surveyed carts containing spices of every colour and tasted freshly baked bread—not round and thick, but flat and puffy, dipped in a white, creamy sauce so refreshing he wanted to eat it by the tubful.

He ate fried fish and caramelised squash, colourful treats both salty and sweet and was nearly full when he spotted the fruit vendor. His stand contained only one type of fruit, bright yellow, long and round, covered in green spines. Carefully, he selected one and tried to smell it without stabbing himself in the nose. The flowery, sweet scent overwhelmed him. He could taste it in his mouth, imagine himself licking sticky fruit juice off golden skin.

A sense of joy washed over him, accompanied by a faint tingle in his groin.

Momentarily disoriented, he gripped Hestia's arm for support, breathing deep. She steadied him. "That's thorn fruit."

"Never heard of it."

"It's sweet. Has a chemical in it that reacts with the skin, makes it sensitive... Let's just say it's used for a lot more than making fabulous desserts."

"Let's buy all of them."

Hestia laughed and paid for three. The vendor placed them in a net bag. Hestia took it and walked off. Tiernan followed. They moved away from the market, heading for the town square, which turned out to be more of a circle. New buildings contrasted old buildings, intricately carved stone next to steel and glass.

In the centre of the circle sat a large fountain depicting a dragon breathing water, coins flashing at its feet. The smell of burning bodies wafted over him. The sky darkened, smoke lingering in noxious clouds. Smouldering pyres surrounded him, containing charred human remains. He shook his head vigorously and the image cleared. No smoke. No bodies. Hestia led him away, heading towards what he could only assume was the royal palace. No other building matched its detail and grandeur.

They entered the palace. Men with guns long as their torsos stood by the entrance, monitoring tourists in silence. The tiled floors and painted stone columns made him feel at home. He wasn't sure where he was going, but he felt drawn to a long hall, stretching endlessly, lined with portraits of those who'd once occupied the palace— the royal family of Rian. One painting captured his attention. Its subject was younger than most, smiling mischievously when the others were intent on looking as serious as possible. Tiernan read the plaque beside it.

The Lost Prince of Rian

Prince Anowki Amari, only child of King Ermalin, age twelve. Prince Anowki disappeared days before the uprising of year 3, during which the royal family were executed. His remains were never found.

The room spun violently. He leaned against Hestia and closed his eyes.

Fires burned all over the courtyard. At the centre of each pyre was a figure shrouded in thick black cloth, cloaked in flame. Smoke billowed from beneath the fabric and rose into the night air. He watched from the palace window, counting the bodies. He heard someone approach and abruptly closed the silk drapes.

"Kai? What's going on out there? Why are the windows covered?" Prince Anowki wore dark purple robes. His thick black hair was cut short, in a state of regrowth after being recently shaved in celebration of his twelfth birthday. His brown eyes were concerned. Distressed.

"The priests are burning more slaves. It's better if you don't look."

The prince pursed his lips. "My father thinks they're working with demons. Spreading the plague. That's what the Ancient Ones told him."

When the Ancient Ones first descended from the sky, bringing with them means of extracting water from salt and irrigating the desert, their divine presence had been a blessing. Now, not so much. They despised the Oterai, who'd been kept as slaves for generations, blaming them for the recent outbreak.

He placed a hand on Anowki's shoulder. "The Ancient Ones have far too much influence over your father. Your mother is trying to fix that."

Anowki threw his arms around him. "I'm worried about Nika."

Anowki wasn't alone in his concern. So far, all the slaves who'd been burned came from lower-class families, mainly because King Ermalin was reluctant to piss off anyone who had money, but no telling how long that would go on. Nineteen-year-old Nika was owned by the royal family. The flames would come for him last.

"Don't worry. I'll take care of Nika."

"Will you help him escape?"

An alarm sounded. A distant, mournful wail. It was an appropriate noise, encapsulating how he felt about the situation. He took another peek outside. The bodies were no longer covered; charred skeletons engulfed in bright, writhing flames. He let the drapes fall back into place and guided Anowki away from the window.

"Let's hope it doesn't come to that. Your father will return to his senses. He has to."

TIERNAN AWOKE COVERED in sweat. Someone had been considerate enough to strip him down to his underwear, but it didn't help much against the scorching heat. He got up, disoriented, and peered out the window to the street below. A sign for the inn jutted outwards from the side of the building.

The creaking of floorboards sounded in an adjoining room and Tiernan opened the door to investigate. He found Auryn seated at a table, lying with his upper body against it. A fan sat on the table, rotating at top speed. "You made it back." Tiernan sat across from him. "What happened to me?"

"You passed out. Your mama carried you back."

"Must have been the heat." He was too hot and tired to consider other options. "What're you doing up?" he asked, though the answer was obvious. Auryn suffered worse than he did. It probably never got this hot up north.

"It's too hot to sleep, even with the air conditioning on, and I can't open the window without inhaling sand."

"Whose idea was it to come to the desert in the middle of summer?"

Auryn filled a glass from a pitcher of ice water and handed it to him. "Not mine."

Tiernan drank slowly, gathering his courage before speaking, "I think I lived here before. Lifetimes ago." He wondered how he died. Maybe it explained his aversion to snakes or his deeply irrational fear of being caught in a volcanic eruption. "I'm so confused."

Hestia emerged from a third bedroom, making her way to the sink before splashing cold water over her face. "You're going to be confused for a while. Remembering too much, too quickly, tends to drive people psychotic. Dealing with one lifetime's worth of shit is hard enough. Surely both of you can attest to that."

"Why bother remembering, then?"

"Doesn't matter much what happened, at least at this point in your awakening. What's important is the people you shared these experiences with, reconnecting with those we love." *Those we love...*

"Do you remember a prince?" he asked Auryn.

"I don't recall much, beyond crashing in the desert. Bright lights. Gunfire. Waking up in a hospital bed on an alien spaceship. I remember *knowing* another member of the crew was alive... being unable to get to him... kept apart..." Auryn closed his eyes momentarily, appearing deep in thought. A shy smile lit up his face. "Your prince wasn't blond, was he?"

"Black hair. Dark eyes."

"I've got nothing, sorry."

"Both of you want the same thing," said Hestia.

"What's that?" asked Tiernan.

"To see the Anorians humiliated and held accountable for every atrocity they've committed. It's a long list. A plague tore through this country over two thousand years ago and victims were quarantined on an island up north, where Auryn lives. The Anorians healed the afflicted and took the opportunity to pose as gods."

"How can I help?" asked Tiernan.

"The Anorians are involved with the Church," said Hestia. She poured herself a glass of water and sipped it slowly. "I'd like you to find evidence of their interactions."

"You're going to get me in trouble again."

"At least trouble isn't boring," said Auryn, reinforcing his fondness for the man.

Chapter Twenty-Eight

AURYN DROPPED TIERNAN off with assurances they'd see each other soon. He apologised for being unable to spend more time with his nephew, but he needed to get back to work.

A month after the explosion, Emperor Haken came to the Farm. His arrival was unexpected and for once Auryn was grateful Keita wasn't around.

Auryn claimed to have no memory of events leading up to the incident, allowing Haken to enlighten him. Haken told the story of how Auryn ended up in the hospital with such conviction he almost believed it. Auryn had been driving in the middle of nowhere and hit an Ibaran improvised explosive device. He was lucky to be alive. His survival and miraculous recovery were a testament to his faith, divine blessings. Haken's ability to look him in the eye and speak such cogent bullshit both impressed him and turned his stomach.

His job required flying outside the quarantine zone, making him privy to knowledge the sun was alive and well.

THREE MONTHS AGO

Haken's arrival made Auryn extremely nervous. All high-ranking military officials had been required to fill out a questionnaire about job satisfaction. At the time, five days had passed since he'd try to kill himself and been revived by a man with wings. *I need your help. I can reunite you with your family.* One of the questions asked, "Is there anything about your job you'd change?" He should have written, "Nothing." like everyone else. "I'm humbled by the opportunity to serve His Holiness." Instead, he'd responded with a ten thousand word essay on the utter absurdity of *farming* animals when they could be growing meat in laboratories or raising insects. He asked for better conditions for the animals. Better pay for the workers who did all the harvesting in the greenhouses, without whom they'd have nothing.

"I appreciate your honesty," said Haken, "but you're missing the point. We're not hurting the planet. We're not devastating the environment. We're just raising delicious livestock. You wouldn't get the same thing out of a lab. It would lack soul. The energy produced by a living creature can't be replicated without life. Real meat is full of energy. Consuming it should be an act of pleasure and exhilaration. It should make you feel *bright*—in awe of the miracle of life, beaming with admiration for your creator."

"Forgive my ignorance, your Holiness."

"There's nothing to forgive, my son. A man born without eyes is not to blame for his inability to see."

"I'm unworthy of your graciousness."

"Nonsense. You deserve better than this place. I want you to assist me in the capital. I've tasked my son with completing important errands, but he's worse than useless. A total loser. I can't depend on him for anything. Elia has always been a stubborn brat when it comes to doing what he's told.

"I want you to keep an eye on him. When he's unable to get things done, you can step in on his behalf. He trusts you. I trust you." It was unusual for Haken to place his trust in someone who'd insisted Reisen Kaneko was harmless even after Reisen allegedly developed a fondness for blowing up buildings.

"I'd be honoured, sir." Aggnaroth would be thrilled. Auryn had collected as much evidence as he could at the Farm. Filmed how the Anorians treated humans who were *supposed* to be protected from cannibalistic aliens. Universal Law existed for a reason. Violators would be fined and imprisoned, or banished, depending on the severity of the crime. If he was promoted to Head Babysitter, he'd have the chance to compile more evidence against the bastards.

"There's one more thing I'd like you to do for me."

"Anything, Your Holiness."

"Find a way to lure Reisen Kaneko out of hiding. I'm going to wipe that punk's memory and send him to an off-world colony, where we can keep a close eye on him. Put him back to work."

He bowed low to the ground. "Yes, sir."

A few days later he got a call from Haken saying he needed someone to fly to Abyon and Elia refused to do it. *"Too much effort", he says! Had I known my son would grow to be so spoiled, I would have sent him to live at the orphanage with you.* Auryn had only one question. "Where's Abyon?" The name didn't sound familiar. Was it somewhere in Ibara? Terasyn and Ibara were supposedly spying on each other, but Auryn had seen little evidence of such activity over the years.

"Meet me at the airfield in an hour. I'll explain."

Auryn anxiously awaited Haken's arrival, unsure what the emperor expected of him.

"I'm going to tell you something not many people are aware of. There aren't many I trust with a secret of this magnitude." Auryn felt a slight pang of guilt for recording the conversation, similar to the twinge of remorse felt when piercing live bait with a fish hook, and equally short-lived. "Jaden, the Emperor of Ibara, works with a powerful demon named Aggnaroth. Aggnaroth can see into the past, predict the future, and influence the people of Ibara. His magick is the reason Ibarans live so long. In exchange, the demon demands total darkness.

"Aggnaroth instructed Jaden to build huge machines capable of blocking out the sun. Their reach covers the entire island." Haken bowed his head solemnly. "I'd rather be blamed for taking away the sun than terrify my people with the knowledge their enemy has a demon on their side. My people have enough to fear as is." *What a humanitarian.* "I need you to fly to Abyon. Abyon is in Rian, south of here, across the ocean, where Jaden's demonic machines no longer have any effect.

"I've always been averse to involving outsiders, but I need to learn more about inkworm. I need to find out how to cure the afflicted. I have no doubt Jaden's responsible for spreading the ghastly parasite." *You know he's not, you lying sack of shit. And Jaden wants nothing to do with the stuff, according to Aggnaroth. Especially after his daughter got infected.* "Jaden is a malignant tumour on the womb of goodness."

"I couldn't agree more, Your Highness. It would be my pleasure to assist you in the war against darkness."

"I knew I could count on you, Auryn. Thank you."

PRESENT DAY

Emperor Haken's grey eyes lit up with excitement at the sight of the azurelite Auryn brought back with him, purchased from a representative of the Altricial who happened to be Auryn's sister-in-law. Haken had big plans for the crystal, exploring its uses as a power source immune to electromagnetic disturbance. The amount of power generated by azurelite was massive. A small chunk could supposedly power a large city for years. He knew the Anorians had done experiments with azurelite, but they'd never gotten their hands on a steady supply, until now.

"The Altricial have sent you a gift, Your Holiness. I told them of your difficulties treating inkworm and they generously offered this tincture." He removed a glass vial from his pocket and handed it to Haken. It contained a viscous gold substance, so bright it almost glowed. "It's made from the resin of *Kalinara,* a sacred tree. It's a natural antibiotic, rich in pranic energy. It should appease the worms for around three months. They were kind enough to include a cutting of the tree. Your gardener is attending to it."

Haken beamed. "I can't tell you how good it feels to finally have someone I can rely on." There was a time in the not too distant past when hearing the emperor speak to him in such a way would have filled him with pride, accomplishment, and a sense of importance. Now his words were hollow.

"Would you like to join my family for dinner?" Haken's question had only one correct answer. To say no would mean Auryn had something better to do than spend time with his sovereign, which Haken's ego wasn't equipped to handle. "It would be an honour."

Rows of flowers lined the hallway from the throne room to the dining room. They grew from plant beds sculpted into the walls, nurtured by artificial lighting and nutrient-rich water. Haken had an obsession with flowers, demanding a fresh bouquet every morning. Vines crossed the ceiling, dangling flowers of white, pink, and purple.

He'd walked this hallway a hundred times and never thought anything of them, beyond their aesthetic appeal, but since his exposure to inkworm, the scent of the blossoms filled him with an overwhelming sense of nostalgia. At first, he accredited it to his childhood in Calder, assuming it was a plant he'd encountered in the outside world, but something told him that wasn't right. The memory stemmed from a deeper, darker place. A place he hadn't worked up the courage to explore in depth, but the more he resisted the tug of unknown tides, the stronger they became.

Apart from an endless supply of food, dinner consisted mainly of awkward silence. Auryn sat beside Elia, who received frequent scowls from Haken. To Elia's left, the empress shifted food around her plate without ever putting it in her mouth, muttering about a shoe sale. Most meat was served almost entirely raw, barely kissed by fire, if at all.

Halfway through dessert, Haken nodded off, sleeping upright in his chair while emitting soft snores.

The empress nibbled a forkful of chocolate cake, "Red, black, strappy heels..."

"Quit talking to yourself," growled Elia. "You sound insane."

"It's the only intelligent conversation I get around here."

"I'm sorry we can't match your intellectual prowess on the topic of footwear. Perhaps a change in subject is advisable."

"The only thing you're qualified to speak of in any detail is accomplishing nothing."

"For your information, I accomplished a lot today. I had a full body massage this morning, and Miss Camila was extra friendly. I got my hair trimmed, thanks for noticing. I spent two hours volunteering, most of which entailed servicing a chef at the soup kitchen. Talk about strenuous labour. I lost count of how many times I made her come. You would've been impressed. Oh, and I judged a hot dog eating contest. The guy who won threw up so much afterwards. You should've seen the size of the chunks." Elia raised his fork, prodding the last piece of steak on his mother's plate. "Are you going to eat that?"

The empress lifted her plate, smashing it on the floor. Emperor Haken awoke with a start, a bewildered expression on his face. The empress rose from her seat and stalked off, snarling. "I wish I'd swallowed you."

Auryn stared at the remains of his blood orange soufflé.

Haken leaned forwards, rubbing an eye. He withdrew the vial of serum from his pocket, placing it on the table. "Give this to the infected and report back with the results. Take Auryn with you. I'll tend to your mother."

"YOU THINK THIS stuff'll work?" Elia sat beside Auryn as the doctor prepared the injection, looking sceptical.

"I hope so. I don't want to be the one to inform your father if it doesn't."

"Too bad that idiot Kaneko isn't around. I'm sure he could figure it out."

"Perhaps Emperor Jaden could be persuaded to turn him over."

"Not much chance of that. I bet the only reason he's protecting Kaneko is the satisfaction of knowing how much it torments my father. A man after my own heart."

"There must be something we can do to bring him in." Auryn always gave the impression he was eager to apprehend Reisen. He'd even worked with the team who hunted him for a while, diligently leading them in the wrong direction.

"You get right on that." Elia captured him in a headlock, rubbing his fist against his scalp so hard it burned. Auryn elbowed the prince in the stomach and squirmed free. For as long as he could remember, he'd wanted a big brother—someone to teach him how to win fights and blow things up, someone he could look up to. Without a brother he felt incomplete. Prince Elia was the closest thing he had, which was better than nothing. Guilt lodged in his chest. The contact lenses he wore recorded everything, providing proof of Elia's involvement.

The doctor drew back the curtain, revealing the patient—a recent victim of an Ibaran biological warfare attack, or so the paperwork said. The patient, Cpt. Devon Hansy, a seventy-five-year-old male, writhed in agony, even under heavy doses of painkillers. His sunken eyes fixated on the ceiling and slime leaked like frothy ink from the corner of his mouth.

Auryn knew the injection would work—he trusted Hestia—but after the deed was done and the drooling continued, he experienced a moment of doubt. Only when Devon sat up, coughing up chunks of sludge, did Auryn dare breathe. He exhaled, lightheaded with relief.

Devon wept. "Praise His Holiness. Praise Him."

YEAR 2045
Thirty Years Ago

Hallowed Mountain Military Complex

Auryn woke up and turned onto his side, glancing at the clock. Far too early to get up, yet Reisen had disappeared from his side. The sound of the TV droned from the living area. He got up to find Reisen seated on the couch, fixated on the TV—a Terasian convoy being attacked by a... No, there had to be a mistake.

"What are you watching?" He sat beside Reisen, heart thudding.

"It was in our mailbox. I have no idea who it's from. There was no note. It's Ibaran surveillance footage of a low-flying Ibaran plane dropping an inkworm bomb on our troops. I've watched it a dozen times and have no idea what relevance it has. I don't see anything strange. Do you?"

He drew in a deep breath. "That's not an Ibaran plane. It's one of ours."

Reisen reached for his hand. "Well, shit."

Chapter Twenty-Nine

IT TOOK TWO days for Tiernan to reach the combination of desperation and courage required to see Ari. The state of desolation was initiated by waking up in the morning with an erection. As soon as he noticed and went to do something about it, his dick softened in his hand. After briefly considering castration as a viable alternative to living a life of frustration and shame, he forced himself out of the house and to the hospital.

Ari spotted him in the waiting room, breaking into a bright smile, white teeth flashing, warming Tiernan's insides. "Hey. I wasn't expecting to see you so soon." Ari lowered his voice. "How'd it go with your mom?"

"All right." Tiernan shifted anxiously in his chair. "Can I talk to you about something, uh, health related?"

"Of course. Come to my office."

Ari's office contained a large desk, an examination table, and wall-to-wall laboratory equipment, including flasks of fluids Tiernan couldn't begin to identify, bubbling in transparent tubes. An infected rat glowered at them from across the room, snapping its jaws at the bars of its cage.

"That's Basil," said Ari.

"Acts just like him." Tiernan stood in front of Basil's cage, wrinkling his nose at the rat. "What's the matter with him?"

"He's got worms."

Tiernan moved away from the cage to take a seat on the edge of the examination table. "If only Basil had the same excuse." He sat with his hands on his lap, staring at them, balling his fingers into fists.

"Tell me what's wrong."

"It just—doesn't work."

"What doesn't?"

Tiernan's shoulders sagged. He sighed heavily, pressing a clammy hand to his forehead. "You're the Magus. Figure it out. How many body parts can you name that stop functioning without killing you, yet make you wish you were dead?"

"You mean—"

"Don't say it out loud, for Goddess's sake."

"Tiernan, I can tell you right now there's nothing physically wrong with you. Psychological factors like stress and guilt can cause all kinds of problems. Get out of your head for a while. Putting pressure on yourself only makes it worse."

"Easy for you to say. How do I fix it?"

"By dealing with what's bothering you." Ari sat beside him. "Are you familiar with saraii mushrooms?"

"Never heard of them. Are they the fun kind?"

"Yes, but they can be beneficial in treating emotional trauma. You feel relaxed. Entertained. Content. Makes it easier to talk about things you'd rather avoid and deal with the aftermath." Ari reached over, taking his hand. "Let me help. Not as a healer, but as someone who cares about you. Do you have time right now?"

"Sure, but...do we have to do it here?"

"No. We can go wherever you'd be most comfortable. I'll need permission to leave, but that shouldn't be a problem."

"Fine." Tiernan gave in, exhausted.

Ari slid off the table and headed for rows of drawers, removing a container of dried mushrooms. "I give small doses of these to certain permanent residents of the psychiatric ward. Does wonders for their dispositions."

"I'm holding you fully accountable if I become some homeless drug addict forced to sell my body in exchange for my next fix."

Ari grinned reassuringly. "At least you'll have lots of clients."

DIRECTOR MAGUS AVA Thrush had the steadiest hands in the hospital and worked flawlessly under pressure. Her knowledge of spellcraft and potion brewing surpassed what most Magus could acquire in several lifetimes. She was firm, but reasonable. Ari knocked on her door, awaiting a response.

"Come in."

He approached her desk and cleared his throat before speaking. "Would you mind if I took the rest of the day off?"

Ava adjusted her glasses, focusing on the ancient tome in front of her—a glossary of medicinal plants he couldn't identify written in a language he couldn't understand. "What for?"

"I'd like to spend some time with a friend. He's not doing well."

"I didn't realise you had any friends." The teasing was justified. Ari spent almost all his time at the hospital and wasn't known for socialising with his co-workers. A childhood spent working long hours for a megalomaniacal tyrant crippled his ability to relate to most people. He preferred to spend time in the lab doing something constructive, putting hard-earned skills to good use.

"I don't often meet people as charming as you."

Ava snorted and looked up, meeting his gaze. "Go ahead. Must be serious if you're willingly taking a break."

"He's in a lot of emotional pain. It's affecting his physical well-being."

Ava nodded, returning to her reading. "Until tomorrow, then."

"GO FIND AN object that means a lot to you," Ari instructed Tiernan. Tiernan looked at him quizzically and then wandered off, leaving him to continue preparing a cup of medicinal tea. Ari mixed peppermint, chamomile, and a bit of ginger to settle the stomach. He added a dose of dried mushrooms last.

Tiernan returned with Mae's stuffed rabbit. *Nika.* The name resonated strangely in Ari's head, even now.

"Why do I need this?" asked Tiernan.

"Just keep it close." Ari gave the mushrooms another minute to soak, then handed the teacup to Tiernan. "Drink all of it."

Tiernan did as he was told, grimacing at the taste—a hint of wet dog. "How long does it take to work?"

"Around ten minutes. It'll last about three-and-a-half hours."

"Mn." Tiernan stared at the floor, rubbing the back of his neck.

"Do you have any extra blankets?"

A puzzled expression returned to Tiernan's face, and Ari accompanied him to a storage closet. He removed piles of blankets and pillows before depositing them on the living room floor.

Ari arranged the bedding to form a makeshift nest and settled atop it. Tiernan stretched out beside him. They lay in silence, listening to the sound of rain beating against the house. Thunder rumbled in the distance, the sound of giants colliding. He watched Tiernan for signs the medicine was kicking in, noticing nothing until the man squirmed uncomfortably.

"It's warm." Tiernan tugged at the collar of his shirt, fanning himself.

Ari got up, opening a window partway, enough to let in more wind than water. "Better?"

Tiernan sat facing the breeze, legs crossed, eyes closed, nodding in acknowledgement. When he opened his eyes again, a few minutes later, his pupils had swelled in size, turning Tiernan's blue eyes black, swollen with enlightenment.

"How do you feel?" asked Ari.

Tiernan gazed around the room, cringing, probably hallucinating by now. "These weasels need to leave."

"Hey. They're not hurting anything." *Weasels, huh?* Stealthy. Cunning. Traitorous. If the animal kingdom had spies, some of the most successful would be weasels. They were also helpful healers, when so inclined, and their presence was a good omen.

"But they'll eat Nika."

"As if we'd let them. Can I see Nika for a moment?"

Tiernan handed the rabbit over reluctantly. Ari cast a protective spell around Nika, surrounding him with a bubble of light, then passed him back.

Tiernan eyed Nika sceptically, shaking him. "You made him very shiny."

"He's weasel-proof now." Ari touched Tiernan's shoulder lightly, trying to reassure him. It was far too early for him to be feeling anxious. He wanted Tiernan to be relaxed when the time came to have a serious conversation.

"The king wanted to burn him," muttered Tiernan.

"Burn Nika?"

"Had to take him far away." Tiernan rocked slowly, turning Nika over in his hands.

"He's safe now." Ari placed his hands atop Tiernan's and met his gaze, smiling encouragingly. They lowered Nika to the floor, setting him aside. A ripple of black silk caught Tiernan's attention. Distress drained from his face, replaced with a sense of childlike wonderment. He bent forwards, running his fingers over the sheet.

"Woah." Tiernan grinned widely—a welcome sight. "The colours are all melty." He closed his eyes, stretching out. "Ooooh."

Whatever Tiernan saw kept him entertained for over an hour. When he finally opened his eyes, he smiled crookedly, a glint in his eyes. "That's like travelling through space, without throwing up."

"I'm glad you told me what's bothering you." Ari took the opportunity to start, unsure if he'd get another chance for Tiernan to be as relaxed as he was.

"It's driving me crazy." Tiernan inhaled deeply, exhaling slowly.

Ari took his hand, clasping their fingers together. "How long has it been an issue?"

"Around four months."

"What was going on when it started?"

"The Altricial...they threatened to kill Mae if I didn't do what they said. I didn't know her at the time, but I couldn't let them hurt her. She was just a kid. They used Finnegan's Lace to re-landscape my back and the nesting pockets to hatch infectious butterflies. They're the source of the outbreak in Enra. 5,000 dead, and counting..." Tiernan tensed. "That's a lot of bodies. Dead kids. Worst part is...if I had the chance to go back and make a different choice, I wouldn't. I couldn't."

"You're under an enormous amount of stress. People react to stress in strange ways. When did you first notice?"

"In the cave." Tiernan paused, hesitating, sighing heavily before continuing. "I was anxious...thought getting off might help. I tried, but I kept thinking about earlier... The butterflies... Impaled him... Can't even remember his name... Fuck..."

Ari gripped Tiernan's hand tighter, struck by the powerlessness of confronting a wound he couldn't heal with magick or ointment, only time and patience. "I'm sorry."

"It never works. Every time I try...nothing. I try to think about good things...but all I see is corpses of people who've died because of me."

He drew Tiernan into a hug. "We're going to fix that."

Tiernan slumped against him, resting his head against Ari's shoulder. "Maybe that witch Lamashtu cursed me when she touched me..."

"She touched you?"

"Her hands were cold...damp... She cleaned every inch of me. Some kind of cleansing ritual..."

He couldn't hold Tiernan any tighter without hurting him. "Please tell me that bitch is dead. It'll save me the trouble of hunting her down."

"I think so... The bridge exploded...she fell."

He felt the thud of Tiernan's heart. *Twenty beats per minute*. Normally cause for alarm, but in Tiernan's case revealed an alarmingly efficient and perfectly healthy heart. He could sense nothing wrong, but the lowest healthy resting heart rate he'd seen in a human was twenty-five.

"I can't imagine what Lamashtu put you through." Ari caressed the back of Tiernan's neck, a sense of worthlessness creeping back over him. He couldn't cut Tiernan open and extract the source of pain, nor prescribe a treatment he was confident in. He could only try.

"It wasn't all bad... Aisha was there... King Karnifer got overthrown. They cut his head off and fed it to the seagulls. It was the only way to appease them. Those birds are horrible... They ate someone alive, you know... I hope they get sucked into a tornado and dumped in a volcano."

"That sounds a bit like overkill to me." He stroked the pale hair at the nape of Tiernan's neck, grateful to be able to do something soothing, something human.

Tiernan rested his head on Ari's shoulder, tracing invisible lines on the floor. "There used to be a forest here. The trees must have burned down." Tiernan's finger moved to the next point of interest. "This road leads to a field with a tree where the butterflies live. They destroy everything they touch. Only the tree is immune."

He took Tiernan's hand, guiding it to a different part of the floor. "Where does this road go?"

"To the sea." Tiernan pulled away, crawling back into their nest. He paused, staring at Nika. "Mae..." Tiernan lowered his head. A sob rose from the depths of his throat, followed by a rough choke.

"Don't fight it." Ari rubbed the back of Tiernan's neck.

"Should've killed myself...maybe they would've let her live. Maybe she'd have gotten out of there before she got sick. Rian wouldn't be under fucking quarantine."

"Don't say that. Regardless of what happened, Mae wouldn't have lived much longer. Her heart couldn't take it. She was better off with you."

Tiernan shook his head, clutching Nika. "She trusted me. I did nothing."

"There's nothing you could have done. I know that hurts, but it doesn't make you responsible. I see patients like Mae all the time, where I can't do anything but permanently ease their suffering. I understand the sense of powerlessness and failure, but you have to let it go. You can't cling to all that negativity and expect to function normally, mentally or physically."

"I can't do this."

Ari touched Tiernan's cheeks, speaking firmly. "Yes, you can. Listen to me. No more satisfying your emotionally masochistic urges. Blaming yourself won't change what happened. What it will do is make you less prepared to deal with shit in the future, make you forget what it's like to feel normal. Maybe you're all right with that, but I'm not."

"Why do you care so much?"

"I don't know why it matters, only that it does. I need you to be okay." He kissed Tiernan's forehead and Tiernan melted into him, boneless, body wracked with sobs.

Tiernan pressed against him, grief passing through him with an occasional shudder, eventually calming. Ari held him for hours, long after the medicine wore off and Tiernan gave in to emotional exhaustion, falling asleep with his head on Ari's arm, head inclined towards his chest. He looked so peaceful, Ari didn't dare move and risk disturbing him, even after his arm went numb.

ARI AWOKE TO the sound of rain. A breeze blew through an open window, rustling the sheets. There was enough moonlight to read the time on his watch.

"What time is it?" asked Tiernan. He was stretched out on his side beside Ari, facing away from him. He'd taken his shirt off at some point, naked from the waist up.

"12:05 PM."

"Mnh."

"How do you feel?"

"Okay. A bit hungover."

"That's normal." Ari touched Tiernan's bare back, tracing the scars carved into his pale skin, contemplating the acts of violence which fuelled their birth. His hands wandered, searching for knots, working his way down to the symmetrical indents at the left and right of Tiernan's tailbone, locating a large knot beside the left dimple. He pressed the underside of his thumb to Tiernan's lower back and applied pressure to the knot, rubbing in a circular motion. He worked at it, determined to relax the stubborn muscle fibres, drawing a sharp gasp from Tiernan. "Did I hurt you?"

"No..." Tiernan swallowed thickly. "You're making me hard."

Ari froze. "Want me to stop?"

The answer was immediate and definitive, emphasised by a squirm of Tiernan's hips. "Don't you dare."

"Turn over." Tiernan did as instructed. Ari kissed him deeply, the way he always did in his dreams, using the heat of their mouths to reassure himself it was real. He slipped Tiernan a hint of tongue before eying Tiernan's exposed torso where a light sweat rose on Tiernan's skin. Ari's gaze settled on the tented fabric of Tiernan's sweatpants, admiring a dark stain of precome. "Mm. I see what you mean."

Ari pulled Tiernan's pants off before settling between his legs and stroking his muscular inner thighs. "You have such a beautiful dick. I feel spoiled." He stroked Tiernan from root to tip, twisting his hand around the flushed tip of his cock.

Tiernan groaned softly, arched his back, and then closed his eyes shut tight. His breath came in ragged gasps.

"Deep breaths." Ari gently squeezed the lower half of Tiernan's cock, massaging him, while his free hand rubbed its head. He focused as much on pleasuring Tiernan as he did opening blocked energy channels. It amazed him how much energy accumulated in the genitals; Tiernan's cock pulsed with more than blood, electric in his grasp.

He stroked faster. Normally he'd try to draw the moment out, to cast Tiernan onto the edge of explosion and reel him in again, and again. But Tiernan needed this and Ari had no desire to deprive him.

Ari gripped harder, pushing Tiernan closer. "Gonna come for me?"

Tears formed in the corners of Tiernan's eyes, clinging stubbornly. "Ngh... Fuck...Yes." Tiernan groaned deeply, and it was over—the accumulation of months of turmoil and frustration, vented in milky globules on his chest. He rolled onto his side, burying his face in a pillow, lying like that for a while, breathing heavily.

"Thank you." Tiernan's voice was thick with sleep, muffled by the pillow. He'd expelled an enormous amount of energy, clearly leaving him exhausted.

"My pleasure." Ari kissed the back of Tiernan's neck. "Go back to sleep."

"What about you?"

"I'm good. Sleep."

"Bossy," muttered Tiernan, drifting off.

A ROOSTER CROWED next door. The full moon remained visible despite streaks of dawn creeping over the horizon. Ari glanced at his watch, frowning at the time. He needed to get back to the hospital and prepare Anton Dane's weekly treatment—a combination of vitamins, minerals, and proteins to combat chronic exhaustion. Anton's condition had no known cause and it drove Ari crazy. He'd initially suspected Anton's mother might be draining the boy's energy as some ritual component, but nothing he'd seen gave him reason to doubt Mrs. Dane was as mystified and concerned as he was.

Ari sat up and looked for his pants. "I should get back to work."

Tiernan turned to face him. "Hang on." Tiernan's hand slid beneath his shirt, trailing down Ari's chest, caressing his skin with a serpentine motion, descending lower and lower. The muscles in Ari's thighs tensed.

Tiernan couldn't pull Ari's underwear down fast enough. In the seconds it took Tiernan to wrap his hand around him there an instance of hunger so unbearable it stung, like the sharp pang of an empty stomach. Tiernan's fingers were agile and quick, pumping his cock as if trying to quell invisible flames, serving only to fuel their glow.

Ari lay back against the bed, breathing hard, skin alight wherever Tiernan's touched him. Tiernan licked the tip of Ari's cock, sweeping his tongue over its sensitive underside. Ari shuddered and brushed Tiernan's long blond hair away from his face, overwhelmed with delight at watching him swallow his length, uncannily adept at finding all his sensitive spots. Tiernan worked his way down until his nose was buried in the thick, dark hair at the base of Ari's cock, head bobbing as he sucked.

It didn't take long for the onslaught of sensation to overwhelm him, filling Tiernan's mouth with the product of his efforts, unaccustomed to such intensity.

He lay next to Tiernan, regarding him sternly, stroking a flushed cheek. "I want you to do three things for me."

"Sounds like a lot of work," muttered Tiernan.

"It is, but I'll ensure you're suitably rewarded."

"Go on."

"First, eat something today, even if you're not hungry."

"Okay."

"Second, spend at least half an hour outside. Bonus points if you talk to someone." Ari forced himself to get up, fighting the temptation to stay home from work for the first time in his life. "Third, I expect you to spend an inordinate amount of time playing with yourself."

Tiernan's skin flushed a deeper, darker red. "I think I can manage that."

"I'll see you tonight."

DETERMINED TO DO something constructive and minimise the likelihood of dwelling on destructive thoughts, Tiernan got up and continued harvesting his garden, loading a wheelbarrow with as many fruits and vegetables as it could carry. He brought the load to Ainsley's only homeless shelter and set aside a dozen tomatoes, which he brought to Misha.

He sat beside Misha in the stable, feeding him the tomatoes one at a time, listening to the grunts of pleasure the velver made as he chewed noisily, juice everywhere. Tiernan scratched his old friend behind the ears, briefly falling asleep against him, soothed by the wavelike rise and fall of Misha's massive body. He was woken by a startled stable hand, who'd come to give Misha a massage. The stable hand left in a hurry, tripping over herself, repeating apologies like prayers.

He moved on, heading for the market. His favourite stall belonged to butcher Barry Greenwald and his daughter Mara. Mara's beauty was matched by her deadliness; she kept a metal war club beneath the counter. Tiernan had seen her use it on multiple occasions, usually on some idiot who misinterpreted her proficiency at customer service as interest in being groped and harassed, and he always admired her technique. He purchased a few links of garlic sausage and some bacon, noticing a crowd gathering nearby.

"What happened?" he asked Mara.

"Someone was teasing Branson's boy. Called him something he shouldn't've." Branson was a weaver who sold his wares in the market. His 18-year-old son, Walter, couldn't read, write, or do basic arithmetic, and was by far one of the most pleasant and affectionate people Tiernan had ever met. "Dezmodeus knocked the bastard out a few minutes ago. Guess he hasn't woken up yet."

Tiernan moved towards the crowd, grateful it wasn't any bigger—the noise and growing sea of human bodies put him on edge. A man with balding, patchy hair sat on the ground, hands over his nose, blood pouring down his face. "My node! You broke my node!" The man staggered to his feet, glaring murderously.

"Get the fuck out of here before I break the rest of you." Dezi made a shooing gesture, his knuckles torn and bleeding.

The man limped off. The crowd dispersed, allowing Tiernan to breathe better.

"You didn't have to hit him." Walter frowned at Dezi.

"I know. I wanted to. Maybe it'll inspire him to re-evaluate his vocabulary."

Walter sighed and shook his head, shuffling off. "Thanks, Dezi."

"Anytime." Dezi noticed Tiernan, raising a hand in greeting. "Hello, Tiernan."

Tiernan nodded. "Dezmodeus."

Dezi grinned widely, purple eyes glinting. "You look a lot more relaxed than the last time I saw you."

Tiernan's cheeks warmed. "I feel a bit better."

"Good."

"How's things with you?"

"Same old, same old. Debating whether or not to throw myself in a tar pit."

Tiernan couldn't tell if Dezi was serious or not, regarding him with confusion.

"Sorry, bad joke. Are you hungry?"

"Not really, but I should eat something."

"Have you tried the Malaqua's chicken skewers?"

"I haven't."

"You're in for a treat, then. This stuff is like an orgasm for your mouth."

Dezi bought them each a skewer. They sat on a bench, devouring the juicy morsels, which did indeed make his taste buds explode with pleasure on more than one occasion.

"I'm leaving next week," declared Dezi between mouthfuls. "Going to head up north for a bit, then meet up with the Altricial in Rian to buy a few black-market items. Should be an interesting trip."

"Sounds dangerous."

"I'll be careful." Dezi took the last bite, eyes closing in contentment as he chewed. "When I get back, we should do something. Maybe invite your uncle along. He's a good guy. Reminds me of your father."

"I'd like that."

Dezi stood and stretched. "I should get back to the shop. Stay out of trouble."

"Likewise."

"I'm always on my best behaviour."

Tiernan shook his head. "And I'm the patron saint of sugar cubes and tulips."

A frown crossed Dezi's face, accompanied by a wounded look. "Your old man used to say that." He shuffled off, shaking his head. "I miss that motherfucker."

ARI'S MORNING HAD been relatively uneventful. Anton's condition remained the same, neither worsening nor showing signs of improvement. He treated a broken leg, swollen tonsils, and an ear infection. In the afternoon things derailed. A young boy arrived with his left arm torn part of the way off. He was already in hypovolemic shock, blue lips standing stark against ghostly skin. Ari managed to close the wound, but the damage was already done, too much blood had been lost.

His next patient also died within less than ten minutes of arrival, an older female, badly burned. Ari's stomach was usually made of steel, but the smell of charred hair and scorched flesh always made him queasy. He managed to retain his lunch, but not without a battle, swallowing the chunky bile that rose in his throat.

In the evening Ari delivered a stillborn baby and amputated a maggot-infested, gangrenous leg on a patient who soon went into cardiac arrest and died. He was ready to leave when a teenage girl was brought in, her body mangled and crushed by a velver and the carriage it was pulling. Even Ava got involved, trying to keep the girl's guts where they belonged, but the patient's heart gave way.

He walked to Tiernan's house in a bit of a daze, trying to process the day's events without dwelling on them. He knocked on Tiernan's door. Ari must've looked worse than he thought, because the look on Tiernan's face was one of obvious alarm.

"What's wrong?" asked Tiernan.

"One of those days." Ari stepped inside, removing his shoes and hanging up his coat.

"Care to elaborate?"

"Not right now." He wanted to hear about Tiernan. Focus on something other than having the life sucked out of him. "I'd rather hear about your day."

Tiernan looked well rested. He'd gotten out of the shower not too long ago, hair still damp. He smelled so damn good, if Ari didn't feel like crap, he would've been all over him. "I did everything you asked me to do. I gardened and went for a walk. Dezmodeus bought me lunch. And you'll be pleased to know my cock got plenty of exercise."

A monstrous weight descended on Ari, as if the air itself was crushing him. "Dezmodeus Azmodian?"

"Yeah. He's the guy who stole my uncle."

Ari took a deep breath. "He's the psycho who brainwashed my parents."

"Shit. He's a friend of the family. Or something. I think he was sleeping with my mom. And possibly my dad."

Ari didn't usually talk about Dezmodeus. Doing so made him feel sick, but his anger refused to be ignored, spilling out of him in a torrent. "I used to help him prepare potions and medicinal ingredients. I was four years old when I first started. He was constantly fucked up on anything he could get to numb his pain and behaved like a tyrannical jackass. He injected me with stimulants, so I could work 50 plus hour shifts and blamed me every time he messed something up. I've been told for as long as I can remember that I need to forgive him, but I can't." He shook his head in defiance. "I hate him." Taboo words spoken in anger. His ancestors would be *really* impressed.

"Forgiving doesn't mean forgetting, but you can't force it. Maybe with time you'll feel differently. Until then, you have every right to be angry." Tiernan took Ari's hand, caressing it with his thumb. "I can stop talking to Dezmodeus if it bothers you."

"You don't have to do that, but don't trust him. You sure your mother and your uncle are both who they say they are?"

"I'm sure."

"Don't lend him any money. He'll never pay you back." There were a thousand things he could warn Tiernan about. *Don't use his jewellery cleaning services.*

Don't pay full price for Haloweed—it's fucking dandelion root. Don't buy a hairless cat from him.

"Good to know."

"My parents gave him their house in exchange for Dezmodeus's assurance they'd get a nice place to live in the afterlife."

"It's a valid concern."

He stared strangely at Tiernan for suggesting there was anything remotely logical about *giving* your house away to someone who claimed to own property in the land of the dead.

Tiernan hugged him, holding him so tightly it squeezed some of the anger out of him.

Ari nuzzled into his neck. "Sorry. I'm a bit of a wreck today."

"How can I help?"

"Take me to bed. I want to sleep for ten hours."

"Sounds like a plan."

They undressed and got into bed, Tiernan's chest pressed to Ari's back, arms around him. For a while, he was all that mattered.

ARI SLEPT FOR nine hours, which was almost as good as ten, and awoke next to a gorgeous blond who was just as hard as him. Tiernan stroked them both in unison and kissed him hungrily. Ari's lips burned from the force of Tiernan's ravenous mouth—a pleasant, lingering sting. Even after he'd showered and dressed and left feeling drunk and annoyed he couldn't spend the day in bed with Tiernan, his lips still tingled.

He went to the bank first, then the pet shop, and then the general store. Fully armed, he continued down the street, halting in front of the apothecary.

Ari hadn't spoken to Dezmodeus in over six years, since his sudden exit from the Emerald Star. He'd left Ainsley in the back of a farmer's wagon and travelled to Kerrick, on the other side of the country. He lacked a specific goal in mind, apart from getting as far away from Dezi as possible. Ironic that they should end up in the same place. He knew he was supposed to forgive Dezi, that carrying such animosity in his heart went against the teachings of the Wren, but he couldn't.

Dezi lived in the back of the apothecary, peddling rare potion-making ingredients that were often the focus of murder trials. He found Dezi at his desk, sorting through stacks of parchment. He appeared to be in his late 20's, but Ari knew he was much older. Dezi's bespectacled purple eyes were tired and rimmed with dark shadows easily mistaken for kohl.

"Here's how this is going to work," said Ari, approaching the desk. "If you don't stay the fuck away from Tiernan Aran I'm going to nail your hands and feet to the floor, extract the testes from your scrotum, fill your empty sac with razor ants, and stitch it back up again." Ari set a jar of razor ants on the counter. They clamoured across the glass, massive mandibles snapping.

Dezi leaned back in his chair and crossed his arms. "Nice to see you, too."

Ari reached into the confines of his robes, removing a hammer, placing it on the desk.

"This is criminal harassment," protested Dezi, a maniacal twinkle in his eyes. "I taught you well."

Ari placed another object on the desk. "This is a 6-1/2" railroad spike."

"I'm afraid I can't agree to those conditions."

"Why? What do you want from Tiernan?" Money, probably.

"To spend time together. That's all."

"What?"

"He's my son."

Ari stared at Dezi in disbelief, choking on his spit. "You're full of shit. His father killed himself!"

Dezi sighed. "Tiernan's mother underwent a procedure allowing for three-parent children."

"Do I look like I was repeatedly dropped on my head as an infant?"

"Hey, if I was lying I wouldn't choose an excuse that sounds batshit insane."

"You might be counting on me thinking as much, you sick fuck. What kind of procedure are you talking about?"

"It involves programming embryonic stem cells and mitochondrial DNA and a bunch of complicated shit I'm not getting into."

"Why isn't Tiernan aware of this?" Ari was annoyed with himself for considering the possibility Dezi might be telling the truth. *Don't believe anything he says. You know better.*

"I messed up. When Tiernan was three, I took him to an illegal cockatrice fight and decapitated a bookie in front of him."

"Sounds plausible."

"Yeah, well, Dem was pissed. Said I wasn't allowed around Tiernan. Something about being a terrible influence. Shouldn't have listened, but I did."

"I don't believe you." It had to be a lie. Ari shook his head, refusing to be manipulated.

"He's got a birthmark beneath his left hip bone and dimples on his lower back, assuming you've seen him naked by now."

"Any temple maiden could've told you that."

"He thinks strawberries are yucky and hates nap time." Dezi's eyes filled with tears. *Unbelievable.* Ari sensed genuine grief radiating off Dezi, but that didn't mean he wasn't putting on a convincing performance, thinking about dead pets and lost lovers. "Please."

Ari wanted to believe him, growing angry with himself for being sucked in. "For fuck's sake. If you're lying, having your balls devoured by ants will be the least of your concerns."

Dezi nodded. "Fair enough."

Ari wished he could leave, but he needed to ask. Needed the nagging to stop. "Does the name Nika mean anything to you?"

"How badly do you want to find out?"

Ari dropped a bag of gold in front of him. Dezi's eyes lit up with such intensity he could've sworn the old goat was part dragon.

"Nika was Prince Anowki of Rian's slave. He was named after a type of desert hare because his mother gave birth less than ten minutes after her water broke."

Dezi had been fascinated by the Oterai for as long as Ari had known him. He'd grown up hearing Dezi tell tales of dragons and dragon hunters. According to Dezi, long ago, when the Oterai ruled Rian, they lived peacefully with dragons. It wasn't until Rian was invaded that the first reports of dragons attacking humans were found. "Why do you ask?"

"There was a little girl... Mae. She had a toy rabbit named Nika and spoke of dragons."

"Mae was the reincarnation of Prince Anowki."

"How the fuck do you know that?"

"Hestia Aran told me. She knew Anowki two thousand years ago, when everything went to shit in Rian. She helped him escape. He's been born at least a dozen times since then. The kid dies a lot. Rarely makes it to adulthood. Combination of bad luck and poor decision making. When she came across Mae, she recognised the prince's soul. Using Mae to manipulate Tiernan was her idea. She wanted them to be together."

"*Why?*"

"Your boyfriend was the prince's bodyguard. They grew rather close."

"I don't believe you." Ari shook his head. He should never have come. He knew better than to trust Dezi. He needed to leave. "I don't believe any of this."

"Makes no difference to me." Dezi shrugged, taking out a long, bone pipe, packing the bowl with a blend of mind-altering substances.

"I meant what I said—if you hurt Tiernan, you're done."

"Stop scaring me. I'm supposed to be taking it easy. High blood pressure." Dezi lit his pipe, disappearing in a cloud of smoke. Some things never changed. Ari turned to leave. Coming here had been a mistake. What information had he gained? Dezi *might* be Tiernan's father and Mae was *supposedly* the Prince of Rian in a previous life, neither of which changed anything. Dezi was still an asshole and Mae was still dead. "Oh. If you're going to be joining the family, I suppose I should attempt to be nice to you, so here's a tip for free – you're not the only one trying to unlock the worm's secrets, but you have an advantage over the others."

"Why's that?" Ari knew better than to ask, but curiosity got the best of him.

"You're its favourite snack."

ARI CHEWED ANOTHER piece of maple candy and savoured the sweetness, enjoying the hint of dried apricot. He'd drawn too much of his own blood and grown queasy.

You're its favourite snack. The worm's response to blood fascinated him. His blood, specifically. He'd used samples generously donated by his colleagues and the worms gorged on it, growing stronger. His own blood produced a much different effect. When exposed to it, the worms shrivelled and died.

At first, he'd obsessed over what the worms were reacting to. Blood was made of red and white blood cells, platelets, and plasma– salt, protein, sugar, and fat. None of these things proved singularly responsible, leaving him faced with the possibility of blood's only other ingredient– pranic energy.

There was still so much he didn't understand. His head spun with possibilities. He thought about what happened when he'd been bitten, the vision, Tiernan's tongue in his mouth. What *was* that? Where had it come from? He needed to know more, to see more, no matter how foolish it was. He knew better, but rejected common sense in the pursuit of answers.

Instead of giving Basil the rat the pleasure of biting him again, he injected himself with the black sludge.

He walked through the temple, on his way to see what the holy chefs had prepared for lunch, lost in thoughts of pastries with smoked salmon and mushroom and a fat garlicy hunk of prime rib roast. He passed Elder Edrith's office, halting at the sight of a man seated in the hall, head in his hands. He noticed the striking white-blond hair first head in hands, striking white-blond hair. "Tiernan?"

The man raised his head. Not Tiernan—a bit older. Demetrius. Tiernan's father. Had to be. "Who're you?" Demetrius looked annoyed at having his solitude interrupted.

He swallowed thickly. "Cappa Andali, sir."

Demetrius' gaze softened instantly. "Tiernan's Cappa?"

"Yes, sir." Cappa's cheeks warmed. He was surprised Tiernan mentioned him. He sat beside Demetrius, hoping he wouldn't mind. Eight years had passed since Demetrius was last on active duty. Cappa wondered what brought him to the temple, but didn't dare ask. "It's a pleasure meeting you, sir. Tiernan told me about how you both took on the Tangorian bandits. Wish I could've seen that."

"I'd say single-handedly burning all of Jarai's defensive towers is equally impressive. Nicely done, son."

"I can't believe Tiernan told you about that."

"He tells me everything." A slight crook in Demetrius' grin indicated he meant everything.

Cappa's face grew hotter. "He has no shame."

Elder Edrith threw open his door, growling. "Demetrius. Get in here."

Demetrius stood up. "Tiernan really likes you, Cappa. Don't let him convince you otherwise."

"Thank you, sir." Cappa exhaled slowly, face on fire.

A DENSE FOG settled over Ari. He wasn't sure how long he spent staring into nothingness. A knock at the door brought him crashing back to reality. He cleared his throat, shaking the lingering haze from his head. "Come in."

Tiernan walked into the room, carrying a bag of fragrant food, making his mouth water.

"You look hungry," said Tiernan, setting the bag down, handing him a wooden container full of thinly cut, tender, barbequed beef and wild rice.

"Starving," he muttered, devouring the feast.

When he finished eating, Tiernan made his way over to Basil's cage and peered inside. "How's Basil?"

"Tiernan ..."

"Hmn?"

Ari couldn't contain it any longer, asking the questioning burning holes in his brain. "Were you involved with someone named Cappa?"

"Yeah. He was a paladin. Died a long time ago. Why?"

"The worm... It triggers something. Both times I've come into contact with it I've seen flashes of Cappa's life. First kissing you, then talking to your father. He knew details about a mission Cappa had been on. He knew you were... together."

Tiernan drew in a deep breath. "You remind me of Cappa. He liked ordering me around."

Ari's face warmed. "I can't help it. Makes me feel good to know a paladin thinks I'm worth listening to." He patted the examination table. "Sit down."

Tiernan sat on the edge of the table, flushed and speechless.

Ari bit down lightly on the lobe of Tiernan's ear, making him groan. "You make me feel invincible."

"I never told Cappa how I felt about him," murmured Tiernan, kissing Ari's mouth. "I'm not making that mistake with you." He swallowed thickly and summoned his courage. "Only the brightest light can banish unruly shadows. You are that extent."

"You are that extent," repeated Ari. "Worth coming back for."

Chapter Thirty

YEAR 2025 CE
2,075 Years Ago

Earth

The heat stifled him, sticking to Reisen like an oppressive film and saturating the blue fabric of his uniform with sweat. He took a gulp of cold water before pressing the bottle against his forehead.

"The air conditioning should be fixed soon," said Gina Danforth, public affairs officer for Project Minokawa at NASA. "Please leave your clothes on for the time being."

It's like she can read my mind.

"Better tell building maintenance to hurry. Our Canadian is melting." Colonel Branden Anderson, a member of the U.S. Air Force, spoke with a slight southern accent. Reisen sighed with relief as Bran placed a water bottle on the back of his neck, the condensation a treat against overheated skin. Bran was an aeronautics engineer from Savannah, Georgia, and one hell of a test pilot. His blond hair, blue eyes, and muscular physique drew inevitable comparisons to Captain America, which were met with an appropriate degree of modesty. At 32, he was also the youngest member of the crew. A decade younger than Reisen.

"I want to review a few things before going to the press room."

No one expected that by the year 2025, humans would be ready to enter the next phase of space exploration. Their ship was nothing as grand as Starship Enterprise, but the Minokawa had a fully functional gravity wheel, graphene skin, and ion drive, all made possible by advances in disruptive technology. Such advances wouldn't have been possible without a combination of private industry and taxes collected from the legalisation of marijuana in the United States and Canada. The Minokawa was designed for short-range space exploration and testing the logistics of long-term survival aboard a spaceship. An onboard garden, for which Reisen was responsible, provided enough oxygen and food for a crew of nine. At least that was the goal. Whether it worked as well in practice as it did in theory and test exercises remained to be seen.

"I'm aware some of you take press conferences more seriously than others, and I'd like to establish a few ground rules." Gina looked directly at Reisen as she said it. Here we go... "This should go without saying, but watch your language." He sunk lower in his chair. "No jokes about bodily functions, masturbation, or sex."

"You're determined to suck all the fun out of this, aren't you?"

"I mean it, Kaneko. If anyone raises the subject of sexual relations between crew members, your response will be what?"

"NASA has no official policy against sex in space, but the NASA Astronaut Code of Professional Responsibility emphasises maintaining professional standards. We're there to work, not fu—fool around. With our demanding *work schedules and monk-like dedication to our craft, sex will undoubtedly be the furthest thing from our minds." Gina appeared satisfied by his response, but the warmth of Bran's hand on his thigh was a reminder there was no way in hell he was going three years without getting laid.*

Reisen awoke on the basement floor. He sat up, wiping tears from his eyes and drool from the corner of his mouth. Naida's condition was steadily declining, requiring more time and effort to care for her. It drained him to the point where even Keita had started asking if he was all right, allowing some small measure of concern to penetrate a wall of indignation. His son rarely spoke to him. When he did it was in as few syllables as possible, usually "no," "yes," or "okay." Keita preferred spending time with his mother. They spent hours listening to music and playing cards

Only lately, with Naida's psychological condition deteriorating, Reisen kept her sedated most of the time and his son now spent most of his time on the couch, smoking marijuana and playing video games. He could almost be mistaken for a normal teenager. He longed to join him, but it stood to reason the moment he caved in and smoked a joint all hell would break loose. Naida's heart would fail or the house would catch on fire or Aggnaroth would show up to inform him the zombie apocalypse was upon them.

He dragged his feet up the basement stairs, one agonising step at a time, trying to think good thoughts.

Richard Dean Anderson in a brown leather jacket and Calgary Flames cap.

Nanaimo bars.

MC1R. *Moksgm'ol.*

ALL DAY BREAKFAST.

Joe Carter hitting the home run that won the Toronto Blue Jays the 1993 World Series. Their second consecutive victory. Carter bounded around the plates with such enthusiasm he'd been terrified he'd miss one. "Don't worry," his father reassured him. "He won't miss."

Circle. Circle. Triangle. Square. Circle. Square. Triangle.

Vancouver winters. The smell of rain.

Haleakalā Observatory, 10,000 feet in the air. Bran. Wrapping the freezing American in a blanket, because they never thought to bring warm clothes to Hawai'i. Watching the sun rise above the clouds, listening to Sigur Rós, thinking, *I want this to be my Groundhog Day.*

God, no. That wasn't helping. Made the pain worse. Reisen stumbled towards the fridge. Crashed into it. He tugged the door open and chugged cold coca tea straight out of a jug. Anything to get his energy levels back up. Hopefully he'd stay awake long enough to have a conversation with his son before slipping into temporary oblivion. He cut several handfuls of wheatgrass, shoving them into a grinder. He swallowed several ounces of the frothy green fluid, grimacing. Sometimes it tasted like freshly cut peas, an English garden. This batch landed closer to the lawn clippings end of the spectrum.

"You okay?" Keita peered at him from across the kitchen.

"Yes."

"Doesn't look like it."

"Need sleep. That's all."

"Go to bed."

"Sit with me for a bit." Keita frowned. Nodded. The teenager's appearance evoked memories of Reisen's Scottish mother. His Japanese father.

Reisen stumbled into the living room and sat on the couch. He looked at the television and smiled. "Playing Little Nemo, eh?"

"It's weird. This kid dreams about drugging animals with candy and stealing their skins after they fall asleep."

"Hey, man. Nemo's the dream master. He can do whatever he wants. Besides, he doesn't skin all the animals. Some he enslaves."

Keita grunted. His pyjama-clad character belly-flopped onto the back of a snail, impaling himself on its spiky purple shell, depleting the last of his health squares, dying.

"Takes time and patience to get good at some of these games. When I was a kid, video game developers had a slightly sadistic streak. If you want an exercise in pain and frustration, try playing *The Adventures of Bayou Billy*."

"No, thanks."

"Or you could try going on a *real* adventure and go buy me a can of cherries. I'll make cheesecake."

"I'm not going outside."

"It may seem like a terrible idea, but it's so much cooler out there than it is in here."

"I hate the cold."

"That's not what I... Never mind. Look, I know it's not easy, I know it stresses you out, but you can't let that stop you. I'm worried you're going to get tired of staring at the TV and start sewing corsets out of human skin. You can't isolate yourself like this. It's not healthy."

"You're one to talk. Look at you! You spend 90% of your time in the basement, losing a battle you have no hope of winning, trying to save someone who no longer recognises their own name. You're not doing it for Mom anymore. You're doing it for yourself, because you can't let her go."

"There has to be a way."

"If there was, don't you think you'd have figured it out by now? You've exhausted every option. Tried every experiment. Subjected her to every possible combination of medicine and magick and insanity you can come up with. Nothing works. She's getting worse and all you can do is convince yourself this is somehow acceptable. You're hurting her. She would have been happy to go years ago, but she's more afraid of you feeling like a gigantic failure than she is of dying."

"She told you that?" An invisible blade piercing his left side, digging downwards into his guts.

"She said she was afraid of disappointing you. She doesn't want you to feel like you wasted the last thirteen years on her." The blade twisted in his side. Bleeding out. "I'm not saying you have to do it tonight...just think about it."

"I'll put it on my to-do list." He staggered to his feet and wobbled in the direction of his bedroom.

"Hey... Reisen...get some sleep."

He grunted noncommittally.

"Reisen!"

"I heard you. Sheesh." He closed the door, pressing his back to it. Maybe it would be good to sleep. He flopped on the bed, burying his face in his pillow. The urge to scream rose from a void in his chest, catching half-formed in his throat.

KEITA ATTEMPTED TO navigate around an angry snake, stunning it with a barrage of candy to the head, but it regained consciousness and stole his last life. Just as well. He needed a break. The strange game, written in a language he didn't understand, required a lot of mental energy to play. He had to pay close attention. Had to try hard to remain calm and not scream and throw things at the TV, which wasn't easy when he kept falling in the same stupid hole.

Keita entered the bathroom and undressed before stepping into the shower. Hot water streamed down his body, the perfect temperature. Despite the soothing stream, his body tensed with annoyance. Why go outside when he didn't have to? There was no telling what could be out there, or how he might react.

The doorbell rang, scaring him, the shrill noise piercing his body like an electric shock. *Aggnaroth*. Had to be. No one else ever visited. He turned the shower off, jumped out, and wrapped a towel around his waist. The doorbell chimed again, making him cringe. He stalked towards the door and tugged it open, glaring.

His eyes widened. Not Aggnaroth. Auryn. He threw himself outside, into Auryn's arms, bare feet freezing on the cold porch, worth every second of pain.

"Keita." Auryn hugged him. Keita clung to the man, disappearing into the thick fur of Auryn's coat. He could have stayed buried there forever, lost in him.

"I can't believe you're here."

Auryn drew him inside, out of the cold. "Figured it was about time I saw how you and your daddy are getting along. Is he around?" Auryn removed his boots and hung his coat by the door.

"He's asleep, or at least he'd better be. He's been acting like a lunatic."

"I see nothing's changed."

"He won't let my mom go, even though it's hopeless. He doesn't sleep. Barely eats. Torments himself over his inability to do anything." It all came pouring out of him. The terrible truth. "I'm more worried about him than I am about her."

"I've seen how he gets. Can't blame you for being concerned."

"I'll be right back. Going to go put some clothes on." He left, dressing in record time, hurrying back to Auryn, sitting beside him on the couch.

"Reisen would spend eternity trying to fix this, like some twisted form of punishment." Keita rested his head against Auryn's shoulder, closing his eyes. "I want him to stop hurting himself."

"Reisen has always been stubborn. Monomaniacal."

"Is that another way of saying he's a selfish jerk?"

"Not exactly. He's prone to obsessing over things. If it's not one thing, it's another. He needs something concrete to anchor to, otherwise he gets lost inside his head. Wanders into dark places. I think it's more of a survival mechanism than an act of selfishness."

"I never thought about it that way. Guess it helps to have something to focus on." The lure of distraction was a familiar concept. Working with Arandano and Winkie gave him a reason to get out of bed in the morning. Means of diverting his attention from unpleasant things. He'd never fully understood Auryn's reason for insisting on his involvement, until now.

"Reisen's been through a lot, Kei." Auryn's fingers grazed the back of his neck, sending a ripple of warmth down his spine. "Dwelling on the past isn't good for him."

"Point taken." He looked Auryn over intently, noting an obvious improvement. Unlike the last time he'd seen him, he looked good. Healthy. It stung that it took the complete removal of him from Auryn's life for the man to regain his health, as if he'd recovered from an excruciating illness, cut out a malignant growth. "How are you holding up?"

"Well, I'm no longer stationed at the Farm. I've been working for Emperor Haken."

"Doing what?" A hint of relief. Maybe his absence hadn't made all the difference. Maybe he wasn't the source of infection.

"Lately I've been flying out of the country, running errands Haken doesn't trust Prince Elia to complete."

He pictured soaring through the air at incredible speed. Climbing higher and higher. The planet's frozen bulk growing smaller and smaller. An infinite array of stars. "That sounds nice."

"Yeah? I'll have to take you with me sometime."

"How high do you go?"

"High enough to rearrange your perspective."

"I'd like that," he muttered and pressed a cheek to Auryn's leg, resting his head in his lap.

"Someone needs to make sure Reisen holds it together. Let Aggnaroth know if he starts acting stranger than usual. I'm talking monster-proofing the kitchen and walking around mumbling about giving the fat kid his glasses back."

Keita stretched out over the couch, trying not to think about how good Auryn smelled. "Reisen told me you guys used to be together. I don't know what you saw in him."

Auryn's cheeks darkened. "He's not perfect, Kei, but neither am I. Your daddy was the first person to make me feel like it was okay to be different. To question things. To feel things normal people aren't supposed to feel."

"When did you realise you're...different?"

"I always suspected, but it wasn't until I met Reisen that I knew for sure. I couldn't stop staring at him. I was afraid he'd notice and report me for being a pervert."

"How come you never told me?"

"I didn't want you to think I was a deviant or worry about me taking advantage of you. I wanted you to feel safe."

"It wouldn't have made me trust you any less."

"Didn't want to risk it."

A door opened down the hall. Reisen emerged, dragging his feet. He shambled into view, pushing his long hair away from his face, tired eyes struggling to maintain focus. He looked at Auryn and stumbled back.

"Think I might be dreaming..."

"Want me to pinch you?" asked Keita.

"Why not? Can't hur—Ow."

"Sorry to drop by unannounced." Auryn tensed, awkwardly meeting Reisen's gaze.

"Please tell me you see him too." Reisen sat on the floor in front of them, head in his hands.

"See who?"

Auryn shoved him lightly. "Keita. That's enough."

Keita sat up, sighing. "Can't sleep?"

"I tried. No luck. Too many things rattling around inside my brain. It's like a tin box full of possessed marbles."

"Reisen. Come with me." Auryn got off the couch, hauling Reisen to his feet.

"God, you smell good." They disappeared down the hall. "This is the best psychotic episode I've had in a long time."

AURYN CLOSED THE door to Reisen's room behind him. He stood face-to-face with the man, awkwardly searching for words that refused to materialise, beginning to panic until Reisen flung his arms around him and hugged him close.

"Ryn..."

"Hmn?"

"Thank you."

"For what?"

"Taking care of Keita."

"I'm pretty sure he's the one who took care of me. I was kind of a mess for a while."

He guided Reisen over to the bed, lying down with him. Reisen closed his eyes, breathing slowing. After a minute, Auryn wondered if he'd fallen asleep, but Reisen spoke up again. "What happened to your son? Keita told me he died, but he didn't know much about it."

"Danicka..." Bile rose in his throat. He hated the sound of his late wife's name. Hated the inevitable dose of anger, guilt, and shame which accompanied it. He could hardly stand thinking it, let alone saying it. "She... I... I wasn't a very good husband. Physically, I was present, but mentally, emotionally... I was elsewhere. Danicka... I think she felt ignored. Like she didn't matter. I wasn't exactly receptive to her needs. She got sick. I knew something was off, but didn't want to deal with it. Didn't care as much as I should have. I came home from work one day and she..." He shook his head, pressing his forehead to Reisen's shoulder. "She killed him. She said she couldn't stand the thought of him growing up to be like me. I don't remember doing it, but I drowned her in the bathtub."

Reisen lowered his head, dissolving into a flood of tears. "I'm so sorry."

"It was a long time ago." He tried to resonate reassurance, as if the passage of time had eroded his pain, but the wound still sounded fresh. Gangrenous. "Some lessons are harder than others."

"Some teachers are assholes," muttered Reisen.

"Elia covered the whole thing up. Even deleted the security footage." He hadn't known until he started working at the Farm that his apartment had been under surveillance. That all private residences in the capital were under surveillance.

"Bless his black heart." Reisen rubbed his eyes. "How do you know he's protecting you and not manipulating you?"

"What do you mean?"

"You don't remember killing Danicka and you're one of the least murderous people I know. I find it hard to believe you'd do something like that. Elia terrorising you into admiring him is a much more likely scenario."

Auryn appreciated Reisen's attempt to console him, but knew he was wrong. Maybe he couldn't recall any specifics, but he remembered how he felt afterwards—the overwhelming weight of guilt, the knowledge that everything had gone horribly wrong and it was all his fault. "You're biased. You hate Elia and you think I'm adorable." He realised his mistake right away, clearing his throat, cursing himself for being presumptuous. "Or used to, anyway."

"Still do." Reisen kissed his cheek. "Can you take Keita for a few days? He needs to get out of this house. Hasn't left since he showed up."

"I can, but I don't like the idea of you being here alone."

"I've gone this long without burning the place down. Give me a little credit. Take him somewhere warm."

"Are you sure?"

"I'll be fine. I can call Aggy if I need anything. He loves an excuse to come over and lose horrifically at *Smash Brothers*."

He eyed Reisen sceptically.

"Don't look at me like that." Reisen took his hand, entwining their fingers. "I want Keita to know the truth. If I tell him we're in the dark because asshole aliens have blocked out the sun with holographic projectors, he's going to think I've lost it. He doesn't know anything... We haven't talked about the shit that went down before all this... I don't think he remembers much... I'm afraid to ask."

"Why?"

"I don't want him to hate me. He may not remember now, but if I start asking questions, it might trigger something."

Auryn hunted for any memory of what Reisen might be referring to, but found nothing. What little he did recall came in brief flashes. A fountain spewing green water. Trees covered in moss. Insects glowing in the dark. A shiny aluminium airplane. Reisen laughing, his nose covered in blue ice cream.

"Reisen... How old are you?"

"2,115. Give or take a year or two. Don't worry, I'm not a vampire. The Anorians altered my genes. Rude."

"The Minokawa crashed... they took you..."

"Those hellpigs shot us down. They executed everyone except you and me."

Auryn shuddered. "What makes us so special?"

"We're aethers. Old souls. The Anorians would rather put us to work than kill us. It's the only reason I'm still alive. That and Elia has admitted to having *zero* interest in fucking my corpse."

He could have lain in bed with Reisen all day, but the man could barely keep his eyes open. "I should go. I'm keeping you awake."

"I love when you keep me awake," murmured Reisen. "I missed you."

"I missed you, too." He kissed Reisen's forehead and retreated, sliding out of bed. "Get some sleep."

"Make sure Keita says goodbye to Naida."

KEITA SAT AT the edge of the couch, head craned towards the hall, listening. His heart beat wildly. He knew it was only a matter of time before Reisen and Auryn got back together. There was nothing he could do to stop it. It shouldn't have mattered. He had no right to protest. No reason to be upset. Auryn didn't want him. It wasn't as if Reisen was stealing him. Auryn belonged with Reisen and it frustrated Keita more than he thought possible.

A door opened down the hall. He slid towards the middle of the couch, trying to look disinterested. Auryn sat next to him. His clothing looked undisturbed, smelled the same. Keita breathed a shaky sigh of relief. His eyes burned, filling with tears. This wasn't how he wanted Auryn to see him. Why did he always have to be so pathetic? *Stupid. Stupid. Stupid.*

Auryn gripped him by the shoulders, "Keita. What's wrong?"

Everything was wrong, but he said the first thing that came to mind. "I hate being here without you."

Auryn drew him into a hug, rubbing his back. "Come with me, then. Just for a few days. Your daddy shouldn't be left unsupervised long."

"Really?" Keita pressed his face to Auryn's shoulder, breathing deep.

"I need to make a phone call. Go pack a few things and say goodbye to your mama."

Keita packed hastily, tossing a few pairs of clothes and necessities. When he finished, he could still hear Auryn talked on the phone and headed for the basement.

"Mom?" She hadn't said anything in weeks. He wasn't sure if she could hear or not. Moments of lucidity had grown further and further apart until she no longer gave any indication of understanding anything around her. There was nothing of her left, just an empty shell resembling his mother. Still, he kissed her forehead, feeling terrible for wishing her body would fail and she would be free. It would be an act of mercy for everyone involved, especially Reisen.

When he emerged from the basement, Auryn had hung up the phone.

"Ready?"

"Yeah. Let's go." Keita's heart thudded wildly. Stomach acid rose in his throat. He got as far as the front door before he stopped, shaking. "I haven't been outside since I got here." It wasn't worth the risk. What if they got separated? What if Auryn got hurt or sick or killed? What if Reisen went crazier than usual while they were gone? His brain dredged up every excuse it could find to feel anxious, no matter how absurd, revolting against him, engaging in full-on mutiny. What if the funny-tasting berries he ate four days ago made him sick and he needed a bathroom, but there wasn't one because he was outside the Goddamn house? WHAT IF HE STARTED SHAKING LIKE THIS IN PUBLIC?

Everyone would know something was wrong with him. Everyone would know he was a freak.

Auryn stood with him by the door, resting a hand on his shoulder. "Breathe. Take all the time you need."

Keita forced himself to take deep, slow breaths, berating himself with each inhalation. *Pathetic. Useless. Weird.* "It shouldn't be so hard. Why do I feel like going outside is the worst fucking thing that can happen to a person when I know damn well it's not?"

"I don't know, Kei. What I do know is I'm not going to let anyone hurt you and we can come back whenever you want."

"Where are we going?"

"An island to the south."

"*South*?" There was nothing south, only endless fields of ice and snow.

"I think you might like it."

"Isn't it cold there?"

"No. It's quite warm. Compared to here, anyway."

Keita stepped forwards, exiting the house.

Chapter Thirty-One

KEITA WORRIED FLYING would be hard on his nerves, but found it weirdly exhilarating. Instead of feeling out of place, he felt safe. In control, despite everything that could go wrong. His brain miraculously chose to ignore dying in a horrific plane crash as a potential source of anxiety, for which he was immensely grateful.

The plane climbed higher and higher. Auryn handed him a pair of glasses with black lenses. "What're these for?" It was so dark outside; he couldn't see anything as-is.

"Put them on. Trust me."

Keita did as he was told, thoroughly confused until they climbed to 60,000 ft and the sun became visible in the distance, flooding the sky with brightness. He'd always wanted to see the sun, yet his focus was drawn to Auryn, the sun pale in comparison to his light.

"What stops the light from reaching the ground?" asked Keita, forcing himself to look out the window.

"Emperor Haken told me it's because the Ibarans block out the sun with hologram towers. He neglected to mention sharing control of this technology with the Emperor of Ibara. Turns out, Emperor Haken and Emperor Jaden are brothers, working for a company owned by their father. They're part of an alien race known as the Anorians and are occupying the planet illegally."

"How do they get away with this?"

"No one has presented any evidence against them." Auryn smiled reassuringly, making him feel weightless. "We're going to change that."

LANDING WAS LIKE arriving on another planet. The ocean went on forever, then out of nowhere Keita spotted land beneath them, partially shrouded in fog. Auryn avoided the fog, touching down on the southern part of the island. Everything about the island was new—the smell of salt in the air, the warmth of the sun on his face, the sound of nearby waves. It should have terrified Keita, but for the first time in a long time he felt more excitement than fear.

They entered a massive two-story wooden house. Keita had never seen a house built out of wood. Its beauty eroded his apprehension over staying in a strange place. "Whose house is this?"

"Aggnaroth's brother, Dezmodeus. He owns houses all over the place."

Dezmodeus... The name sounded familiar, but Keita couldn't place it. He marvelled at the craftsmanship involved in creating such an aesthetically pleasing living space. A grand set of stairs were framed by ornately carved bannisters depicting fish fighting their way upstream, leaping over rocks, curls of water crashing around them. Keita admired the ripples in the walls, the natural grain of the wood striking in its simplicity. He finished unpacking his things, taking one of ten bedrooms—whomever built the house clearly had accommodating lots of people in mind. Auryn took the room next to him, close but not close enough.

"Want to go for a walk?" asked Auryn. "I've been assured there's nothing out there that can eat us."

Keita smiled at Auryn's attempt to ease his anxiety and took a deep breath. "All right."

Auryn handed him a bottle from his backpack. "Put this on wherever the sun's going to touch you—your hands, your ears, everything. Otherwise, it'll burn you."

Keita applied the bottle's contents, questioning his wisdom in agreeing to wander around a strange island under the mercy of a blazing sun. Auryn did the same, taking no chances.

Once outside, Keita relaxed a bit, sticking close to Auryn. They walked along the beach, sand sticking to Keita's bare feet.

"Has Reisen told you anything about Aggnaroth's plan?" asked Auryn, pocketing his hands.

"No. He hasn't mentioned it."

"We've collected a decent amount of evidence against the Anorians. The problem is getting it to someone who can turn it over to the proper authorities. Aggnaroth has someone in mind, but we're not sure where he is. We need to get the evidence off the planet before we can do anything. In order to do that, once your mama passes, Reisen's going to turn himself in."

"What?"

"Haken wants to send Reisen to an off-world colony. He also wants to erase his memory, so he'll have no idea who he is. Fortunately, the chip Aggnaroth is implanting in Reisen's body to store the evidence will have the ability to shock Reisen with enough spiritual energy to restore his memory. You can erase an experience from the mind, but the soul retains information, internalising every experience. It remembers. It's like saving data from your computer on a backup drive. Even if the computer gets wiped, the data still exists."

"How do you know the Anorians won't kill him?" There were so many things that could go wrong. Haken could kill Reisen, despite everything. The chip could malfunction. The thought of Reisen forgetting him all over again bothered him.

"Dezmodeus insists they won't. He says Reisen's more dangerous to the Anorians dead than alive and they're well aware of that."

Despite Auryn's reassurance, Keita remained sceptical. "Isn't there anything else we can do?"

"Well... Aggnaroth suggested using Jaden's daughter, Jada, to help. She's in love with him and finds her family's behaviour deplorable, but Dezmodeus won't allow it. Says he'd rather sew his mouth to Haken's asshole and spend eternity choking on shit than trust an Anorian."

"Dezmodeus..." He'd seen something in the temple... something he'd forgotten about. A man with wings. *Fuck things up again, Dezmodeus, and I'll cut your cock off.* "Did Elia cut his wings off?"

Auryn's eyes widened in surprise. "Yes. You remember that?"

"Sort of." He could recall the sound of metal on bone. Trying to stop the bleeding. Failing. "I tried to help."

"What else do you remember?"

"That's about it." Something strange had happened at the temple. He'd received no diving blessing. More like a curse. "Why do I have someone else's memories?"

"They're from a previous lifetime. You were part of a crew working against the Anorians around two thousand years ago when they first established their presence on the island."

Aliens. Reincarnation. Keita could see why Reisen hadn't discussed any of this with him. He would've called

Aggy and informed him Reisen's brain had finally melted. "Who else was in the crew?"

"At first it was just you and me. I was an astronaut from a planet called Earth. I worked with Reisen and fell in love with him. Our spaceship was brought down by the Anorians. We were both forced to serve in the Anorian military, but I was rescued. Reisen wasn't. We tried to get him back, but..." Auryn shook his head solemnly. "Dezmodeus joined next, then Aggnaroth. We eventually picked up three more—Kai, Nika, and Anowki."

The energy required to process the information, and refrain from throwing a fit over the fact Auryn had been in love with Reisen for the last two thousand fucking years, wore him out.

"I'm sorry. I know it's a lot. We don't have to talk about it anymore." Auryn stopped and pulled him close, hugging him, water lapping at their feet.

Keita pressed his face to Auryn's shoulder, breathing him in. He wished he could move back in with Auryn, but he'd seen the unfortunate affect his presence had on the man, the stress he'd put on him. If Haken found out he was still alive, Auryn would be screwed.

They made their way back to the house. Keita's neck tingled with a faint streak of red and he was glad he'd taken Auryn's advice to apply sunblock.

Auryn cooked garlic shrimp and made crab dip loaded with cheese. Keita gorged himself to the point of almost bursting, regretting nothing.

When the time came for bed, he debated asking, but finally worked up the courage. "Can I sleep with you?"

"Sure."

He'd slept with Auryn over a thousand times, but never felt so nervous crawling into bed with him. Time spent without him had done nothing to diminish his feelings. Any anger towards Auryn had long-since evaporated.

They both wore pyjama pants, naked from the waist up. He noticed something he'd never seen before—faint, pinkish raised markings, mostly on Auryn's chest. "What happened?"

"There was an explosion. I was injured." Auryn rolled onto his back and stared at the ceiling. "I attached a bomb to the undercarriage of the vehicle and detonated it after I dropped you off. You made everything I'd endured up to that point worthwhile, but without you... Without you, there was no point. I was stressed out... not thinking straight. I expected the explosion to kill me."

Keita touched Auryn's cheek, his heart pounding. He'd known there was something wrong with Auryn, but never expected him to do something as extreme as kill himself. He wasn't sure how to respond and blurted out the first thing that came to mind. "I'm glad you're still here."

"It was a mistake. Won't happen again."

"Tell me the next time you feel that bad. Don't suffer alone. I don't know what I could've done to help, but I would've tried."

"I didn't want you to worry."

"I'd rather worry about you than lose you."

"Okay." Auryn turned back towards him, cheeks flushed with colour.

Keita tried not to stare at the scars on his chest. "Thanks for bringing me here. It's nice."

"Thanks for coming with me. It was Reisen's idea. He figured you could use a change of scenery. It's not too stressful?"

"No."

"Good."

Keita closed his eyes and listened to the ocean. "I like the sound of the waves." It soothed him, washing away unwelcome thoughts.

"Me, too." Auryn shifted a little closer. "When Reisen's gone, do you want to stay in Ibara?"

"I'd rather be close to you." Keita quickly elaborated. "If that's okay. I don't want to cause any trouble."

"I'll make it work." Auryn yawned, prompting him to do the same. "Things aren't the same without you."

A fuzzy sensation spread through Keita's body, warming him. Auryn didn't want him, but still wanted him around. Not as a lover, but a friend. All Keita had to do was get over his stupid obsession. Move on. Banish every impure thought from his mind. As if that wasn't something he'd been trying to do for seven years. He'd just have to try harder.

A GUNSHOT RANG out and Keita heard himself scream with a voice that wasn't his own. He woke up, panicked, thrashing, concerned with only one thing. Auryn. Was Auryn okay?

Auryn sat up next to him, dazed. "Keita?"

Auryn appeared unharmed, but he'd definitely heard something. Keita bolted out of bed and ran for the front door. A large window showed the well-manicured front yard and dense forest beyond. No sign of activity in the driveway. No strange vehicles. The house was silent, apart from the sound of wind and waves. No creak of intruders, no indication of life apart from his own frantic heartbeat pulsing in his ears.

"Whatcha doin'?" asked Auryn, joining him at the door, his eyes still half-closed.

"I heard a noise..." Keita felt like an idiot. There was no sign of anything amiss, yet he was shaking and unconvinced they weren't under attack. "Must be nothing... Sorry."

Auryn put an arm around him. "We can go outside and take a look."

"It's stupid... Sorry."

"Stop apologising. And it's not stupid. If it'll help you worry less, it's worth it." Auryn led the way upstairs and out onto the upper balcony, which wrapped all the way around the top floor of the house. With a better view of the driveway, he confirmed an absence of visible threats and reminded himself to breathe, sticking close to Auryn. They moved to the back of the house, where the ocean became visible, illuminated by a curious object hovering above the water, bright and pale, like a night sun.

"What is that thing?" asked Keita, gesturing towards the glowing orb.

"The moon." Auryn grinned. "I can't think of anything more beautiful."

"I can." He wanted to hold Auryn so badly his arms ached. *We all want things we can't have, Kei.* "Can we stay out here for a bit?"

"Sure."

He sat with Auryn in a cushioned area overlooking the water. "Do you remember a lot from before?"

"No. Aggnaroth had to tell me everything. When I was injured, he injected me with inkworm to speed up the healing process, but the memories that surfaced were from when I was little. I was born in a country south of here, called Calder. When I was four, Dezmodeus abducted me. Left me on the doorstep of an orphanage in

Terasyn, hoping when I grew up I'd be in a position to spy on Haken. Going any further back is hard. Everything is fragmented. Random images. Rarely more than a single moment in time." Auryn wrapped an arm around him. "But I remember you. You dyed your hair the same colour it is now."

"How do you know it's me?" Maybe Aggnaroth was wrong; a case of mistaken identity.

"Every soul has a unique vibration...like a fingerprint. The guy I saw didn't look much like you, apart from the hair, but he *felt* like you. Does that make sense?"

"Sort of."

"I remember sitting at a desk, working on a computer. Trying to, anyway. I had a bad headache... everything was too bright... I could barely see. I got upset. Next thing you know, you're there, and it all didn't seem so bad."

He touched Auryn's forehead gingerly and tried to visualise what might have happened, recalling the desperate panic he'd woken in earlier. "Your head... someone shot you." He shuddered, leaning into Auryn. "I was afraid you were going to die."

Auryn smiled reassuringly. "Apparently I'm hard to kill."

"Good thing." Keita clung to him, grateful just to be with him.

KEITA AWOKE IN bed, taking a moment to orient himself. He'd fallen asleep outside. Auryn must've carried him inside. He sat up, wondering where Auryn had gone. The smell of pancakes hit him, answering his question. He got up and headed downstairs, stomach growling.

"Morning."

"Morning. Did you sleep okay?"

"Yeah." There'd been no more bad dreams. Only blissful nothingness.

Auryn's phone went off and he answered it, brows furrowed in annoyance. "Hello? Ah, okay." There was a long pause. "I see. We'll head back right away. Thanks, Aggnaroth."

Keita's anxiety flared. He guessed the news before Auryn told him.

"Aggnaroth went over to check on Reisen and found him cremating your momma in the backyard."

Keita closed his eyes. "Finally."

Auryn's arms tightened around him. The information was not unexpected—he'd seen how sick his mother was when he left—yet it still stung.

Chapter Thirty-Two

KEITA PREPARED HIMSELF for the worst, but Reisen hadn't moved since Aggnaroth found him. He sat in the backyard, wearing a white shirt and a black tie beneath a heavy black jacket. Naida's remains lay on a pyre, reduced to bones and ash.

Auryn approached first, placing a hand on Reisen's shoulder. "Rase."

Reisen stared at the remains, fixated, frowning deeply, "It's odd... The things that stick in your mind... refusing to be expunged, while others just fade away."

Keita exchanged helpless expressions with Auryn. "Reisen, I'm sorry about Naida. You did everything you could."

"I failed miserably, but thanks." Reisen drank from a flask, shuddering.

Keita snatched the flask from him, sniffing its contents. "What're you drinking?"

"I have no idea, but I'm sure it's fine. I scraped the mould off."

Keita took a swig, breathed fire. He coughed harshly, seeing purple dots. "It's disgusting."

"Might be an acquired taste." Reisen reclaimed the flask and pocketed it. "I'd like your help with something, Keita."

"What?"

Reisen got up and placed an urn next to Naida's bones. He held out a pair of smoothly worn wooden sticks, one paler than the other, offering them to Keita. "We're keeping Naida's bones. You can help me collect them. We start from the feet and work our way up."

"*Why?*"

Reisen regarded him blankly. "Otherwise she'll be upside down."

Keita sighed and watched the way Reisen used the sticks to pick up bones, squeezing the tips together to capture them. It took him a while to get the hang of it, shakily moving his mother one piece at a time.

He managed to wrangle a particularly large bone, but his grasp was precarious.

"Pass it to me," said Reisen.

Keita handed it over, the cold getting to him, fingers going numb. Reisen expertly took the bone and reverently placed it in the urn.

Acknowledging Keita's discomfort, Reisen sped up, grabbing certain pieces, leaving others. He reached Naida's neck, retrieving a triangular shaped bone. The bone went into the urn and Reisen covered it with a piece of skull, muttering to himself. He seemed satisfied, placing the lid on the urn.

"Can we please go inside? I'm freezing my balls off."

"Go ahead. I'll be in shortly."

REISEN STUMBLED INTO the living room, burning all over as his skin warmed from the cold. He lay on the floor and stared at the ceiling. It rippled in calming waves. The carpet was warm and fuzzy and soft. Reisen wanted to cover himself with it, to amalgamate with it, become more carpet than man. *Cousin It.*

He shut his eyes, trying to think of anything other than Naida.

Fishing with Bran on the Skeena River. Fresh sockeye.

Mario Maker. Those fucking kaiza levels. Ain't no one got time for that shit.

Zihuantanejo.

John Lithgow screaming at a sasquatch, tears rolling down Reisen's eight-year-old face.

Madmartigan.

Walking with his father, near their house in Vancouver. Early evening. Snow falling in thick chunks. No wind. Warm and happy.

Keita stretched out next to him on one side, Auryn on the other.

Reisen closed his eyes. "This carpet is amazing." He ran his fingers through it, enjoying the soft, shaggy strands. "It's like a Wookie mated with a muskox."

He tried to resist the temptation for self-abasement, but such a spectacular failure deserved every bit of shit he could give himself. Naida had trusted him to fix things. Trusted him to keep her safe.

It started at the back of his throat—a tightly knotted wad of grief expanding like damp cotton, spreading up through his sinus cavities. It anchored between his eyes, sparking a throb—the steady march of armoured, blistered feet. His resistance crumbled and exposed the inner sanctum of his defences, crippling his efforts to repel the attack. The tears felt like sandpaper on his face, scraping his eyes.

Reisen rolled onto his stomach, pressing his face to the floor. "Goddamnit."

He gritted his teeth, shutting his eyes tight. Darkness surrounded him, washing him into a void. He floated—weightless, breathless, choking on shadows.

He regained awareness gradually, becoming first aware of a painful throbbing in his forehead, then its cause—smashing his head against the floor, with no memory of deciding to publicly abuse himself, the fucking Wookie carpet cushioning the blows.

Auryn grabbed him, pinning his arms behind his back.

He expected Keita to yell, to tell him how stupid and selfish he was being, to rub the painfully obvious in his face, but he said nothing, hugging him instead. Keita's willingness to take pity on him indicated unprecedented levels of patheticness.

He wasn't sure how long they stayed like that, but the tears came and went, drying on his face.

Auryn's pocket vibrated and he let go of Reisen to answer his phone. "Hello? All right. Yes, I'll be there. Okay. Bye." Auryn leaned in for a hug, first him, then Keita. "I have to get going, but I'll be back tomorrow." Auryn gazed at Reisen intently, blue eyes narrowing. "Be on your best behaviour."

"I always am."

"That's what I'm afraid of. Don't give Keita any trouble—I'm serious."

"I'll be a model prisoner, I swear."

Auryn rolled his eyes.

"See you tomorrow." Keita showed Auryn out and returned to the living room. He sat next to Reisen, drawing his knees to his chest.

"How was your trip?" asked Reisen.

"It was nice. Flying isn't as terrible as I thought it would be. Thanks for suggesting it to Auryn."

"You're welcome." It took every bit of self-control he possessed not to ask the obvious questions. *Is it awkward being around him? Do you want to kiss him? Because it's totally understandable if you do. He's always been yours. I was only ever borrowing him.* He wondered how Auryn dealt with it. If he ever looked at Keita and felt things he tried to ignore. "I'm way too coherent. Must fix." He struggled to his feet and headed for the kitchen.

"Want to play something afterward? Maybe that racing game where everyone throws shells at you?"

"Hell yes. You might actually be able to beat me." Keita was quite good, but Reisen had every track in every game memorised. It wasn't a guarantee of success, because shit could go wrong fast, especially if there was a blue shell involved, but it gave him an advantage. *The people of earth may be gone, but Rainbow Road lives on.*

Chapter Thirty-Three

TWO DAYS LATER

Dezmodeus forbade Aggnaroth from telling Jada anything, warning him to keep his distance, threatening to "take care of her" if she knew too much. He talked Dezi out of doing anything irrational, which for his brother presented a significant challenge.

Aggnaroth's mind emptied, all thought replaced by the sight of Jada in fishnet stockings, the strands of fabric decorated with ornate flowers made of colourful sequins. He bit the inside of his bottom lip, fighting the urge to kiss her thighs.

Jada dumped a load of clothes into her suitcase. She stared at the mountain of garments, frowning. "I always overpack. I'm only going to be gone two days." She was going to an Anorian outpost on Eevire, the moon. An opportunity to shop and socialise with others who were more like her.

"There is no shame in being overprepared." Aggnaroth watched her adoringly. It did not matter what she was doing. He found her fascinating.

"Do you want me to bring you back anything?"

"No, thank you. But..."

"But?"

There would be no coming back from this. If he was wrong... if Jada went running to her father and told him everything... he would deserve whatever Dezmodeus did to him, provided Jaden did not get to him first. "I was wondering if you could do me a small favour while you are there."

"Of course. What is it?"

Maybe recording what her father is going to do to me will help our cause.

"There is an Anorian soldier... Goes by the name of Dirge." Dirge was not actually Anorian, but enjoyed explosions and mayhem enough to convincingly play the part. "There is a small chance he may be stationed on Eevire." *He would want to stay close.* "If he is around, I would like you to ask him something important."

Jada nodded and wrapped her arms around his neck, kissing the corner of his mouth. "What would you like me to ask?"

Aggnaroth leaned into her. *Maybe Dezmodeus can earn money by charging people to view my corpse. Come one, come all. View the incredible bird man. This freak of nature died in a way I dare not describe with children around. Never trust a fucking alien princess, kids.* "First, please tell him that Aggnaroth sent you and everyone is accounted for, except the patron saint of sugar cubes and tulips."

He avoided using Demetrius's real name, not out of distrust, but in case anyone questioned Jada. The less she knew, the better. She could not reveal who they were trying to find if no one could identify who that individual was. "Ask Dirge if he knows where he is. He will want proof that I sent you, so you will have to show him this." He removed his phone from his pocket—the one Jaden did not know about—and sent a photo to Jada. Tiernan Aran. Dirge would not recognise him, but he would know exactly who it was.

AGGNAROTH FAIRED POORLY in Jada's absence. He lay awake at night, wondering how he was going to tell Dezmodeus what he had done. When she returned, the wait between welcoming her home and getting her alone was excruciating.

"I found Dirge. You were right." Jada beamed. "He asked if I had proof you'd sent me and I showed him the photo. I've never seen a grown man squeal so much. Dirge said his saintliness is a resident of Dakha prison on Eevire."

Prison? His heart thudded painfully. He was correct in assuming the Nephilim could no longer bypass Anorian security.

"Dakha is where high-security prisoners are sent." The prisoner was not Reisen Kaneko, not someone whose love of blowing things up was almost entirely fictionalised. The prisoner was dangerous and the Anorians were taking no chances. "It's hidden on the side of the moon that never sees the sun." An inconvenient place to arrange a prison break. They had limited resources and a small number of people who would be useful in a combat situation. *Hestia. Tiernan. Ari. Keita. Auryn.* It was not enough.

Jada's fingers ran through his hair, massaging his scalp. "Dirge said the guy you're searching for is eighteen. Born in prison." In this case, *born* likely meant shoved into a lab grown body. "Does that help?"

"It does. Thank you. It means a lot." He grazed Jada's neck with parted lips, overwhelmed with gratitude. Now the hard part. He needed to figure out how to break the news to Dezmodeus without endangering Jada and giving himself a substantial headache. Maybe he would get lucky. Dezmodeus's love for the man who had been

Demetrius Aran would prevail and his brother would be willing to forget any perceived transgressions. Not much chance of that, but he could dream.

THREE DAYS LATER

Inkworm victims were restricted to an isolated wing of the hospital. Their appearance frightened and demoralised staff and no matter how many steps were taken to allay the fear of contagion, other patients rioted at the suggestion of breathing the same air as the infected.

At 1:05 in the morning, Aggnaroth made his way through the quiet halls of the infected wing and entered a small, private room. The man Haken selected had not been sick long. Less than a month. Most signs of infection were obvious—decaying eyes, withered skin, pockmarked with oozing craters, extremities black and rotting. Other were not so readily observable, particularly a bright golden aura. A warm glow typically reserved for the enlightened. A bi-product of infection.

He prepared the injection—venom from the Altricial's butterflies, extracted by Hestia Aran, who had given it to Dezmodeus, who gave it to him. He sensed his brother's soul lurking nearby, ready to invade a temporary host. Dezmodeus found astral projection easy and effortless while Aggnaroth found the effort required to leave his body exhausting, and the freedom terrifying. He felt like he was floating in space, painfully cold and unable to breathe, fighting for air, only a thin silver cord connecting him to his body. It required a courageous, curious nature, which he lacked. It made sense that his brother excelled at etheric travel. Dezmodeus hated his body and would take any excuse he could get to leave.

Dezmodeus also excelled at possession, even if he found it in poor taste, making him the obvious choice.

Aggnaroth found a suitable vein and let the green-hued fluid flow, preparing the body for invasion. He murmured an apology under his breath, though he was doing the man a favour. Sudden eviction meant the soul escaped unscathed, not the usual case with an inkworm infection. It took several minutes to achieve the full effect.

A low groan. A trickle of black slime from chapped, shivering lips. Aggnaroth stared intently at the man's twisted face. "Dezmodeus?"

"Mother*fucker*. This body sucks worse than mine." The eviction of the body's previous residence was permanent, but Dezmodeus would not stay long.

Aggnaroth sweated from head to toe. He should have told Dezmodeus sooner, but he thought it best to wait until his brother's capacity for rage was limited. No time like the present. "Jada found Dirge. He said Dem is being held prisoner on Eevire. He is around eighteen."

His brother foamed at the mouth, making furious noises. Aggnaroth pressed a finger to his lips, like a dutiful librarian. "Shhh. Save your strength."

He was in so much trouble.

EMPEROR HAKEN WORE his finest furs—the pelt of an extinct ice leopard accented with bits of fluffy white ermine. His audience was limited to less than fifty people, all of whom could be depended on to keep quiet if nothing went as planning or broadcast news of His Holy Majesty's inherent superiority if everything worked out. A bunch of royal ass kissers, a classification from which Auryn knew he was tragically unexempt.

Crystal glasses of carbonated spring water circulated on silver trays, accompanied by cucumber sandwiches with lemon dill goat cheese and crunchy seaweed snacks. Painfully wholesome.

When the time came, they gathered in the Great Hall. The scent of flowers wafted over him; the strange dangly ones. His heart ached.

Haken guided a wheelchair-bound man into the room. Ravaged by inkworm, the man sat with his head cocked to the side, drooling dark sludge. Solemn, sympathetic murmurs ripped through the crowd, empty and disingenuous.

Haken's long-sleeved shirt disguised a tiny needle, ready to inject its contents at the push of a button. Auryn had watched the royal physician attach it, all the while listening to the elderly woman praise His Royal Holiness, Source of Everything. She chose to ignore the truth, opting instead for comforting lies.

He recorded everything.

Haken cleared his throat, standing confidently with a hand on the infected man's shoulder. "This is Francolin Altir. He's been infected for several weeks. Today he will be cured." Haken was taking a gamble. There was a chance something could go wrong, even though they knew the serum worked, hence the importance of an audience of a few loyal followers instead of a nationwide television broadcast.

"I believe I've finally unlocked the mystery of this unholy affliction. It seems all it requires is a little illumination." Light emanated from Haken's right hand, the left delving into the pocket of his fur coat to activate the magic button.

And just like that, proof of divinity. The sickly, shrivelled husk of a human transformed into a healthy receptacle of divine radiation. No outward signs of infection were visible. Scrubbed clean.

Cries of adulation swept through the crowd, but tapered off as the man in the wheelchair began to laugh. Frenetic. Off-kilter. A sound more animal than human.

"What's so funny, dear child?" Haken looked confused, a hint of unease infiltrating his voice.

Francolin rose from the metal chair, stretching. "Seriously, people. Trusting this guy with your souls is like trusting a two-year-old with a rusty coat hanger to perform an abortion." He acted fast, while the crowd was still gaping, mouths frozen in disbelief, palace guards equally stunned, weapons still holstered. He picked up the wheelchair by the armrests and brought it crashing down on Haken. A quick blow to the temple. A shattering of bone. Pounding and pounding, metal warping.

It took 162 shots to bring him down.

AURYN FOCUSED ON Haken's remains, still recording, carefully capturing the extent of the damage. A rusty smear of blood covered the floor, accented with bright bits of bone and grey-pink globs of brain. The emperor had been reduced to mush.

Elia paced beside him, guts sticking to his expensive shoes. "What a mess." He appeared unconcerned, even bemused. Police had been instructed to round up Francolin's family, but he had none—the only reason Aggnaroth agreed to help.

Not even the empress seemed to care Haken was gone. He'd been told what to expect, but it still struck him as odd that Haken's death was regarded so casually. As crazy as it sounded, Dezi claimed the royal family had an entire warehouse full of bodies, spare copies ready to be inhabited should their current incarnations come to an unfortunate end. This practice wasn't unusual on planets with spiritually developed populations, but on Ankari it was forbidden.

Two hours after Emperor Haken was murdered, he walked into the room, frowning at the gore still covering the floor. "Nasty business, that. Can anyone explain why Francolin Altir wanted to kill me?"

"Perhaps the injection healed his body, but not his mind," suggested Auryn.

"The way he spoke..." Haken clenched a fist. "No respect. He sounded liked that fool Kaneko."

Elia crossed his arms. "Surely Kaneko isn't the only one who'd talk to you like that. You must have a long list of suspects."

"Is Dezmodeus still skulking around Calder?" asked Haken.

Elia snorted. "Dezmodeus wouldn't dare pull a stunt like that. He values his cock too much."

Auryn breathed deeply, kneeling in front of Haken. "Let me bring you Reisen Kaneko, your Holiness. It would be an honour to present you with a gift to commemorate your resurrection."

"Pull that off, my son, and I'll give you everything you've ever wanted."

"All I ask for is your blessing."

"How thoughtful." Haken scowled at Elia from across the room. "Why can't you be more like Auryn?"

"Because I'm not terrified of displeasing you," replied Elia. Elia nudged the remains of Haken's colon with the toe of his shoe. "You should talk to the doctor about taking something to help you be more regular." Elia kicked Haken's colon with the side of his foot, sending it flying across the room, splattering pearl white walls. "There's an awful lot of shit in here."

A WEEK LATER

Reisen focused on his breathing, trying not to panic, not to think about what would happen if something went wrong. He got the sense that Aggnaroth wasn't 100% confident with performing the procedure, but hoped he was just being paranoid. Good to be getting it out of the way, at least. Maybe he'd have a chance of sleeping without artificial assistance.

Aggnaroth showed up first, followed by Auryn, halting Keita's incessant pacing of the living room. Everything was ready. He splashed cold water over his face and exiting the bathroom, cringing at the sound of the doorbell. He wasn't expecting any additional party members.

He stalked towards the front door, eying it suspiciously. "Who goes there?"

"Dezi."

Reisen's stomach sank. He didn't have the patience to deal with Dezi right now. "Go away."

"That's not very polite. What would your fellow Canadians say if they weren't all incinerated?"

Auryn approached, regarding him strangely. "Who's at the door?"

"Dezimonster."

"Let him in."

Reisen stepped in front of the door, not prepared to do that, even under orders from a handsome blond. "I don't want to."

"You're a little old to be acting like a four-year-old, Kaneko," replied Dezi. "Don't drag me into one of your infantilism fantasies."

"Shut your face!"

"Reisen." Auryn looked unprepared to tolerate further crap.

"Whaaat?"

"I'm opening the door."

Reisen groaned, retreating.

Dezmodeus stepped inside. "Nice to know southern hospitality's not dead."

UNSURE WHO ELSE to expect, Keita stepped into the living room. A man, almost the size of Aggnaroth, stood by the door, looking sickly and frail.

"Who are you?" he asked, realising only after posing the question that the man had the same pointed ears as Aggnaroth.

"I am Dezmodeus Azmodian. Aggnaroth's brother."

Dezmodeus didn't look much like his brother. He had no wings and appeared unable to stand up straight, his shoulders hunched, dark lines beneath his eyes. He looked as if he'd been seriously injured... Or had his wings sawn off.

Keita rang a mop through a bucket of hot water, wiping the last smear of blood off the floor. Tufts of dark feathers stuck to the bristles in leechlike clumps. Dezmodeus was asleep in the medical bay, heavily sedated. Keita dumped the dirty water and headed for the Captain's quarters, slightly woozy. Healing Dezi required more energy than expected.

He knocked on the door; it slid open. A blond man sat at a round table, head in his hands. Keita stood beside him, placing a hand on the man's shoulder. "I cleaned up the mess."

"Much appreciated." The man's accent was a faint, familiar drawl. His chest rose and fell with a heavy sigh. Keita hated seeing him like this. Hated everyone responsible for making him feel this way. "Was Reisen with them?" Especially Reisen.

"Yes. The piece of shit just stood there." The captain winced at his response as if he'd been struck and Keita wished he'd lied.

"It's not his fault."

The man's willingness to defend Reisen burned like hot knives in his chest, severing his restraint. "He had the nerve to lecture me when I was healing Dezi, told me to focus on what I was doing. Fucking asshole." He wanted to stop talking, but trying to dam the flood of words only made them flow faster. "How can you defend him? He's one of them now! Reisen's not the same person you fell in love with, Bran! What's it going to take for you to see that?" Keita shook his head, trying to clear it, focus falling on Dezmodeus. "It's you…"

"You remember me?" Dezmodeus looked touched.

"Prince Elia cut your wings off."

Reisen grunted softly. "That's what happens when you steal 332 billion dollars-worth of azurelite from a psychopath."

"You saved my life." Dezmodeus bowed his head, then turned to Reisen. "I didn't steal anything."

"Bullshit."

"Piss off, Kaneko."

Aggnaroth emerged from the bathroom, clearing his throat. "I see everyone is getting along nicely."

"How long have you been in there?" asked Dezmodeus. "I hope you turned the fan on."

"Why does this piece of shit need to be here?" Reisen pointed a finger at Dezmodeus, on the edge of hysterics.

Dezmodeus rolled his eyes. "It's all about shit with you, Kaneko. You should probably talk to someone about that."

Aggnaroth chewed his bottom lip nervously. "He knows the procedure better than I do. I wanted to tell you, but Dezi said it was not a good idea."

"Are you fucking kidding me?" Reisen never got this angry.

"Reisen. That's not necessary." Auryn curved his arms around Reisen, hugging him loosely.

"Sorry I dislike the idea of a pathological criminal cutting me open!"

"No one is faulting you for that," replied Auryn.

"Hey," grumbled Dezi.

"Give us a minute, please." Auryn took Reisen by the arm, disappearing with him into a spare bedroom.

"That went better than expected." Aggnaroth sank into a chair and rubbed the bridge of his nose.

Dezmodeus hissed at his brother. "The only reason I'm not stomping your ass is because it'll upset Keita."

"Why are you mad?" Keita asked Dezi.

"Because this cockweed is a fucking moron who went flipshit for the enemy. He can't even use his dick and it's still making him act like a stupid motherfucker." Dezi picked up an ashtray, hurling it at Dezmodeus, barely missing him.

"There was no other way," protested Aggnaroth. "And I would appreciate it if you did not talk about mother like that."

Keita lit a joint, grateful he was an only child.

"Do you get along with Reisen?" asked Dezi.

Keita found the question odd. "Why do you ask?"

"Because I'm surprised you haven't smothered him in his sleep."

"Can't say I haven't been tempted." He couldn't identify the source of his rage. It was easy to blame Reisen for being negligent, but the more he thought about it, the more he realised it didn't bother him that much. Sure, he could have lived without being tortured by men who enjoyed their jobs far too much, but that crap brought him to Auryn, and being with Auryn was way better than being with Reisen. "Is it that obvious?"

"No. But the two of you have a history. We're not supposed to carry grudges from one lifetime to another. We're supposed to forgive and forget. But some blades cut deeper than others. They leave scars death can't erase."

"You're saying Reisen pissed me off in a previous lifetime?" *Reisen's not the same person you fell in love with, Bran! What's it going to take for you to see that?*

"Exactly."

"What did he do?"

"The same thing he'd do to me if I told you." Dezi stretched and stood up slowly, wincing. "God, I'm starving. What do you have to eat around here?"

"I DON'T TRUST him." Reisen sat on the edge of the bed, shaking. Auryn had rarely seen him this worked up. He knew Dezi's reputation was unsavoury at best, but Dezi's relentless quest for gold was driven by the need to raise enough money for Aggy's freedom. Auryn understood doing terrible things for a good reason.

"I understand," said Auryn. "Do you want to call it off?"

"No. We've sacrificed too much to get this far."

"Dezi hates the Anorians as much as you do. He's not going to compromise the mission for some personal vendetta." Auryn touched the side of Reisen's face, grazing his cheek. "He won't hurt you."

"I don't want to forget you."

He wrapped Reisen in a hug, the closeness of him a shock to the system. Fighting the urge to kiss him required every bit of self-control he had.

Someone knocked at the door and Keita walked into the room, quickly averting his eyes. "Dezmodeus wants to know if his services are still required," said Keita, fixated on the wall.

They weren't doing anything wrong, but guilt stuck to him like sap, spreading with every attempt at removal.

Reisen stood up. "Let's get this over with."

THE TINY CHIP of azurelite containing a copy of the evidence they'd gathered against the Anorians was inserted into an incision in Reisen's back. It also carried instructions to shock Reisen with enough pranic energy to restore his memory, when activated by a specific trigger. Aggnaroth healed the wound, leaving no trace of a scar. The chip would be undetectable by Anorian scanning equipment.

Auryn studied Reisen, still out from the anaesthetic Dezi gave him at the beginning of the procedure. Not that transferring data to the chip was painful, but Reisen didn't want to be awake when Dezi sliced him open.

After an hour or so, Reisen stirred, dark eyes flickering open and shut, the faint sound of protest rising from his throat. "I don't wanna go to space..." Reisen shook his head. "It's cold and it smells funny."

"No one's making you go anywhere," assured Auryn.

"Wish I could say the same," grumbled Dezi. "The shit I do for love."

Chapter Thirty-Four

THERE WERE FEW places Dezmodeus hated more than Fenton. The environment was hostile to life, the soil eroded and stripped of nutrients, the water polluted and foul. Sulphur dioxide hissed from vents in the ground, killing large swathes of vegetation, rendering half the country inhospitable. The people were hungry, diseased, and crippled by war. Like something out of a film about mutant rednecks. Only one thing could motivate him to set foot in this cesspool.

Hestia.

Dezi entered Hearthbane Forest repeating one thought in his mind, a mantra—if he pulled this off, Hestia would reward him. Generously. Not with gold, but something far more valuable. He'd be hurting for days, but the jerk-off material would last forever.

A miasma of noxious energy gathered ahead, taking up permanent residence in the gnarled, leafless trees. It produced a fog of forgetfulness. People easily lost track of where they were going and wandered aimlessly, unfazed by starvation, dehydration, and exhaustion. Most wanderers never realised the miasma was killing them. Those who did usually didn't care.

He unshouldered his backpack, unzipped it, and removed a gas mask, carefully fitting it to his face. He ensured the seal was tight and drew his hood over his head.

The absence of animals in the trees was unnerving. No birds. No bears. Not even a bloody squirrel. Nothing survived. Human bodies lay where they'd fallen, skin leathery and preserved, each wrinkle and crease etched into peaceful blackened faces.

This wasn't his first trip to the spirit gate, but the path was never the same. The route he'd taken last time, a narrow path through the trees, was now a sheer rock face. His gas mask made it impossible to detect the acidic tang in the air that would lead him to water. All he could smell was rubber, forcing him to rely on whispers of the trees to guide him. Trees never lied. Except when they did. After passing the same tree twice, he unsheathed a machete, hacking through the dense branches. *Fucking pathological asshat.*

He reached the lakeshore despite a lack of assistance and the miasma cleared. He removed his mask, making his way around Lake Tyron until reaching a tilted shack with an equally dilapidated dock. A small boat was moored at the dock, the only way to the middle of the lake. He banged on the door of the shack, rattling it.

"Hold on. No need ta break me door down." A voice rose from inside. The door creaked open. A short, wide-set man with an oversized head, greenish skin tone, and wispy black hair peered up at him. "Oh. It's ye."

"Damn right it's me. We're going for a ride."

"Can't. Motor's conked out on me boat. Need parts ta fix it."

"Then you'd better think of another way to get me out there, or I'm going to tear your shitty shack down."

"I have paddles, if ye feel like rowing."

"That'll take all bloody day."

The Boatmaster smiled. "Most likely."

Dezi rowed cautiously, iridium-plated paddles dipping into the acidic water. If anything went wrong, the first item on his agenda was using the bug-eyed Boatmaster as sacrificial bait. The Boatmaster sat at the bow, tensely scanning the water. Dezi didn't want to think about the creatures that lived down there, with skin like metal and teeth like butcher knives. The farther away from shore they got, the worse his nerves got.

"Lotsa bubbles ahead," said the Boatmaster. "Might wanna speed up."

"Fuck you. Why don't you row for a while?"

"Can't. Bad shoulder."

More ripples appeared in the water. Dezi rowed faster, muscles screaming.

By the time they reached the middle of the lake his entire body ached and burned and not in a good way. He stumbled onto a small moss-covered island and threw up. The only thing living here was a giant old swamp cypress. At the flared base of its trunk a hole sat between tendrils of exposed root.

"Wait here," he told the Boatman. "I won't be gone long."

"Can't. Got somethin' I need ta do. Be back for ye in a while."

"The hell do you think you're going with a broken motor and fucked-up shoulder?"

The Boatman pulled the cord on his motor and it roared to life. "Seems to be okay now."

Dezi gritted his teeth and turned towards the tree. *Cockweed.*

DEZI SLIPPED INTO the hole, sliding down into darkness. The narrow passage made him uneasy enough to be glad he wasn't fucking claustrophobic. He hit the ground hard and skidded to a halt, glasses askew. Thousands of glowing worms lit up the cave ceiling like blue stars. He picked himself up, groaning softly, and continued onwards, soon reaching the end of the small cave.

Instead of a rock wall, a thick membrane stretched across the cavern. On the other side of the translucent film a garden was visible, bathed in a dreamlike haze, out of focus. He clawed at the membrane as he pushed forwards, trying to tear a hole through it. It surrounded him, cutting off his air. He fought like hell, kicking and scratching like a feral cat, finally breaking free into the sunshine. He lay in a garden filled with colourful wildflowers—fireweed and lupines, vivid gashes of purple and red. He closed his eyes, breathing deeply and basking in the relief of occupying a body that no longer felt possessed by nails. He stretched his wings and stood tall, grinning like a lunatic.

The air thrummed with energy, a higher vibration than the physical realm, inducing a sense of lightness. His true form had long hair, down to his shoulders. He picked himself up and headed for the castle, home of General Asheron Sariel, once commander of the Nephilim armies, now a recluse who refused to leave the spirit world. Asheron also happened to be Hestia's father, his father in-law.

The guards allowed him to pass, recognising him. Asheron's assistant greeted him at the door, agreeing to allow him to have a brief word with Asheron once he was finished his nap. They met in the solarium, sitting at a table, surrounded by windows. The table was loaded with warm croissants and pats of garlic butter; steaming apple strudel; pitchers of peach cider.

Asheron eyed him with the usual annoyance. The man's skin and hair were the whitest he'd ever seen, his eyes deep purple. At almost eight feet tall, Asheron was massive. He greeted Dezi in the usual way.

"Have you found Dem?" asked Asheron.

"Yes..." Dezi twitched and fought the urge to grind his teeth. "We have reason to believe he's being held prisoner on Eevire."

"Prison, you say?" Asheron tilted his head and stared off into the distance. His mouth opened, but no words came out. He stopped gaping, head bobbed tiredly, eyes half-lidded. Spending so much time in the spirit realm made Asheron unstable and disconnected. Dezi was already losing him. Time to get to the point.

"Do you remember King Ermalin's son—Prince Anowki?" asked Dezi.

"The boy... Reisen shot him."

"Yuh, that's the one. His most recent incarnation passed away. I'd like to retrieve his soul before the Anorians get around to processing him."

"I'll allow it." Thank fuck he'd caught Asheron on a good day. They could just as easily be having a conversation about the migration routes of isosceles triangles.

He followed Asheron down the hall, into a ritual chamber. They stood before a wall of shimmering gelatin, much like the barrier he'd crossed before, but thicker. Unlike the spirit gate, he lacked the strength to enter the land of the dead on his own. He'd need to be quick; the rift would only remain open for a few hours. If he failed to make it back on time, there'd be no guarantee Asheron would be inclined to open it again anytime soon.

Asheron pressed a hand to the wall, submerging it in the gel. Flashes of lightning forked from Asheron's fingertips, branching vein-like throughout the barrier and creating a narrow opening.

Dezi rushed through the gap, entering the land of the dead. Aphelion.

A waning moon hung low in the sky, swollen with reflected light. Dead leaves swirled around Dezi's feet, crunching beneath the soles of his shoes. The detritus added to a sense of realism, an attempt to recreate the mortal world, adding to the confusion of the souls who arrived here.

He removed the blue agate marble Hestia had given him from his pocket. Mae had played with it, imbuing the stone with her energy. He searched for her signature among the thousands of dead until he found it. He traced it to its source, ascending the steps to an old house. It looked like it had been constructed by the same master craftsman who built the Boatmaster's shitty shack. The building was full of badly patched holes and collapsing inward; the carpenter was no Mekani Sedgewren.

The inside of the house was equally underwhelming. Paint peeled off the walls, littering decaying floorboards with faded flecks of yellow. Nearly every wall was full of holes. Rats, or some other large rodent, had eaten most of the exposed insulation and their droppings were everywhere, dried and odourless.

Dezi entered a child's bedroom and rapped on a thick oak wardrobe, awaiting a response. From somewhere deep inside the wardrobe he heard a faint *tap, tap.*

The door burst open. Mae launched at him, knocking him to the floor, her teeth flashing and faded tiger print pyjamas clinging to her sickly frame. Dezi covered his eyes with an arm. "Don't eat me!"

Mae sniffed him and rolled off, crouching cat-like on the floor, bare feet covered in dirt. "I wasn't gonna."

Recently deceased souls often clung to their previous incarnation until they were ready to move on, once the shock and trauma dissipated. "Good, because I can tell you right now, I'd taste like crap. I eat way too much junk food."

"Wouldn't that make you sweet?"

"Too sweet. I'll rot the teeth right out of your pretty little head." Dezi sat up.

"You're weird."

Dezi knelt in front of Mae, gazing deep into her eyes. "Mae, do you remember Tiernan?"

The dead girl looked confused. "How do you know my name?"

"You're very special, Mae. I've come a long way to find you. I need you to think carefully. Do you remember being in a cave?"

Mae closed her eyes. She muttered something, incoherent at first, regurgitated sound. Her body rocked slowly from side to side. "Nika was there. Nika goes everywhere with me. Except..." She opened her eyes, staring at her empty hands. "I gave Nika to Tiernan. Tiernan took good care of Nika when the king wanted to burn him. Tiernan would never let him burn."

Dezi leaned in closer, gently touching Mae's arm. "Would you like to see Tiernan, Mae?"

"Yes!" Mae's damp eyes lit up, gleaming excitedly, and Dezi knew he had her.

"I have a new body lined up for you. It'll be ready soon. You can be with Tiernan again. Nika will be there too, the little shit."

Mae glared murderously. "Don't call Nika names."

"Or what?"

"I'll kick your butt." She looked like she meant it.

"All right, all right. I'll be nice." Dezi smiled and took Mae by the hand, tugging her in the direction of the light. "Let's get out of this dump."

THE AIRPLANE SHUDDERED. Dezmodeus held his breath. He imagined the plane crashing. His body strewn across the desert in pieces, scavenger food. How long would it take before the sand swallowed him? Hours? Days?

He'd caught a commercial flight, direct from Fenton to Rian. Not the wisest idea, in retrospect, but it was the fastest way.

The plane was half-empty. Dezi's body ached. Sitting for too long was hard on him. His muscles disliked remaining stationary as much as they hated movement. A sharp pain radiated from the crown of his head to his toes, like hot, stabbing coals trapped beneath his skin. His back hurt the worst, along the length of his spine and around his shoulders. As far as extreme body modification went, having your wings cut off wasn't something Dezi would endorse.

Mae sat next to the window, chattering incessantly, "How come we're in Rian?"

Dezi avoided the question. "Do you remember living here?"

"Sorta. The Ancient Ones... They made my father do bad things."

"They didn't make him do anything. He believed those asshole aliens were gods and wanted to appease them, even if it meant being a murderous pig."

"Be quiet, Dezi! He made a mistake."

"Wiping your ass with poison ivy is a mistake. Eating *vaneru* out of season is a mistake. Destroying a specific group of people because you think they're a bunch of demon-worshipping degenerates is genocide, kid."

"Genocide? What's that mean?"

"It means King Ermalin was a huge dick. Like the Ancient Ones."

"No! The Ancient Ones are bad! They tricked my parents into burning people and trapped everyone who got sick on an island."

"Dick, dick, dick."

"You're a dick!" Mae puffed up her cheeks. "A big fat one."

"You're the fattest one of all." Dezi jabbed Mae in the chest with a finger. "The King of Dick."

The people sitting behind him murmured among themselves, waving over an airline attendant. "Excuse me. The man in front of us is talking to himself. It's bothering my wife."

The attendant frowned at him. "I'm sorry, sir, but I'm going to have to ask you to be quiet. You're disturbing the other passengers."

Dezi shifted in his seat, pain spiking. He glanced at the dead girl beside him, then back to the stewardess, grunting softly. "Not half as much as they disturb me."

DEZMODEUS COULDN'T SLEEP. There was too much on his mind and his body felt like it had been fed through a wood chipper, sliced into a thousand pieces and stitched back together again with razor wire. He sat up, rifling through his things. The tent shuddered in the wind, desert sand blasting the canopy. He'd driven from the airport to the middle of nowhere and set up camp. Until the sun came up, there was nothing he could do but wait.

Dezi took a handful of painkillers and lay back down, curling into a foetal position.

"You don't like being in a body, do you?" Mae peered at him from within the depths of her sleeping bag. It was completely unnecessary for a dead kid to have a bed, but the brat insisted.

"I've got nothing against the practice in general. It's *this* body I dislike."

"How come it hurts so much?"

"I stole something from the Ancient Ones, or so they thought. Made them kinda mad. They cut off my wings."

Mae groaned. "It's hopeless. Why do they have to be so mean?"

"They can't go on like this forever. Shitting all over Universal Law." The Anorians were occupying a restricted planet. Type 1. No extraterrestrial contact permitted, except for the Nephilim. Interaction with humans was a long-standing, highly respected traditional in Nephilim culture. Their intentions were, for the most part, primarily philanthropic. The same couldn't be said of the Anorians. They couldn't resist the allure of preying on unsuspecting souls and the possibility of getting their grubby little hands on a steady azurelite supply.

A human planet was the perfect place to mask delinquent behaviour. Depravity was expected at this stage of spiritual development and largely ignored by the extraterrestrial community—nothing about a nursery full of screaming babies stood out as unusual.

At some point he slept, waking up with Mae holding his hand. *Damn kid.* He squinted at his watch, vision failing him, eventually establishing it was still too bloody early to get up.

"Dezi."

"Yuh?"

"I'm worried." Mae's voice quavered.

"I'm not a therapist, kid."

"What's that?"

"Someone who's paid to care about your problems."

"I can pay you. Uncle Nedri's buried not far from here. He's got all kinds of good stuff he's not using anymore."

"What's troubling you, my child?"

"What if Tiernan doesn't know it's me? I'll be in a new body and new bodies make people forget. How can I remind him when I don't remember who I am?"

"If you keep stressing about shit you have no control over you're going to turn into an adult. Trust things are gonna be okay. You could go your whole life without remembering anything and Tiernan wouldn't love you any less."

"Will I be a girl or a boy? Something else, maybe?"

"I don't know. Does it matter?"

Mae fell momentarily silent. "No."

Dezi scratched a phantom itch near his shoulder blade, where his left wing used to be. Over fifty years without wings and his body still hadn't gotten the memo. "Then don't worry about it."

"Nika's gonna be there, too?"

Dezi groaned softly, hoping he'd get his money's worth. "Yes, yes. Nika stays close to Tiernan."

"Good."

Mae yawned and closed her eyes. "Thanks, Dezi."

DEZMODEUS WAS DONE with the desert. Done with barely being able to breathe; all that dusty, dry-ass air. Done with getting sand in everything. Done with the relentless heat. He loaded the last of their supplies into the all-terrain vehicle and slumped against the steering wheel, waiting for the nausea to subside.

Mae reached over from the passenger seat to pat him on the back, "There, there."

He swatted her hand away. "Get off me."

Mae huffed at him, folding her arms across her chest. She was quiet for a minute, blissfully silent, but the reprieve was short-lived.

"I know what'll make you feel better." The dead girl leaned forwards in her seat, scanning the horizon while her face scrunched in concentration. She pointed southwest. "Go that way! We'll visit Uncle Nedri and get you some gold."

Dezi turned the keys in the ignition and hit the gas. He wasn't sure what he'd find or whether it would be worth the effort. He was in no condition to be single-handedly launching a major archaeological excavation and many tombs of Rian's ancient leaders were rigged with traps and other equally unpleasant things designed to deter thieves. There wasn't much time to be fucking around, looking for treasure—the Altricial were expecting him. Still, it was worth investigating.

It was a few hour's drive to Uncle Nedri's resting place. Dezi withered in the hot sun and sat in the shade to rest while Mae located the tomb's entrance, well-disguised among the sand.

He dozed off unintentionally and awoke with a pile of trinkets at his feet. A gold statue of the sun. Glimmering gemstones. A bronze tablet. Old coins. And most intriguing of all, a large multi-faceted sphere. Each facet had a unique symbol carved on it; hundreds of tiny diagrams covered the object. A puzzle box.

"What am I supposed to do with this?" he murmured, tracing a bony finger over the sphere's smooth surface. These things were fucking impossible to open. Not only did the symbols have to be activated in the right sequence, but only those with Oterai blood could activate the locking mechanism. The box had something inside it. He felt its weight shift as he turned the sphere over in his hands. "What's in it?"

"I dunno," said Mae. "It wasn't there last time."

"What do you mean?"

"It's not Uncle Nedri's. Dunno where it came from, but he doesn't need more junk."

"You're saying someone broke in and gave him this?"

"Yes."

"And nothing is missing from inside the tomb?"

"Nope."

Dezi rubbed his forehead and collected his loot. He'd worry about the box later. They'd gone out of their way and needed to get to the Altricial camp before dark.

When they finally arrived at the Altricial camp, Dezi was ready to collapse. He spent a few minutes rehydrating and regaining his senses, then made his way to the centre of the encampment, entering the main tent in search of

Ilyana, head of the Altricial. Members were assassins trained in the art of alchemy and the dark arts, though the efficiency of their training was debatable; none of the Altricial could see the dead girl who accompanied him.

Ily sat on a velvet stool, examining a tiny tree. *Kalinara.* The shape of the tree looked deliberately crafted—the use of wire and pressure to create a dramatic bend, but he suspected the curve was natural. The bark had a rich blue tint and a velvety texture. Needled branches extended only from the outer curve, emitting a faint, sweet scent. They too had a bluish hue, supporting bunches of purple berries.

The stoneware dish in which it sat was shallow and rectangular, with claw feet. Golden images engraved in the ancient black material were faded and unrecognisable, shiny lines branching into nowhere. The berries were round and plump, ready to be harvested, crushed, and steam distilled, if he understood her explanation correctly. The resulting essential oil would be enough for nearly a hundred doses. A natural antibiotic, rich in energy. The Church gave it to paladins, providing steady income for the Altricial.

Ilyana raised a hand to her mouth, looking as if she was going to be sick. She turned her head away and wretched.

"Hope you're not contagious," he murmured.

"I'm pregnant."

Despite the heat, despite the shrill ache in his body, despite everything, Dezi smiled. "Congratulations."

Chapter Thirty-Five

THREE WEEKS LATER

A thousand things could go wrong. The possibilities tormented Keita since he'd first heard news of Reisen's insane plan, but he was determined not to let his reservations show. He'd managed to hold his shit together all day.

It wasn't until Reisen hugged him goodbye that Keita started to shake.

"You should be happy to have the place all to yourself," teased Reisen.

Keita shook his head, speaking quietly. "I don't like this."

Reisen hugged him tighter. "The Anorians understand something most people don't. If you discover a witch in your midst, you don't burn her. You don't antagonise someone with the ability to curse your ass. No, if you're smart, you put her to work. You use her abilities to your advantage."

"Are you calling yourself a witch?"

"Something like that." Reisen released him, removing a tiny metal box from his pocket. "I'm giving you a duplicate of the chip Dezmodeus made, in case something happens."

Keita took the box, unsure how he felt about being placed in such a stressful position, apart from being strangely flattered Reisen chose him over Auryn.

"I'll see you soon."
All he could do was hope Reisen was right.

Idyn Star Newspaper
Year 2073, Cern 18

Reisen Kaneko Brought to Justice

At 4:48 this morning the world became a safer place. An elaborate undercover operation lead by General Auryn Tyrus drew terrorist Reisen Kaneko out of hiding. Kaneko was lured to an abandoned house on the outskirts of the stone forest under the pretence of procuring a large quantity of inkworm. He was apprehended by a tactical team lead by General Tyrus.

News of the operation's success was broadcast across Terasyn, resulting in celebrations across the country. His Holiness Emperor Haken confirmed Kaneko's capture, stating, "We've eliminated the threat of inexplicable violence. We can finally avenge the souls of those we've lost to Kaneko and enter a more enlightened phase of civilisation."

Under His Holiness Emperor Haken's orders, Kaneko will be executed by lethal injection at the hour of redemption.

The Anorians didn't interrogate Reisen. He'd been prepared to break a few ribs, maybe lose a few teeth, be tickled voraciously, but they didn't touch him. He spent the hours following his "capture" locked in a room at the palace where his greatest torture was being surrounded by pictures of Haken and his family. He even had a private bathroom which smelled like lilacs. At one point he lay down on a velvet couch and managed to fall asleep, napping until Prince Elia's arrival. Elia let himself in, standing before Reisen, arms crossed.

"Reisen Kaneko." Elia was like the inexplicable offspring of Ted Bundy and Hannibal Lecter, charming and inclined to cut your face off. "My father would like to see you."

"About time." Reisen stood up and stretched. "I was starting to feel ignored."

No guards accompanied them, sending the message Elia was unafraid, though they both knew otherwise. It was comforting to know he wasn't the only one scared shitless.

Haken sat on his throne, wearing a seal fur coat, drinking blood from a gold chalice, blond hair slicked back. "Reisen, my old friend."

"Haken, you relentless pile of shit." He was glad Auryn wasn't here for this. "How's it hangin'?"

"I'm glad you're here."

"Awe, I feel all warm and fuzzy inside."

"I could use your help."

"Is your wisteria wilting?"

Haken retrieved a tablet from his side, displaying a photograph of a sickly looking tree. "You think you can lure me back to the dark side with a tree?"

"This is *Kalinara*. It's used to treat inkworm. It's not doing well."

"God damnit." Reisen sighed heavily. It was easy to pretend to be enticed by the offer. *Kalinara* was beautiful and the allure of creating an elixir capable of placating the cranky-ass worms was strong.

"Your memory will be erased and you will be transferred to our base on Eevire. You will only work with inkworm under strict supervision. I don't want a repeat of this foolishness."

"You'll have to find someone else to blame next time you blow something up."

Reisen reached up, adjusting the bun on his head, searching. There were other places he could hide things, but this was by far the most convenient. He withdrew a tiny needle from the mass of hair and injected himself before anyone had the chance to react. If the Anorians were going to take everything from him, he preferred to go down on his own terms. 1.5 ML of carnelian root was enough to scramble his brains sufficiently to satisfy his alien overlords, though they would undoubtedly inject him again, just to be sure. Not everything would be gone, just—

A tornado swept through his mind, sucking everything into a swirling vortex of numbness. He fought against it for the same reason he fought against falling asleep under anaesthetic, the thrill of seeing how long he could ward off the inevitable, the terror of having no control over what came next. Memories surged to the surface, only to be swallowed by the storm.

Gene Chandler proclaiming his dukedom.

French bulldogs.

The orchestral version of "Gerudo Valley," all that bouncy brass and pounding percussion.

David Bowie in Labyrinth. Those grey leggings. An overwhelming sense of disappointment when he found out that wasn't his real hair.

His mom and dad, laughing in the rain.

Bran. Their first kiss, under a bald cypress tree. Bran tasted of lemon and mint and made him believe in the impossible, something deeper than love, something intrinsic to his being, engraved in his soul.

The flashing of cameras. "Reisen! Are you dating Branden Anderson?"

They'd only been gone three months when they encountered the anomaly. A large, flat, puddle of a glistening, silver substance. It surrounded them, ingesting them, regurgitating them elsewhere.

A reign of fire. Crashing.

His eyes rolled back in his head, body listing, Haken's voice drifting in from far away, "Bring me some scissors."

About the Author

Kale is a resident of northern Alberta, which serves as the inspiration for a world trapped in perpetual winter. She's an avid reader with an English degree from the University of Calgary. In her spare time, Kale loves playing video games, making chainmaille, watching anime, and cultivating a steadily expanding bonsai collection.

Email: kalenight@gmail.com

Twitter: @kale_night

Website: www.abrokenwinter.com

Also Available from NineStar Press

Connect with NineStar Press

www.ninestarpress.com

www.facebook.com/ninestarpress

www.facebook.com/groups/NineStarNiche

www.twitter.com/ninestarpress

www.tumblr.com/blog/ninestarpress